Decorations, gifts, Christmas trees,
sleigh bells, snow and mistletoe—
Christmas is such a fabulous time
of year to fall in love!

Christmas Treasures

*Three classic Christmas
romances by three bestselling,
favourite authors*

Christmas Treasures

BETTY NEELS

CAROLINE ANDERSON

HELEN BROOKS

*First published in Great Britain 2006
by Harlequin Mills & Boon Limited, Eton House,
18-24 Paradise Road, Richmond, Surrey TW9 1SR*

CHRISTMAS TREASURES © by Harlequin Books S.A. 2006

The publisher acknowledges the copyright holders of the
individual works as follows:

Always and Forever © Betty Neels 2001
The Perfect Christmas © Caroline Anderson 2001
Christmas at His Command © Helen Brooks 2002

ISBN 13: 978 0 263 85110 6
ISBN 10: 0 263 85110 9

059-1006

Printed and bound in Spain
by Litografía Rosés S.A., Barcelona

Always and Forever

BETTY NEELS

Betty Neels spent her childhood and youth in Devonshire before training as a nurse and midwife. She was an army nursing sister during the war, married a Dutchman, and subsequently lived in Holland for fourteen years. She lived with her husband in Dorset, and had a daughter and grandson. Her hobbies were reading, animals, old buildings and writing. Betty started to write on retirement from nursing, incited by a lady in a library bemoaning the lack of romantic novels. Betty Neels has sold over thirty-five million copies of her books, world-wide.

CHAPTER ONE

THERE was going to be a storm; the blue sky of a summer evening was slowly being swallowed by black clouds, heavy with rain and thunder, flashing warning signals of flickering lightning over the peaceful Dorset countryside, casting gloom over the village. The girl gathering a line of washing from the small orchard behind the house standing on the village outskirts paused to study the sky before lugging the washing basket through the open door at the back of the house.

She was a small girl, nicely plump, with a face which, while not pretty, was redeemed by fine brown eyes. Her pale brown hair was gathered in an untidy bunch on the top of her head and she was wearing a cotton dress which had seen better days.

She put the basket down, closed the door and went in search of candles and matches, then put two old-fashioned oil lamps on the wooden table. If the storm was bad there would be a power cut before the evening was far advanced.

This done to her satisfaction, she poked up the elderly Aga, set a kettle to boil and turned her attention to the elderly dog and battle-scarred old tomcat, waiting patiently for their suppers.

She got their food, talking while she did so because the eerie quiet before the storm broke was a little unnerving, and then made tea and sat down to drink it as the first heavy drops of rain began to fall.

With the rain came a sudden wind which sent her round the house shutting windows against the deluge. Back in the kitchen, she addressed the dog.

'Well, there won't be anyone coming now,' she told him, and gave a small shriek as lightning flashed and thunder drowned out any other sound. She sat down at the table and he came and sat beside her, and, after a moment, the cat got onto her lap.

The wind died down as suddenly as it had arisen but the storm was almost overhead. It had become very dark and the almost continuous flashes made it seem even darker. Presently the light over the table began to flicker; she prudently lit a candle before it went out.

She got up then, lighted the lamps and took one into the hall before sitting down again. There was nothing to do but to wait until the storm had passed.

The lull was shattered by a peal on the doorbell, so unexpected that she sat for a moment, not quite believing it. But a second prolonged peal sent her to the door, lamp in hand.

A man stood in the porch. She held the lamp high in order to get a good look at him; he was a very large man, towering over her.

'I saw your sign. Can you put us up for the night? I don't care to drive further in this weather.'

He had a quiet voice and he looked genuine. 'Who's we?' she asked.

'My mother and myself.'

She slipped the chain off the door. 'Come in.' She peered round him. 'Is that your car?'

'Yes—is there a garage?'

'Go round the side of the house; there's a barn—the door's open. There's plenty of room there.'

He nodded and turned back to the car to open its door and help his mother out. Ushering them into the hall, the girl said, 'Come back in through the kitchen door; I'll leave it unlocked. It's across the yard from the barn.'

He nodded again, a man of few words, she supposed, and he went outside. She turned to look at her second guest. The woman was tall, good-looking, in her late fifties, she supposed, and dressed with understated elegance.

'Would you like to see your room? And would you like a meal? It's a bit late to cook dinner but you could have an omelette or scrambled eggs and bacon with tea or coffee?'

The older woman put out a hand. 'Mrs Fforde—spelt with two ffs, I'm afraid. My son's a doctor; he was driving me to the other side of Glastonbury, taking a shortcut, but driving had become impossible. Your sign was like something from heaven.' She had to raise her voice against the heavenly din.

The girl offered a hand. 'Amabel Parsons. I'm sorry you had such a horrid journey.'

'I hate storms, don't you? You're not alone in the house?'

'Well, yes, I am, but I have Cyril—that's my dog— and Oscar the cat.' Amabel hesitated. 'Would you like to come into the sitting room until Dr Fforde comes? Then you can decide if you would like something to eat. I'm afraid you will have to go to bed by candlelight...'

She led the way down the hall and into a small room, comfortably furnished with easy chairs and a small round table. There were shelves of books on either side of the fireplace and a large window across which

Amabel drew the curtains before setting the lamp on the table.

'I'll unlock the kitchen door,' she said and hurried back to the kitchen just in time to admit the doctor.

He was carrying two cases. 'Shall I take these up?'

'Yes, please. I'll ask Mrs Fforde if she would like to go to her room now. I asked if you would like anything to eat…'

'Most emphatically yes. That's if it's not putting you to too much trouble. Anything will do—sandwiches…'

'Omelettes, scrambled eggs, bacon and eggs? I did explain to Mrs Fforde that it's too late to cook a full meal.'

He smiled down at her. 'I'm sure Mother is longing for a cup of tea, and omelettes sound fine.' He glanced round him. 'You're not alone?'

'Yes,' said Amabel. 'I'll take you upstairs.'

She gave them the two rooms at the front of the house and pointed out the bathroom. 'Plenty of hot water,' she added, before going back to the kitchen.

When they came downstairs presently she had the table laid in the small room and offered them omelettes, cooked to perfection, toast and butter and a large pot of tea. This had kept her busy, but it had also kept her mind off the storm, still raging above their heads. It rumbled away finally in the small hours, but by the time she had cleared up the supper things and prepared the breakfast table, she was too tired to notice.

She was up early, but so was Dr Fforde. He accepted the tea she offered him before he wandered out of the door into the yard and the orchard beyond, accompanied by Cyril. He presently strolled back to stand in the door-way and watch her getting their breakfast.

Amabel, conscious of his steady gaze, said briskly, 'Would Mrs Fforde like breakfast in bed? It's no extra trouble.'

'I believe she would like that very much. I'll have mine with you here.'

'Oh, you can't do that.' She was taken aback. 'I mean, your breakfast is laid in the sitting room. I'll bring it to you whenever you're ready.'

'I dislike eating alone. If you put everything for Mother on a tray I'll carry it up.'

He was friendly in a casual way, but she guessed that he was a man who disliked arguing. She got a tray ready, and when he came downstairs again and sat down at the kitchen table she put a plate of bacon, eggs and mushrooms in front of him, adding toast and marmalade before pouring the tea.

'Come and sit down and eat your breakfast and tell me why you live here alone,' he invited. He sounded so like an elder brother or a kind uncle that she did so, watching him demolish his breakfast with evident enjoyment before loading a slice of toast with butter and marmalade.

She had poured herself a cup of tea, but whatever he said she wasn't going to eat her breakfast with him...

He passed her the slice of toast. 'Eat that up and tell me why you live alone.'

'Well, really!' began Amabel and then, meeting his kindly look, added, 'It's only for a month or so. My mother's gone to Canada,' she told him. 'My married sister lives there and she's just had a baby. It was such a good opportunity for her to go. You see, in the summer we get quite a lot of people coming just for bed and breakfast, like you, so I'm not really alone. It's different in the winter, of course.'

He asked, 'You don't mind being here by yourself? What of the days—and nights—when no one wants bed and breakfast?'

She said defiantly, 'I have Cyril, and Oscar's splendid company. Besides, there's the phone.'

'And your nearest neighbour?' he asked idly.

'Old Mrs Drew, round the bend in the lane going to the village. Also, it's only half a mile to the village.' She still sounded defiant.

He passed his cup for more tea. Despite her brave words he suspected that she wasn't as self-assured as she would have him believe. A plain girl, he considered, but nice eyes, nice voice and apparently not much interest in clothes; the denim skirt and cotton blouse were crisp and spotless, but could hardly be called fashionable. He glanced at her hands, which were small and well shaped, bearing signs of housework.

He said, 'A lovely morning after the storm. That's a pleasant orchard you have beyond the yard. And a splendid view...'

'Yes, it's splendid all the year round.'

'Do you get cut off in the winter?'

'Yes, sometimes. Would you like more tea?'

'No, thank you. I'll see if my mother is getting ready to leave.' He smiled at her. 'That was a delicious meal.' But not, he reflected, a very friendly one. Amabel Parsons had given him the strong impression that she wished him out of the house.

Within the hour he and his mother had gone, driving away in the dark blue Rolls Royce. Amabel stood in the open doorway, watching it disappear round the bend in

the lane. It had been providential, she told herself, that
they should have stopped at the house at the height of
the storm; they had kept her busy and she hadn't had
the time to be frightened. They had been no trouble—
and she needed the money.

It would be nice, she thought wistfully, to have someone like Dr Fforde as a friend. Sitting at breakfast with
him, she'd had an urgent desire to talk to him, tell him
how lonely she was, and sometimes a bit scared, how
tired she was of making up beds and getting breakfast
for a succession of strangers, keeping the place going
until her mother returned, and all the while keeping up
the façade of an independent and competent young
woman perfectly able to manage on her own.

That was necessary, otherwise well-meaning people
in the village would have made it their business to dis-
suade her mother from her trip and even suggest that
Amabel should shut up the house and go and stay with
a great-aunt she hardly knew, who lived in Yorkshire
and who certainly wouldn't want her.

Amabel went back into the house, collected up the
bedlinen and made up the beds again; hopefully there
would be more guests later in the day...

She readied the rooms, inspected the contents of the
fridge and the deep freeze, hung out the washing and
made herself a sandwich before going into the orchard
with Cyril and Oscar. They sat, the three of them, on an
old wooden bench, nicely secluded from the lane but
near enough to hear if anyone called.

Which they did, just as she was on the point of going
indoors for her tea.

The man on the doorstep turned round impatiently as
she reached him.

'I rang twice. I want bed and breakfast for my wife, son and daughter.'

Amabel turned to look at the car. There was a young man in the driver's seat, and a middle-aged woman and a girl sitting in the back.

'Three rooms? Certainly. But I must tell you that there is only one bathroom, although there are handbasins in the rooms.'

He said rudely, 'I suppose that's all we can expect in this part of the world. We took a wrong turning and landed ourselves here, at the back of beyond. What do you charge? And we do get a decent breakfast?'

Amabel told him, 'Yes.' As her mother frequently reminded her, it took all sorts to make the world.

The three people in the car got out: a bossy woman, the girl pretty but sulky, and the young man looking at her in a way she didn't like...

They inspected their rooms with loud-voiced comments about old-fashioned furniture and no more than one bathroom—and that laughably old-fashioned. And they wanted tea: sandwiches and scones and cake. 'And plenty of jam,' the young man shouted after her as she left the room.

After tea they wanted to know where the TV was.

'I haven't got a television.'

They didn't believe her. 'Everyone has a TV set,' complained the girl. 'Whatever are we going to do this evening?'

'The village is half a mile down the lane,' said Amabel. 'There's a pub there, and you can get a meal, if you wish.'

'Better than hanging around here.'

It was a relief to see them climb back into the car and

drive off presently. She laid the table for their breakfast and put everything ready in the kitchen before getting herself some supper. It was a fine light evening, so she strolled into the orchard and sat down on the bench. Dr Fforde and his mother would be at Glastonbury, she supposed, staying with family or friends. He would be married, of course, to a pretty girl with lovely clothes—there would be a small boy and a smaller girl, and they would live in a large and comfortable house; he was successful, for he drove a Rolls Royce...

Conscious that she was feeling sad, as well as wasting her time, she went back indoors and made out the bill; there might not be time in the morning.

She was up early the next morning; breakfast was to be ready by eight o'clock, she had been told on the previous evening—a decision she'd welcomed with relief. Breakfast was eaten, the bill paid—but only after double-checking everything on it and some scathing comments about the lack of modern amenities.

Amabel waited politely at the door until they had driven away then went to put the money in the old tea caddy on the kitchen dresser. It added substantially to the contents but it had been hard earned!

The rooms, as she'd expected, had been left in a disgraceful state. She flung open the window, stripped beds and set about turning them back to their usual pristine appearance. It was still early, and it was a splendid morning, so she filled the washing machine and started on the breakfast dishes.

By midday everything was just as it should be. She made sandwiches and took them and a mug of coffee out to the orchard with Cyril and Oscar for company, and sat down to read the letter from her mother the postman had brought. Everything was splendid, she wrote. The baby was thriving and she had decided to stay another few weeks, if Amabel could manage for a little longer—*For I don't suppose I'll be able to visit here for a year or two, unless something turns up.*

Which was true enough, and it made sense too. Her mother had taken out a loan so that she could go to Canada, and even though it was a small one it would have to be paid off before she went again.

Amabel put the letter in her pocket, divided the rest of her sandwich between Cyril and Oscar and went back into the house. There was always the chance that someone would come around teatime and ask for a meal, so she would make a cake and a batch of scones.

It was as well that she did; she had just taken them out of the Aga when the doorbell rang and two elderly ladies enquired if she would give them bed and breakfast.

They had come in an old Morris, and, while well-spoken and tidily dressed, she judged them to be not too free with their money. But they looked nice and she had a kind heart.

'If you would share a twin-bedded room?' she suggested. 'The charge is the same for two people as one.' She told them how much and added, 'Two breakfasts, of course, and if you would like tea?'

They glanced at each other. 'Thank you. Would you serve us a light supper later?'

'Certainly. If you would fetch your cases? The car can go into the barn at the side of the house.'

Amabel gave them a good tea, and while they went for a short walk, she got supper—salmon fish cakes, of tinned salmon, of course, potatoes whipped to a satiny smoothness, and peas from the garden. She popped an egg custard into the oven by way of afters and was rewarded by their genteel thanks.

She ate her own supper in the kitchen, took them a pot of tea and wished them goodnight. In the morning she gave them boiled eggs, toast and marmalade and a pot of coffee, and all with a generous hand.

She hadn't made much money, but it had been nice to see their elderly faces light up. And they had left her a tip, discreetly put on one of the bedside tables. As for the bedroom, they had left it so neat it was hard to see that anyone had been in it.

She added the money to the tea caddy and decided that tomorrow she would go to the village and pay it into the post office account, stock up on groceries and get meat from the butcher's van which called twice a week at the village.

It was a lovely morning again, and her spirits rose despite her disappointment at her mother's delayed return home. She wasn't doing too badly with bed and breakfast, and she was adding steadily to their savings. There were the winter months to think of, of course, but she might be able to get a part-time job once her mother was home.

She went into the garden to pick peas, singing cheerfully and slightly off key.

Nobody came that day, and the following day only a solitary woman on a walking holiday came in the early evening; she went straight to bed after a pot of tea and left the next morning after an early breakfast.

After she had gone, Amabel discovered that she had taken the towels with her.

Two disappointing days, reflected Amabel. I wonder what will happen tomorrow?

She was up early again, for there was no point in lying in bed when it was daylight soon after five o'clock. She breakfasted, tidied the house, did a pile of ironing before the day got too hot, and then wandered out to the bench in the orchard. It was far too early for any likely person to want a room, and she would hear if a car stopped in the lane.

But of course one didn't hear a Rolls Royce, for it made almost no sound.

Dr Fforde got out and stood looking at the house. It was a pleasant place, somewhat in need of small repairs and a lick of paint, but its small windows shone and the brass knocker on its solid front door was burnished to a dazzling brightness. He trod round the side of the house, past the barn, and saw Amabel sitting between Cyril and Oscar. Since she was a girl who couldn't abide being idle, she was shelling peas.

He stood watching her for a moment, wondering why he had wanted to see her again. True, she had interested him, so small, plain and pot valiant, and so obviously terrified of the storm—and very much at the mercy of undesirable characters who might choose to call. Surely she had an aunt or cousin who could come and stay with her?

It was none of his business, of course, but it had seemed a good idea to call and see her since he was on his way to Glastonbury.

He stepped onto the rough gravel of the yard so that she looked up.

She got to her feet, and her smile left him in no doubt that she was glad to see him.

He said easily, 'Good morning. I'm on my way to Glastonbury. Have you quite recovered from the storm?'

'Oh, yes.' She added honestly, 'But I was frightened, you know. I was so very glad when you and your mother came.'

She collected up the colander of peas and came towards him. 'Would you like a cup of coffee?'

'Yes, please.' He followed her into the kitchen and sat down at the table and thought how restful she was; she had seemed glad to see him, but she had probably learned to give a welcoming smile to anyone who knocked on the door. Certainly she had displayed no fuss at seeing him.

He said on an impulse, 'Will you have lunch with me? There's a pub—the Old Boot in Underthorn—fifteen minutes' drive from here. I don't suppose you get any callers before the middle of the afternoon?'

She poured the coffee and fetched a tin of biscuits.

'But you're on your way to Glastonbury…'

'Yes, but not expected until teatime. And it's such a splendid day.' When she hesitated he said, 'We could take Cyril with us.'

She said then, 'Thank you; I should like that. But I must be back soon after two o'clock; it's Saturday…'

They went back to the orchard presently, and sat on the bench while Amabel finished shelling the peas. Oscar had got onto the doctor's knee and Cyril had sprawled under his feet. They talked idly about nothing much and Amabel, quite at her ease, now answered his carefully put questions without realising just how much she was telling him until she stopped in mid-sentence, aware that her tongue was running away with her. He saw that at once and began to talk about something else.

They drove to the Old Boot Inn just before noon and found a table on the rough grass at its back. There was a small river, overshadowed by trees, and since it was early there was no one else there. They ate home-made pork pies with salad, and drank iced lemonade which the landlord's wife made herself. Cyril sat at their feet with a bowl of water and a biscuit.

The landlord, looking at them from the bar window, observed to his wife, 'Look happy, don't they?'

And they were, all three of them, although the doctor hadn't identified his feeling as happiness, merely pleasant content at the glorious morning and the undemanding company.

He drove Amabel back presently and, rather to her surprise, parked the car in the yard behind the house, got out, took the door key from her and unlocked the back door.

Oscar came to meet them and he stooped to stroke him. 'May I sit in the orchard for a little while?' he asked. 'I seldom get the chance to sit quietly in such peaceful surroundings.'

Amabel stopped herself just in time from saying, 'You poor man,' and said instead, 'Of course you may, for as long as you like. Would you like a cup of tea, or an apple?'

So he sat on the bench chewing an apple, with Oscar on his knee, aware that his reason for sitting there was to cast an eye over any likely guests in the hope that before he went a respectable middle-aged pair would have decided to stay.

He was to have his wish. Before very long a middle-aged pair did turn up, with mother-in-law, wishing to stay for two nights. It was absurd, he told himself, that he should feel concern. Amabel was a perfectly capable young woman, and able to look after herself; besides, she had a telephone.

He went to the open kitchen door and found her there, getting tea.

'I must be off,' he told her. 'Don't stop what you're doing. I enjoyed my morning.'

She was cutting a large cake into neat slices. 'So did I. Thank you for my lunch.' She smiled at him. 'Go carefully, Dr Fforde.'

She carried the tea tray into the drawing room and went back to the kitchen. They were three nice people—polite, and anxious not to be too much trouble. 'An evening meal?' they had asked diffidently, and had accepted her offer of jacket potatoes and salad, fruit tart and coffee with pleased smiles. They would go for a short walk presently, the man told her, and when would she like to serve their supper?

When they had gone she made the tart, put the potatoes in the oven and went to the vegetable patch by the orchard to get a lettuce and radishes. There was no hurry, so she sat down on the bench and thought about the day.

She had been surprised to see the doctor again. She had been pleased too. She had thought about him, but she hadn't expected to see him again; when she had looked up and seen him standing there it had been like seeing an old friend.

'Nonsense,' said Amabel loudly. 'He came this morning because he wanted a cup of coffee.' What about taking you out to lunch? asked a persistent voice at the back of her mind.

'He's probably a man who doesn't like to eat alone.'

And, having settled the matter, she went back to the kitchen.

The three guests intended to spend Sunday touring around the countryside. They would return at tea time and could they have supper? They added that they would want to leave early the next morning, which left Amabel with almost all day free to do as she wanted.

There was no need for her to stay at the house; she didn't intend to let the third room if anyone called. She would go to church and then spend a quiet afternoon with the Sunday paper.

She liked going to church, for she met friends and acquaintances and could have a chat, and at the same time assure anyone who asked that her mother would be coming home soon and that she herself was perfectly content on her own. She was aware that some of the older members of the congregation didn't approve of her mother's trip and thought that at the very least some friend or cousin should have moved in with Amabel.

It was something she and her mother had discussed at some length, until her mother had burst into tears, declaring that she wouldn't be able to go to Canada. Amabel had said at once that she would much rather be on her own, so her mother had gone, and Amabel had written her a letter each week, giving light-hearted and slightly optimistic accounts of the bed and breakfast business.

Her mother had been gone for a month now; she had phoned when she had arrived and since then had written regularly, although she still hadn't said when she would be returning.

Amabel, considering the matter while Mr Huggett, the church warden, read the first lesson, thought that her

mother's next letter would certainly contain news of her
return. Not for the world would she admit, even to herself, that she didn't much care for living on her own.
She was, in fact, uneasy at night, even though the house
was locked and securely bolted.

She kept a stout walking stick which had belonged to
her father by the front door, and a rolling pin handy in
the kitchen, and there was always the phone; she had
only to lift it and dial 999!

Leaving the church presently, and shaking hands with
the vicar, she told him cheerfully that her mother would
be home very soon.

'You are quite happy living there alone, Amabel? You
have friends to visit you, I expect?'

'Oh, yes,' she assured him. 'And there's so much to
keep me busy. The garden and the bed and breakfast
people keep me occupied.'

He said with vague kindness, 'Nice people, I hope,
my dear?'

'I'm careful who I take,' she assured him.

It was seldom that any guests came on a Monday;
Amabel cleaned the house, made up beds and checked
the fridge, made herself a sandwich and went to the orchard to eat it. It was a pleasant day, cool and breezy,
just right for gardening.

She went to bed quite early, tired with the digging,
watering and weeding. Before she went to sleep she allowed her thoughts to dwell on Dr Fforde. He seemed
like an old friend, but she knew nothing about him. Was
he married? Where did he live? Was he a GP, or working
at a hospital? He dressed well and drove a Rolls Royce,
and he had family or friends somewhere on the other

side of Glastonbury. She rolled over in bed and closed
her eyes. It was none of her business anyway...

The fine weather held and a steady trickle of tourists
knocked on the door. The tea caddy was filling up nicely
again; her mother would be delighted. The week slid
imperceptibly into the next one, and at the end of it there
was a letter from her mother. The postman arrived with
it at the same time as a party of four—two couples sharing a car on a brief tour—so that Amabel had to put it
in her pocket until they had been shown their rooms and
had sat down to tea.

She went into the kitchen, got her own tea and sat
down to read it.

It was a long letter, and she read it through to the
end—and then read it again. She had gone pale, and
drank her cooling tea with the air of someone unaware
of what they were doing, but presently she picked up
the letter and read it for the third time.

Her mother wasn't coming home. At least not for several months. She had met someone and they were to be
married shortly.

*I know you will understand. And you'll like him.
He's a market gardener, and we plan to set up a garden centre from the house. There's plenty of room and
he will build a large glasshouse at the bottom of the
orchard. Only he must sell his own market garden
first, which may take some months.*

*It will mean that we shan't need to do bed and
breakfast any more, although I hope you'll keep on
with it until we get back. You're doing so well. I know
that the tourist season is quickly over but we hope to
be back before Christmas.*

The rest of the letter was a detailed description of her husband-to-be and news too, of her sister and the baby.

You're such a sensible girl, her mother concluded, *and I'm sure you're enjoying your independence. Probably when we get back you will want to start a career on your own.*

Amabel was surprised, she told herself, but there was no reason for her to feel as though the bottom had dropped out of her world; she was perfectly content to stay at home until her mother and stepfather should return, and it was perfectly natural for her mother to suppose that she would like to make a career for herself.

Amabel drank the rest of the tea, now stewed and cold. She would have plenty of time to decide what kind of career she would like to have.

That evening, her guests in their rooms, she sat down with pen and paper and assessed her accomplishments. She could cook—not quite cordon bleu, perhaps, but to a high standard—she could housekeep, change plugs, cope with basic plumbing. She could tend a garden... Her pen faltered. There was nothing else.

She had her A levels, but circumstances had never allowed her to make use of them. She would have to train for something and she would have to make up her mind what that should be before her mother came home. But training cost money, and she wasn't sure if there would be any. She could get a job and save enough to train...

She sat up suddenly, struck by a sudden thought. Waitresses needed no training, and there would be tips. In one of the larger towns, of course. Taunton or Yeovil? Or what about one of the great estates run by the

National Trust? They had shops and tearooms and house guides. The more she thought about it, the better she liked it.

She went to bed with her decision made. Now it was just a question of waiting until her mother and her stepfather came home.

CHAPTER TWO

IT WAS almost a week later when she had the next letter, but before that her mother had phoned. She was so happy, she'd said excitedly; they planned to marry in October—Amabel didn't mind staying at home until they returned? Probably in November?

'It's only a few months, Amabel, and just as soon as we're home Keith says you must tell us what you want to do and we'll help you do it. He's so kind and generous. Of course if he sells his business quickly we shall come home as soon as we can arrange it.'

Amabel had heard her mother's happy little laugh. 'I've written you a long letter about the wedding. Joyce and Tom are giving a small reception for us, and I've planned such a pretty outfit—it's all in the letter...'

The long letter when it arrived was bursting with excitement and happiness.

You have no idea how delightful it is not to have to worry about the future, to have someone to look after me—you too, of course. Have you decided what you want to do when we get home? You must be so excited at the idea of being independent; you have had such a dull life since you left school...

But a contented one, reflected Amabel. Helping to turn their bed and breakfast business into a success, knowing that she was wanted, feeling that she and her mother were making something of their lives. And now she must start all over again.

It would be nice to wallow in self-pity, but there were two people at the door asking if she could put them up for the night...

Because she was tired she slept all night, although the moment she woke thoughts came tumbling into her head which were better ignored, so she got up earlier than usual and went outside in her dressing gown with a mug of tea and Cyril and Oscar for company.

It was pleasant sitting on the bench in the orchard in the early-morning sun, and in its cheerful light it was impossible to be gloomy. It would be nice, though, to be able to talk to someone about her future...

Dr Fforde's large, calm person came into her mind's eye; he would have listened and told her what she should do. She wondered what he was doing...

Dr Fforde was sitting on the table in the kitchen of his house, the end one in a short terrace of Regency houses in a narrow street tucked away behind Wimpole Street in London. He was wearing a tee shirt and elderly trousers and badly needed a shave; he had the appearance of a ruffian—a handsome ruffian. There was a half-eaten apple on the table beside him and he was taking great bites from a thick slice of bread and butter. He had been called out just after two o'clock that morning to operate on a patient with a perforated duodenal ulcer; there had been complications which had kept him from his bed and now he was on his way to shower and get ready for his day.

He finished his bread and butter, bent to fondle the sleek head of the black Labrador sitting beside him, and went to the door. It opened as he reached it. The young-ish man who came in was already dressed, immaculate in a black alpaca jacket and striped trousers. He had a sharp-nosed foxy face, and dark hair brushed to a satin smoothness.

He stood aside for the doctor and wished him a severe good morning.

'Out again, sir?' His eye fell on the apple core. 'You had only to call me. I'd have got you a nice hot drink and a sandwich...'

The doctor clapped him on the shoulder. 'I know you would, Bates. I'll be down in half an hour for one of your special breakfasts. I disturbed Tiger; would you let him out into the garden?'

He went up the graceful little staircase to his room, his head already filled with thoughts of the day ahead of him. Amabel certainly had no place in them.

Half an hour later he was eating the splendid breakfast Bates had carried through to the small sitting room at the back of the house. Its French windows opened onto a small patio and a garden beyond where Tiger was me-andering round. Presently he came to sit by his master, to crunch bacon rinds and then accompany him on a brisk walk through the still quiet streets before the doctor got into his car and drove the short distance to the hos-pital.

Amabel saw her two guests on their way, got the room ready for the next occupants and then on a sudden im-pulse went to the village and bought the regional weekly paper at the post office. Old Mr Truscott, who ran it and knew everyone's business, took his time giving her her change.

'Didn't know you were interested in the *Gazette*, nothing much in it but births, marriages and deaths.' He fixed her with a beady eye. 'And adverts, of course. Now if anyone was looking for a job it's a paper I'd recommend.'

Amabel said brightly, 'I dare say it's widely read, Mr Truscott. While I'm here I'd better have some more air mail letters.'

'Your ma's not coming home yet, then? Been gone a long time, I reckon.'

'She's staying a week or two longer; she might not get the chance to visit my sister again for a year or two. It's a long way to go for just a couple of weeks.

Over her lunch she studied the jobs page. There were heartening columns of vacancies for waitresses: the basic wage was fairly low, but if she worked full-time she could manage very well... And Stourhead, the famous National Trust estate, wanted shop assistants, help in the tearooms and suitable applicants for full-time work in the ticket office. And none of them were wanted until the end of September.

It seemed too good to be true, but all the same she cut the ad out and put it with the bed and breakfast money in the tea caddy.

A week went by, and then another. Summer was almost over. The evenings were getting shorter, and, while the mornings were light still, there was the ghost of a nip in the air. There had been more letters from Canada from her mother and future stepfather, and her sister, and during the third week her mother had telephoned; they were married already—now it was just a question of selling Keith's business.

'We hadn't intended to marry so soon but there was no reason why we shouldn't, and of course I've moved in with him,' she said. 'So if he can sell his business soon we shall be home before long. We have such plans...!'

There weren't as many people knocking on the door now; Amabel cleaned and polished the house, picked the last of the soft fruit to put in the freezer and cast an eye over the contents of the cupboards.

With a prudent eye to her future she inspected her wardrobe—a meagre collection of garments, bought with an eye to their long-lasting qualities, in good taste but which did nothing to enhance her appearance.

Only a handful of people came during the week, and no one at all on Saturday. She felt low-spirited—owing to the damp and gloomy weather, she told herself—and even a brisk walk with Cyril didn't make her feel any better. It was still only early afternoon and she sat down in the kitchen, with Oscar on her lap, disinclined to do anything.

She would make herself a pot of tea, write to her mother, have an early supper and go to bed. Soon it would be the beginning of another week; if the weather was better there might be a satisfying number of tourists—and besides, there were plenty of jobs to do in the garden. So she wrote her letter, very bright and cheerful, skimming over the lack of guests, making much of the splendid apple crop and how successful the soft fruit had been. That done, she went on sitting at the kitchen table, telling herself that she would make the tea.

Instead of that she sat, a small sad figure, contemplating a future which held problems. Amabel wasn't a girl given to self-pity, and she couldn't remember the last time she had cried, but she cried now, quietly and without fuss, a damp Oscar on her lap, Cyril's head pressed against her legs. She made no attempt to stop; there was no one there to see, and now that the rain was coming down in earnest no one would want to stop for the night.

Dr Fforde had a free weekend, but he wasn't particularly enjoying it. He had lunched on Saturday with friends, amongst whom had been Miriam Potter-Stokes, an elegant young widow who was appearing more and more frequently in his circle of friends. He felt vaguely sorry for her, admired her for the apparently brave face she was showing to the world, and what had been a casual friendship now bid fair to become something more serious—on her part at least.

He had found himself agreeing to drive her down to Henley after lunch, and once there had been forced by good manners to stay at her friend's home for tea. On the way back to London she had suggested that they might have dinner together.

He had pleaded a prior engagement and gone back to his home feeling that his day had been wasted. She was an amusing companion, pretty and well dressed, but he had wondered once or twice what she was really like. Certainly he enjoyed her company from time to time, but that was all...

He took Tiger for a long walk on Sunday morning and after lunch got into his car. It was no day for a drive into the country, and Bates looked his disapproval.

'Not going to Glastonbury in this weather, I hope, sir?' he observed.

'No, no. Just a drive. Leave something cold for my supper, will you?'

Bates looked offended. When had he ever forgotten to leave everything ready before he left the house?

'As always, sir,' he said reprovingly.

It wasn't until he was driving west through the quiet city streets that Dr Fforde admitted to himself that he knew where he was going. Watching the carefully nurtured beauty of Miriam Potter-Stokes had reminded him of Amabel. He had supposed, in some amusement, because the difference in the two of them was so marked. It would be interesting to see her again. Her mother would be back home by now, and he doubted if there were many people wanting bed and breakfast now that summer had slipped into a wet autumn.

He enjoyed driving, and the roads, once he was clear of the suburbs, were almost empty. Tiger was an undemanding companion, and the countryside was restful after the bustle of London streets.

The house, when he reached it, looked forlorn; there were no open windows, no signs of life. He got out of the car with Tiger and walked round the side of the house; he found the back door open.

Amabel looked up as he paused at the door. He thought that she looked like a small bedraggled brown hen. He said, 'Hello, may we come in?' and bent to fondle the two dogs, giving her time to wipe her wet cheeks with the back of her hand. 'Tiger's quite safe with Cyril, and he likes cats.'

Amabel stood up, found a handkerchief and blew her nose. She said in a social kind of voice, 'Do come in.

Isn't it an awful day? I expect you're on your way to Glastonbury. Would you like a cup of tea? I was just going to make one.'

'Thank you, that would be nice.' He had come into the kitchen now, reaching up to tickle a belligerent Oscar under the chin. 'I'm sorry Tiger's frightened your cat. I don't suppose there are many people about on a day like this—and your mother isn't back yet?'

She said in a bleak little voice, 'No...' and then to her shame and horror burst into floods of tears.

Dr Fforde sat her down in the chair again. He said comfortably, 'I'll make the tea and you shall tell me all about it. Have a good cry; you'll feel better. Is there any cake?'

Amabel said in a small wailing voice, 'But I've been crying and I don't feel any better.' She gave a hiccough before adding, 'And now I've started again.' She took the large white handkerchief he offered her. 'The cake's in a tin in the cupboard in the corner.'

He put the tea things on the table and cut the cake, found biscuits for the dogs and spooned cat food onto a saucer for Oscar, who was still on top of a cupboard. Then he sat down opposite Amabel and put a cup of tea before her.

'Drink some of that and then tell me why you are crying. Don't leave anything out, for I'm merely a ship which is passing in the night, so you can say what you like and it will be forgotten—rather like having a bag of rubbish and finding an empty dustbin...'

She smiled then. 'You make it sound so—so normal...' She sipped her tea. 'I'm sorry I'm behaving so badly.'

He cut the cake and gave her a piece, before saying

matter-of-factly, 'Is your mother's absence the reason? Is she ill?'

'Ill? No, no. She's married someone in Canada...'

It was such a relief to talk to someone about it. It all came tumbling out: a hotch-potch of market gardens, plans for coming back and the need for her to be independent as soon as possible.

He listened quietly, refilling their cups, his eyes on her blotched face, and when she had at last finished her muddled story, he said, 'And now you have told me you feel better about it, don't you? It has all been bottled up inside you, hasn't it? Going round inside your head like butter in a churn. It has been a great shock to you, and shocks should be shared. I won't offer you advice, but I will suggest that you do nothing—make no plans, ignore your future—until your mother is home. I think that you may well find that you have been included in their plans and that you need no worries about your future. I can see that you might like to become independent, but don't rush into it. You're young enough to stay at home while they settle in, and that will give you time to decide what you want to do.'

When she nodded, he added, 'Now, go and put your hair up and wash your face. We're going to Castle Cary for supper.'

She gaped at him. ' I can't possibly...'

'Fifteen minutes should be time enough.'

She did her best with her face, and piled her hair neatly, then got into a jersey dress, which was an off the peg model, but of a pleasing shade of cranberry-red, stuck her feet into her best shoes and went back into the kitchen. Her winter coat was out of date and shabby, and for once she blessed the rain, for it meant that she could wear her mac.

Their stomachs nicely filled, Cyril and Oscar were already half asleep, and Tiger was standing by his master, eager to be off.

'I've locked everything up,' observed the doctor, and ushered Amabel out of the kitchen, turned the key in the lock and put it in his pocket, and urged her into the car. He hadn't appeared to look at her at all, but all the same he saw that she had done her best with her appearance. And the restaurant he had in mind had shaded rose lamps on its tables, if he remembered aright…

There weren't many people there on a wet Sunday evening, but the place was welcoming, and the rosy shades were kind to Amabel's still faintly blotchy face. Moreover, the food was good. He watched the pink come back into her cheeks as they ate their mushrooms in garlic sauce, local trout and a salad fit for the Queen. And the puddings were satisfyingly shrouded in thick clotted cream…

The doctor kept up a gentle stream of undemanding talk, and Amabel, soothed by it, was unaware of time passing until she caught sight of the clock.

She said in a shocked voice, 'It's almost nine. You will be so late at Glastonbury…'

'I'm going back to town,' he told her easily, but he made no effort to keep her, driving her back without more ado, seeing her safely into the house and driving off again with a friendly if casual goodbye.

The house, when he had gone, was empty—and too quiet. Amabel settled Cyril and Oscar for the night and went to bed.

It had been a lovely evening, and it had been such a

relief to talk to someone about her worries, but now she had the uneasy feeling that she had made a fool of herself, crying and pouring out her problems like a hysterical woman. Because he was a doctor, and was used to dealing with awkward patients, he had listened to her, given her a splendid meal and offered sensible suggestions as to her future. Probably he dealt with dozens like her...

She woke to a bright morning, and around noon a party of four knocked on the door and asked for rooms for the night, so Amabel was kept busy. By the end of the day she was tired enough to fall into bed and sleep at once.

There was no one for the next few days but there was plenty for her to do. The long summer days were over, and a cold wet autumn was predicted.

She collected the windfalls from the orchard, picked the last of the beans for the freezer, saw to beetroots, carrots and winter cabbage and dug the rest of the potatoes. She went to the rickety old greenhouse to pick tomatoes. She supposed that when her stepfather came he would build a new one; she and her mother had made do with it, and the quite large plot they used for vegetables grew just enough to keep them supplied throughout the year, but he was bound to make improvements.

It took her most of the week to get the garden in some sort of order, and at the weekend a party of six stayed for two nights, so on Monday morning she walked to the villager to stock up on groceries, post a letter to her mother and, on an impulse, bought the local paper again.

Back home, studying the jobs page, she saw with regret that the likely offers of work were no longer in it. There would be others, she told herself stoutly, and she must remember what Dr Fforde had told her—not to rush into anything. She must be patient; her mother had said that they hoped to be home before Christmas, but that was still weeks away, and even so he had advised her to do nothing hastily…

It was two days later, while she was putting away sheets and pillowcases in the landing cupboard, when she heard Cyril barking. He sounded excited, and she hurried downstairs; she had left the front door unlocked and someone might have walked in…

Her mother was standing in the hall, and there was a tall thickset man beside her. She was laughing and stooping to pat Cyril, then she looked up and saw Amabel.

'Darling, aren't we a lovely surprise? Keith sold the business, so there was no reason why we shouldn't come back here.'

She embraced Amabel, and Amabel, hugging her back, said, 'Oh, Mother—how lovely to see you.'

She looked at the man and smiled—and knew immediately that she didn't like him and that he didn't like her. But she held out a hand and said, 'How nice to meet you. It's all very exciting, isn't it?'

Cyril had pushed his nose into Keith's hand and she saw his impatient hand push it away. Her heart sank.

Her mother was talking and laughing, looking into the rooms, exclaiming how delightful everything looked. 'And there's Oscar.' She turned to her husband. 'Our cat, Keith. I know you don't like cats, but he's one of the family.'

He made some non-committal remark and went to fetch the luggage. Mrs Parsons, now Mrs Graham, ran upstairs to her room, and Amabel went to the kitchen to get tea. Cyril and Oscar went with her and arranged themselves tidily in a corner of the kitchen, aware that this man with the heavy tread didn't like them.

They had tea in the sitting room and the talk was of Canada and their journey and their plans to establish a market garden.

'No more bed and breakfast,' said Mrs Graham. 'Keith wants to get the place going as soon as possible. If we can get a glasshouse up quickly we could pick up some of the Christmas trade.'

'Where will you put it?' asked Amabel. 'There's plenty of ground beyond the orchard.'

Keith had been out to look around before tea, and now he observed, 'I'll get that ploughed and dug over for spring crops, and I'll put the glasshouse in the orchard. There's no money in apples, and some of the trees look past it. We'll finish picking and then get rid of them. There's plenty of ground there—fine for peas and beans.'

He glanced at Amabel. 'Your mother tells me you're pretty handy around the house and garden. The two of us ought to be able to manage to get something started— I'll hire a man with a rotavator who'll do the rough digging; the lighter jobs you'll be able to manage.'

Amabel didn't say anything. For one thing she was too surprised and shocked; for another, it was early days to be making such sweeping plans. And what about her mother's suggestion that she might like to train for something? If her stepfather might be certain of his plans, but why was he so sure that she would agree to them? And she didn't agree with them. The orchard had always been there, long before she was born. It still produced a good crop of apples and in the spring it was so beautiful with the blossom...

She glanced at her mother, who looked happy and content and was nodding admiringly at her new husband.

It was later, as she was getting the supper that he came into the kitchen.

'Have to get rid of that cat,' he told her briskly. 'Can't abide them, and the dog's getting on a bit, isn't he? Animals don't go well with market gardens. Not to my reckoning, anyway.'

'Oscar is no trouble at all,' said Amabel, and tried hard to sound friendly. 'And Cyril is a good guard dog; he never lets anyone near the house.'

She had spoken quietly, but he looked at her face and said quickly, 'Oh, well, no hurry about them. It'll take a month or two to get things going how I want them.'

He in his turn essayed friendliness. 'We'll make a success of it, too. Your mother can manage the house and you can work full-time in the garden. We might even take on casual labour after a bit—give you time to spend with your young friends.'

He sounded as though he was conferring a favour upon her, and her dislike deepened, but she mustn't allow it to show. He was a man who liked his own way and intended to have it. Probably he was a good husband to her mother, but he wasn't going to be a good stepfather...

Nothing much happened for a few days; there was a good deal of unpacking to do, letters to write and trips to the bank. Quite a substantial sum of money had been transferred from Canada and Mr Graham lost no time in making enquiries about local labour. He also went up to London to meet men who had been recommended as likely to give him financial backing, should he require it.

In the meantime Amabel helped her mother around the house, and tried to discover if her mother had meant her to have training of some sort and then changed her mind at her husband's insistence.

Mrs Graham was a loving parent, but easily dominated by anyone with a stronger will than her own. What was the hurry? she wanted to know. A few more months at home were neither here nor there, and she would be such a help to Keith.

'He's such a marvellous man, Amabel, he's bound to make a success of whatever he does.'

Amabel said cautiously, 'It's a pity he doesn't like Cyril and Oscar...'

Her mother laughed. 'Oh, darling, he would never be unkind to them.'

Perhaps not unkind, but as the weeks slipped by it was apparent that they were no longer to be regarded as pets around the house. Cyril spent a good deal of time outside, roaming the orchard, puzzled as to why the kitchen door was so often shut. As for Oscar, he only came in for his meals, looking carefully around to make sure that there was no one about.

Amabel did what she could, but her days were full, and it was obvious that Mr Graham was a man who rode roughshod over anyone who stood in his way. For the sake of her mother's happiness Amabel held her tongue; there was no denying that he was devoted to her mother, and she to him, but there was equally no denying that he found Amabel, Cyril and Oscar superfluous to his life.

It wasn't until she came upon him hitting Cyril and then turning on an unwary Oscar and kicking him aside that Amabel knew that she would have to do something about it.

She scooped up a trembling Oscar and bent to put an arm round Cyril's elderly neck. 'How dare you? Whatever have they done to you? They're my friends and I love them,' she added heatedly, 'and they have lived here all their lives.'

Her stepfather stared at her. 'Well, they won't live here much longer if I have my way. I'm the boss here. I don't like animals around the place so you'd best make up your mind to that.'

He walked off without another word and Amabel, watching his retreating back, knew that she had to do something—and quickly.

She went out to the orchard—there were piles of bricks and bags of cement already heaped near the bench, ready to start building the glasshouse—and with Oscar on her lap and Cyril pressed against her she reviewed and discarded several plans, most of them too far-fetched to be of any use. Finally she had the nucleus of a sensible idea. But first she must have some money, and secondly the right opportunity...

As though a kindly providence approved of her efforts, she was able to have both. That very evening her stepfather declared that he would have to go to London in the morning. A useful acquaintance had phoned to say that he would meet him and introduce him to a wholesaler who would consider doing business with him once he was established. He would go to London early in the morning, and since he had a long day ahead of him he went to bed early.

Presently, alone with her mother, Amabel seized what seemed to be a golden opportunity.

'I wondered if I might have some money for clothes, Mother. I haven't bought anything since you went away...'

'Of course, love. I should have thought of that myself. And you did so well with the bed and breakfast business. Is there any money in the tea caddy? If there is take whatever you want from it. I'll ask Keith to make you an allowance; he's so generous...'

'No, don't do that, Mother. He has enough to think about without bothering him about that; there'll be enough in the tea caddy. Don't bother him.' She looked across at her mother. 'You're very happy with him, aren't you, Mother?'

'Oh, yes, Amabel. I never told you, but I hated living here, just the two of us, making ends meet, no man around the place. When I went to your sister's I realised what I was missing. And I've been thinking that perhaps it would be a good idea if you started some sort of training...'

Amabel agreed quietly, reflecting that her mother wouldn't miss her...

Her mother went to bed presently, and Amabel made Oscar and Cyril comfortable for the night and counted the money in the tea caddy. There was more than enough for her plan.

She went to her room and, quiet as a mouse, got her holdall out of the wardrobe and packed it, including undies and a jersey skirt and a couple of woollies; autumn would soon turn to winter...

She thought over her plan when she was in bed; there seemed no way of improving upon it, so she closed her eyes and went to sleep.

She got up early, to prepare breakfast for her stepfather, having first of all made sure that Oscar and Cyril weren't in the kitchen. Once he had driven away she got her own breakfast, fed both animals and got dressed. Her mother came down, and over her coffee suggested that she might get the postman to give her a lift to Castle Cary.

'I've time to dress before he comes, and I can get my hair done. You'll be all right, love?'

It's as though I'm meant to be leaving, reflected Amabel. And when her mother was ready, and waiting for the postman, reminded her to take a key with her— 'For I might go for a walk.'

Amabel had washed the breakfast dishes, tidied the house, and made the beds by the time her mother got into the post van, and if she gave her mother a sudden warm hug and kiss Mrs Graham didn't notice.

Half an hour later Amabel, with Oscar in his basket, Cyril on a lead, and encumbered by her holdall and a shoulder bag, was getting into the taxi she had requested. She had written to her mother explaining that it was high time she became independent and that she would write, but that she was not to worry. *You will both make a great success of the market garden and it will be easier for you both if Oscar, Cyril and myself aren't getting under your feet,* she had ended.

The taxi took them to Gillingham where—fortune still smiling—they got on the London train and, once there, took a taxi to Victoria bus station. By now Amabel realised her plans, so simple in theory, were fraught with possible disaster. But she had cooked her goose. She bought a ticket to York, had a cup of tea, got water for Cyril and put milk in her saucer for Oscar and then climbed into the long-distance bus.

It was half empty, and the driver was friendly. Amabel perched on a seat with Cyril at her feet and Oscar in his basket on her lap. She was a bit cramped, but at least they were still altogether...

It was three o'clock in the afternoon by now, and it was a hundred and ninety-three miles to York, where they would arrive at about half past eight. The end of the journey was in sight, and it only remained for Great-Aunt Thisbe to offer them a roof over their heads. A moot point since she was unaware of them coming...

'I should have phoned her,' muttered Amabel, 'but there was so much to think about in such a hurry.'

It was only now that the holes in her hare-brained scheme began to show, but it was too late to worry about it. She still had a little money, she was young, she could work and, most important of all, Oscar and Cyril were still alive...

Amabel, a sensible level-headed girl, had thrown her bonnet over the windmill with a vengeance.

She went straight to the nearest phone box at the bus station in York; she was too tired and light-headed from her impetuous journey to worry about Great-Aunt Thisbe's reaction.

When she heard that lady's firm, unhurried voice she said without preamble, 'It's me—Amabel, Aunt Thisbe. I'm at the bus station in York.'

She had done her best to keep her voice quiet and steady, but it held a squeak of panic. Supposing Aunt Thisbe put down the phone...

Miss Parsons did no such thing. When she had been told of her dead nephew's wife's remarriage she had disapproved, strongly but silently. Such an upheaval: a strange man taking over from her nephew's loved memory, and what about Amabel? She hadn't seen the girl for some years—what of her? Had her mother considered her?

She said now, 'Go and sit down on the nearest seat, Amabel. I'll be with you in half an hour.'

'I've got Oscar and Cyril with me.'

'You are all welcome,' said Aunt Thisbe, and rang off.

Much heartened by these words, Amabel found a bench and, with a patient Cyril crouching beside her and Oscar eyeing her miserably from the little window in his basket, sat down to wait.

Half an hour, when you're not very happy, can seem a very long time, but Amabel forgot that when she saw Great-Aunt Thisbe walking briskly towards her, clad in a coat and skirt which hadn't altered in style for the last few decades, her white hair crowned by what could best be described as a sensible hat. There was a youngish man with her, short and sturdy with weatherbeaten features.

Great-Aunt Thisbe kissed Amabel briskly. 'I am so glad you have come to visit me, my dear. Now we will go home and you shall tell me all about it. This is Josh, my right hand. He'll take your luggage to the car and drive us home.'

Amabel had got to her feet. She couldn't think of anything to say that wouldn't need a long explanation, so she held out a hand for Josh to shake, picked up Oscar's basket and Cyril's lead and walked obediently out into the street and got into the back of the car while Aunt Thisbe settled herself beside Josh.

It was dark now, and the road was almost empty of traffic. There was nothing to see from the car's window but Amabel remembered Bolton Percy was where her aunt lived, a medieval village some fifteen miles from York and tucked away from the main roads. It must be ten years since she was last here, she reflected; she had been sixteen and her father had died a few months earlier...

The village, when they reached it, was in darkness, but her aunt's house, standing a little apart from the row of brick and plaster cottages near the church, welcomed them with lighted windows.

Josh got out and helped her with the animals and she followed him up the path to the front door, which Great-Aunt Thisbe had opened.

'Welcome to my home, child,' she said. 'And yours for as long as you need it.'

CHAPTER THREE

THE next hour or two were a blur to Amabel; her coat was taken from her and she was sat in a chair in Aunt Thisbe's kitchen, bidden to sit there, drink the tea she was given and say nothing—something she was only too glad to do while Josh and her aunt dealt with Cyril and Oscar. In fact, quite worn out, she dozed off, to wake and find Oscar curled up on her lap, washing himself, and Cyril's head pressed against her knee.

Great-Aunt Thisbe spoke before she could utter a word.

'Stay there for a few minutes. Your room's ready, but you must have something to eat first.'

'Aunt Thisbe—' began Amabel.

'Later, child. Supper and a good night's sleep first. Do you want your mother to know you are here?'

'No, no. I'll explain…'

'Tomorrow.' Great-Aunt Thisbe, still wearing her hat, put a bowl of fragrant stew into Amabel's hands. 'Now eat your supper.'

Presently Amabel was ushered upstairs to a small room with a sloping ceiling and a lattice window. She didn't remember getting undressed, nor did she feel surprised to find both Oscar and Cyril with her. It had been a day like no other and she was beyond surprise or questioning; it seemed quite right that Cyril and Oscar should share her bed. They were still all together, she thought with satisfaction. It was like waking up after a particularly nasty nightmare.

When she woke in the morning she lay for a moment, staring up at the unfamiliar ceiling, but in seconds memory came flooding back and she sat up in bed, hampered by Cyril's weight on her feet and Oscar curled up near him. In the light of early morning yesterday's journey was something unbelievably foolhardy—and she would have to explain to Great-Aunt Thisbe.

The sooner the better.

She got up, went quietly to the bathroom, dressed and the three of them crept downstairs.

The house wasn't large, but it was solidly built, and had been added to over the years, and its small garden had a high stone wall. Amabel opened the stout door and went outside. Oscar and Cyril, old and wise enough to know what was wanted of them, followed her cautiously.

It was a fine morning but there was a nip in the air, and the three of them went back indoors just as Great-Aunt Thisbe came into the kitchen.

Her good morning was brisk and kind. 'You slept well? Good. Now, my dear, there's porridge on the Aga; I dare say these two will eat it. Josh will bring suitable food when he comes presently. And you and I will have a cup of tea before I get our breakfast.

'I must explain…'

'Of course. But over a cup of tea.'

So presently Amabel sat opposite her aunt at the kitchen table, drank her tea and gave her a carefully accurate account of her journey. 'Now I've thought about it, I can see how silly I was. I didn't stop to think, you see—only that I had to get away because my—my stepfather was going to kill...' She faltered. 'And he doesn't like me.'

'Your mother? She is happy with him?'

'Yes—yes, she is, and he is very good to her. They don't need me. I shouldn't have come here, only I had to think of something quickly. I'm so grateful to you, Aunt Thisbe, for letting me stay last night. I wondered if you would let me leave Oscar and Cyril here today, while I go into York and find work. I'm not trained, but there's always work in hotels and people's houses.'

The sound which issued from Miss Parsons' lips would have been called a snort from a lesser mortal.

'Your father was my brother, child. You will make this your home as long as you wish to stay. As to work— it will be a godsend to me to have someone young about the place. I'm well served by Josh and Mrs Josh, who cleans the place for me, but I could do with company, and in a week or two you can decide what you want to do.

'York is a big city; there are museums, historical houses, a wealth of interest to the visitor in Roman remains—all of which employ guides, curators, helpers of all kinds. There should be choice enough when it comes to looking for a job. The only qualifications needed are intelligence, the Queen's English and a pleasant voice and appearance. Now go and get dressed, and after breakfast you shall telephone your mother.'

'They will want me to go back—they don't want me, but he expects me to work for him in the garden.'

'You are under no obligation to your stepfather, Amabel, and your mother is welcome to come and visit you at any time. You are not afraid of your stepfather?'

'No—but I'm afraid of what he would do to Oscar and Cyril. And I don't like him.'

The phone conversation with her mother wasn't entirely satisfactory—Mrs Graham, at first relieved and glad to hear from Amabel, began to complain bitterly at what she described as Amabel's ingratitude.

'Keith will have to hire help,' she pointed out. 'He's very vexed about it, and really, Amabel, you have shown us a lack of consideration, going off like that. Of course we shall always be glad to see you, but don't expect any financial help—you've chosen to stand on your own two feet. Still, you're a sensible girl, and I've no doubt that you will find work—I don't suppose Aunt Thisbe will want you to stay for more than a week or two.' There was a pause. 'And you've got Oscar and Cyril with you?'

'Yes, Mother.'

'They'll hamper you when you look for work. Really, it would have been better if Keith had had them put down.'

'Mother! They have lived with us for years. They don't deserve to die.'

'Oh, well, but they're neither of them young. Will you phone again?'

Amabel said that she would and put down the phone. Despite Great-Aunt Thisbe's sensible words, she viewed the future with something like panic.

Her aunt took one look at her face, and said, 'Will you walk down to the shop and get me one or two things, child? Take Cyril with you—Oscar will be all right here—and we will have coffee when you get back.'

It was only a few minutes' walk to the stores in the centre of the village, and although it was drizzling and windy it was nice to be out of doors. It was a small village, but the church was magnificent and the narrow main street was lined with small solid houses and crowned at its end by a large brick and plaster pub.

Amabel did her shopping, surprised to discover that the stern-looking lady who served her knew who she was.

'Come to visit your auntie? She'll be glad of a bit of company for a week or two. A good thing she's spending the winter with that friend of hers in Italy...'

Two or three weeks, decided Amabel, walking back, should be enough time to find some kind of work and a place to live. Aunt Thisbe had told her that she was welcome to stay as long as she wanted to, but if she did that would mean her aunt would put off her holiday. Which would never do... She would probably mention it in a day or two—especially if Amabel lost no time in looking for work.

But a few days went by, and although Amabel reiterated her intention of finding work as soon as possible her aunt made no mention of her holiday; indeed she insisted that Amabel did nothing about it.

'You need a week or two to settle down,' she pointed out, 'and I won't hear of you leaving until you have decided what you want to do. It won't hurt you to spend the winter here.'

Which gave Amabel the chance to ask, 'But you may have made plans...'

Aunt Thisbe put down her knitting. 'And what plans would I be making at my age, child? Now, let us say no more for the moment. Tell me about your mother's wedding?'

So Amabel, with Oscar on her lap and Cyril sitting

between them, told all she knew, and presently they fell
to talking about her father, still remembered with love
by both of them.

Dr Fforde, immersed in his work though he was, nevertheless found his thoughts wandering, rather to his surprise, towards Amabel. It was some two weeks after she
had left home that he decided to go and see her again.
By now her mother and stepfather would be back and
she would have settled down with them and be perfectly
happy, all her doubts and fears forgotten.

He told himself that was his reason for going: to reassure himself that, knowing her to be happy again, he
could dismiss her from his mind.

It was mid-afternoon when he got there, and as he
parked the car he saw signs of activity at the back of
the house. Instead of knocking on the front door he
walked round the side of the house to the back. Most of
the orchard had disappeared, and there was a large concrete foundation where the trees had been. Beyond the
orchard the ground had been ploughed up; the bench had
gone, and the fruit bushes. Only the view beyond was
still beautiful.

He went to the kitchen door and knocked.

Amabel's mother stood in the doorway, and before
she could speak he said, 'I came to see Amabel.' He
held out a hand. 'Dr Fforde.'

Mrs Graham shook hands. She said doubtfully, 'Oh,
did you meet her when she was doing bed and breakfasts? She's not here; she's left.'

She held the door wide. 'Come in. My husband will
be back very shortly. Would you like a cup of tea?'

'Thank you.' He looked around him. 'There was a dog...'

'She's taken him with her—and the cat. My husband won't have animals around the place. He's starting up a market garden. The silly girl didn't like the idea of them being put down—left us in the lurch too; she was going to work for Keith, help with the place once we get started—we are having a big greenhouse built.'

'Yes, there was an orchard there.'

He accepted his tea and, when she sat down, took a chair opposite her.

'Where has Amabel gone?' The question was put so casually that Mrs Graham answered at once.

'Yorkshire, of all places—and heaven knows how she got there. My first husband's sister lives near York—a small village called Bolton Percy. Amabel went there— well, there wasn't anywhere else she could have gone without a job. We did wonder where she was, but she phoned when she got there... Here's my husband.'

The two men shook hands, exchanged a few minutes' conversation, then Dr Fforde got up to go.

He had expected his visit to Amabel's home to reassure him as to her future; it had done nothing of the sort. Her mother might be fond of her but obviously this overbearing man she had married would discourage her from keeping close ties with Amabel—he had made no attempt to disguise his dislike of her.

Driving himself back home, the doctor reflected that Amabel had been wise to leave. It seemed a bit drastic to go as far away as Yorkshire, but if she had family there they would have arranged her journey. He reminded himself that he had no need to concern himself about her; she had obviously dealt with her own future in a sensible manner. After all, she had seemed a sensible girl...

Bates greeted him with the news that Mrs Potter-Stokes had telephoned. 'Enquiring if you would take her to an art exhibition tomorrow evening which she had already mentioned.'

And why not? reflected Dr Fforde. He no longer needed to worry about Amabel. The art exhibition turned out to be very avant-garde, and Dr Fforde, escorting Miriam Potter-Stokes, listening to her rather vapid remarks, trying to make sense of the childish daubs acclaimed as genius, allowed his thoughts to wander. It was time he took a few days off, he decided. He would clear his desk of urgent cases and leave London for a while. He enjoyed driving and the roads were less busy now.

So when Miriam suggested that he might like to spend the weekend at her parents' home, he declined firmly, saying, 'I really can't spare the time, and I shall be out of London for a few days.'

'You poor man; you work far too hard. You need a wife to make sure that you don't do too much.'

She smiled up at him and then wished that she hadn't said that. Oliver had made some rejoinder dictated by good manners, but he had glanced at her with indifference from cold blue eyes. She must be careful, she reflected; she had set her heart on him for a husband...

Dr Fforde left London a week later. He had allowed himself three days: ample time to drive to York, seek out the village where Amabel was living and make sure that she was happy with this aunt and that she had some definite plans for her future. Although why he should concern himself with that he didn't go into too deeply.

A silly impetuous girl, he told himself, not meaning a word of it.

He left after an early breakfast, taking Tiger with him, sitting erect and watchful beside him, sliding through the morning traffic until at last he reached the M1. After a while he stopped at a service station, allowed Tiger a short run, drank a cup of coffee and drove on until, mindful of Tiger's heavy sighs, he stopped in a village north of Chesterfield.

The pub was almost empty and Tiger, his urgent needs dealt with, was made welcome, with a bowl of water and biscuits, while the doctor sat down before a plate of beef sandwiches, home-made pickles and half a pint of real ale.

Much refreshed, they got back into the car presently, their journey nearing its end. The doctor, a man who, having looked at the map before he started a journey, never needed to look at it again, turned off the motorway and made his way through country roads until he was rewarded by the sight of Bolton Percy's main street.

He stopped before the village stores and went in. The village was a small one; Amabel's whereabouts would be known...

As well as the severe-looking lady behind the counter there were several customers, none of whom appeared to be shopping with any urgency. They all turned to look at him as he went in, and even the severe-looking lady smiled at his pleasant greeting.

An elderly woman at the counter spoke up. 'Wanting to know the way? I'm in no hurry. Mrs Bluett—' she indicated the severe lady '—she'll help you.'

Dr Fforde smiled his thanks. 'I'm looking for a Miss Amabel Parsons.'

He was eyed with even greater interest.

'Staying with her aunt—Miss Parsons up at the End House. End of this street; house stands on its own beyond the row of cottages. You can't miss it. They'll be home.' She glanced at the clock. 'They sit down to high tea around six o'clock, but drink a cup around half past three. Expecting you, is she?'

'No...' Mrs Bluett looked at him so fiercely that he felt obliged to add, 'We have known each other for some time.' She smiled then, and he took his leave, followed by interested looks.

Stopping once more a hundred yards or so down the street, he got out of the car slowly and stood just for a moment looking at the house. It was red brick and plaster, solid and welcoming with its lighted windows. He crossed the pavement, walked up the short path to the front door and knocked.

Miss Parsons opened it. She stood looking at him with a severity which might have daunted a lesser man.

'I have come to see Amabel,' observed the doctor mildly. He held out a hand. 'Fforde—Oliver Fforde. Her mother gave me this address.'

Miss Parsons took his hand and shook it. 'Thisbe Parsons. Amabel's aunt. She has spoken of you.' She looked round his great shoulder. 'Your car? It will be safe there. And a dog?'

She took another good luck at him and liked what she saw. 'We're just about to have a cup of tea. Do bring the dog in—he's not aggressive? Amabel's Cyril is here...'

'They are already acquainted.' He smiled. 'Thank you.'

He let Tiger out of the car and the pair of them followed her into the narrow hallway.

Miss Parsons marched ahead of them, opened a door and led the way into the room, long and low, with windows at each end and an old-fashioned fireplace at its centre. The furniture was old-fashioned too, beautifully kept and largely covered by photos in silver frames and small china ornaments, some of them valuable, and a quantity of pot plants. It was a very pleasant room, lived in and loved and very welcoming.

The doctor, treading carefully between an occasional table and a Victorian spoon-back chair, watched Amabel get to her feet and heaved a sigh of relief at the pleased surprise on her face.

He said, carefully casual, 'Amabel...' and shook her hand, smiling down at her face. 'I called at your home and your mother gave me this address. I have to be in York for a day or two and it seemed a good idea to renew our acquaintance.'

She stared up into his kind face. 'I've left home...'

'So your stepfather told me. You are looking very well.'

'Oh, I am. Aunt Thisbe is so good to me, and Cyril and Oscar are happy.'

Miss Parsons lifted the teapot. 'Sit down and have your tea and tell me what brings you to York, Dr Fforde. It's a long way from London—you live there, I presume?'

The doctor had aunts of his own, so he sat down, drank his tea meekly and answered her questions without telling her a great deal. Tiger was sitting beside him, a model of canine obedience, while Cyril settled near him. Oscar, of course, had settled himself on top of the bookcase. Presently the talk became general, and he made no effort to ask Amabel how she came to be so far from her home. She would tell him in her own good time, and he had two days before he needed to return to London.

Miss Parsons said briskly, 'We have high tea at six o'clock. We hope you will join us. Unless you have some commitments in York?'

'Not until tomorrow morning. I should very much like to accept.'

'In that case you and Amabel had better take the dogs for a run while I see to a meal.'

It was dark by now, and chilly. Amabel got into her mac, put Cyril's lead on and led the way out of the house, telling him, 'We can go to the top of the village and come back along the back lane.'

The doctor took her arm and, with a dog at either side of them, they set off. 'Tell me what happened,' he suggested.

His gentle voice would have persuaded the most unwilling to confide in him and Amabel, her arm tucked under his, was only too willing. Aunt Thisbe was a dear, loving and kind under her brusque manner, but she hadn't been there; Dr Fforde had, so there was no need to explain about Cyril and Oscar or her stepfather...

She said slowly, 'I did try, really I did—to like him and stay at home until they'd settled in and I could suggest that I might train for something. But he didn't like me, although he expected me to work for him, and he hated Cyril and Oscar.'

She took a breath and began again, not leaving anything out, trying to keep to the facts and not colouring them with her feelings.

When she had finished the doctor said firmly, 'You

did quite right. It was rather hazardous of you to under-
take the long journey here, but it was a risk worth taking.'

They were making their way back to the house, and
although it was too dark to see he sensed that she was
crying. He reminded himself that he had adopted the role
of advisor and impersonal friend. That had been his intention and still was. Moreover, her aunt had offered her
a home. He resisted a desire to take her in his arms and
kiss her, something which, while giving him satisfaction
would possibly complicate matters. Instead he said
cheerfully, 'Will you spend the afternoon with me tomorrow? We might drive to the coast.'

Amabel swallowed tears. 'That would be very nice,'
she told him. 'Thank you.' And, anxious to match his
casual friendliness, she added, 'I don't know this part of
the world, do you?'

For the rest of the way back they discussed Yorkshire
and its beauties.

Aunt Thisbe was old-fashioned; the younger genera-
tion might like their dinner in the evening, but she had
remained faithful to high tea. The table was elegantly
laid, the teapot at one end, a covered dish of buttered
eggs at the other, with racks of toast, a dish of butter
and a home-made pâté. There was jam too, and a pot of
honey, and sandwiches, and in the centre of the table a
cakestand bearing scones, fruitcake, oatcakes and small
cakes from the local baker, known as fancies.

The doctor, a large and hungry man, found everything
to his satisfaction and made a good meal, something
which endeared him to Aunt Thisbe's heart, so that when
he suggested he might take Amabel for a drive the following day she said at once that it was a splendid idea.

Here was a man very much to her liking; it was a pity that it was obvious that his interest in Amabel was only one of impersonal kindness. The girl had been glad to see him, and heaven knew the child needed friends. A pity that he was only in York for a few days and lived so far away...

He washed the dishes and Amabel dried them after their meal. Aunt Thisbe, sitting in the drawing room, could hear them talking and laughing in the kitchen. Something would have to be done, thought the old lady. Amabel needed young friends, a chance to go out and enjoy herself; life would be dull for her during the winter. A job must be found for her where she would meet other people.

Aunt Thisbe felt sharp regret at the thought of the holiday she would have to forego: something which Amabel was never to be told about.

Dr Fforde went presently, making his goodbyes with beautiful manners, promising to be back the following afternoon. Driving to York with Tiger beside him, he spoke his thoughts aloud. 'Well, we can put our minds at rest, can we not, Tiger? She will make a new life for herself with this delightful aunt, probably find a pleasant job and meet a suitable young man and marry him.' He added, 'Most satisfactory.' So why did he feel so dissatisfied about it?

He drove to a hotel close to the Minster—a Regency townhouse, quiet and elegant, and with the unobtrusive service which its guests took for granted. Tiger, accommodated in the corner of his master's room, settled down for the night, leaving his master to go down to the bar for a nightcap and a study of the city.

The pair of them explored its streets after their breakfast. It was a fine day, and the doctor intended to drive to the coast that afternoon, but exploring the city would give him the opportunity of getting to know it. After all, it would probably be in York where Amabel would find a job.

He lunched in an ancient pub, where Tiger was welcomed with water and biscuits, and then went back to the hotel, got into his car and drove to Bolton Percy.

Amabel had spent the morning doing the small chores Aunt Thisbe allowed her to do, attending to Oscar's needs and taking Cyril for a walk, but there was still time to worry about what she should wear for her outing. Her wardrobe was so scanty that it was really a waste of time to worry about it.

It would have to be the pleated skirt and the short coat she had travelled in; they would pass muster for driving around the country, and Dr Fforde never looked at her as though he actually saw her. It had been lovely to see him again, like meeting an old friend—one who listened without interrupting and offered suggestions, never advice, in the friendliest impersonal manner of a good doctor. He was a doctor, of course, she reminded herself.

He came punctually, spent ten minutes talking to Miss Parsons, suggested that Cyril might like to share the back seat with Tiger, popped Amabel into the car and took the road to the coast.

Flamborough stood high on cliffs above the North Sea, and down at sea level boats sheltered in the harbour. Dr Fforde parked the car, put the dogs on their leads and walked Amabel briskly towards the peninsula. It was breezy, but the air was exhilarating, and they seemed to be the only people around.

When they stopped to look out to sea, Amabel said

happily, 'Oh, this is marvellous; so grand and beautiful—fancy living here and waking up each morning and
seeing the sea.'

They walked a long way, and as they turned to go
back Dr Fforde said, carefully casual, 'Do you want to
talk about your plans, Amabel? Perhaps your aunt has
already suggested something? Or do you plan to stay
with her indefinitely?'

'I wanted to ask you about that. There's a problem.
You won't mind if I tell you about it, and perhaps you
could give me some advice. You see I was told quite
unwittingly, by Mrs Bluett who owns the village shop,
that Aunt Thisbe had plans to spend the winter in Italy
with a friend. I haven't liked to ask her, and she hasn't
said anything, but I can't allow her to lose a lovely holiday like that because I'm here. After all, she didn't expect me, but she's so kind and she might feel that she
should stay here so that I've got a home, if you see what
I mean.'

They were standing facing each other, and she stared
up into his face. 'You can see that I must get a job very
quickly, but I'm not sure how to set about it. I mean,
should I answer advertisements in the paper or visit an
agency? There's not much I can do, and it has to be
somewhere Cyril and Oscar can come too.'

He said slowly, 'Well, first you must convince your
aunt that you want a job—and better not say that you
know of her holiday. Go to York, put your name down
at any agencies you can find...' He paused, frowning.
'What can you do, Amabel?'

'Nothing, really,' she said cheerfully. 'Housework,
cooking—or I expect I could be a waitress or work in a
shop. They're not the sort of jobs people want, are they?

And they aren't well paid. But if I could get a start somewhere, and also somewhere to live…'

'Do you suppose your aunt would allow you to live at her house while she was away?'

'Perhaps. But how would I get to work? The bus service is only twice weekly, and there is nowhere in the village where I could work.' She added fiercely, 'I must be independent.'

He took her arm and they walked on. 'Of course. Now, I can't promise anything, Amabel, but I know a lot of people and I might hear of something. Do you mind where you go?'

'No, as long as I can have Cyril and Oscar with me.'

'There is no question of your returning home?'

'None whatever. I'm being a nuisance to everyone, aren't I?'

He agreed silently to that, but he didn't say so. She was determined to be independent, and for some reason which he didn't understand he wanted to help her.

He asked, 'Have you some money? Enough to pay the rent and so on?'

'Yes, thank you. Mother let me have the money in the tea caddy, and there is still some left.'

He decided it wasn't worth while asking about the tea caddy. 'Good. Now we are going to the village; I noticed a pub as we came through it—the Royal Dog and Duck. If it is open they might give us tea.'

They had a splendid meal in the snug behind the bar: a great pot of tea, scones and butter, cream and jam, great wedges of fruitcake and, in case that wasn't enough, a dish of buttered toast. Tiger and Cyril, sitting under the table, provided with water and any tidbits which came their way, were tired after their walk, and dozed quietly.

He drove back presently through the dusk of late autumn, taking side roads through charming villages—Burton Agnes, with its haunted manor and Norman church, through Lund, with its once-upon-a-time cockpit, on to Bishop Burton, with its village pond and little black and white cottages, and finally along country roads to Bolton Percy.

The doctor stayed only as long as good manners dictated, although he asked if he might call to wish them goodbye the following morning.

'Come for coffee?' invited Miss Parsons.

The stiff breeze from yesterday had turned into a gale in the morning, and he made that his excuse for not staying long over his coffee. When Amabel had opened the door to him he had handed her a list of agencies in York, and now he wanted to be gone; he had done what he could for her. She had a home, this aunt who was obviously fond of her, and she was young and healthy and sensible, even if she had no looks to speak of. He had no further reason to be concerned about her.

All the same, driving down the M1, he was finding it difficult to forget her. She had bidden him goodbye in a quiet voice, her small hand in his, wished him a safe journey and thanked him. 'It's been very nice knowing you,' she had told him.

It had been nice knowing her, he conceded, and it was a pity that their paths were unlikely to cross in the future.

That evening Amabel broached the subject of her future to her aunt. She was careful not to mention Aunt Thisbe's holiday in Italy, pointing out with enthusiasm her great wish to become independent.

'I'll never be grateful enough to you,' she assured her aunt, 'for giving me a home—and I love being here with you. But I must get started somewhere, mustn't I? I know I shall like York, and there must be any number of jobs for someone like me—I mean, unskilled labour. And I won't stop at that. You do understand, don't you, Aunt?'

'Yes, of course I do, child. You must go to York and see what there is there for you. Only you must promise me that if you fall on hard times you will come here.' She hesitated, then, 'And if I am not here, go to Josh and Mrs Josh.'

'I promise, Aunt Thisbe. There's a bus to York tomorrow morning, isn't there? Shall I go and have a look round—spy out the land...?'

'Josh has to take the car in tomorrow morning; you shall go with him. The bus leaves York in the afternoon around four o'clock, but if you miss it phone here and Josh will fetch you.'

It was a disappointing day. Amabel went from one agency to the next, and was entered on their books, but there were no jobs which would suit her; she wasn't a trained lady's maid, or a cashier as needed at a café, she had neither the training nor the experience to work at a crêche, nor was she suitable as a saleslady at any of the large stores—lack of experience. But how did one get experience unless one had a chance to learn in the first place?

She presented a brave face when she got back to her aunt's house in the late afternoon. After all, this was only the first day, and her name was down on several agencies' books.

Back in London, Dr Fforde immersed himself in his work, assuring Bates that he had had a most enjoyable break.

'So why is he so gloomy?' Bates enquired of Tiger. 'Too much work. He needs a bit of the bright lights—needs to get out and about a bit.'

So it pleased Bates when his master told him that he would be going out one evening. Taking Mrs Potter-Stokes to the theatre, and supper afterwards.

It should have been a delightful evening; Miriam was a charming companion, beautifully dressed, aware of how very attractive she was, sure of herself, and amusing him with anecdotes of their mutual friends, asking intelligent questions about his work. But she was aware that she hadn't got his full attention. Over supper she exerted herself to gain his interest, and asked him prettily if he had enjoyed his few days off. 'Where did you go?' she added.

'York…'

'York?' She seized on that. 'My dear Oliver, I wish I'd known; you could have called on a great friend of mine—Dolores Trent. She has one of those shops in the Shambles—you know, sells dried flowers and pots and expensive glass. But she's hopeless at it—so impractical, breaking things and getting all the money wrong. I had a letter from her only a few days ago—she thinks she had better get someone to help her.'

She glanced at the doctor and saw with satisfaction that he was smiling at her. 'How amusing. Is she as attractive as you, Miriam?'

Miriam smiled a little triumphant smile, the evening was a success after all.

Which was what the doctor was thinking…

CHAPTER FOUR

WHEN Amabel came back from walking Cyril the next morning she was met at the door by her aunt.

'A pity. You have just missed a phone call from your nice Dr Fforde. He has heard of a job quite by chance from a friend and thought you might be interested. A lady who owns a shop in the Shambles in York—an arty-crafty place, I gather; she needs someone to help her. He told me her name—Dolores Trent—but he doesn't know the address. You might like to walk through the Shambles and see if you can find her shop. Most thoughtful of him to think of you.'

Josh drove her in after lunch. She was, her aunt had decreed, to spend as long as she wanted in York and phone when she was ready to return; Josh would fetch her.

She walked through the city, found the Shambles and started to walk its length. It was a narrow cobbled street, lined by old houses which overhung the lane, almost all of which were now shops: expensive shops, she saw at once, selling the kind of things people on holiday would take back home to display or give as presents to someone who needed to be impressed.

She walked down one side, looking at the names over the doors and windows, pausing once or twice to study some beautiful garment in a boutique or look at a display of jewellery. She reached the end and started back on the other side, and halfway down she found what she was looking for. It was a small shop, tucked between a bookshop and a mouthwatering patisserie, its small window displaying crystal vases, great baskets of dried silk flowers, delicate china and eye-catching pottery. Hung discreetly in one corner was a small card with 'Shop Assistant Required' written on it.

Amabel opened the door and went inside.

She supposed that the lady who came to meet her through the bead curtain at the back of the shop was Dolores Trent; she so exactly fitted her shop. Miss Trent was a tall person, slightly overweight, swathed in silky garments and wearing a good deal of jewellery, and she brought with her a cloud of some exotic perfume.

'You wish to browse?' she asked in a casual manner. 'Do feel free…'

'The card in the window?' said Amabel. 'You want an assistant. Would I do?'

Dolores Trent looked her over carefully. A dull little creature, she decided, but quite pleasant to look at, and she definitely didn't want some young glamorous girl who might distract customers from buying.

She said sharply, 'You live here? Have you references? Have you any experience?'

'I live with my aunt at Bolton Percy, and I can get references. I've no experience in working in a shop, but I'm used to people. I ran a bed and breakfast house…'

Miss Trent laughed. 'At least you sound honest. If you come here to work, how will you get here? Bolton Percy's a bit rural, isn't it?'

'Yes. I hope to find somewhere to live here.'

Several thoughts passed with quick succession through Dolores Trent's head. There was that empty room behind the shop, beyond the tiny kitchenette and the cloakroom; it could be furnished with odds and ends from the attic at home. The girl could live there, and since she would have rent-free accommodation there would be no need to pay her the wages she would be entitled to…

Miss Trent, mean by nature, liked the idea.

'I might consider you, if your references are satisfactory. Your hours would be from nine o'clock till five, free on Sundays. I'd expect you to keep the shop clean and dusted, unpack goods when they arrive, arrange shelves, serve the customers and deal with the cash. You'd do any errands, and look after the shop when I'm not here. You say you want to live here? There's a large room behind the shop, with windows and a door opening onto a tiny yard. Basic furniture and bedding. There's a kitchenette and a cloakroom which you can use. Of course you do understand that if I let you live here I won't be able to pay you the usual wages?'

She named a sum which Amabel knew was not much more than half what she should have expected. On the other hand, here was shelter and security and independence.

'I have a dog and a cat. Would you object to them?'

'Not if they stay out of sight. A dog would be quite a good idea; it's quiet here at night. You're not nervous?'

'No. Might I see the room?'

It was a pleasant surprise, quite large and airy, with two windows and a small door opening onto a tiny square of neglected grass. But there were high walls surrounding it; Cyril and Oscar would be safe there.

Dolores Trent watched Amabel's face. The girl needed the job and somewhere to live, so she wasn't likely to leave at a moment's notice if she found the work too hard or the hours too long. Especially with a dog and a cat...

She said, 'Provided your references are okay, you can come on a month's trial. You'll be paid weekly. After the month it will be a week's notice on either side.' As they went back to the shop she said, 'I'll phone you when I've checked the references.'

Amabel, waiting for Josh to fetch her in answer to her phone call, was full of hope. It would be a start: somewhere to live, a chance to gain the experience which was so necessary if she wanted to get a better job. She would have the chance to look around her, make friends, perhaps find a room where Cyril and Oscar would be welcome, and find work which was better paid. But that would be later, she conceded. In the meantime she was grateful to Dr Fforde for his help. It was a pity she couldn't see him and tell him how grateful she was. But he had disappeared back into his world, somewhere in London, and London was vast...

Convincing Aunt Thisbe that the offer of work from Miss Trent was exactly what she had hoped for was no easy task. Aunt Thisbe had said no word of her holiday, only reiterating her advice that Amabel should spend the next few weeks with her, wait until after Christmas before looking for work...

It was only after Amabel had painted a somewhat overblown picture of her work at Miss Trent's shop, the advantages of getting one foot in the door of future prospects, and her wish to become independent, that Miss Parsons agreed reluctantly that it might be the chance of a lifetime. There was the added advantage that, once in

York, the chance of finding an even better job was much greater than if Amabel stayed at Bolton Percy.

So Amabel sent off her references and within a day or so the job was hers, if she chose to take it. Amabel showed her aunt the letter and it was then that Aunt Thisbe said, 'I shall be sorry to see you go, child. You must spend your Sundays here, of course, and any free time you have.' She hesitated. 'If I am away then you must go to Josh and Mrs Josh, who will look after you. Josh will have a key, and you must treat the house as your home. If you need the car you have only to ask...'

'Will you be away for long?' asked Amabel.

'Well, dear, I have been invited to spend a few weeks with an old friend who has an apartment in Italy. I hadn't made up my mind whether to go, but since you have this job and are determined to be independent...'

'Oh, Aunt Thisbe, how lovely for you—and hasn't everything worked out well? I'll be fine in York and I'll love to come here, if Mrs Josh won't mind. When are you going?'

'You are to start work next Monday? I shall probably go during that week.'

'I thought I'd ask Miss Trent if I could move in on Sunday...'

'A good idea. Josh can drive you there and make sure that everything is all right. Presumably the shop will be empty?'

'I suppose so. I'd have all day to settle in, and if it's quiet Cyril and Oscar won't find it so strange. They're very adaptable.'

So everything was settled. Miss Trent had no objection to Amabel moving in on Sunday. The key would be next door at the patisserie, which was open on

Sundays, and the room had been furnished; she could go in and out as she wished and she was to be ready to open the shop at nine o'clock on Monday morning. Miss Trent sounded friendly enough, if a trifle impatient.

Amabel packed her case and Miss Parsons, with brisk efficiency, filled a large box with food: tins of soup, cheese, eggs, butter, bread, biscuits, tea and coffee and plastic bottles of milk and, tucked away out of sight, a small radio. Amabel, for all her brave face, would be lonely.

Aunt Thisbe decided that she would put off her holiday until the following week; Amabel would spend Sunday with her and she would see for herself if she could go away with a clear conscience... She would miss Amabel, but the young shouldn't be held back.

She would have liked to have seen the room where Amabel was to live, but she sensed that Amabel didn't want that—at least not until she had transformed it into a place of which her aunt would approve. And there were one or two things she must tell Josh—that nice Dr Fforde might return. It wasn't very likely, but Aunt Thisbe believed that one should never overlook a chance.

Saying goodbye to Aunt Thisbe wasn't easy. Amabel had been happy living with her; she had a real affection for the rather dour old lady, and knew that the affection was reciprocated, but she felt in her bones that she was doing the right thing. Her aunt's life had been disrupted by her sudden arrival and that must not be made permanent. She got into the car beside Josh and turned to smile and wave; she would be back on Sunday, but this was the real parting.

There were few people about on an early Sunday

morning: tourists strolling along the Shambles, peering into shop windows, church goers. Josh parked the car away from the city centre and they walked, Amabel with the cat basket and Cyril on his lead, Josh burdened with her case and the box of food.

They knew about her at the patisserie; she fetched the key and opened the shop door, led the way through the shop and opened the door to her new home.

Miss Trent had said that she would furnish it, and indeed there was a divan bed against one wall, a small table by the window with an upright chair, a shabby easy chair by the small electric fire and a worn rug on the wooden floor. There was a pile of bedding and a box of cutlery, and a small table lamp with an ugly plastic shade.

Josh put the box down on the table without saying a word, and Amabel said, too brightly, 'Of course it will look quite different once I've arranged things and put up the curtains.'

Josh said, 'Yes, miss,' in a wooden voice. 'Miss Parsons said we were to go next door and have a cup of coffee. I'll help you sort out your things.'

'I'd love some coffee, but after that you don't need to bother, Josh. I've all the rest of the day to get things how I want. And I must take Cyril for a walk later. There's that park by St Mary Abbot's Church, and then I must take a look round the shop.'

They had their coffee and Josh went away, promising to return on the Sunday morning, bidding her to be sure and phone if she needed him or her aunt. She sensed that he didn't approve of her bid for independence and made haste to assure him that everything was fine...

In her room presently, with the door open and Cyril

and Oscar going cautiously around the neglected patch of grass, Amabel paused in her bedmaking to reflect that Miss Trent was certainly a trusting kind of person. 'You would have thought,' said Amabel to Oscar, peering round the open door to make sure that she was there, 'that she would have wanted to make sure that I had come. I might have stolen whatever I fancied from the shop.'

Well, it was nice to be trusted; it augered well for the future...

Dolores Trent had in fact gone to Harrogate for the weekend, with only the briefest of thoughts about Amabel. The girl would find her own way around. It had been tiresome enough finding someone to help out in the shop. Really, she didn't know why she kept the place on. It had been fun when she had first had it, but she hadn't realised all the bookwork there would be, and the tiresome ordering and unpacking...

If this girl needed a job as badly as she had hinted, then she could take over the uninteresting parts and leave Dolores to do the selling. It might even be possible to take more time for herself; the shop was a great hindrance to her social life...

Amabel arranged the odds and ends of furniture to their best advantage, switched on the fire, settled her two companions before it and unpacked the box of food. Aunt Thisbe had been generous and practical. There were tins of soup and a tin opener with them, tins of food for Oscar and Cyril, and there was a fruitcake— one of Mrs Josh's. She stowed them away, together with the other stores, in an empty cupboard she found in the tiny kitchenette.

She also found a saucepan, a kettle, some mugs and

plates and a tin of biscuits. Presumably Miss Trent made herself elevenses each morning. Amabel opened a tin of soup and put the saucepan on the gas ring, then went to poke her nose into the tiny cloakroom next to the kitchenette. There was a small geyser over the washbasin; at least there would be plenty of hot water.

She made a list while she ate her soup. A cheap rug for the floor, a pretty lampshade, a couple of cushions, a vase—for she must have flowers—and a couple of hooks so that she could hang her few clothes. There was no cupboard, nowhere to put her undies. She added an orange box to the list, with a question mark behind it. She had no idea when she would have the chance to go shopping. She supposed that the shop would close for the usual half-day during the week, though Miss Trent hadn't mentioned that.

She made Oscar comfortable in his basket, switched off the fire, got Cyril's lead and her coat and left the shop, locking the door carefully behind her. It was mid-afternoon by now, and there was no one about. She walked briskly through the streets to St Mary's, where there was a park, and thought there would be time each morning to take Cyril for a quick run before the shop opened. They could go again after the shop closed. There was the grass for him and Oscar during the day; she could leave the door open...

And there were Sundays to look forward to...

On the way back she wondered about Dr Fforde; she tried not to think about him too often, for that was a waste of time. He had come into her life but now he had gone again. She would always be grateful to him, of course, but she was sensible enough to see that he had no place in it.

When she reached the shop she saw that the patisserie was closing its doors, and presently, when she went to look, the shop lights had been turned out. It seemed very quiet and dark outside, but there were lights here and there above the shops. She took heart from the sight of them.

After she had had her tea she went into the shop, turned on the lights and went slowly from shelf to shelf, not touching but noting their order. She looked to see where the wrapping paper, string and labels were kept, for she felt sure Miss Trent would expect her to know that. She wasn't going to be much use for a few days, but there were some things she would be expected to discover for herself.

She had her supper then, let Oscar and Cyril out for the last time, and got ready for bed. Doing the best she could with a basin of hot water in the cloakroom, she pondered the question of baths—or even showers. The girl at the patisserie had been friendly; she might be able to help. Amabel got into her bed, closely followed by her two companions, and fell instantly asleep.

She was up early—and that was another thing, an alarm clock, she thought as she dressed—opened the door onto the grass patch and then left the shop with Cyril. The streets were empty, save for postmen and milkmen, but there were signs of life when she returned after Cyril's run in the park. The shops were still closed, but curtains were being drawn above them and there was a delicious smell of baking bread from the patisserie.

Amabel made her bed, tidied the room, fed the animals and sat down to her own breakfast—a boiled egg, bread and butter and a pot of tea. Tomorrow, she promised herself, she would buy a newspaper when she went out with Cyril, and, since the patisserie opened at half past eight, she could get croissants or rolls for her lunch.

She tidied away her meal, bade the animals be good and shut and locked the door to the shop. They could go outside if they wanted, and the sun was shining...

She was waiting in the shop when Miss Trent arrived. Beyond a nod she didn't reply to Amabel's good morning, but took off her coat, took out a small mirror and inspected her face.

'I don't always get here as early as this,' she said finally. 'Open the shop if I'm not here, and if I'm not here at lunchtime just close the shop for half an hour and get yourself something. Have you had a look round? Yes? Then put the "Open" sign on the door. There's a feather duster under the counter; dust off the window display then unpack that box under the shelves. Be careful, they are china figures. Arrange them on the bottom shelf and mark the price. That will be on the invoice inside the box.'

She put away the mirror and unlocked the drawer in the counter. 'What was your name?' When Amabel reminded her, she said, 'Yes, well, I shall call you Amabel—and you'd better call me Dolores. There probably won't be any customers until ten o'clock. I'm going next door for a cup of coffee. You can have yours when I get back.'

Which was half an hour later, by which time Amabel had dealt with the china figures, praying silently that there would be no customers.

'You can have fifteen minutes,' said Dolores. 'There's coffee and milk in the kitchenette; take it into your room if you want to.'

Cyril and Oscar were glad to have her company, even

if only for a few minutes, and it made a pleasant break in the morning.

There were people in the shop by now, picking things up and putting them down again, taking their time choosing what they would buy. Dolores sat behind the counter, paying little attention to them and leaving Amabel to wrap up their purchases. Only occasionally she would advise a customer in a languid manner.

At one o'clock she told Amabel to close the door and lock it.

'Open up again in half an hour if I'm not back,' she said. 'Did I tell you that I close on Wednesday for a half-day? I shall probably go a bit earlier, but you can shut the shop and then do what you like.'

Amabel, while glad to hear about the half-day, thought that her employer seemed rather unbusinesslike. She closed the shop and made herself a sandwich before going to sit on the patch of grass with Oscar and Cyril for company.

She was glad when it was one o'clock on Wednesday; standing about in the shop was surprisingly tiring and, although Dolores was kind in a vague way, she expected Amabel to stay after the shop shut so that she could unpack any new goods or rearrange the windows. Dolores herself did very little, beyond sitting behind the counter holding long conversations over the phone. Only when a customer showed signs of serious buying did she exert herself.

She was good at persuading someone to buy the more expensive glass and china, laughing and chatting in an animated way until the sale was completed, then made no effort to tell Amabel how to go on, seeming content to let her find things out for herself. Amabel supposed that she must make a living from the shop, although it was obvious that she had very little interest in it.

It was a temptation to phone Aunt Thisbe and ask if Josh would fetch her for her half-day, but there were things she wished to do. Shopping for food and material for a window curtain, a new lampshade, flowers... Next week, when she had been paid, she would find a cheerful bedspread for the bed and a cloth for the table.

She did her shopping and took Cyril for a walk, and then spent the rest of her day rearranging her room, sitting by the electric fire eating crumpets for her tea and reading the magazine Dolores had left behind the counter.

Not very exciting, reflected Amabel, but it was early days, and there was Sunday to look forward to. She wrote a letter to her mother, read the magazine from end to end and allowed her thoughts to wander to Dr Fforde.

Sunday came at last, bringing Josh and the prospect of a lovely day and the reality of a warm welcome from Aunt Thisbe.

Warm as well as practical. Amabel was despatched to the bathroom to lie in a pine-scented bath—'For that is something you must miss,' said Miss Parsons. 'Come down when you are ready and we will have coffee and you shall tell me everything.'

Amabel, pink from her bath, settled before the fire in her aunt's drawing room with Oscar and Cyril beside her, and gave a detailed account of her week. She made it light-hearted.

'It's delightful working in such a pleasant place,' she pointed out. 'There are some lovely things in the shop, and Miss Trent—she likes to be called Dolores—is very kind and easygoing.'

'You are able to cook proper meals?'

'Yes, and I do—and the room looks so nice now that I have cushions and flowers.'

'You are happy there, Amabel? Really happy? You have enough free time and she pays you well?'

'Yes, Aunt. York is such a lovely city, and the people in the other shops in the Shambles are so friendly...'

Which was rather an exaggeration, but Aunt Thisbe must be convinced that there was no reason why she shouldn't go to Italy...

She would go during the following week, Miss Parsons told Amabel, and Amabel was to continue to spend her Sundays at End House; Josh would see to everything...

Amabel, back in her room with another box of food and a duvet her aunt had declared she didn't want, was content that she had convinced the old lady that she was perfectly happy; they would write to each other, and when Aunt Thisbe came back in the New Year they would review the future.

A week or two went by. Amabel bought a winter coat, a pretty cover for the duvet, a basket for Cyril and a cheap rug. She also saved some money—but not much.

After the first two weeks Dolores spent less and less time at the shop. She would pop in at opening time and then go and have her hair done, or go shopping or meet friends for coffee. Amabel found it odd, but there weren't many customers. Trade would pick up again at Christmas, Dolores told her.

Amabel, aware that she was being underpaid and overworked, was nonetheless glad to have her days filled. The few hours she spent in her room once the shop was closed were lonely enough. Later, she promised herself, once she felt secure in her job, she would join a club or go to night school. In the meantime she read and knitted and wrote cheerful letters home.

And when she wasn't doing that she thought about Dr Fforde. Such a waste of time, she told herself. But there again, did that matter? It was pleasant to remember… She wondered what he was doing and wished she knew more about him. Wondered too if he ever thought of her…

To be truthful, he thought of her very seldom; he led a busy life and time was never quite his own. He had driven to Glastonbury once or twice to see his mother, and since the road took him past Amabel's home he had slowed the car to note the work being carried out there. He had thought briefly of calling to see Mrs Graham, but decided against it. There was no point now that Amabel was in York and happy. He hoped that she had settled down by now. Perhaps when he had time to spare he would drive up and go to see her…

He was seeing a good deal of Miriam, and friends were beginning to invite them together to dinner parties. He often spent evenings with her at the theatre when he would much rather have been at home, but she was amusing, and clever enough to appear to have a sincere interest in his work. Hardly aware of it, he was being drawn into her future plans…

It wasn't until one evening, returning home after a long day at the hospital to be met by Bates with a message from Miriam—she—and he—were to join a party of theatregoers that evening, he was to call for her at seven-thirty and after the theatre he would take her out to supper—that he realised what was happening.

He stood for a moment without speaking, fighting down sudden anger, but when he spoke there was nothing of it in his voice.

'Phone Mrs Potter-Stokes, please, and tell her that I am unable to go out this evening.' He smiled suddenly as an idea drowned the anger. 'And, Bates, tell her that I shall be going away.'

There was no expression on Bates's foxy face, but he felt a deep satisfaction. He didn't like Mrs Potter-Stokes and, unlike the doctor, had known for some time that she was set on becoming Mrs Fforde. His 'Very good, Doctor,' was the model of discretion.

As for Dr Fforde, he ate a splendid supper and spent the rest of the evening going through his diary to see how soon he could get away for a couple of days. He would go first to Miss Parsons' house, for Amabel might have chosen to ignore the chance of working in a shop in York. In any case her aunt would know where she was. It would be interesting to meet again...

Almost a week later he set off for York, Tiger beside him. It was a sullen morning, but once he was clear of the endless suburbs the motorway was fairly clear and the Rolls ate up the miles. He stopped for a snack lunch and Tiger's need for a quick trot, and four hours after he had left his home he stopped before Miss Parsons' house.

Of course no one answered his knock, and after a moment he walked down the narrow path beside the house to the garden at the back. It appeared to be empty, but as he stood there Josh came out of the shed by the bottom hedge. He put down the spade he was carrying and walked up the path to meet him.

'Seeking Miss Amabel, are you? House is shut up.

Miss Parsons is off to foreign parts for the winter and Miss Amabel's got herself a job in York—comes here of a Sunday; that's her day off.'

He studied the doctor's face. 'You'll want to know where she's working. A fancy shop in the Shambles. Lives in a room at the back with those two animals of hers. Brings them here of a Sunday, spends the day at End House, opens the windows and such, airs the place, has a bath and does her washing and has her dinner with us. Very independent young lady, anxious not to be a nuisance. Says everything is fine at her job but she doesn't look quite the thing, somehow...'

Dr Fforde frowned. 'She got on well with her aunt? They seemed the best of friends...'

'And so they are. I'm not knowing, mind, but I fancy Miss Amabel took herself off so's Miss Parsons didn't have to alter her plans about her holiday.'

'I think you may be right. I'll go and see her, make sure everything is as it should be.'

'You do that, sir. Me and the missus aren't quite easy. But not knowing anyone to talk to about it...'

'I'm here for a day or two, so I'll come and see you again if I may?'

'You're welcome, sir. You and your dog.' Josh bent to stroke Tiger. 'Miss Amabel does know to come here if needful.'

'I'm glad she has a good friend in you, Josh.'

Dr Fforde got back into his car. It was mid afternoon and drizzling; he was hungry, and he must book in at the hotel where he had stayed before, but before doing so he must see Amabel.

She was on her hands and knees at the back of the shop, unpacking dozens of miniature Father Christmases intended for the Christmas market. Dolores was at the hairdresser and would return only in time to lock the till, tell her to close the shop and lock up.

She was tired and grubby, and there hadn't been time to make tea. Dolores expected everything to be cleared away before she got back. At least there had been no customers for a while, but Amabel was becoming increasingly worried at the amount of work Dolores expected her to do. It had been fine for the first few weeks, but Dolores's interest was dwindling. She was in the shop less, and dealing with the customers and sorting out the stock was becoming increasingly difficult. To talk to her about it was risky; she might so easily give Amabel a week's notice, and although she might find work easily enough there were Oscar and Cyril to consider...

She unwrapped the last of the little figures and looked up as someone came into the shop.

Dr Fforde stood in the doorway looking at her. His instant impression was that she wasn't happy, but then she smiled, her whole face alight with pleasure.

He said easily, 'Josh told me where you were. He also told me that Miss Parsons is away.' He glanced round him. 'You live here? Surely you don't run the place on your own?'

She had got to her feet, dusting off her hands, brushing down her skirt.

'No. Dolores—that is, Miss Trent—is at the hairdresser. Are you just passing through?'

'I'm here for a couple of days. When do you close this shop?'

'Five o'clock. But I tidy up after that.'

'Will you spend the evening with me?'

She had bent to stroke Tiger's head. 'I'd like that, thank you. Only I have to see to Oscar and Cyril, and take Cyril for a walk, so I won't be ready until about six o'clock.'

'I'll be here soon after five…'

Dolores came in then, assuming her charming manner at the sight of a customer. 'Have you found something you like? Do take a look round.'

She smiled at him, wondering where he came from; if he was on his own she might suggest showing him what was worth seeing in the city—the patisserie wasn't closed yet…

'I came to see Amabel,' he told her. 'We have known each other for some time, and since I am here for a day or two…'

'You're old friends?' Dolores asked artlessly. 'I expect you know York well? You don't live here?'

'No, but I have been here before. We met some time ago, in the West Country.'

Still artless, Dolores said, 'Oh, I thought you might be from London—I've friends there.' An idea—an unlikely idea—had entered her head. 'But I don't suppose you would know them. I came up here after my divorce, and it was an old schoolfriend—Miriam Potter-Stokes—who persuaded me to do something instead of sitting aimlessly around…'

She knew her wild guess had been successful when he said quietly, 'Yes, I know Miriam. I must tell her how successful you are.'

'Do, please. I must be off. Amabel, close at five o'clock. There'll be a delivery of those candlesticks before nine o'clock tomorrow morning, so be sure to be ready for it.' She gave the doctor a smiling nod. 'Nice to have met you. I hope you enjoy your stay here.'

She wasted no time when she reached her home, but poured herself a drink and picked up the phone.

'Miriam, listen and don't interrupt. Do you know where this Oliver of yours is? You don't? He's a big man, handsome, rather a slow voice, with a black dog? He's in my shop. On the best of terms with Amabel, the girl who works for me. It seems they've known each other for some time.' She gave a spiteful little laugh. 'Don't be too sure that Oliver is yours, Miriam.'

She listened to Miriam's outraged voice, smiling to herself. Miriam was an old schoolfriend, but it wouldn't hurt her to be taken down a peg. Dolores said soothingly, 'Don't get so upset, darling. He's here for a few days; I'll keep an eye on things and let you know if there's anything for you to worry about. Most unlikely, I should think. She's a small dull creature and she wears the most appalling clothes. I'll give you a ring tomorrow some time.'

When Dolores had gone the doctor said, 'Where do you live, Amabel? Surely not here?'

'Oh, but I do. I have a room behind the shop.'

'You shall show it to me when I come back.' He glanced at his watch. 'In half an hour.'

She said uncertainly, 'Well...'

'You're glad to see me, Amabel?'

She said without hesitating, 'Oh, yes, I am.'

'Then don't dither,' he said.

He came closer, and, looking down into her face, took

her hands in his. 'There is a Nigerian proverb which says, ''Hold a true friend with both your hands,''' he said. He smiled and added gently, 'I'm your true friend, Amabel.'

CHAPTER FIVE

CLOSING the shop, tidying up, feeding Oscar and Cyril, doing her face and hair, Amabel was conscious of a warm glow deep inside her person. She had a friend, a real friend. She was going to spend the evening with him and they would talk. There was so much she wanted to talk about...

He had said that he would be back at half past five, so at that time she shut her room door and went back into the shop to let him in, stooping to pat Tiger. 'I still have to take Cyril for a walk,' she told him as she led the way to her room.

He stood in the middle of it, looking round him, absently fondling Cyril. He didn't allow his thoughts to show on his face, but remarked placidly, 'Having access to space for Oscar and Cyril is an advantage, isn't it? They're happy here with you?'

'Well, yes. It's not ideal, but I'm lucky to have found it. And I have you to thank for that. I couldn't thank you before because I didn't know where you lived.'

'A lucky chance. Can we leave Oscar for a few hours?'

'Yes, he knows I take Cyril out in the evening. I'll get my coat.'

She was longing for a cup of tea; the afternoon had been long and she hadn't had the chance to make one. She was hungry too. He had told her that they were true

87

friends, but she didn't know him well enough to suggest
going to a café, and besides, Cyril needed his run.

They set off, talking of nothing much at first, but presently, walking briskly through the park, she began to
answer his carefully put questions with equally careful
answers.

They had been walking steadily for half an hour when
he stopped and caught her by the arm. 'Tea,' he said.
'Have you had your tea? What a thoughtless fool I am.'

She said quickly, 'Oh, it doesn't matter, really it
doesn't,' and added, 'It was such a lovely surprise when
you came into the shop.'

He turned her round smartly. 'There must be somewhere we can get a pot of tea.'

So she got her tea, sitting at a very small table in a
chintzy teashop where shoppers on their way home were
still lingering. Since she was hungry, and the doctor
seemed hungry too, she tucked into hot buttered toast,
hot mince pies and a slice of the delicious walnut cake
he insisted that she have.

'I thought we'd have dinner at my hotel,' he told her.
'But if you're not too tired we might take a walk through
the streets. York is such a splendid place, and I'd like
to know more of it.'

'Oh, so would I. But about going to the hotel for dinner—I think it would be better if I didn't. I mean, there's
Cyril, and I'm not—that is—I didn't stop to change my
dress.'

'The hotel people are very helpful about dogs. They'll
both be allowed to stay in my room while we dine. And
you look very nice as you are, Amabel.'

He sounded so matter-of-fact that her doubts melted
away, and presently they continued with their walk.

None of the museums or historical buildings was open, but they wouldn't have visited them anyway; they walked the streets—Lendal Street, Davey Gate, Parliament Street and Coppergate, to stare up at Clifford's Tower, then back through Coppergate and Fosse Gate and Pavement and so to the Shambles again, this time from the opposite end to Dolores's shop. They lingered for a while so that she could show him the little medieval church where she sometimes went, before going on to the Minster, which they agreed would need leisurely hours of viewing in the daylight.

The hotel was close by, and while Amabel went away to leave her coat and do the best she could with her face and hair the doctor went with the dogs. He was waiting for her when she got back to the lounge.

'We deserve a drink,' he told her, 'and I hope you are as hungry as I am.'

It wasn't a large hotel, but it had all the unobtrusive perfection of service and comfort. They dined in a softly lit restaurant, served by deft waiters. The *maître d'* had ushered them to one of the best tables, and no one so much as glanced at Amabel's dowdy dress.

They dined on tiny cheese soufflés followed by roast beef, Yorkshire pudding, light as a feather, crisp baked potatoes and baby sprouts, as gently suggested by the doctor. Amabel looked as though a good meal wouldn't do her any harm, and she certainly enjoyed every mouthful—even managing a morsel of the lemon mousse which followed.

Her enjoyment was unselfconscious, and the glass of claret he ordered gave her face a pretty flush as well as loosening her tongue. They talked with the ease of two people who knew each other well—something which

Amabel, thinking about it later, found rather surprising—and presently, after a leisurely coffee, the doctor went to fetch the dogs and Amabel her coat and they walked back to the shop.

The clocks were striking eleven as they reached the shop door. He took the key from her, opened the door and handed her Cyril's lead.

'Tomorrow is Wednesday—you have a half-day?' When she nodded he said, 'Good. Could you be ready by half past one? We'll take the dogs to the sea, shall we? Don't bother with lunch; we'll go next door and have coffee and a roll.'

She beamed up at him. 'Oh, that would be lovely. Dolores almost always goes about twelve o'clock on Wednesdays, so I can close punctually, then there'll only be Oscar to see to.' She added anxiously, 'I don't need to dress up?'

'No, no. Wear that coat, and a scarf for your head; it may be chilly by the sea.'

She offered a hand. 'Thank you for a lovely evening: I have enjoyed it.'

'So have I.' He sounded friendly, and as though he meant it—which of course he did. 'I'll wait until you're inside and locked up. Goodnight, Amabel.'

She went through the shop and turned to lift a hand to him as she opened the door to her room and switched on the light. After a moment he went back to his hotel. He would have to return to London tomorrow, but he could leave late and travel through the early part of the night so that they could have dinner together again.

'Am I being a fool?' he enquired of Tiger, whose gruff rumble could have been either yes or no...

It was halfway through the busy morning when

Dolores asked casually, 'Did you have a pleasant evening with your friend, Amabel?'

Amabel warmed to her friendly tone. 'Oh, yes, thank you. We went for a walk through the city and had dinner at his hotel. And this afternoon we're going to the sea.'

'I dare say you found plenty to talk about?'

'Yes, yes, we did. His visit was quite unexpected. I really didn't expect to see him again...'

'Does he come this way often? It's quite a long journey from London.'

'Well, yes. He came just before I started work here—my mother told him where I was and he looked me up.'

She had answered readily enough, but Dolores was prudent enough not to ask any more questions. She said casually, 'You must wrap up; it will be cold by the sea. And you can go as soon as he comes for you; I've some work I want to do in the shop.'

She's nicer than I thought, reflected Amabel, going back to her careful polishing of a row of silver photo frames.

Sure enough, when the doctor's large person came striding towards the shop, Dolores said, 'Off you go, Amabel. He can spend ten minutes in the shop while you get ready.'

While Amabel fed Oscar, got Cyril's lead and got into her coat, tidied her hair and made sure that she had everything in her handbag, Dolores invited the doctor to look round him. 'We're showing our Christmas stock,' she told him. 'It's always a busy time, but we close for four days over the holiday. Amabel will be able to go to her aunt's house. She's away at present, Amabel told me, but I'm sure she'll be back by then.' She gave him a sly glance. 'I dare say you'll manage to get a few days off?'

'Yes, I dare say.'

'Well, if you see Miriam give her my love, won't you? Are you staying here long?'

'I'm going back tonight. But I intend to return before Christmas.'

Amabel came then, with Cyril on his lead. She looked so happy that just for a moment Dolores had a quite unusual pang of remorse. But it was only a pang, and the moment they had gone she picked up the phone.

'Miriam—I promised to ring you. Your Oliver has just left the shop with Amabel. He's driving her to the sea and spending the rest of the day with her. What is more, he told me that he intends returning to York before Christmas. You had better find yourself another man, darling!'

She listened to Miriam raging for a few minutes. 'I shouldn't waste your breath getting into a temper. If you want him as badly as all that then you must think of something. When you have, let me know if I can help.'

Miriam thought of something at once. When Dolores heard it she said, 'Oh, no, I can't do that.' For all her mischief-making she wasn't deliberately unkind. 'The girl works very well, and I can't just sack her at a moment's notice.'

'Of course you can; she's well able to find another job—plenty of work around before Christmas. When he comes tell Oliver she's found a better job and you don't' know where it is. Tell him you'll let him know if you hear anything of her; he won't be able to stay away from his work for more than a couple of days at a time. The girl won't come to any harm, and out of sight is out of mind...'

Miriam, most unusually for her burst into tears, and Dolores gave in; after all, she and Miriam were very old friends...

The doctor and his little party had to walk to where he had parked the car, and on the way he marshalled them into a small pub in a quiet street to lunch upon a sustaining soup, hot crusty bread and a pot of coffee—for, as he explained, they couldn't walk on empty stomachs. That done, he drove out of the city, north through the Yorkshire Moors, until he reached Staithes, a fishing village between two headlands.

He parked the car, tucked Amabel's hand under his arm and marched her off into the teeth of a strong wind, the dogs trotting happily on either side of them. They didn't talk; the wind made that difficult and really there was no need. They were quite satisfied with each other's company without the need of words.

The sea was rough, grey under a grey sky, and once away from the village there was no one about. Presently they turned round, and back in the village explored its streets. The houses were a mixture of cottages and handsome Georgian houses, churches and shops. They lingered at the antiques shops and the doctor bought a pretty little plate Amabel admired before they walked on beside the Beck and finally turned back to have tea at the Cod and Lobster pub.

It was a splendid tea; Amabel, her cheeks pink, her hair all over the place and glowing with the exercise, ate the hot buttered parkin, the toast and home-made jam and the fruit cake with a splendid appetite.

She was happy—the shop, her miserable little room, her loneliness and lack of friends didn't matter. Here she was, deeply content, with someone who had said that he was her friend.

They didn't talk about themselves or their lives; there were so many other things to discuss. The time flew by and they got up to go reluctantly.

Tiger and Cyril, nicely replete with the morsels they had been offered from time to time, climbed into the car, went to sleep and didn't wake until they were back in York. The doctor parked the car at his hotel, led the dogs away to his room and left Amabel to tidy herself. It was no easy task, and she hardly felt at her best, but it was still early evening and the restaurant was almost empty.

They dined off chicken *à la king* and lemon tart which was swimming in cream, and the doctor talked comfortably of this and that. Amabel wished that the evening would go on for ever.

It didn't of course. It was not quite nine o'clock when they left the hotel to walk back to the shop. The girl who worked in the patisserie was still there, getting ready to leave. She waved as they passed and then stood watching them. She liked Amabel, who seemed to lead a very dull and lonely life, and now this handsome giant of a man had turned up...

The doctor took the key from Amabel, opened the shop door and then gave it back to her.

'Thank you for a lovely afternoon—Oliver. I feel full of fresh air and lovely food.'

He smiled down at her earnest face. 'Good. We must do it again, some time. When she looked uncertain, he added, 'I'm going back to London tonight, Amabel. But I'll be back.'

He opened the door and pushed her inside, but not before he had given her a quick kiss. The girl in the patisserie saw that, and smiled. Amabel didn't smile, but she glowed from the top of her head to the soles of her feet.

He had said that he would come back…

Dolores was in a friendly mood in the morning; she wanted to know where Amabel had gone, if she had had a good dinner, and was her friend coming to see her again?

Amabel, surprised at the friendliness, saw no reason to be secretive. She gave a cheerful account of her afternoon, and when Dolores observed casually, 'I dare say he'll be back again?' Amabel assured her readily enough that he would.

Any niggardly doubts Dolores might have had about Miriam's scheme were doused by the girl in the patisserie who served her coffee.

'Nice to see Amabel with a man,' she observed chattily. 'Quite gone on her, I shouldn't doubt. Kissed her goodbye and all. Stood outside the shop for ages, making sure she was safely inside. He'll be back, mark my words! Funny, isn't it? She's such a plain little thing, too…'

This was something Miriam had to know, so Dolores sent Amabel to the post office to collect a parcel and picked up the phone.

She had expected rage, perhaps tears from Miriam, but not silence. After a moment she said, 'Miriam?'

Miriam was thinking fast; the girl must be got rid of, and quickly. Any doubts Dolores had about that must be quashed at once. She said in a small broken voice,

'Dolores, you must help me. I'm sure it's just a passing infatuation—only a few days ago we spent the evening together.' That there wasn't an atom of truth in that didn't worry her; she had to keep Dolores's sympathy.

She managed a sob. 'If he goes back to see her and she's gone he can't do anything about it. I know he's got commitments at the hospital he can't miss.' Another convincing lie. 'Please tell him that she's got another job but you don't know where? Or that she's got a boy-friend? Better still tell him that she said she would join her aunt in Italy. He wouldn't worry about her then. In fact that's what she will probably do...'

'That cat and dog of hers—' began Dolores.

'Didn't you tell me that there was a kind of handyman who does odd jobs for the aunt? They'll go to him.'

Put like that, it sounded a reasonable solution. 'You think she might do that?' Dolores was still doubtful, but too lazy to worry about it. She said, 'All right, I'll sack her—but not for a day or two. There's more Christmas stock to be unpacked and I can't do that on my own.'

Miriam gave a convincing sob. 'I'll never be able to thank you enough. I'm longing to see Oliver again; I'm sure everything will be all right once he's back here and I can be with him.'

Which was unduly optimistic of her. Oliver, once back home, made no attempt to contact her. When she phoned his house it was to be told by a wooden-voiced Bates that the doctor was unavailable.

In desperation she went to his consulting rooms, where she told his receptionist that he was expecting her when he had seen his last patient, and when presently he came into the waiting room from his consulting room she went to meet him.

'Oliver—I know I shouldn't be here. Don't blame your receptionist; I said you expected me. Only it is such a long time since we saw each other.'

She lifted her face to his, aware that she was at her most attractive. 'Have I done something to annoy you? You are never at home when I phone; that man of yours says you're not available.' She put a hand on his sleeve and smiled the sad little smile she had practised before her mirror.

'I've been busy—am still. I'm sorry I haven't been free to see you, but I think you must cross me off your list, Miriam.' He smiled at her. 'I'm sure there are half a dozen men waiting for the chance to take you out.'

'But they aren't you, Oliver.' She laughed lightly. 'I don't mean to give you up, Oliver.' She realised her mistake when she saw the lift of his eyebrows, and added quickly, 'You are a perfect companion for an evening out, you know.'

She wished him a light-hearted goodbye then, adding, 'But you'll be at the Sawyers' dinner party, won't you? I'll see you then.'

'Yes, of course.' His goodbye was friendly, but she was aware that only good manners prevented him from showing impatience.

The sooner Dolores got rid of that girl the better, thought Miriam savagely. Once she was out of the way she would set about the serious business of capturing Oliver.

But Dolores had done nothing about sacking Amabel. For one thing she was too useful at this busy time of the year, and for another Dolores's indolence prevented her from making decisions. She was going to have to do something about it, because she had said she would, but later.

Then an ill-tempered and agitated phone call from Miriam put an end to indecision. A friend of Miriam's had mentioned casually that it was a pity that Oliver would be away for her small daughter's—his goddaughter's—birthday party. He'd be gone for several days, he had told her. The birthday was in three days' time...

'You must do something quickly—you promised.' Miriam managed to sound desperately unhappy, although what she really felt was rage. But it wouldn't do to lose Dolores's sympathy. She gave a sob. 'Oh, my dear, I'm so unhappy.'

And Dolores, her decision made for her, promised. 'The minute I get to the shop in the morning.'

Amabel was already hard at work, unwrapping Christmas tree fairies, shaking out their gauze wings and silky skirts, arranging them on a small glass shelf. She wished Dolores good morning, the last of the fairies in her hand.

Dolores didn't bother with good morning. She disliked unpleasantness if it involved herself, and the quicker it was dealt with the better.

'I'm giving you notice,' she said, relieved to find that once she had said it it wasn't so difficult. 'There's not enough work for you, and besides, I need the room at the back. You can go this evening, as soon as you've packed up. Leave your bits and pieces; someone can collect them. You'll get your wages, of course.'

Amabel put the last fairy down very carefully on the shelf. Then she said in a small shocked voice, 'What have I done wrong?'

Dolores picked up a vase and inspected it carefully.

'Nothing. I've just told you; I want the room and I've no further use for you in the shop.' She looked away from Amabel. 'You can go back to your aunt, and if you want work there'll be plenty of casual jobs before Christmas.'

Amabel didn't speak. Of what use? Dolores had made herself plain enough; to tell her that her aunt was still away, and that she had had a card from Josh that morning saying that he and Mrs Josh would be away for the next ten days and would she please not go and visit them as usual next Sunday, would be useless.

Dolores said sharply, 'And it's no use saying anything. My mind's made up. I don't want to hear another word.'

She went to the patisserie then, to have her coffee, and when she came back told Amabel that she could have an hour off to start her packing.

Amabel got out her case and began to pack it, explaining to Cyril and Oscar as she did so. She had no idea where she would go; she had enough money to pay for a bed and breakfast place, but would they take kindly to the animals? There wouldn't be much time to find somewhere once she left the shop at five o'clock. She stripped the bed, packed what food she had in a box and went back to the shop.

When five o'clock came Dolores was still in the shop.

She gave Amabel a week's wages, told her that she could give her name for a reference if she needed to, and went back to sit behind the counter.

'Don't hang about,' she said. 'I want to get home.'

But Amabel wasn't going to hurry. She fed Oscar and Cyril and had a wash, made a cup of tea and a sandwich, for she wasn't sure where the next meal would come from, and then, neatly dressed in her new winter coat, with Cyril on his lead, Oscar in his basket and carrying her case, she left the shop.

She didn't say anything. Good evening would have been a mockery; the evening was anything but good. She closed the shop door behind her, picked up her case, waved to the girl in the patisserie, and started off at a brisk pace, past the still lighted shops.

She didn't know York well, but she knew that she wasn't likely to find anywhere cheap in and around the main streets. If she could manage until Josh and his wife got back...

She reached the narrow side streets and presently saw a café on a street corner. It was a shabby place, but it had a sign in its window saying 'Rooms to Let'. She went inside and went to the counter, where a girl lounged reading a magazine.

The place was almost empty; it smelled of fried food and wasn't too clean, but to Amabel it was the answer to her prayers.

The girl was friendly enough. Yes, there was a room, and she could have it, but she didn't know about the dog and cat. She went away to ask and came back to say that there was a room on the ground floor where the animals could stay with her, but only at night; during the day she would have to take them with her. 'And since we're doing you a favour we'll have to charge more.'

A lot more. But at least it was a roof over their heads. It was a shabby roof, and a small ill-furnished room, but there was a wash handbasin and a window opening onto a window box which had been covered by wire netting, and that solved Oscar's problems.

Amabel handed over the money, left her case, locked the door and went out again, intent on finding a cafeteria. Presently, feeling all the better for a meal, still accompanied by Oscar in his basket and Cyril, she bought a take away meat pie and milk, carrying them to her room.

Oscar, let out of his basket at last, made a beeline for the window box, and then settled down to eat the meat in the pie while Cyril wolfed the crust, washing it down with the milk before climbing onto the bed.

Amabel washed in tepid water, cleaned her teeth, got into her nightie and then into bed. She was tired, too tired to think rationally, so she closed her eyes and went to sleep.

She was up early, asked for tea and toast from the girl at the counter and took Cyril out for five minutes. Since she didn't dare to leave Oscar he went too, grumbling in his basket.

Assuring the girl they would be back in the evening, she locked the door and set off into the cold bright morning.

It was apparent by midday that a job which would admit Cyril and Oscar was going to be hard to find. Amabel bought a carton of milk and a ham roll and found a quiet corner by St Mary's, where she fed Oscar and Cyril from the tin she had in her shoulder bag before letting a timid Oscar out to explore the flowerbeds. With a cat's good sense he stayed close to her, and soon got back into his basket and settled down again. He was a wise beast and he was aware that they were, the three of them, going through a sticky patch...

The afternoon was as disappointing as the morning, and the café, when Amabel got back to it, looked uninviting. But it spelled security of a sort, and tomorrow was another day.

Which turned out to be most unfortunately, just like the previous one. The following morning, when Amabel went to her frugal breakfast in the café, the girl at the counter leaned across to say, 'Can't put you up any longer. Got a regular booked the room for a week.'

Amabel chewed toast in a dry mouth. 'But there's another room I can rent?'

'Not with them animals. Be out by ten o'clock, will you? So's I can get the bed changed.'

'But just for a few nights?'

'Not a hope. The boss turned a blind eye for a couple of nights but that's it. Tried the Salvation Army, have you? There's beds there, but you'd have to find somewhere for that dog and cat.'

It was another fine morning, but cold. Amabel found a sheltered seat in the park and sat down to think. She discarded the idea of going home. She had escaped once; it might not be as easy again, and nothing was going to make her abandon Cyril and Oscar.

It was a question of waiting for eight days before Josh and his wife returned, and, however careful she was, there wasn't enough money in her purse to buy them bed and board for that time. She would try the Salvation Army—after five o'clock the girl had said—and hope that they would allow Cyril and Oscar to stay with her.

She had bought a local paper, so now she scanned the vacancies in the jobs columns. She ticked off the most promising, and set off to find the first of them. It was a tiresome business, for her suitcase was quite heavy and Oscar's basket got in the way. Each time she was re-

jected. Not unkindly, but with an indifference which
hurt.

It was after four o'clock when she finally gave up and
started on her way to the Salvation Army shelter. She
had to pass the end of the Shambles to reach it, and on
an impulse she turned aside and went through the half-
open door of the little church she had sometimes visited.
It was quiet inside and there was no one there. It was
cold too, and dimly lighted, but there was peace there...

Amabel sat down in one of the old-fashioned high-
backed pews, put Oscar's basket beside her, and, with
her case on the other side and Cyril at her feet, allowed
the tranquillity of the little church to soothe her.

She said aloud, 'Things are never as bad as they
seem,' and Cyril thumped his tail in agreement. Presently, tired from all the walking, he went to sleep. So
did Oscar, but Amabel sat without moving, trying to
make plans in her tired head which, despite her efforts,
was full of thoughts of Oliver. If he were there, she
thought dreamily, he would know exactly what to do...

The doctor had reached York shortly after lunch, booked
a room at the hotel and, with the faithful Tiger loping
beside him, made his way to Dolores's shop. She was
sitting behind the counter, reading, but she looked up as
he went in and got to her feet. She had known that
sooner or later he would come, but she still felt a momentary panic at the sight of him. Which was silly of
her; he stood there in the doorway, large and placid, and
his quiet greeting was reassuring.

'I've come to see Amabel,' he told her. 'Will you
allow her to have an hour or two off? Or perhaps the
rest of the afternoon? I can't stay in York long...'

'She's not here…'

'Oh, not ill, I hope?'

'She's gone. I didn't need her any more.' There was no expression on his face, but she took a step backwards. 'She's got an aunt to go to.'

'When was this? She had a week's notice, presumably?'

Dolores picked up a vase on the counter and put it down again. She said again, 'There's this aunt…'

'You sent her packing at a moment's notice?' The doctor's voice was quiet, but she shivered at the sound of it. 'She took the cat and dog with her?'

'Of course she did.'

'Did you know that her aunt was away from home?'

Dolores shrugged. 'She did mention it.' She would have to tell him something to make him see that it was useless looking for the girl. 'Amabel said something about going to stay with friends of her mother—somewhere near…' She paused for a moment, conjuring up names out of the back of her head. 'I think she said Nottingham—a Mrs Skinner…'

She heaved a sigh of relief; she had done that rather well.

He stood looking at her, his face inscrutable, his eyes cold. 'I don't believe you. And if any harm comes to Amabel I shall hold you responsible.'

He left the shop, closing the door quietly behind him, and Dolores flew to the kitchenette and reached for the bottle of whisky she kept hidden away there. Which meant that she missed seeing the girl at the patisserie go to the door and call to the doctor.

'Hi—you looking for Amabel? Poor kid got the sack

at a moment's notice—told she wasn't wanted by that Dolores, I suppose...'

'You spoke to her?'

'Didn't have a chance. Had me hands full of customers. She waved though—had her case and that dog and cat, going heaven knows where. Haven't seen hair nor hide of her since...'

'How long ago?'

'Two days?'

'Dolores said that she had gone away to friends.'

The girl sniffed. 'Don't you believe it—that woman will tell you anything she thinks you want to hear.'

'Yes. You think Amabel is still in York? I'm going to drive to her aunt's house now; there's a man, Josh...'

'I've seen 'im once or twice of a Sunday—brings her back here—she goes there on her free day.'

The doctor thanked her. 'Probably she is there—and thank you. I'll let you know if I find her.'

'You do that—I liked her.'

She watched him go. He was a man to satisfy any girl's dreams, not to mention the money. That was a cashmere coat, and a silk tie costing as much as one of her dresses...

Of course there was no one at Miss Parsons' house, and no response from Josh's cottage when he knocked. He was equally unsuccessful at the village shop—Josh was away, he was told, and there had been no sign of Amabel.

The doctor drove back to York, parked the car once more at the hotel and set off with Tiger to scour the city. He was worried, desperately concerned as to Amabel's whereabouts. He forced himself to think calmly as he systematically combed the streets of the inner city.

He didn't believe for one moment that Amabel had left York, and he thought it unlikely that she would have had enough money to get her home. And to go home was the most unlikely thing she would do. She was here, still in York. It was just a question of finding her...

He stopped at several of the smaller shops to ask if anyone had seen her and was told in one of them—a shabby little café—that there had been a girl with a dog. She had bought a roll and had coffee two days ago. A slender clue, but enough to take the doctor through the streets once more.

It was as he reached the lower end of the Shambles for the second time that his eye lighted on the little church close by. He remembered then that Amabel had told him that she had gone there from time to time. He went through its open door and stood just inside, aware of the quiet and the cold, and he saw Amabel, a small vague figure in the distance.

He heaved a great sigh and went quietly to where she was sitting. 'Hello, Amabel,' he said in a calm voice, 'I thought I might find you here.'

She turned her head slowly as Cyril got to his feet, wagging his tail and whining with pleasure. 'Oliver—Oliver, is it really you?'

She stopped because she was crying, and he went and sat down beside her and put a great arm around her shoulders. He sat quietly and let her weep, and when her sobs became sniffs offered a handkerchief.

'So sorry,' said Amabel. 'You were a surprise—at least, I was thinking about you, and there you were.'

He was relieved to hear that her voice, while still watery, was quite steady.

'Are you staying in York?' she asked politely. 'It's nice to see you again. But don't let me keep you.'

The doctor choked back a laugh. Even in dire circumstances, Amabel, he felt sure, would always be polite. He said gently, 'Amabel, I went to the shop and that woman—Dolores—told me what she had done. I've spent hours looking for you, but we aren't going to talk about it now. We are going to the hotel, and after a meal and a good night's sleep we will talk.'

'No,' said Amabel quite forcibly. 'I won't. What I mean is, thank you, but no. Tomorrow…'

He had Oscar's basket, and her case. Now he said, 'One day at a time, Amabel.'

CHAPTER SIX

SEVERAL hours later Amabel, fed and bathed and in bed, with Cyril curled up on the floor and Oscar stretched out on her feet, tried to sort out the evening so that it made sense. As it was, it had been a fairy tale dream. In no other way could she account for the last few hours.

How had Oliver been able to conjure a private sitting room out of thin air? A tray of tea, food for Oscar and Cyril? Her case had been unpacked and its contents whisked away to be washed and pressed, she was in a bedroom with a balcony where Oscar could feel free, had had a delicious meal and a glass of wine, and Oliver urging her to eat and drink and not ask questions but to go to bed since they must leave early in the morning.

She had obeyed sleepily, thanked him for her supper and said goodnight, then spent ages in the bath. And it had all seemed perfectly normal—just as a dream was always normal. In the morning she must find a way of leaving, but now she would just close her eyes...

She opened them to thin sunshine through the drawn curtains and a cheerful girl with a tray of tea.

'Dr Fforde asks that you dress quickly and meet him in the sitting room in twenty minutes—and I'm to take the dog with me so that he can have a run with the doctor's dog.'

Amabel drank her tea, put Oscar on the balcony and went into the sitting room. She showered and dressed with all speed, anxious not to keep Oliver waiting, so

108

her hair didn't look its best and her make-up was perfunctory, but she looked rested and ready for anything.

The doctor was at a window, looking out onto the street below. He turned round as she went in and studied her. 'That's better. You slept well?'

'Yes. Oh, yes, I did. It was like heaven.' She bent to stroke Cyril's head. 'Thank you for taking him out. And thank you for letting me stay here. It's like a dream.'

Breakfast was brought in then, and when they had sat down at the table she said, 'I expect you are in a hurry. The maid asked me to be quick. I'm very grateful, Oliver, for your kindness.' She added, 'There are several jobs I shall go and see about this morning.'

The doctor loaded toast with marmalade. 'Amabel, we are friends, so let us not talk nonsense to each other. You are a brave girl, but enough is enough. In half an hour or so we are leaving York. I have written to Josh so that he will know what has happened when he comes back home, and we will let Miss Parsons know as soon as possible.'

'Know what?'

'Where you will be and what you will be doing.'

'I'm not going home.'

'No, no, of course not. I am hoping that you will agree to do something for me. I have a great-aunt recovering from a slight stroke. Her one wish is to return to her home, but my mother hasn't been able to find someone who will live with her for a time. No nursing is needed, but a willingness to talk and be talked to, join in any small amusement she may fancy, help her to make life enjoyable. She is old, in her eighties, but she loves her garden and her home. She has a housekeeper and a housemaid who have both been with her for years. And don't think that I'm asking you to do this because you happen to be between jobs…'

Which sounded so much better, reflected Amabel, than being out of work, or even destitute. He was asking for her help and she owed him a great deal. Besides, he was her friend, and friends help each other when they were needed.

She said, 'If your great-aunt would like me to be with her, then I'll go to her. But what about Cyril and Oscar?'

'She has a house in the country; she likes animals and they will be welcome there. I should point out that she is a very old lady and liable to have another stroke, so the prospect for you is not a permanent one.'

Amabel drank the last of her coffee. 'Well, I expect for someone like me, with no special skills, it would be hard to find permanent work. But I must write to Aunt Thisbe and tell her.'

'Better still, if you have her phone number you can ring her up.'

'May I? When we get to wherever we are going?'

He crossed the room to the telephone on a side table. 'You have the number with you?' He held out a hand and she handed him the grubby slip of paper she had carried everywhere with her. He got the receptionist and waited for her to get the number, then handed Amabel the phone.

Aunt Thisbe's voice was loud and clear, demanding to know who it was.

'It's me. Amabel. There's nothing wrong, but I must tell you—that is, I must explain—'

The phone was taken from her. 'Miss Parsons? Oliver Fforde. Perhaps I can set your mind at rest. Amabel is with me and quite safe. She will explain everything to you, but I promise you that you have no need to worry about her.' He handed the phone back. 'I'll take the dogs for a quick walk—tell Miss Parsons that you will phone again this evening.'

Aunt Thisbe's firm voice begging her to take her time and tell her what had happened collected Amabel's wits for her. She gave a fairly coherent account of what had been happening. 'And Oliver has told me that he has a job waiting for me with an old aunt and has asked me to take it. And I've said I would because I should like to repay his kindness.'

'A sensible decision, child. An opportunity to express your thanks and at the same time give you a chance to decide what you intend to do. I heard Oliver saying that you will phone again this evening. This has changed things, of course. I was thinking of returning for Christmas, so that you would have somewhere to come over the holiday period, but now that there is no need of that and so I shall stay here for another few weeks. But remember, Amabel, if you need me I will return at once. I am very relieved that Oliver has come to your aid. A good man, Amabel, and one to be trusted.'

Amabel put down the phone as Oliver returned. He said briskly, 'I've put the dogs in the car. If you will get your coat, we'll be off.'

He shovelled Oscar into his basket. 'I must be back at the hospital by three o'clock, so I'll drop you off on the way.' He added impatiently, 'I'll explain as we go.'

Since it was obvious to her that he had no intention of saying anything more until it suited him, Amabel did as she was told.

Consumed by curiosity, and a feeling of uncertainty about her future, Amabel had to wait until they were

travelling fast down the M1 before the doctor had anything to say other than enquiries as to her comfort.

'We are going to Aldbury in Hertfordshire. It's a small
village a few miles from Berkhamsted. My mother is
there, arranging for my aunt's return, and she will explain everything to you—time off, salary and so on—
and stay overnight to see you settled in. She is very
relieved that you have agreed to take the job and you
will be very welcomed, both by her and by Mrs
Twitchett, the housekeeper, and Nelly.'

Amabel said, 'Your great-aunt might not like me.'

'There is nothing about you to dislike, Amabel.'

A remark which did nothing for her ego. She had
never had delusions about herself, but now she felt a
nonentity...

The doctor glanced at her as he spoke, at her unassuming profile as she looked steadily ahead. She looked
completely unfazed, accepting the way in which he had
bulldozed her into an unknown future. He had had no
chance to do otherwise; there had been no time, and to
have left her there alone in York would have been unthinkable. He said, 'I've rushed you, haven't I? But
sometimes one has to take a chance!'

Amabel smiled. 'A lucky chance for me. I'm so grateful, and I'll do my best with your great-aunt. Would you
tell me her name?'

'Lady Haleford. Eighty-seven years old, widowed for
ten years. No children. Loves her garden, birds, the
country and animals. She likes to play cards and cheats.
Since her stroke she has become fretful and forgetful and
at times rather peevish.' He added, 'No young society,
I'm afraid.'

'Well, I have never gone out much, so that doesn't matter.'

When he could spare the time, he reflected, he would take her out. Dinner and dancing, a theatre or concert. He didn't feel sorry for her, Amabel wasn't a girl one could pity, but she deserved some fun and he liked her. He was even, he had to admit, becoming a little fond of her in a brotherly sort of way. He wanted to see her safely embarked on the life she wanted so that she would have the chance to meet people of her own age, marry... He frowned. Time enough for that...

They travelled on in silence, comfortable in each other's company, and after a while he asked, 'Do you want to stop? There's a quiet pub about ten miles ahead; we can let the dogs out there.'

The pub stood back from the road and the car park was almost empty. 'Go on inside,' the doctor told her. 'I'll see to the dogs and make sure Oscar's all right. We can't stay long.'

As long as it's long enough to find the Ladies' thought Amabel, wasting no time.

They had beef sandwiches and coffee, saw to the dogs and got back into the car. Oscar, snoozing in his basket, was hardly disturbed. Life for him had had its ups and downs lately, but now he was snug and safe and Amabel's voice reassured him.

Travelling in a Rolls Royce was very pleasant, reflected Amabel, warm and comfortable and sliding past everything else on the road. And Oliver drove with relaxed skill. She supposed that he was a man who wasn't easily put out.

When he turned off the motorway he said, 'Not long now,' and sure enough, a few miles past Berkhamsted, he took a side turning and then a narrow lane and slowed as they reached Aldbury. It was a charming village, having its origin in Saxon times. There was a village green, a duck pond and a pub close by, and standing a little apart was the church, and beyond the village there was a pleasing vista of parkland and woods. Amabel, staring round her, knew that she would like living here, and hoped that it might be in one of the brick and timber cottages they were passing.

The doctor drove to the far side of the pond and stopped before a house standing on its own. Its front door opened directly onto the pavement—and it was brick and timber, as the others. It had a thatched roof, just as those did, but it was considerably larger and yet looked just as cosy.

He got out and opened Amabel's door. 'Come in and meet my mother again,' he invited. 'I'll come for the dogs and Oscar in a moment.'

The house door had been opened and a short stout woman stood there, smiling. She said comfortably, 'So here you are, Master Oliver, and the young lady...'

'Miss Amabel Parsons. Amabel, this is Mrs Twitchett.'

He bent to kiss her cheek and Amabel offered a hand, aware that as it was being shaken she was being studied closely. She hoped that Mrs Twitchett's smiling nod was a good sign.

The hall was wide with a wood floor, handsomely carpeted, but Amabel had no time to look around her for a door was thrust open and Mrs Fforde came to meet them.

The doctor bent to kiss her. 'No need to introduce

you,' he said cheerfully. 'I'll leave you for a moment and see to the dogs and Oscar.'

'Yes, dear. Can you stay?'

'Ten minutes. I've a clinic in a couple of hours.'

'Coffee? It'll be here when you've seen to the dogs. What about the cat?'

'Oscar is a much-travelled beast; he'll present no problems and the garden is walled.'

He went away and Mrs Fforde took Amabel's arm. 'Come and sit down for a moment. Mrs Twitchett will bring the coffee; I'm sure you must need it. I don't suppose Oliver stopped much on the way?'

'Once—we had coffee and sandwiches.'

'But it's quite a drive, even at his speed. Take off your coat and come and sit down.'

'My husband's aunt, Lady Haleford, is old and frail. I expect Oliver has told you that. The stroke has left her in need of a good deal of assistance. Nothing that requires nursing, you understand, just someone to be there. I hope you won't find it too arduous, for you are young and elderly people can be so trying! She is a charming old lady, though, and despite the fact that she can be forgetful she is otherwise mentally alert. I do hope that Oliver made that clear to you?'

Mrs Fforde looked so anxious that Amabel said at once, 'Yes, he did. I'll do my best to keep Lady Haleford happy, indeed I will.'

'You don't mind a country life? I'm afraid you won't have much freedom.'

'Mrs Fforde, I am so grateful to have a job where Cyril and Oscar can be with me—and I love the country.'

'You will want to let your mother know where you

are?' asked Mrs Fforde gently. 'Presently, when you are settled in, phone her. I shall be staying here overnight and will fetch Lady Haleford in the morning.'

The doctor joined them then, and Mrs Twitchett followed him in with a tray of coffee, Tiger and Cyril sidling in behind her.

'Oscar is in the kitchen,' he observed. 'What a sensible animal he is. Mrs Twitchett and Nelly have already fallen for his charms.' He smiled at Amabel and turned to his mother. 'You'll go home tomorrow? I'll try and get down next weekend. You will discuss everything with Amabel before you go? Good.' He drank his coffee and bent to kiss her cheek. 'I'll phone you…'

He laid a hand on Amabel's shoulder. 'I hope you will be happy with my aunt, Amabel. If there are any problems, don't hesitate to tell my mother.'

'All right—but I don't expect any. And thank you, Oliver.'

He was going again out of her life, and this time it was probably for the last time. He had come to her aid, rescued her with speed and a lack of fuss, set her back on her feet once more and was now perfectly justified in forgetting all about her. She offered her hand and her smile lighted up her face. 'Goodbye, Oliver.'

He didn't reply, only patted her shoulder and a moment later he was gone.

'We will go upstairs,' said Mrs Fforde briskly. 'I'll show you your room, and then we will go over the rest of the house so that you will feel quite at home before Lady Haleford arrives. We should be back in time for lunch and I'll leave soon after that. You're sure you can manage?'

'Yes,' said Amabel gravely. 'I'm sure, Mrs Fforde.'

It might not be easy at first, but she owed Oliver so much...

They went up the staircase, with its worn oak treads, to the landing above, with several doors on either side and a passage leading to the back of the house.

'I've put you next to my aunt's room,' said Mrs Fforde. 'There's a bathroom between—hers. Yours is on the other side of your room. I hope you won't have to get up in the night, but if you are close by it will make that easier.'

She opened a door and they went in together. It was a large room, with a small balcony overlooking the side of the house, and most comfortably furnished. It was pretty chintz curtains matching the bedspread, thick carpeting and a dear little easy chair beside a small table close to the window. The small dressing table had a stool before it and there was a pink-shaded lamp on the bedside table.

Mrs Fforde led the way across the room and opened a door. 'This is your bathroom—rather small, I'm afraid...'

Amabel thought of the washbasin behind the shop. 'It's perfect,' she said.

'And here's the door to my aunt's bathroom...' They went through it, and on into Lady Haleford's room at the front of the house. It was magnificently furnished, its windows draped in damask, the four-poster bed hung with the same damask, the massive dressing table loaded with silver-backed brushes and mirror, little cut-glass bottles and trinkets.

'Has Lady Haleford always lived here?'

'Yes—at least since her husband died. They lived in the manor house before that, of course, but when her son inherited he moved there with his wife and children and she came here. That was ten years ago. She has often told me that she prefers this house to the manor. For one thing the garden here is beautiful and the rooms aren't too large. And, being in the village, she can still see her friends without having to go too far. Until she had her stroke she drove herself, but of course that won't be possible now. Do you drive?'

'Yes,' said Amabel. 'But I'm not used to driving in large towns.'

'It would be driving Lady Haleford to church and back, and perhaps to call on local friends.'

'I could manage that,' said Amabel.

They went round the house in a leisurely manner. It was, she considered, rather large for one old lady and her two staff, but it was comfortable, rather old-fashioned, and it felt like home. Downstairs, beside the drawing room, there was a dining room, the morning room and a small sitting room—all immaculate. The kind of rooms, reflected Amabel, in which one could sit all day.

The last room they went into was the kitchen, as old-fashioned as the rest of the house. Something smelled delicious as they went in, and Mrs Twitchett turned from the Aga to warn them that dinner would be on the table in half an hour. Nelly was doing something at the table, and sitting before the Aga, for all the world as though they had lived there for ever, were Cyril and Oscar, pleased to see her but making no effort to rouse themselves.

'Happen they're tired out,' said Mrs Twitchett. 'They've eaten their fill and given no trouble.'

Amabel stooped to pat them. 'You really don't mind them being here?'

'Glad to have them. Nelly dotes on them. They'll always be welcome in here.'

Amabel had a sudden urge to burst into tears, a foolishness she supposed, but the relief to have a kind home for her two companions was great. They deserved peace and quiet after the last few months...

She smiled uncertainly at Mrs Twitchett and said thank you, then followed Mrs Fforde out of the kitchen.

Over dinner she was told her duties—not onerous but, as Mrs Fforde pointed out, probably boring and tiring. She was to take her free time when and where she could, and if it wasn't possible to have a day off each week she was to have two half-days. She might have to get up at night occasionally, and, as Mrs Fforde pointed out, the job at times might be demanding. But the wages she suggested were twice as much as Dolores had paid her. Living quietly, thought Amabel, I shall be able to save almost all of them. With a little money behind her she would have a chance to train for a career which would give her future security.

The next morning, buoyed up by high hopes, she waited for Mrs Fforde's return with Lady Haleford. All the same she was nervous.

It was a pity that she couldn't know that the doctor, sitting at his desk in his consulting rooms, had spared a moment to think of her as he studied his next patient's notes. He hoped that she would be happy with his great-aunt; the whole thing had been hurriedly arranged and even now she might be regretting it. But something had had to be done to help her.

He stood up to greet his patient and dismissed her from his thoughts.

Mrs Fforde's elderly Rover stopped in front of the door and Amabel went into the hall, standing discreetly at a distance from Mrs Twitchett and Nelly, waiting at the door. She and Cyril had been out early that morning for a walk through the country lanes; now he stood quietly beside her, and Oscar had perched himself close by, anxious not to be overlooked.

Lady Haleford was small and thin, and walked with a stick and the support of Mrs Fforde's arm, but although she walked slowly and hesitantly there was nothing invalidish about her.

She returned Mrs Twitchett's and Nelly's greetings in a brisk manner and asked at once, 'Well, where's this girl Oliver has found to look after me?'

Mrs Fforde guided her into the drawing room and sat her in a high-backed chair. 'Here, waiting for you.' She said over her shoulder, 'Amabel, come and meet Lady Haleford.'

Amabel put a cautionary finger on Cyril's head and went to stand before the old lady.

'How do you do, Lady Haleford?'

Lady Haleford studied her at some length. She had dark eyes, very bright in her wrinkled face, a small beaky nose and a mouth which, because of her stroke, drooped sideways.

'A plain girl,' she observed to no one in particular. 'But looks are only skin-deep, so they say. Nice eyes and pretty hair, though, and young...' She added peevishly, 'Too young. Old people are boring to the young.

You'll be gone within a week. I'm peevish and I forget things and I wake in the night.'

Amabel said gently, 'I shall be happy here, Lady Haleford. I hope you will let me stay and keep you company. This is such a lovely old house, you must be glad to be home again, you will get well again now that you are home.'

Lady Haleford said, 'Pooh,' and then added, 'I suppose I shall have to put up with you.'

'Only for as long as you want to, Lady Haleford,' said Amabel briskly.

'Well, at least you've a tongue in your head,' said the old lady. 'Where's my lunch?'

Her eye fell on Cyril. 'And what's this? The dog Oliver told me about? And there's a cat?'

'Yes. They are both elderly and well-behaved, and I promise you they won't disturb you.'

Lady Haleford said tartly, 'I like animals. Come here, dog.'

Cyril advanced obediently, not much liking to be called dog when he had a perfectly good name. But he stood politely while the old lady looked him over and then patted his head.

Mrs Fforde went home after lunch, leaving Amabel to cope with the rest of the day. Oliver had advised her to let Amabel find her own feet. 'She's quite capable of dealing with any hiccoughs,' he had pointed out, 'and the sooner they get to know each other the better.'

A remark which hadn't prevented him from thinking that perhaps he had made a mistake pitching Amabel into a job she might dislike. She was an independent girl, determined to make a good future for herself; she had only accepted the job with his great-aunt because she had to have a roof over her head and money in her pocket. But he had done his best, he reflected and need waste no more time thinking about her.

But as he had decided not to think any more about Amabel, so Miriam was equally determined to think about him. Dolores had phoned her and told her of his visit. 'I told him that she had left York—I invented an aunt somewhere or other, a friend of her mother's...' She didn't mention that he hadn't believed her. 'He went away and I didn't see him again. Is he back in London? Have you seen him?'

'No, not yet, but I know he's back. I rang his consulting rooms and said I wanted an appointment. He's been back for days. He can't have wasted much time in looking for her. You've been an angel, Dolores, and so clever to fob him off.'

'Anything for a friend, darling. I'll keep my eyes and ears open just in case she's still around.' She giggled. 'Good hunting!'

As far as she was concerned she didn't intend to do any more about it, although she did once ask idly if anyone had seen Amabel or her visitor when she had her coffee in the patisserie. But the girl behind the counter didn't like Dolores; she had treated Amabel shabbily and she had no need to know that that nice man had gone back one evening and told her that Amabel and her companions were safe with him.

Miriam had phoned Oliver's house several times to be told by Bates that his master was not home.

'He's gone away again?' she'd asked sharply.

'No. No, miss. I assume that he's very busy at the hospital.'

He told the doctor when he returned in the evening. 'Mrs Potter-Stokes, sir, has been ringing up on several occasions. I took it upon myself to say that you were at the hospital. She didn't wish to leave a message.' He lowered his eyes. 'I should have told you sooner, sir, but you have been away from home a good deal.'

'Quite right, Bates. If she should phone again, will you tell her that I'm very busy at the moment? Put it nicely.'

Bates murmured assent, concealing satisfaction; he disliked Mrs Potter-Stokes.

It was entirely by chance that Miriam met a friend of her mother's one morning. A pleasant lady who enjoyed a gossip.

'My dear, I don't seem to have seen you lately. You and Oliver Fforde are usually together...' She frowned. 'He is coming to dinner on Thursday, but someone or other told me that you were away.'

'Away? No, I shall be at home for the next few weeks.' Miriam contrived to look wistful. 'Oliver and I have been trying to meet for days—he's so busy; you would never believe how difficult it is to snatch an hour or two together.'

Her companion, a woman without guile and not expecting it in others, said at once, 'My dear Miriam, you must come to dinner. At least you can sit with each other and have a little time together. I'll get another man to make up the numbers.'

Miriam laid a hand on her arm. 'Oh, how kind of you; if only we can see each other for a while we can arrange to meet.'

Miriam went home well satisfied, so sure of her charm and looks that she was positive that Oliver, seeing her again, would resume their friendship and forget that silly girl.

But she was to be disappointed. He greeted her with his usual friendly smile, listened to her entertaining chatter, and with his usual beautiful manners evaded her questions as to where he had been. It was vexing that despite all her efforts he was still no more than one of her many friends.

At the end of the evening he drove her home, but he didn't accept her invitation to go in for a drink.

'I must be up early,' he told her, and wished her a pleasantly cool goodnight.

Miriam went angrily to her bed. She could find no fault in his manner towards her, but she had lost whatever hold she'd thought she had on him. Which made her all the more determined to do something about it. She had always had everything she wanted since she was a small girl, and now she wanted Oliver.

It was several days later that, an unwilling fourth at one of her mother's bridge parties, she heard someone remark, 'Such a pity he cannot spare the time to join us; he's going away for the weekend...'

The speaker turned to Miriam. 'I expect you knew that already, my dear?'

Miriam stopped herself just in time from trumping her partner's ace.

'Yes, yes, I do. He's very fond of his mother...'

'She lives at such a pleasant place. He's going to see an old aunt as well.' She laughed. 'Not a very exciting weekend for him. You won't be with him, Miriam?' The speaker glanced at her slyly.

'No, I'd already promised to visit an old schoolfriend.'

Miriam thought about that later. There was no reason

why Oliver shouldn't visit an old aunt; there was no
reason why she should feel uneasy about it. But she did.

She waited for a day or two and then phoned him,
keeping her voice deliberately light and understanding.
There was rather a good film on; how about them going
to see it together at the weekend?

'I'll be away,' he told her.

'Oh, well, another time. Visiting your mother?'

'Yes. It will be nice to get out of London for a couple
of days.'

He was as pleasant and friendly as he always had
been, but she knew that she was making no headway
with him. There was someone else—surely not that girl
still?

She gave the matter a good deal of thought, and finally
telephoned Mrs Fforde's home; if she was home, she
would hang up, say 'wrong number', or make some excuse, but if she was lucky enough to find her out and
the housekeeper, a garrulous woman, answered, she
might learn something...

She was in luck, and the housekeeper, told that this
was an old friend of the doctor's, was quite ready to
offer the information that he would be staying for the
weekend and leaving early on Sunday to visit Lady
Haleford.

'Ah, yes,' said Miriam encouragingly, 'his great-aunt.
Such a charming old lady.'

The housekeeper went on, 'Back home after a stroke,
madam told me. But they've got someone to live with
her—a young lady, but very competent.'

'I must give Lady Haleford a ring. Will you let me
have her number?'

It was an easy matter to phone and, under the pretext

of getting a wrong number, discover that Lady Haleford lived at Aldbury. It would be wise to wait until after Oliver had been there, but then she would find some reason for calling on the old lady and see for herself what it was about this girl that held Oliver's interest.

Satisfied that she had coped well with what she considered a threat to her future, Miriam relaxed.

Amabel, aware that fate was treating her kindly, set about being as nearly a perfect companion as possible. No easy task, for Lady Haleford was difficult. Not only was she old, she was accustomed to living her life as she wished—an impossibility after her stroke—so that for the first few days nothing was right, although she tolerated Cyril and Oscar, declaring that no one else understood her.

For several days Amabel was to be thoroughly dispirited; she had done nothing right, said nothing right, remained silent when she should have spoken, spoken when she was meant to be silent. It was disheartening, but she liked the old lady and guessed that underneath the peevishness and ill-temper there was a frightened old lady lurking.

There had been no chance to establish any kind of routine. She had had no free time other than brief walks round the garden with Cyril. But Mrs Twitchett and Nelly had done all they could to help her, and she told herself that things would improve.

She had coaxed Lady Haleford one afternoon, swathed in shawls, to sit in the drawing room, and had set up a card table beside her, intent on getting her to play two-handed whist. Her doctor had been that morning, pronounced himself satisfied with her progress and suggested that she might begin to take an interest in life once more.

He was a hearty man, middle-aged and clearly an old friend. He had taken no notice of Lady Haleford's peevishness, told her how lucky she was to have someone so young and cheerful to be with her and had gone away, urging Amabel at the same time to get out into the fresh air.

'Nothing like a good walk when you're young,' he had observed, and Mabel, pining for just that, had agreed with him silently.

Lady Haleford went to sleep over her cards and Amabel sat quietly, waiting for her to rouse herself again. And while she sat, she thought. Her job wasn't easy, she had no freedom and almost no leisure, but on the other hand she had a roof—a comfortable one—over her head, Oscar and Cyril had insinuated themselves into the household and become household pets, and she would be able to save money. Besides, she liked Lady Haleford, she loved the old house and the garden, and she had so much to be thankful for she didn't know where to begin.

With the doctor, she supposed, who had made it all possible. If only she knew where he lived she could write and tell him how grateful she was...

The drawing room door opened soundlessly and he walked in.

Amabel gaped at him, her mouth open. Then she shut it and put a finger to it. 'She's asleep,' she whispered unnecessarily, and felt a warm wave of delight and content at the sight of him.

He dropped a kiss on her cheek, having crossed the room and sat down.

'I've come to tea,' he told her, 'and if my aunt will invite me, I'll stay for supper.'

He sounded matter-of-fact, as though dropping in for tea was something he did often, and he was careful to hide his pleasure at seeing Amabel again. Still plain, but good food was producing some gentle curves and there were no longer shadows under her eyes.

Beautiful eyes, thought the doctor, and smiled, feeling content in her company.

CHAPTER SEVEN

LADY HALEFORD gave a small snort and woke up.

'Oliver—how delightful. You'll stay for tea? Amabel, go and tell Mrs Twitchett. You know Amabel, of course?'

'I saw her as I came in, and yes, I know Amabel. How do you find life now that you are back home, Aunt?'

The old lady said fretfully, 'I get tired and I forget things. But it is good to be home again. Amabel is a good girl and not impatient. Some of the nurses were impatient. You could feel them seething under their calm faces and I can sympathise with them.'

'You sleep well?'

'I suppose so. The nights are long, but Amabel makes tea and we sit and gossip.' She added in an anxious voice, 'I shall get better, Oliver?'

He said gently, 'You will improve slowly, but getting well after illness is sometimes harder than being ill.'

'Yes, it is. How I hate that wheelchair and that horrible thing to help me walk. I won't use it, you know. Amabel gives me an arm...'

The old lady closed her eyes and nodded off for a moment, before adding, 'It was clever of you to find her, Oliver. She's a plain girl, isn't she? Dresses in such dull clothes too, but her voice is pleasant and she's gentle.' She spoke as though Amabel wasn't there, sitting close to her. 'You made a good choice, Oliver.'

The doctor didn't look at Amabel. 'Yes, indeed I did, Aunt.'

Nelly came in with the tea tray then, and he began a casual conversation about his mother and his work and the people they knew, giving Amabel time to get over her discomfort. She was too sensible to be upset by Lady Haleford's remarks, but he guessed that she felt embarrassed...

Tea over, Lady Haleford declared that she would take a nap. 'You'll stay for dinner?' she wanted to know. 'I see you very seldom.' She sounded peevish.

'Yes, I'll stay with pleasure,' he told her. 'While you doze Amabel and I will take the dogs for a quick run.'

'And I shall have a glass of sherry before we dine,' said the old lady defiantly.

'Why not? We'll be back in half an hour or so. Come along, Amabel.'

Amabel got up. 'Is there anything you want before we go, Lady Haleford?' she asked.

'Yes, fetch Oscar to keep me company.'

Oscar, that astute cat, knew on which side his bread was buttered, for he settled down primly on the old lady's lap and went to sleep.

It was cold outside, but there was a bright moon in a starry sky. The doctor took Amabel's arm and walked her briskly through the village, past the church and along a lane out of the village. They each held a dog lead and the beasts trotted beside them, glad of the unexpected walk.

'Well,' said the doctor, 'how do you find your job? Have you settled in? My aunt can be difficult, and now, after her stroke, I expect she is often querulous.'

'Yes, but so should I be. Wouldn't you? And I'm very

happy here. It's not hard work, and you know everyone is so kind.'

'But you have to get up during the night?'

'Well, now and then.' She didn't tell him that Lady Haleford woke up during the early hours most nights and demanded company. Fearful of further probing questions, she asked, 'Have you been busy? You haven't needed to go to York again?'

'No, that is a matter happily dealt with. You hear from your mother and Miss Parsons?'

'Yes, Aunt Thisbe is coming home at the end of January, and my mother seems very happy. The market garden is planted and they have plenty of help.' She faltered for a moment. 'Mother said not to go home and see her yet, Mr Graham is still rather—well, I think he'd rather that I didn't visit them...'

'You would like to see your mother?' he asked gently.

'Yes, but if she thinks it is best for me to stay away then I will. Perhaps later...'

'And what do you intend to do later?'

They turned for home and he tucked her hand under his arm.

'Well, I shall be able to save a lot of money. It's all computers these days, isn't it? So I'll take a course in them and get a good job and somewhere to live.' She added anxiously, 'Your aunt does want me to stay for a while?'

'Oh, most certainly. I've talked to her doctor and he thinks that she needs six weeks or two months living as she does at present, and probably longer.'

They had reached the house again.

'You have very little freedom,' he told her.

She said soberly, 'I'm content.'

They had supper early, for Lady Haleford became easily tired, and as soon as the meal was finished the doctor got up to go.

'You'll come again?' demanded his aunt. 'I like visitors, and next time you will tell me about yourself. Haven't you found a girl to marry yet? You are thirty-four, Oliver. You've enough money and a splendid home and the work you love; now you need a wife.'

He bent to kiss her. 'You shall be the first to know when I find her.' And to Amabel he said, 'No, don't get up. Mrs Twitchett will see me out.' He put a hand on Amabel's shoulder as he passed her chair, and with Tiger at his heels was gone.

His visit had aroused the old lady; she had no wish to go to bed, she said pettishly. And it was a pity that Oliver could visit her so seldom. She observed, 'He is a busy man, and I dare say has many friends. But he needs to settle down. There are plenty of nice girls for him to choose from, and there is that Miriam...' She was rambling a bit. 'The Potter-Stokes widow—been angling for him for an age. If he's not careful she'll have him.' She closed her eyes. 'Not a nice young woman...'

Lady Haleford dozed for a while so Amabel thought about Oliver and the prospect of him marrying. She found the idea depressing, although it was the obvious thing for a man in his position to do. Anyway, it was none of her business.

A week went by, almost unnoticed in the gentle routine of the old house. Lady Haleford improved a little, but not much. Some days her testiness was enough to cast a blight over the entire household, so that Mrs Twitchett burnt the soup and Nelly dropped plates and Amabel had to listen to a diatribe of her many faults.

Only Cyril and Oscar weathered the storm and her fierce little rages, sitting by her chair and allowing her peevish words to fly over their heads.

But there were days when she was placid, wanting to talk, play at cards, and walk slowly round the house, carefully hitched up under Amabel's arm.

Her doctor came, assured her that she was making steady progress, warned Amabel to humour her as much as possible and went away again.

Since humouring her meant getting up in the small hours to read to the old lady, or simply to talk until she drowsed off to a light sleep, Amabel had very little time for herself. At least each morning she took Cyril for a walk while Lady Haleford rested in her bed after break-fast before getting up, and she looked forward to her half-hour's freedom each day, even when it was cold and wet.

On this particular morning it was colder and wetter than it had been for several days, and Amabel, trudging back down the village street with Cyril beside her, looked rather as though she had fallen into a ditch and been pulled out backwards. Her head down against the wind and rain, she didn't see the elegant little sports car outside Lady Haleford's gate until she was beside it.

Even then she would have opened the door and gone inside if the woman in the car hadn't wound down the window and said in an anxious voice, 'Excuse me—if you could spare a moment? Is this Lady Haleford's house? My mother is a friend of hers and asked me to look her up as I was coming this way. But it's too early to call. Could I leave a message with someone?'

She smiled charmingly while at the same time study-ing Amabel's person. This must be the girl, reflected

Miriam. Plain as a pikestaff and looks like a drowned rat. I can't believe that Oliver is in the least bit interested in her. Dolores has been tricking me... She spent a moment thinking of how she would repay her for that, then said aloud, at her most charming, 'Are you her granddaughter or niece? Perhaps you could tell her?'

'I'm Lady Haleford's companion,' said Amabel, and saw how cold the lovely blue eyes were. 'But I'll give her a message if you like. Would you like to come back later, or come and wait indoors? She has been ill and doesn't get up early.'

'I'll call on my way back,' said Miriam. She smiled sweetly. 'I'm sorry you're so wet standing there; I am thoughtless. But perhaps you don't mind the country in winter. I don't like this part of England. I've been in York for a while, and after that this village looks so forlorn.'

'It's very nice here,' said Amabel. 'But York is lovely; I was there recently.'

Her face ringed by strands of wet hair, she broke into a smile she couldn't suppress at the remembrance of the doctor.

Miriam said sharply, 'You have happy memories of it?'

Amabel, lost in a momentary dream, didn't notice the sharpness. 'Yes.'

'Well, I won't keep you.' Miriam smiled and made an effort to sound friendly. 'I'll call again.'

She drove away and Amabel went indoors. She spent the next ten minutes drying herself and Cyril and then went to tidy herself before going to Lady Haleford's room.

The old lady was in a placid mood, not wanting to

talk much and apt to doze off from time to time. It wasn't until she was dressed and downstairs in her normal chair by the drawing room fire that she asked, 'Well, what have you been doing with yourself, Amabel?'

Glad of something to talk about, Amabel told her of her morning's encounter. 'And I'm so sorry but she didn't tell me her name, and I forgot to ask, but she said that she'll be back.'

Lady Haleford said worriedly, 'I do have trouble remembering people... What was she like? Dark? Fair? Pretty?'

'Fair and beautiful, very large blue eyes. She was driving a little red car.'

Lady Haleford closed her eyes. 'Well, she'll be back. I don't feel like visitors today, Amabel, so if she does call make my apologies—and ask her name.'

But of course Miriam didn't go back, and after a few days they forgot about her.

Miriam found it just impossible to believe that Oliver could possibly have any interest in such a dull plain girl, but all the same it was a matter which needed to be dealt with. She had begun to take it for granted that he would take her to the theatre, out to dine, to visit picture galleries, and even when he had refused on account of his work she had been so sure of him...

Her vanity prevented her from realising that he had merely been fulfilling social obligations, that he had no real interest in her.

She would have to change her tactics. She stopped phoning him with suggestions that they should go to the theatre or dine out, but she took care to be there at a mutual friend's house if he were to be there, too. Since

Christmas was approaching, there were dinner parties and social gatherings enough.

Not that he was always to be found at them. Oliver had many friends, but his social life depended very much on his work so that, much to Miriam's annoyance, she only saw him from time to time, and when they did meet he was his usual friendly self, but that was all. Her pretty face and charm, her lovely clothes and witty talk were wasted on him.

When they had met at a friend's dinner party, and she'd asked casually what he intended to do for Christmas, he'd told her pleasantly that he was far too busy to make plans.

'Well, you mustn't miss our dinner party,' she'd told him. 'Mother will send you an invitation.'

The days passed peacefully enough at Aldbury. Lady Haleford had her ups and downs—indeed it seemed to Amabel that she was slowly losing ground. Although perhaps the dark days of the winter made the old lady loath to leave her bed. Since her doctor came regularly, and assured Amabel that things were taking their course, she spent a good many hours sitting in Lady Haleford's room, reading to her or playing two-handed patience.

All the same she was glad when Mrs Fforde phoned to say that she would be coming to spend a day or two. 'And I'm bringing two of my grandchildren with me— Katie and James. We will stay for a couple of days before I take them to London to do the Christmas shopping. Lady Haleford is very fond of them and it may please her to see them. Will you ask Mrs Twitchett to come to the phone, Amabel? I leave it to you to tell my aunt that we shall be coming.'

It was a piece of news which pleased the old lady mightily. 'Two nice children,' she told Amabel. 'They must be twelve years old—twins, you know. Their mother is Oliver's sister.' She closed her eyes for a moment and presently added, 'He has two sisters; they're both married, younger than he.'

They came two days later; Katie was thin and fair, with big blue eyes and a long plait of pale hair and James was the taller of the two, quiet and serious. Mrs Fforde greeted Amabel briskly.

'Amabel—how nice to see you again. You're rather pale—I dare say that you don't get out enough. Here are Katie and James. Why not take them into the garden for a while and I will visit Lady Haleford? Only put on something warm.' Her eyes lighted on Cyril, standing unexpectedly between the children.

'They are happy, your cat and dog?'

'Yes, very happy.'

'And you, Amabel?'

'I'm happy too, Mrs Fforde.'

Oscar, wishing for a share of the attention, went into the garden too, and, although it was cold, it was a clear day with no wind. They walked along its paths while the children told Amabel at some length about their shopping trip to London.

'We spend Christmas at Granny's,' they explained. 'Our aunt and uncle and cousins will be there, and Uncle Oliver. We have a lovely time and Christmas is always the same each year. Will you go home for Christmas, Amabel?'

'Oh, I expect so,' said Amabel, and before they could ask any more questions added, 'Christmas is such fun, isn't it?'

They stayed for two days, and Amabel was sorry to see them go, but even such a brief visit had tired Lady Haleford, and they quickly slipped back into the placid pattern of their days.

Now that Christmas was near Amabel couldn't help wishing that she might enjoy some of the festivities, so it was a delightful surprise when Lady Haleford, rather more alert than she had been, told her that she wanted her to go to Berkhamstead and do some Christmas shopping. 'Sit down,' she commanded, 'and get a pen and some paper and write down my list.'

The list took several days to complete, for Lady Haleford tended to doze off a good deal, but finally Amabel caught the village bus, her ears ringing with advice and instructions from Mrs Twitchett, the list in her purse and a wad of banknotes tucked away safely.

It was really rather exciting, and shopping for presents was fun even if it was for someone else. It was a long list, for Lady Haleford's family was a large one: books, jigsaw puzzles, games for the younger members, apricots in brandy, a special blend of coffee, Stilton cheese in jars, a case of wine, boxes of candied fruits, and mouth-watering chocolates for the older ones.

Amabel, prowling round the small grocer's shop which seemed to stock every luxury imaginable, had enjoyed every minute of her shopping. She had stopped only briefly for a sandwich and coffee, and now, with an hour to spare before the bus left, she did a little shopping for herself.

High time too, she thought, stocking up on soap and toiletries, stockings and a thick sweater, shampoos and toothpaste. And then presents: patience cards for Lady Haleford, a scarf for Mrs Twitchett, a necklace for Nelly, a new collar for Cyril and a catnip mouse for Oscar. It was hard to find a present for her mother; she chose a blouse, in pink silk, and, since she couldn't ignore him, a book token for her stepfather.

At the very last minute she saw a dress, silvery grey in some soft material—the kind of dress, she told herself, which would be useful for an occasion, and after all it was Christmas... She bought it and, laden with parcels, went back to Aldbury.

The old lady, refreshed by a nap, wanted to see everything. Amabel drank a much needed cup of tea in the kitchen and spent the next hour or so carefully unwrapping parcels and wrapping them up again. Tomorrow, said Lady Haleford, Amabel must go into the village shop and get coloured wrapping paper and labels and write appropriate names on them.

The village shop was a treasure store of Christmas goods. Amabel spent a happy half-hour choosing suitably festive paper and bore it back for the old lady's approval. Later, kneeling on the floor under Lady Haleford's eyes, she was glad of her experience in Dolores's shop, for the gifts were all shapes and sizes. Frequently it was necessary to unwrap something and repack it because Lady Haleford had dozed off and got muddled...

The doctor, coming quietly into the room, unnoticed by a dozing Lady Haleford and, since she had her back to the door, by Amabel, stood in the doorway and watched her. She wasn't quite as tidy as usual, and half obscured by sheets of wrapping paper and reels of satin ribbon. Even from the back, he considered, she looked flustered...

The old lady opened her eyes and saw him and said,

'Oliver, how nice. Amabel, I've changed my mind. Unwrap the Stilton cheese and find a box for it.'

Amabel put down the cheese and looked over her shoulder. Oliver smiled at her and she smiled back, a smile of pure delight because she was so happy to see him again.

Lady Haleford said with a touch of peevishness, 'Amabel—the cheese…'

Amabel picked it up again and clasped it to her bosom, still smiling, and the doctor crossed the room and took it from her.

'Stilton—who is it for, Aunt?' He eyed the growing pile of gaily coloured packages. 'I see you've done your Christmas shopping.'

'You'll stay for lunch?' said Lady Haleford. 'Amabel, go and tell Mrs Twitchett.' When Amabel had gone she said, 'Oliver, will you take Amabel out? A drive, or tea, or something? She has no fun and she never complains.'

'Yes, of course. I came partly to suggest that we have dinner together one evening.'

'Good. Mrs Twitchett told me that the child has bought a new dress. Because it's Christmas, she told her. Perhaps I don't pay her enough…'

'I believe she is saving her money so that she can train for some career or other.'

'She would make a good wife…' The old lady dozed off again.

It was after lunch, when Lady Haleford had been tucked up for her afternoon nap, that the doctor asked Amabel if she would have dinner with him one evening. They were walking the dogs, arm-in-arm, talking easily like two old friends, comfortable with each other, but she stopped to look up at him.

'Oh, that would be lovely. But I can't, you know. It would mean leaving Lady Haleford for a whole evening, and Nelly goes to her mother's house in the village after dinner—she's got rheumatism, her mother, you know—and that means Mrs Twitchett would be alone...'

'I think that something might be arranged if you would leave that to me.'

'And then,' continued Amabel, 'I've only one dress. I bought it the other day, but it's not very fashionable. I only bought it because it's Christmas and I...really, it was a silly thing to do.'

'Since you are going to wear it when we go out I don't find it in the least silly.' He spoke gently. 'Is it a pretty dress?'

'Pale grey. Very plain. It won't look out of date for several years.'

'It sounds just the thing for an evening out. I'll come for you next Saturday evening—half past seven.'

They walked back then, and presently he went away, giving her a casual nod. 'Saturday,' he reminded her, and bent to kiss her cheek. Such a quick kiss that she wasn't sure if she had imagined it.

She supposed that she wasn't in the least surprised to find that Lady Haleford had no objection to her going out with the doctor. Indeed, she seemed to find nothing out of the ordinary in it, and when Amabel enquired anxiously about Nelly going to her mother, she was told that an old friend of Mrs Twitchett's would be spending the evening with her.

'Go and enjoy yourself,' said that lady. 'Eat a good dinner and dance a bit.'

So when Saturday came Amabel got into the grey dress, took pains with her face and her hair and went downstairs to where the doctor was waiting. Lady Haleford had refused to go to bed early; Mrs Twitchett would help her, she had told Amabel, but Amabel was to look in on her when she got home later. 'In case I am still awake and need something.'

Amabel, the grey dress concealed by her coat, greeted the doctor gravely, pronounced herself ready, bade the old lady goodnight, bade Oscar and Cyril to be good and got into the car beside Oliver.

It was a cold clear night with a bright moon. There would be a heavy frost by morning, but now everything was silvery in the moonlight.

'We're not going far,' said the doctor. 'There's rather a nice country hotel—we can dance if we feel like it.'

He began to talk about this and that, and Amabel, who had been feeling rather shy, lost her shyness and began to enjoy herself. She couldn't think why she should have felt suddenly awkward with him; after all, he was a friend—an old friend by now...

He had chosen the hotel carefully and it was just right. The grey dress, unassuming and simple but having style, was absorbed into the quiet luxury of the restaurant.

The place was festive, without being overpoweringly so, and the food was delicious. Amabel ate prawns and Caesar salad, grilled sole and straw potatoes and, since it was almost Christmas, mouthwatering mince pies with chantilly cream. But not all at once.

The place was full and people were dancing. When the doctor suggested that she might like to dance she got up at once. Only as they reached the dance floor she hesitated. 'It's ages since I danced,' she told him.

He smiled down at her. 'Then it's high time you did now,' he told her.

She was very light on her feet, and she hadn't forgotten how to dance. Oliver looked down onto her neat head of hair and wondered how long it would be before she discovered that she was in love with him. He was prepared to wait, but he hoped that it wouldn't be too long…!

The good food, the champagne and dancing had transformed a rather plain girl in a grey dress into someone quite different. When at length it was time to leave, Amabel, very pink in the cheeks and bright of the eye, her tongue loosened by the champagne, told him that she had never had such a lovely evening in her life before.

'York seems like a bad dream,' she told him, 'and supposing you hadn't happened to see me, what would I have done? You're my guardian angel, Oliver.'

The doctor, who had no wish to be her guardian angel but something much more interesting, said cheerfully, 'Oh, you would have fallen on your feet, Amabel, you're a sensible girl.'

And all the things she suddenly wanted to say to him shrivelled on her tongue.

'I've had too much champagne,' she told him, and talked about the pleasures of the evening until they were back at Lady Haleford's house.

He went in with her, to switch on lights and make sure all was well, but he didn't stay. She went to the door with him and thanked him once again for her lovely evening.

'I'll remember it,' she told him.

He put his arms round her then, and kissed her hard, but before she could say anything he had gone, closing the door quietly behind him.

She stood for a long time thinking about that kiss, but presently she took off her shoes and crept upstairs to her room. There, was no sound from Lady Haleford's bedroom and all was still when she peeped through the door; she undressed and prepared for bed, and was just getting into bed when she heard the gentle tinkling of the old lady's bell. So she got out of bed again and went quietly to see what was the matter.

Lady Haleford was now wide awake, and wanted an account of the evening.

'Sit down and tell me about it,' she commanded. 'Where did you go and what did you eat?'

So Amabel stifled a yawn and curled up in a chair by the bed to recount the events of the evening. Not the kiss, of course.

When she had finished Lady Haleford said smugly, 'So you had a good time. It was my suggestion, you know—that Oliver should take you out for the evening. He's so kind, you know—always willing to do a good turn. Such a busy man, too. I'm sure he could ill spare the time.' She gave a satisfied sigh. 'Now go to bed Amabel. We have to see to the rest of those Christmas presents tomorrow.'

So Amabel turned the pillow, offered a drink, turned the night light low and went back to her room. In her room she got into bed and closed her eyes, but she didn't go to sleep.

Her lovely evening had been a mockery, a charitable action undertaken from a sense of duty by someone whom she had thought was her friend. He was still her friend, she reminded herself, but his friendship was mixed with pity.

Not to be borne, decided Amabel, and at last fell asleep as the tears dried on her cheeks.

Lady Haleford had a good deal more to say about the evening out in the morning; Amabel had to repeat everything she had already told her and listen to the old lady's satisfied comments while she tied up the rest of the parcels.

'I told Oliver that you had bought a dress...'

Amabel cringed. Bad enough that he had consented to take her out; he probably thought that she had bought it in the hope that he might invite her.

She said quickly, 'We shall need some more paper. I'll go and buy some...'

In the shop, surrounded by the village ladies doing their weekly shopping, she felt better. She was being silly, she told herself. What did it matter what reason Oliver had had for asking her out for the evening? It had been a lovely surprise and she had enjoyed herself, and what had she expected, anyway?

She went back and tied up the rest of the presents, and recounted, once again, the previous evening's events, for the old lady protested that she had been told nothing.

'Oh, you spent five minutes with me when you came in last night, but I want to know what you talked about. You're a nice girl, Amabel, but I can't think of you as an amusing companion. Men do like to be amused, but I dare say Oliver found you pleasant enough; he can take his pick of pretty women in London.'

All of which did nothing to improve Amabel's spirits.

Not being given to self-pity, she told herself to remember that Lady Haleford was old and had been ill and didn't mean half of what she said. As for her evening out, well, that was a pleasant memory and nothing more. If she should see the doctor again she would take care to let him see that, while they were still friends, she neither expected nor wanted to be more than that.

I'll be a little cool, reflected Amabel, and in a few weeks I expect I'll be gone from here. Being a sensible girl, she fell to planning her future…

This was a waste of time, actually, for Oliver was planning it for her; she would be with his aunt for several weeks yet—time enough to think of a way in which they might see each other frequently and let her discover for herself that he was in love with her and wanted to marry her. He had friends enough; there must be one amongst them who needed a companion or something of that sort, where Cyril and Oscar would be acceptable. And where he would be able to see her as frequently as possible…

The simplest thing would be for her to stay at his house. Impossible—but he lingered over the delightful idea…

He wasn't the only one thinking about Amabel's future. Miriam, determined to marry Oliver, saw Amabel as a real threat to her plans.

She was careful to be casually friendly when she and Oliver met occasionally, and she took care not to ask him any but the vaguest questions about his days. She had tried once or twice to get information from Bates, but he professed ignorance of his employer's comings and goings. He told her stolidly that the doctor was either at his consulting room or at the hospital, and if she phoned and wanted to speak to him at the weekend Bates informed her that he was out with the dog.

Oliver, immersed in his work and thoughts of Amabel,

dismissed Miriam's various invitations and suggestions
that they might spend an evening together with good-
mannered friendliness; he didn't believe seriously that
Miriam wanted anything more than his company from
time to time; she had men-friends enough.

He underestimated her, though. Miriam drove herself
to Aldbury, parked the car away from the centre of the
village and found her way to the church. The village
shop would have been ideal ground from which to glean
information, but there was the risk of meeting Amabel.
Besides, people in the village might talk.

The church was old and beautiful, but she didn't waste
time on it. Someone—the vicar, she supposed—was
coming down the aisle towards her, wanting to know if
he could help her...

He was a nice elderly man, willing to talk to this
charming lady who was so interested in the village. 'Oh,
yes,' he told her, 'there are several old families living in
the village, their history going back for many years.'

'And those lovely cottages with thatched roofs—one
of them seems a good deal larger than the rest?'

'Ah, yes, that would be Lady Haleford's house. A
very old family. She has been ill and is very elderly. She
was in hospital for some time, but now I'm glad to say
she is at home again. There is a very charming young
woman who is her companion. We see her seldom, for
she has little spare time, although Lady Haleford's
nephew comes to visit his aunt and I have seen the pair
of them walking the dogs. He was here recently, so I'm
told, and took her out for the evening...! How I do ramble on, but living in a small village we tend to be interested in each other's doings. You are touring this part
of the country?'

'Yes, this is a good time of year to drive around the countryside. I shall work my way west to the Cotswolds,' said Miriam, untruthfully. 'It's been delightful talking to you, Vicar, and now I must get back to my car and drive on.'

She shook hands and walked quickly back to her car, watched by several ladies in the village shop, whose sharp eyes took in every inch of her appearance.

She drove away quickly and presently pulled up on the grass verge the better to think. At first she was too angry to put two thoughts together. This was no passing attraction on Oliver's part; he had been seeing this girl for some time now and his interest was deep enough to cause him to seek her out. Miriam seethed quietly. She didn't love Oliver; she liked him enough to marry him and she wanted the things the marriage would bring to her: a handsome husband, money, a lovely home and the social standing his name and profession would give her.

She thumped the driving wheel in rage. Something would have to be done, but what?

CHAPTER EIGHT

QUIET though the routine of Lady Haleford's household was, Christmas, so near now, was not to be ignored. Cards were delivered, gifts arrived, visitors called to spend ten minutes with the old lady, and Amabel trotted round the house arranging and rearranging the variety of pot plants they brought with them.

It was all mildly exciting, but tiring for the invalid, so that Amabel needed to use all her tact and patience, coaxing callers to leave after the briefest of visits, and even then Lady Haleford exhibited a mixture of lethargy and testiness which prompted her to get the doctor to call.

He was a rather solemn man who had looked after the old lady for years, and he now gave it as his opinion that, Christmas or no Christmas, his patient must revert to total peace and quiet.

'The occasional visitor,' he allowed, and Amabel was to use her discretion in turning away more than that.

Amabel said, 'Lady Haleford likes to know who calls. She gets upset if someone she wishes to see is asked not to visit her. I've tried that once or twice and she gets rather uptight.'

Dr Carr looked at her thoughtfully. 'Yes, well, I must leave that to your discretion, Miss Parsons. Probably to go against her wishes would do more harm than good. She sleeps well?'

'No,' said Amabel. 'Although she dozes a lot during the day.'

'But at night—she is restless? Worried…?'

'No. Just awake. She likes to talk, and sometimes I read to her.'

He looked at her as though he hadn't really seen her before.

'You get sufficient recreation, Miss Parsons?'

Amabel said that, yes, thank you, she did. Because if she didn't he might decide that she wasn't capable enough for the job and arrange for a nurse. Her insides trembled at the thought.

So Amabel met visitors as they were ushered into the hall and, unless they were very close old friends or remote members of Lady Haleford's family, persuaded them that she wasn't well enough to have a visitor, then offered notepaper and a pen in case they wanted to write a little note and plied them with coffee and one of Mrs Twitchett's mince pies.

Hard work, but it left both parties satisfied.

Though it was quite quiet in the house, the village at its doorstep was full of life. There was a lighted Christmas tree, the village shop was a blaze of fairy lights, and carol singers—ranging from small children roaring out the first line of 'Good King Wenceslas' to the harmonious church choir—were a nightly event. And Mrs Twitchett, while making sure that Lady Haleford was served the dainty little meals she picked at, dished up festive food suitable to the season for the other three of them.

Amabel counted her blessings and tried not to think about Oliver.

*   *   *

Dr Fforde was going to Glastonbury to spend Christmas with his mother and the rest of his family. Two days which he could ill spare. He had satisfied himself that his patients were making progress, presented the theatre staff with sherry, his ward sister and his receptionist and the nurse at the consulting rooms with similar bottles, made sure that Bates and his wife would enjoy a good Christmas, loaded the car boot with suitable presents and, accompanied by Tiger, was ready to leave home.

He was looking forward to the long drive, and, more than that, he was looking forward to seeing Amabel, for he intended to call on his aunt on his way.

He had been working hard for the last week or so, and on top of that there had been the obligatory social events. Many of them he had enjoyed, but not all of them. He had found the dinner party given by Miriam's parents particularly tedious, but he had had no good reason to refuse the invitation—although he had been relieved to find that Miriam seemed no longer to look upon him as her future. She had been as amusing and attractive as always, but she had made no demands on his time, merely saying with apparent sincerity that he must be glad to get away from his work for a few days.

It was beginning to snow when he left, very early on the morning of Christmas Eve. Tiger, sitting very upright beside him, watched the heavy traffic. It took some time to get away from London but the doctor remained patient, thinking about Amabel, knowing that he would be seeing her in an hour or so.

The village looked charming as he drove through it and there was a small lighted Christmas tree in the cottage's drawing room window. He got out of the car, opened the door for Tiger, and saw Amabel and Cyril at the far end of the village street. Tiger, scenting friends, was already on his way to meet them. Oliver saw Amabel stop, and for a moment he thought she was going to turn round and hurry away. But she bent to greet Tiger and came towards him. He met her halfway.

There was snow powdering her woolly cap and her coat, and her face was rosy with cold. He thought she looked beautiful, though he was puzzled by her prim greeting.

He said cheerfully, 'Hello. I'm on my way to spend Christmas with the family. How is my aunt?'

'A bit tired,' she told him seriously. 'There have been a great many visitors, although she has seen only a handful of them.'

They were walking back towards the house. 'I expect you'd like to see her? She'll be finishing her breakfast.' Since he didn't speak, the silence got rather long. 'I expect you've been busy?' Annabel finally ventured.

'Yes, I'll go back on Boxing Day.' They had reached the front door when he said, 'What's the matter, Amabel?'

She said, too quickly, 'Nothing. Everything is fine.' And as she opened the door added, 'Would you mind going up to Lady Haleford? I'll dry the dogs and tidy myself.'

Mrs Twitchett came bustling into the hall then, and Amabel slipped away. Oliver wouldn't stay long and she could keep out of his way...

The dogs made themselves comfortable on either side of Oscar in front of the Aga, and when Nelly came in to say that Mr Oliver would have a cup of coffee before he went away Amabel slipped upstairs. Lady Haleford would be ready to start the slow business of dressing.

'Go away,' said the old lady as Amabel went into her room. 'Go and have coffee with Oliver. I'll dress later.' When Amabel looked reluctant, she added, 'Well, run along. Surely you want to wish him a happy Christmas?'

So Amabel went downstairs again, as slowly as possible, and into the drawing room. The dogs and Oscar had gone there with the coffee, sitting before the fire, and the doctor was sitting in one of the big wing chairs.

He got up as she went in, drew a balloon-backed chair closer to his own and invited her to pour their coffee.

'And now tell me what is wrong,' he said kindly. 'For there is something, isn't there? Surely we are friends enough for you to tell me? Something I have done, Amabel?'

She took a gulp of coffee. 'Well, yes, but it's silly of me to mind. So if it's all the same to you I'd rather not talk about it.'

He resisted the urge to scoop her out of her chair and wrap her in his arms. 'It isn't all the same to me...'

She put down her cup and saucer. 'Well, you didn't have to take me out to dinner just because Lady Haleford said that you should—I wouldn't have gone if I'd known...' She choked with sudden temper. 'Like giving a biscuit to a dog...'

Oliver bit back a laugh, not of amusement but of tenderness and relief. If that was all...

But she hadn't finished. 'And I didn't buy a dress because I hoped you would take me out.' She looked at him then. 'You are my friend, Oliver, and that is how I think of you—a friend.'

He said gently, 'I came to take you out for the evening, Amabel. Anything my aunt said didn't influence me in any way. And as for your new dress, that was something I hadn't considered. It was a pretty dress, but you look nice whatever you are wearing.' He would have liked to have said a great deal more, but it was obviously not the right moment. When she didn't speak, he said, 'Still friends, Amabel?'

'Yes—oh, yes, Oliver. I'm sorry I've been so silly.'

'We'll have another evening out after Christmas. I think that you will be here for some time yet.'

'I'm very happy here. Everyone in the village is so friendly, and really I have nothing to do.'

'You have very little time to yourself. Do you get the chance to go out—meet people—young people?'

'Well, no, but I don't mind.'

He got up to go presently. It was still snowing and he had some way to drive still. She went with him to the door, and Tiger, reluctant to leave Cyril and Oscar, pushed between them. Amabel bent to stroke him.

'Go carefully,' she said, 'and I hope that you and your family have a lovely Christmas.'

He stood looking down at her. 'Next year will be different!' He fished a small packet from a pocket. 'Happy Christmas, Amabel,' he said, and kissed her.

He didn't wait to hear her surprised thanks. She stood watching the car until it was out of sight, her mouth slightly open in surprise, clutching the little gaily wrapped box.

The delightful thought that he might come again on his way back to London sent a pleasant glow through her person.

She waited until Christmas morning before she opened the box, sitting up in bed early in the darkness. The box contained a brooch, a true lover's knot, in gold and turquoise—a dainty thing, but one she could wear with her very ordinary clothes.

She got up dressed in the grey dress and pinned the brooch onto it before getting into her coat and slipping out of the house to go to church.

It was dark and cold, and although the snow had stopped it lay thick on the ground. The church was cold too, but it smelled of evergreens and flowers, and the Christmas tree shone with its twinkling lights. There weren't many people at the service, for almost everyone would be at Matins during the morning, but as they left the church there was a pleasant flurry of cheerful talk and good wishes.

Amabel made sure that Lady Haleford was still asleep, had a quick breakfast with Mrs Twitchett and Nelly and took Cyril for his walk. The weather didn't suit his elderly bones and the walk was brief. She settled him next to Oscar by the Aga and went to bid Lady Haleford good morning.

The old lady wasn't in a festive mood. She had no wish to get out of her bed, no wish to eat her breakfast, and she said that she was too tired to look at the gifts Amabel assured her were waiting for her downstairs.

'You can read to me,' she said peevishly.

So Amabel sat down and read. *Little Women* was a soothing book, and very old-fashioned. She found the chapter describing Christmas and the simple pleasures of the four girls and their mother was a sharp contrast to the comfortable life Lady Haleford had always lived.

Presently Lady Haleford said, 'What a horrid old woman I am...'

'You're one of the nicest people I know,' said

Amabel, and, quite forgetting that she was a paid companion, she got up and hugged the old lady.

So Christmas was Christmas after all, with presents being opened, and turkey and Christmas pudding and mince pies, suitably interposed between refreshing naps, and Amabel, having tucked Lady Haleford into her bed, went early to bed herself. There was nothing else to do, but that didn't matter. Oliver would be returning to London the next day, and perhaps he would come and see them again...

But he didn't. It was snowing again, and he couldn't risk a hold-up on the way back to London.

The weather stayed wintry until New Year's Day, when Amabel woke to a bright winter's sun and blue sky. It was still snowy underfoot, and as she sloshed through it with a reluctant Cyril she wondered what the New Year would bring...

As for the doctor, he hardly noticed which day of the week it was, for the New Year had brought with it the usual surge of bad chests, tired hearts and the beginnings of a flu epidemic. He left home early and came home late, and ate whatever food Bates put before him. He was tired, and often frustrated, but it was his life and his work, and presently, when things had settled down again, he would go to Amabel...

Miriam waited for a few days before phoning Oliver. He had just got home after a long day and he was tired, but that was something she hadn't considered. There was a new play, she told him, would he get tickets? 'And we could have supper afterwards. I want to hear all about Christmas...'

He didn't tell her that he was working all day and

every day, and sometimes into the night as well. He said mildly, 'I'm very busy, Miriam, I can't spare the time. There is a flu epidemic...'

'Oh, is there? I didn't know. There must be plenty of junior doctors...'

'Not enough.'

She said with a flash of temper, 'Then I'll get someone who will enjoy my company.'

The doctor, reading the first of a pile of reports on his desk, said absent-mindedly, 'Yes, do. I hope you will have a pleasant evening.'

He put the phone down and then picked it up again. He wanted to hear Amabel's voice. He put it down again. Phone conversations were unsatisfactory, for either one said too much or not enough. He would go and see her just as soon as he could spare the time. He ignored the pile of work before him and sat back and thought about Amabel, in her grey dress, wearing, he hoped, the true lover's knot.

Miriam had put down the phone and sat down to think. If Oliver was busy then he wouldn't have time to go to Aldbury. It was a chance for her to go, talk to the girl, convince her that he had no interest in her, that his future and hers were as far apart as two poles. It would be helpful if she could get Amabel away from this aunt of his, but she could see no way of doing that. She would have to convince Amabel that she had become an embarrassment to him...

There was no knowing when Oliver would go to Aldbury again, and Miriam waited with impatience for the snow to clear away. On a cold bright day, armed with a bouquet of flowers purporting to come from her mother, she set out.

The church clock was striking eleven as she stopped before Lady Haleford's cottage. Nelly answered the door, listened politely to Miriam's tale of her mother's friendship with Lady Haleford and bade her come in and wait. Lady Haleford was still in her room, but she would fetch Miss Parsons down. She left Miriam in the drawing room and went away, and presently Amabel came in.

Miriam said at once, 'Oh, hello—we've met before, haven't we? I came at the wrong time. Am I more fortunate today? Mother asked me to let Lady Haleford have these flowers…'

'Lady Haleford will be coming down in a few minutes,' said Amabel, and wondered why she didn't like this visitor.

She was being friendly enough, almost gushing, and Lady Haleford, when Nelly had mentioned Miriam's name, had said, 'That young woman—very pushy. And I haven't met her mother for years.' She had added, 'But I'll come down.'

Which she did, some ten minutes later, leaving Amabel to make polite conversation that Miriam made no effort to sustain.

But with the old lady she was at her most charming, giving her the flowers with a mythical message from her mother, asking about her health with apparent concern.

The old lady, normally a lady of perfect manners, broke into her chatter. 'I am going to take a nap. Amabel, fetch your coat and take Mrs Potter-Stokes to look round the village or the church if she chooses. Mrs Twitchett will give you coffee in half an hour's time. I will say goodbye now; please thank your mother for the flowers.'

She sat back in her chair and closed her eyes, leaving

Amabel to usher an affronted Miriam out of the room.
In the hall Amabel said, 'Lady Haleford has been very
ill and she tires easily. Would you like to see round the
church?'

Miriam said no, in a snappy voice, and then, mindful
of why she had come, added with a smile, 'But perhaps
we could walk a little way out of the village? The country looks very pretty.'

Amabel got into her coat, tied a scarf over her head
and, with Cyril on his lead, led the way past the church
and into the narrow lane beyond. Being a friendly girl,
with nice manners, she made small talk about the village
and the people who lived in it, aware that her companion
hadn't really wanted to go walking—she was wearing
the wrong shoes for a start.

Annoyed though Miriam was, she saw that this was
her chance—if only there was a suitable opening. She
stepped into a puddle and splashed her shoe and her
tights and the hem of her long coat, and saw the opening...

'Oh, dear. Just look at that. I'm afraid I'm not a country girl. It's a good thing that I live in London and always shall. I'm getting married soon, and Oliver lives
and works there too...'

'Oliver?' asked Amabel in a careful voice.

'A nice name, isn't it? He's a medical man, always
frightfully busy, although we manage to get quite a lot
of time together. He has a lovely house; I shall love
living there.'

She turned to smile at Amabel. 'He's such a dear—
very kind and considerate. All his patients dote on him.
And he's always ready to help any lame dog over a stile.
There's some poor girl he's saved from a most miserable

life—gone out of his way to find her a job. I hope she's grateful. She has no idea where he lives, of course. I mean, she isn't the kind of person one would want to become too familiar with, and it wouldn't do for her to get silly ideas into her head, would it?'

Amabel said quickly, 'I shouldn't think that would be very likely, but I'm sure she must be grateful.'

Miriam tucked a hand under Amabel's arm. 'Oh, I dare say—and if she appeals to him again for any reason I'll talk to her. I won't have him badgered; heaven knows how many he's helped without telling me. Once we're married, of course, things will be different.'

She gave Amabel a smiling nod, noting with satisfaction that the girl looked pale. 'Could we go back? I'm longing for a cup of coffee...'

Over coffee she had a great deal to say about the approaching wedding. 'Of course, Oliver and I have so many friends, and he's well known in the medical profession. I shall wear white, of course...' Miriam allowed her imagination full rein.

Amabel ordered more coffee, agreed that four bridesmaids would be very suitable, and longed for her unwelcome visitor to go. Which, presently, she did.

Lady Haleford, half dozing in her room, opened her eyes long enough to ask if the caller had gone and nodded off again, for which Amabel was thankful. She had no wish to repeat their conversation—besides, Oliver's private life was none of her business. She hadn't liked Miriam, but it had never entered her head that the woman was lying. It all made sense; Oliver had never talked about his home or his work or his friends. And why should he? Mrs Twitchett had remarked on several occasions that he had given unobtrusive help to people.

'He's a very private person,' she had told Amabel. 'Lord knows what goes on in that clever head of his.'

There was no hope of going to see Amabel for the moment; the flu epidemic had swollen to a disquieting level. The doctor treated his patients with seeming tirelessness, sleeping when he could, sustained by Mrs Bates's excellent food and Bates's dignified support. But Amabel was always at the back of his mind, and from time to time he allowed himself to think about her, living her quiet life and, he hoped, sometimes thinking about him.

Of Miriam he saw nothing; she had prudently gone to stay with friends in the country, where there was less danger of getting the flu. She phoned him, leaving nicely calculated messages to let him see that she was concerned about him, content to bide her time, pleased with herself that she had sewn the seeds of doubt in Amabel's mind. Amabel was the kind of silly little fool, she reflected, who would believe every word of what she had said. Head over heels in love with him, thought Miriam, and doesn't even know it.

But here she was wrong; Amabel, left unhappy and worried, thought about Oliver a good deal. In fact he was never out of her thoughts. She *had* believed Miriam when she had told her that she and Oliver were to marry. If Lady Haleford hadn't been particularly testy for the next few days she might have mentioned it to her, but it wasn't until two o'clock one morning, when the old lady was sitting up in her bed wide awake and feeling chatty, that she began to talk about Oliver.

'Time he settled down. I only hope he doesn't marry that Potter-Stokes woman. Can't stand her—but there's no denying that she's got looks and plenty of ambition. He'd be knighted in no time if she married him, for she knows all the right people. But he'd have a fashionable practice and turn into an embittered man. He needs to be loved...'

Amabel, curled up in a chair by the bed, wrapped in her sensible dressing gown, her hair neatly plaited, murmured soothingly, anxious that the old lady should settle down. Now was certainly not the time to tell her about Miriam's news.

Lady Haleford dozed off and Amabel was left with her thoughts. They were sad, for she agreed wholeheartedly with the old lady that Miriam would not do for Oliver. He does need someone to love him, reflected Amabel, and surprised herself by adding *me*.

Once over her surprise at the thought, she allowed herself to daydream a little. She had no idea where Oliver lived—somewhere in London—and she knew almost nothing about his work, but she would love him, and care for him, and look after his house, and there would be children...

'I fancy a drop of hot milk,' said Lady Haleford. 'And you'd better go to bed, Amabel. You looked washed out...'

Which effectively put an end to daydreams, although it didn't stop her chaotic thoughts. Waiting for the milk to heat, she decided that she had been in love with Oliver for a long time, accepting him into her life as naturally as drawing breath. But there was nothing to be done about it; Miriam had made it plain that he wouldn't welcome the prospect of seeing her again.

If he did come to see his aunt, thought Amabel, pouring the milk carefully into Lady Haleford's special mug, then she, Amabel, would keep out of his way, be coolly pleasant, let him see that she quite understood.

These elevating thoughts lasted until she was back in her own bed, where she could cry her eyes out in peace and quiet.

The thoughts stood her in good stead, for Oliver came two days later. It being a Sunday, and Lady Haleford being in a good mood, Amabel had been told that she might go to Matins, and it was on leaving the church that she saw the car outside the cottage. She stopped in the porch, trying to think of a means of escape. If she went back into the church she could go out through the side door and up the lane and stay away for as long as possible. He probably wasn't staying long…

She felt a large heavy arm on her shoulders and turned her head.

'Didn't expect me, did you?' asked the doctor cheerfully. 'I've come to lunch.'

Amabel found her voice and willed her heart to stop thumping. She said, 'Lady Haleford will be pleased to see you.'

He gave her a quick, all-seeing look. Something wasn't quite right…

'I've had orders to take you for a brisk walk before lunch. Up the lane by the church?'

Being with him, she discovered, was the height of happiness. Her high-minded intentions could surely be delayed until he had gone again? While he was there, they didn't make sense. As long as she remembered that they were friends and nothing more.

She said, 'Where's Tiger?'

'Being spoilt in the kitchen. Wait here. I'll fetch him and Cyril.'

He was gone before she could utter, and soon back again with the dogs, tucking an arm in hers and walking her briskly past the church and up the lane. The last time she had walked along it, she reflected, Miriam had been with her.

Very conscious of the arm, she asked, 'Have you been busy?'

'Very busy. There's not been much flu here?'

'Only one or two cases.' She sought for something to talk about. 'Have you seen Lady Haleford yet? She's better—at least I think so. Once the spring is here, perhaps I could drive her out sometimes—just for an hour—and she's looking forward to going into the garden.'

'I spent a few minutes with her. Yes, she is making progress, but it's a long business. I should think you will be here for some weeks. Do you want to leave, Amabel?'

'No, no, of course not. Unless Lady Haleford would like me to go?'

'That is most unlikely. Have you thought about the future?'

'Yes, quite a lot. I—I know what I want to do. I'll go and see Aunt Thisbe and then I'll enrol at one of those places where I can train to use a computer. There's a good one at Manchester; I saw it advertised in Lady Haleford's paper.' She added, to make it sound more convincing, 'I've saved my money, so I can find somewhere to live.'

The doctor, quite rightly, took this to be a spur-of-the-moment idea, but he didn't say so.

'Very sensible. You don't wish to go home?'

'Yes. I'd like to see Mother, but she wrote to me just after Christmas and said that my stepfather still wasn't keen for me to pay a visit.'

'She could come here...'

'I don't think he would like that. I did suggest it.' She added, 'Mother is very happy. I wouldn't want to disturb that.'

They had been walking briskly and had passed the last of the cottages in the lane. The doctor came to a halt and turned her round to face him.

'Amabel, there is a great deal I wish to say to you...'

'No,' she said fiercely. 'Not now—not ever. I quite understand, but I don't want to know. Oh, can't you see that? We're friends, and I hope we always will be, but when I leave here it's most unlikely that we shall meet again.'

He said slowly, 'What makes you think that we shall never meet again?'

'It wouldn't do,' said Amabel. 'And now please don't let's talk about it any more.'

He nodded, his blue eyes suddenly cold. 'Very well.' He turned her round. 'We had better go back, or Mrs Twitchett will be worried about a spoilt lunch.'

He began to talk about the dogs and the weather, and was she interested in paintings? He had been to see a rather interesting exhibition of an early Victorian artist...

His gentle flow of talk lasted until they reached the cottage again and she could escape on the pretext of seeing if the old lady needed anything before lunch. The fresh air had given her face a pleasing colour, but it still looked plain in her mirror. She flung powder onto her nose, dragged a comb through her hair and went downstairs.

Lady Haleford, delighted to have Oliver's company,

asked endless questions. She knew many of the doctor's friends and demanded news of them.

'And what about you, Oliver? I know you're a busy man, but surely you must have some kind of social life?'

'Not a great deal—I've been too busy.'

'That Potter-Stokes woman called—brought flowers from her mother. Heaven knows why; I hardly know her. She tired me out in ten minutes. I sent her out for a walk with Amabel...'

'Miriam came here?' asked Oliver slowly, and looked at Amabel, sitting at the other side of the table.

She speared a morsel of chicken onto her fork and glanced at him quickly. 'She's very beautiful, isn't she? We had a pleasant walk and a cup of coffee—she couldn't stay long; she was on her way to visit someone. She thought the village was delightful. She was driving one of those little sports cars...' She stopped talking, aware that she was babbling.

She put the chicken in her mouth and chewed it. It tasted like ashes.

'Miriam is very beautiful,' agreed the doctor, staring at her, and then said to his aunt, 'I'm sure you must enjoy visitors from time to time, Aunt, but don't tire yourself.'

'I don't. Besides, Amabel may look like a mouse, but she can be a dragon in my defence. Bless the girl! I don't know what I would do without her.' After a moment she added, 'But of course she will go soon.'

'Not until you want me to,' said Amabel. 'And by then you will have become so much better that you won't need anyone.' She smiled across the table at the old lady. 'Mrs Twitchett has made your favourite pudding. Now, there is someone you would never wish to be without!'

'She has been with me for years. Oliver, your Mrs Bates is a splendid cook, is she not? And Bates? He still runs the place for you?'

'My right hand,' said the doctor. 'And as soon as you are well enough I shall drive you up to town and you can sample some of Mrs Bates's cooking.'

Lady Haleford needed her after-lunch nap.

'Stay for tea?' she begged him. 'Keep Amabel company. I'm sure you'll have plenty to talk about...'

'I'm afraid that I must get back.' He glanced at his watch. 'I'll say goodbye now.'

When Amabel came downstairs again he had gone.

Which was only to be expected, Amabel told herself, but she would have liked to have said goodbye. To have explained...

But how did one explain that, since one had fallen in love with someone already engaged to someone else, meeting again would be pointless. And she had lost a friend...

Later that day Lady Haleford, much refreshed by her nap, observed, 'A pity Oliver had to return so soon.' She darted a sharp glance at Amabel. 'You get on well together?'

'Yes,' said Amabel, and tried to think of something to add but couldn't.

'He's a good man.'

'Yes,' said Amabel again. 'Shall I unpick that knitting for you, Lady Haleford?'

The old lady gave her a thoughtful look. 'Yes, Amabel, and then we will have a game of cards. That will distract our thoughts.'

Amabel, surveying her future during a wakeful night, wondered what she should do, but as events turned out she had no need to concern herself with that.

It was several days after Oliver's visit that she had a phone call. She had just come in with Cyril, after his early-morning walk, and, since Nelly and Mrs Twitchett were both in the kitchen, she answered it from the phone in the hall.

'Is that you, Amabel?' Her stepfather's voice was agitated. 'Listen, you must come home at once. Your mother's ill—she's been in hospital and they've sent her home and there's no one to look after her.'

'What was wrong? Why didn't you let me know that she was ill?'

'It was only pneumonia. I thought they'd keep her there until she was back to normal. But here she is, in bed most of the day, and I've enough to do without nursing her as well.'

'Haven't you any help?'

'Oh, there's a woman who comes in to clean and cook. Don't tell me to hire a nurse; it's your duty to come home and care for your mother. And I don't want any excuses. You're her daughter, remember.'

'I'll come as soon as I can,' said Amabel, and took Cyril to the kitchen.

Mrs Twitchett looked at her pale face. 'Something wrong? Best tell us.'

It was a great relief to tell someone. Mrs Twitchett and Nelly heard her out.

'Have to go, won't you love?' Nelly's eye fell on Cyril and Oscar, side by side in front of the Aga. 'Will you take them with you?'

'Oh, Nelly, I can't. He wanted to kill them both; that's

why I left home.' Amabel sniffed back tears. 'I'll have to take them to a kennel and a cattery.'

'No need,' Mrs Twitchett said comfortably. 'They'll stay here until you know what's what. Lady Haleford loves them both, and Nelly will see to Cyril's walks. Now, just you go and tell my lady what it's all about.'

Lady Haleford, sitting up in bed, sipping her early-morning tea and wide awake for once, said immediately, 'Of course you must go home immediately. Don't worry about Cyril and Oscar. Get your mother well again and then come back to us. Will she want you to stay at home for good?'

Amabel shook her head. 'No, I don't think so. You see, my stepfather doesn't like me.'

'Then go and pack, and arrange your journey.'

CHAPTER NINE

THE doctor had driven himself back to London, deep in thought. It was obvious that Miriam had said something to Amabel which had upset her and caused her to retire into her shell of coolness. But she hadn't sounded cool in the lane. The only way to discover the reason for this was to go and see Miriam. She had probably said something as a joke and Amabel had misunderstood her...

He had gone to see her the very next evening and found her entertaining friends. As she had come to meet him he had said, 'I want to talk to you, Miriam.'

She, looking into his bland face and cold eyes, said at once, 'Oh, impossible, Oliver—we're just about to go out for the evening.'

'You can join your friends later. It is time we had a talk, Miriam, and what better time than now?'

She pouted. 'Oh, very well.' Then she smiled enchantingly. 'I was beginning to think that you had forgotten me.'

Presently, when everyone had gone, she sat down on a sofa and patted the cushion beside her. 'My dear, this is nice—just the two of us.'

The doctor sat down in a chair opposite her.

'Miriam, I have never been your dear. We have been out together, seen each other frequently at friends' houses, visited the theatre, but I must have made it plain to you that that was the extent of our friendship.' He asked abruptly, 'What did you say to Amabel?'

Miriam's beautiful face didn't look beautiful any more. 'So that's it—you've fallen in love with that dull girl! I guessed it weeks ago, when Dolores saw you in York. Her and her silly pets. Well, anyway, I've cooked your goose. I told her you were going to marry me, that you had helped her out of kindness and the sooner she disappeared the better...'

She stopped, because Oliver's expressionless face frightened her, and then when he got to his feet said, 'Oliver, don't go. She's no wife for you; you need someone like me, who knows everyone worth knowing, entertains all the right people, dresses well.'

Oliver walked to the door. 'I need a wife who loves me and whom I love.' And he went away.

It was a pity, he reflected that his next few days were so crammed with patients, clinics and theatre lists that it was impossible for him to go and see Amabel. It was a temptation to phone her, but he knew that would be unsatisfactory. Besides, he wanted to see her face while they talked.

He drove back home and went to his study and started on the case notes piled on his desk, dismissing Amabel firmly from his thoughts.

Lady Haleford had summoned Mrs Twitchett to her bedroom and demanded to know how Amabel was to go home. 'I don't know where the girl lives. Didn't someone tell me that she came from York?'

'And so she did, my lady; she's got an aunt there. Left home when her mother brought in a stepfather who don't like her. Somewhere near Castle Cary—she'll need to get the train to the nearest station and get a taxi or a bus, if there is one.'

Mrs Twitchett hesitated. 'And, my lady, could we keep Oscar and Cyril here while she's away? Seeing that her stepfather won't have them? Going to put them down, he was, so she left home.'

'The poor child. Arrange for William down at the village garage to drive her home. I've already told her that of course the animals must stay.'

So Amabel was driven away in the village taxi, which was just as well, for the journey home otherwise would have been long and tedious and she had had no time to plan it.

It was late afternoon when William drew up with a flourish at her home.

There were lights shining from several windows, and she could see a large greenhouse at the side of the house. As they got out of the car she glimpsed another beyond it, where the orchard had been.

The front door opened under her touch and they went into the hall as she saw her stepfather come from the kitchen.

'And about time too,' he said roughly. 'Your mother's in the sitting room, waiting to be helped to bed.'

'This is William, who brought me here by taxi,' said Amabel. 'He's going back to Aldbury, but he would like a cup of tea first.'

'I've no time to make tea…'

Amabel turned to William. 'If you'll come with me to the kitchen, I'll make it. I'll just see Mother first.'

Her mother looked up as she went into the sitting room.

'There you are, Amabel. Lovely to see you again, dear, and have you here to look after me.' She lifted her face for Amabel's kiss. 'Keith is quite prepared to let bygones be bygones and let you live here...'

'Mother, I must give the taxi driver a cup of tea. I'll be back presently and we can have a talk.'

There was no sign of her stepfather. William, waiting patiently in the kitchen, said, 'Not much of a welcome home, miss.'

Amabel warmed the teapot. 'Well, it all happened rather suddenly. Do you want a sandwich?'

William went very soon, feeling all the better for the tea and sandwiches, and the tip he had accepted reluctantly, and Amabel went back to the sitting room.

'Tell me what has been wrong with you, Mother. Do you stay up all day? The doctor visits you?'

'Pneumonia, love, and I went to hospital because Keith couldn't possibly manage on his own.'

'Have you no help?'

'Oh, yes, of course. Mrs Twist has been coming each day, to see to the house and do some of the cooking, and the hospital said a nurse would come each day once I was back home. She came for a day or two, but she and Keith had an argument and he told them that you would be looking after me. Not that I need much attention. In fact he's told Mrs Twist that she need not come any more, now that you are back home.'

'My stepfather told me that there was no one to look after you, that he had no help...'

Her mother said lightly, 'Oh, well, dear, you know what men are—and it does seem absurd for him to pay for a nurse and Mrs Twist when we have you...'

'Mother, I don't think you understand. I've got a job. I came because I thought there was no one to help you. I'll stay until you are better, but you must get Mrs Twist back and have a nurse on call if it's necessary. I'd like to go back to Aldbury as soon as possible. You see, dear, Keith doesn't like me—but you're happy with him, aren't you?'

'Yes, Amabel, I am, and I can't think why you can't get on, the pair of you. But now you are here the least you can do is make me comfortable. I'm still rather an invalid, having breakfast in bed and then a quiet day here by the fire. My appetite isn't good, but you were always a good cook. Keith likes his breakfast early, so you'll have all day to see to the house.'

She added complacently, 'Keith is doing very well already, and now he won't need to pay Mrs Twist and that nurse he can plough the money back. You'll want to unpack your things, dear. Your old room, of course. I'm not sure if the bed is made up, but you know where everything is. And when you come down we'll decide what we'll have for supper.'

Of course the bed wasn't made up; the room was chilly and unwelcoming and Amabel sat down on the bed to get her thoughts sorted out. She wouldn't stay longer than it took to get Mrs Twist back, see the doctor and arrange for a nurse to visit, whatever her stepfather said. She loved her mother, but she was aware that she wasn't really welcome, that she was just being used as a convenience by her stepfather.

She made the bed, unpacked, and went back downstairs to the kitchen. There was plenty of food in the fridge. At least she wouldn't need to go to the shops for a few days...

Her mother fancied an omelette. 'But that won't do for Keith. There's a gammon steak, and you might do some potatoes and leeks. You won't have time to make a pudding, but there's plenty of cheese and biscuits...'

'Have you been cooking, Mother?'

Her mother said fretfully, 'Well, Keith can't cook, and Mrs Twist wasn't here. Now you're home I don't need to do anything.'

The next morning Amabel went to the village to the doctor's surgery. He was a nice man, but elderly and overworked.

'You're mother is almost fit again,' he assured Amabel. 'There is no reason why she shouldn't do a little housework, as long as she rests during the day. She needs some tests done, of course, and pills, and a check-up by the practice nurse. It is a pity that her husband refuses to let her visit; he told me that you would be coming home to live and that you would see to your mother.'

'Has Mother been very ill?'

'No, no. Pneumonia is a nasty thing, but if it's dealt with promptly anyone as fit as your mother makes a quick recovery.'

'I understood from what my stepfather told me on the phone that Mother was very ill and he was without help.' She sighed. 'I came as quickly as I could, but I have a job...'

'Well, I shouldn't worry too much about that. I imagine that a few days of help from you will enable your mother to lead her usual life again. She has help, I believe?'

'My stepfather gave Mrs Twist notice...'

'Oh, dear, then you must get her back. Someone local?'

'Yes.'

'Well, it shouldn't be too difficult to persuade Mr Graham to change his mind. Once she is reinstated, you won't need to stay.'

Something which she pointed out to her stepfather later that day. 'And do please understand that I must go back to my job at the end of week. The doctor told me that Mother should be well by then. You will have to get Mrs Twist to come every day.'

'You unnatural girl.' Keith Graham's face was red with bad temper. 'It's your duty to stay here…'

'You didn't want me to stay before,' Amabel pointed out quietly. 'I'll stay for a week, so that you have time to make arrangements to find someone to help Mother.' She nodded her neat head at him. 'There was no need for me to come home. I love Mother, but you know as well as I do that you hate having me here. I can't think why you decided to ask me to come.'

'Why should I pay for a woman to come and do the housework when I've a stepdaughter I can get for nothing?'

Amabel got to her feet. If there had been something suitable to throw at him she would have thrown it, but since there wasn't she merely said, 'I shall go back at the end of the week.'

But there were several days to live through first, and although her mother consented to be more active there was a great deal to do—the cooking, fires to clean and light, coal to fetch from the shed, beds to make and the house to tidy. Her stepfather didn't lift a finger, only coming in for his meals, and when he wasn't out and about he was sitting by the fire, reading his paper.

Amabel said nothing, for eventually there was only one more day to go…

She was up early on the last morning, her bag packed, and she went down to cook the breakfast Keith demanded. He came into the kitchen as she dished up his bacon and eggs.

'Your mother's ill,' he told her. 'Not had a wink of sleep—nor me neither. You'd better go and see to her.'

'At what time is Mrs Twist coming?'

'She isn't. Haven't had time to do anything about her...'

Amabel went upstairs and found her mother in bed.

'I'm not well, Amabel. I feel awful. My chest hurts and I've got a headache. You can't leave me.'

She moaned as Amabel sat her gently against her pillows.

'I'll bring you a cup of tea, Mother, and phone the doctor.'

She went downstairs to phone and leave a message at the surgery. Her stepfather said angrily. 'No need for him. All she needs is a few days in bed. You can stay on a bit.'

'I'll stay until you get Mrs Twist back. Today, if possible.'

Her mother would eat no breakfast, so Amabel helped her to the bathroom, made the bed and tidied the room and then went back downstairs to cancel the taxi which was to have fetched her in an hour's time. She had no choice but to stay until the doctor had been and Mrs Twist was reinstated.

There was nothing much wrong with her mother, the doctor told her when he came. She was complaining about her chest, but he could find nothing wrong there, and her headache was probably due to the sleepless nights she said she was having.

He said slowly, 'She has worked herself up because you are going away. I think it would be best if you could arrange to stay for another day or two. Has Mr Graham got Mrs Twist to come in?'

'No. He told me that he had had no time. I thought I might go and see her myself. You don't think that Mother is going to be ill again?'

'As far as I can see she has recovered completely from the pneumonia, but, as I say, she has worked herself up into a state—afraid of being ill again. So if you could stay…'

'Of course I'll stay until Mother feels better.' She smiled at him. 'Thank you for coming, Doctor.'

He gave her a fatherly pat. He thought she looked a bit under the weather herself he must remember to call in again in a day or two.

Amabel unpacked her bag, assured her mother that she would stay until Mrs Twist could come, and went to see that lady…

Mrs Twist was a comfortable body with a cheerful face. She listened to Amabel in silence and then said, 'Well, I'm sorry to disoblige you, but I've got my old mum coming today for a week. Once she's gone home again I'll go each day, same as before. Staying long, are you?'

'I meant to go back to my job this morning, but Mother asked me to stay until you could arrange to come back.' She couldn't help adding, 'You will come, won't you?'

'Course I will, love. And a week goes by quick enough. Nice having your ma to chat to.'

Amabel said, yes, it was, and thought how nice that would have been. Only there was precious little time to chat, and when she did sit down for an hour to talk it was her mother who did the talking: about how good Keith was to her, the new clothes she had bought, the holiday they intended to take before the spring brought all the extra work in the greenhouses, how happy she was... But she asked no questions of Amabel.

She said, 'I expect you've got a good job, darling. You were always an independent girl. You must tell me about it one day...I was telling you about our holiday...'

It was strange how the days seemed endless, despite the fact that she had little leisure. She had written a note to Lady Haleford, saying that she would return as soon as she could arrange help for her mother. Since her mother seemed quite well again, it was now just a question of waiting for Mrs Twist's mother to go home. Her mother, however, was disinclined to do much.

'There's no need for me to do anything,' she had said, half laughing, 'while you're here.'

'Mrs Twist does everything when she comes?'

'Oh, yes. Although I do the cooking. But you're such a good cook, love, and it gives you something to do.'

One more day, thought Amabel. She had missed Cyril and Oscar. She had missed Oliver too, but she tried not to think of him—and how could she miss someone she hardly ever saw?

Amabel had been gone for almost two weeks before the doctor felt free to take time off and go to Aldbury. His aunt greeted him with pleasure. 'But you've come to see Amabel? Well, she's not here. The child had to go home; her mother was ill. She expected to be gone for a week. Indeed, she wrote and told me she would be coming back. And then I had another letter saying that she would have to stay another week. Can't think why she didn't telephone.' She added, 'Mrs Twitchett phoned and a man answered her. Very abrupt, she said, told her that Amabel wasn't available.'

It was already late afternoon, and the doctor had a list early on the following morning, a clinic in the afternoon and private patients to see. To get into his car and go to Amabel was something he wanted to do very much, but that wasn't possible; it wouldn't be possible for two days.

He thought about phoning her, but it might make matters worse and in any case there was a great deal he could do. He went back home, sat down at his desk and picked up the phone; he could find out what was happening…

Mrs Graham's doctor was helpful. There was no reason, he said over the phone, why Amabel should stay at home. She had told him very little, but he sensed that her mother's illness had been used to get her to return there. 'If there is anything I can do?' he offered.

'No, no, thanks. I wanted to be sure that her mother really needs her.'

'There's no reason why she shouldn't walk out of the house, but there may be circumstances which prevent her doing that.'

The doctor picked up the phone and heard Miss Parsons' firm voice at the other end.

'I hoped that you might be back…' He talked at some length and finally put the phone down and went in search of Bates. After that, all he had to do was to possess his soul in patience until he could go to Amabel.

He set off early in the morning two days later, with Tiger beside him and Bates to see him on his way.

Life was going to be quite interesting, Bates thought as he went in search of his wife.

Once free of London and the suburbs, Oliver drove fast. He hoped that he had thought of everything. A lot was going to happen during the next few hours, and nothing must go wrong.

It was raining when he reached the house, and now that the apple orchard had gone the house looked bare and lonely and the greenhouses looked alien. He drove round the side of the house, got out with Tiger, opened the kitchen door and went in.

Amabel was standing at the sink, peeling potatoes. She was wearing an apron several sizes too large for her and her hair hung in a plait over one shoulder. She looked pale and tired and utterly forlorn.

This was no time for explanations; the doctor strode to the sink, removed the potato and the knife from her hands and folded his arms around her. He didn't speak, he didn't kiss her, just held her close. He was holding her when Mr Graham came in.

'Who are you?' he demanded.

Oliver gave Amabel a gentle push. 'Go and get your coat and pack your things.' Something in his voice made her disentangle herself from his embrace and look up at his quiet face. He smiled down at her. 'Run along, darling.'

She went upstairs and all she could think of then was that he had called her darling. She should have taken him into the sitting room, where her mother was... Instead she got her case from the wardrobe and began to pack it, and, that done, picked up her coat and went downstairs.

The doctor had watched her go and then turned to Mr

Graham, who began in a blustering voice, 'I don't know why you're here, whoever you are—'

'I'll tell you,' said Oliver gently. 'And when I've finished perhaps you will take me to Amabel's mother.'

She looked up in surprise as they went into the sitting room.

'He's come for Amabel,' said Mr Graham, looking daggers at Oliver. 'I don't know what things are coming to when your daughter's snatched away and you so poorly, my dear.'

'Your doctor tells me that you are fully recovered, Mrs Graham, and I understand that you have adequate help in the house…'

'I'm very upset—' began Mrs Graham. Glancing at the quiet man standing there, she decided that a show of tears wouldn't help. 'After all, a daughter should take care of her mother…'

'And do the housework and the cooking?' From the look of her Amabel has been doing that, and much more besides.

'She ought to be grateful,' growled Mr Graham, 'having a home to come to.'

'Where she is expected to do the chores, cook and clean and shop?' asked Oliver coolly. 'Mr Graham, you make me tired—and extremely angry.'

'Who is going to see to things when she's gone?'

'I'm sure there is adequate help to be had in the village.' He turned away as Amabel came into the room. 'Everything is satisfactorily arranged,' he told her smoothly. 'If you will say goodbye, we will go.'

Amabel supposed that presently she would come to her senses and ask a few sensible questions, even ask for an explanation of the unexpected events taking place around her, but all she said was, 'Yes, Oliver,' in a meek voice, and went to kiss her mother and bid her stepfather a frosty goodbye.

She said tartly, 'There's a lot I could say to you, but I won't,' and she walked out of the room with Oliver. Tiger was in the kitchen, and somehow the sight of him brought her to her senses.

'Oliver—' she began.

'We'll talk as we go,' he told her comfortably, and popped her into the car, settled Tiger in the back seat and got in beside her. Presently he said in a matter-of-fact voice, 'We shall be home in time for supper. We'll stop at Aldbury and get Oscar and Cyril.'

'But where are we going?'

'Home.'

'I haven't got a home,' said Amabel wildly.

'Yes, you have.' He rested a hand on her knee for a moment. 'Darling, *our* home.'

And after that he said nothing for quite some time, which left Amabel all the time in the world to think. Chaotic thoughts which were interrupted by him saying in a matter-of-fact voice, 'Shall we stop for a meal?' and, so saying, stopping before a small pub, well back from the road, with a lane on one side of it.

It was dim and cosy inside, with a handful of people at the bar, and they had their sandwiches and coffee against a background of cheerful talk, not speaking much themselves.

When they had finished the doctor said, 'Shall we walk a little way up the lane with Tiger?'

They walked arm in arm and Amabel tried to think of something to say—then decided that there was no need; it was as though they had everything that mattered.

But not quite all, it seemed, for presently, when they stopped to look at the view over a gate, Oliver turned her round to face him.

'I love you. You must know that, my dear. I've loved you since I first saw you, although I didn't know it at once. And then you seemed so young, and anxious to make a life for yourself; I'm so much older than you...'

Amabel said fiercely, 'Rubbish. You're just the right age. I don't quite understand what has happened, but that doesn't matter...' She looked up into his face. 'You have always been there, and I can't imagine a world without you...'

He kissed her then, and the wintry little lane was no longer a lane but heaven.

In a little while they got back into the car, and Amabel, with a little gentle prompting, told Oliver of her two weeks with her mother.

'How did you know I was there?' she wanted to know, and when he had told her she said, 'Oliver, Miriam Potter-Stokes said that you were going to marry her. I know now that wasn't true, but why did she say that?' She paused. 'Did you think that you would before you met me?'

'No, my darling. I took her out once or twice, and we met often at friends' houses. But it never entered my head to want to marry her. I think that she looked upon me, as she would look upon any other man in my position, as a possible source of a comfortable life.'

'That's all right, then,' said Amabel.

She looked so radiantly happy that he said, 'My dearest, if you continue to look like that I shall have to stop and kiss you.'

An unfulfilled wish since they were on a motorway.

There was no doubt about the warmth of their welcome at Lady Haleford's cottage. They were met in the hall by Mrs Twitchett, Nelly, Oscar and Cyril, and swept into the drawing room, where Lady Haleford was sitting.

She said at once, 'Amabel, I am so happy to see you again, although I understand from Oliver that this visit is a brief one. Still, we shall see more of each other, I have no doubt. I shall miss you and Oscar and Cyril. Oliver shall bring you here whenever he has the time, but of course first of all he must take you to see his mother. You'll marry soon?'

Amabel went pink and Oliver answered for her. 'Just as soon as it can be arranged, Aunt.'

'Good. I shall come to the wedding, and so will Mrs Twitchett and Nelly. Now we will have tea...'

An hour later, once more in the car, Amabel said, 'You haven't asked me...'

He glanced at her briefly, smiling. 'Oh, but I will. Once we are alone and quiet. I've waited a long time, dear love, but I'm not going to propose to you driving along a motorway.'

'I don't know where you live...'

'In a quiet street of Regency houses. There's a garden with a high wall, just right for Oscar and Cyril, and Bates and his wife look after me and Tiger, and now they will look after you three as well.'

'Oh—is it a big house?'

'No, no, just a nice size for a man and his wife and children to live in comfortably.'

Which gave Amabel plenty to think about, staring out of the window into the dark evening through rose-coloured spectacles, soothed by Oliver's quiet voice

from time to time and the gentle fidgets of the three
animals on the back seat.

She hadn't been sure of what to expect, and when she
got out of the car the terrace of houses looked elegant
and dignified, with handsome front doors and steps leading to their basements. But Oliver gave her time to do
no more than glimpse at them. Light streamed from an
open door and someone stood waiting by it.

'We're home,' said Oliver, and took her arm and
tucked it under his.

She had been feeling anxious about Bates, but there
was no need; he beamed at her like a kindly uncle, and
Mrs Bates behind him shook her hand, her smile as wide
as her husband's.

'You will wish to go straight to the drawing room,
sir,' said Bates, and opened a door with a flourish.

As they went in, Aunt Thisbe came to meet them.

'Didn't expect to see me, did you, Amabel?' she asked
briskly. 'But Oliver is a stickler for the conventions, and
quite right too. You will have to bear with me until you
are married.'

She offered a cheek to be kissed, and then again for
Oliver.

'You two will want to talk, but just for a moment there
is something I need to do...' he murmured.

Aunt Thisbe made for the door. 'I'll see about those
animals of yours,' she said, and closed the door firmly
behind her.

The doctor unbuttoned Amabel's coat, tossed it on a
chair and took her in his arms. 'This is a proposal—but
first, this...' he bent his head and kissed her, taking his
time about it.

'Will you marry me, Amabel?' he asked her.

'Will you always kiss me like that?' she asked him.

'Always and for ever, dearest.'

'Then I'll marry you,' said Amabel, 'because I like being kissed like that. Besides, I love you.'

There was only one answer to that...

The Perfect Christmas

CAROLINE ANDERSON

Caroline Anderson has the mind of a butterfly. She's been a nurse, a secretary, a teacher, run her own soft-furnishing business and now she's settled on writing. She says, 'I was looking for that elusive something. I finally realised it was variety, and now I have it in abundance. Every book brings new horizons and new friends, and in between books I have learned to be a juggler. My teacher husband John and I have two beautiful and talented daughters, Sarah and Hannah, umpteen pets and several acres of Suffolk that nature tries to reclaim every time we turn our backs!' Caroline writes for the Mills & Boon Medical Romance® and Romance series.

Look for Caroline Anderson's next marvellous new book, **The Tycoon's Instant Family**, in Mills & Boon Romance in November 2006.

CHAPTER ONE

JULIA glanced at her watch and sighed, her fingers tapping on the steering wheel. She was going to be late on the ward—and today, of all days, with a new consultant surgeon starting, an operations list a mile long and new admissions that had come in over the weekend to sort out.

Something had obviously happened at the roundabout up ahead, bringing the traffic, such as it was, to a grinding halt on the inner ring road. Another minor shunt, probably. It was always happening. If only she'd left earlier, but Katie had been difficult and it was a miracle she was here even now. She glanced at her watch again. It was ten to seven, and if they didn't get moving in the next couple of minutes, she would definitely be late.

She peered ahead into the winter darkness and wished it was daylight so she could see what was going on. If she could only creep forward a little further, she could take the side road and cut through to the hospital that way, but if there were any casualties, she really ought to go and help.

Torn between her various obligations, she hesitated for a moment, but then someone's headlights picked up a running figure darting from car to car, calling out. With a sinking feeling she opened her door and stood up, half out of the car, and the man saw her and ran towards her. 'Got any first-aid experience?' he asked. 'One of the drivers is bleeding badly.'

'I'm a nurse,' she replied, resigning herself to being late. She squeezed her car off the road, locked it and ran towards the roundabout, arriving at the scene just as a solidly built man wrenched open the door of one of the cars and stuck his head inside.

'Where's the casualty?' she asked the man who'd hailed her, and he pointed at the person who'd just opened the door.

'In there. It's a woman. That man's just got the door open—it was jammed.'

'Can someone call the ambulances?' she said, heading for the car at a run, and several people confirmed that it had been done already. Good. Hopefully they'd soon be here and she could get on her way.

Tucking her long fair hair behind her ears, she leant over the man who was obstructing her view of the driver. All she could see was a pair of massive shoulders filling the gap, but the smell of blood was unmistakable. 'Excuse me,' she said, but he didn't move, so she tried again, firming up her voice and injecting more authority. 'Can you let me see her? I'm a nurse.'

He lifted his head a fraction and turned it, and she caught a glimpse of a strong profile in the reflected streetlight before he spoke, his voice deep and calm and confident. 'A nurse? Excellent. I'm a doctor—you can give me a hand. I can't let go of this one—her necklace is embedded in her throat and I think she's nicked her carotid artery judging by the way she's pumping blood out all over me. She reeks of alcohol as well—I think she's been partying. Whatever, I can't let go of her neck and her passenger's injured, too. Can you check him?'

'Sure,' she agreed, glad someone who knew what they were doing was in charge of the bleeding woman.

'What about the people in the other cars? Have you seen any of them?'

'I think they're out and walking around—more shaken up than anything. These two were definitely going faster, judging by the damage to the car and the position of it.'

As she made her way to the passenger side of the car, Julia glanced around. Two people were wandering around looking dazed, staring at their damaged vehicle. It was by the central island of the roundabout, its front quarter smashed, and the car with the injured driver had obviously cut in front of it and was half up the roundabout's grassy centre, the remains of a road sign jutting out from under the bonnet. It had clearly come to an abrupt halt, and it looked as if the driver just simply hadn't seen the roundabout coming.

Two other cars were slewed across the roundabout, adding to the confusion, but the damage to them was slight and the occupants were obviously all right.

She tugged open the passenger door and checked the other occupant of the first car. He was groggy but conscious, bleeding from a cut on his forehead and clutching his knees and moaning. No seat belt, she noticed, and wondered how on earth he hadn't just gone straight through the windscreen. She looked up at her impromptu colleague just as he lifted his head, and her eyes were caught by his, strangely piercing, like sunlight through rain. Her own eyes were grey, but not like that! Not that amazing grey that was almost silver. They took her breath away.

'Knees and head,' she told him after a moment, trying to concentrate, and he nodded.

'Don't think he had a belt on—idiot. He's lucky to be alive. How's his spine?'

'Suspect, I should think,' she said, eyeing the man's crouched position on the edge of the seat. He was slumped at a strange angle, but at least he could feel his knees. He might not think so just at the moment, but that was definitely a good sign.

A siren sounded in the distance, and the paramedics ran up to them. The doctor detailed his findings, Julia did the same, and within a few minutes their patients were handed over and whisked away. Another ambulance had arrived and was checking out the people from the other cars, and the police asked Julia and her companion if they'd seen anything.

'It had happened when I arrived,' she told them, and they took her name and address and let her go. She ran back to her car, wiped her hands on a rag she used for the windscreen and drove to the hospital by the back route, abandoned her car in the car park and arrived on her ward, bloodstained and grubby, a mere half-hour late.

'What on earth have you been doing?' the night sister asked, eyeing her in amazement.

Julia snorted. 'Roadside rescue,' she said succinctly. 'Give me a minute to change into my spare uniform and have a quick scrub, and I'll be with you.'

In fact, it was only her coat that was bloodstained. Her tunic top had escaped, and her trousers were only slightly damp on the knees from kneeling on the road. Still, she changed completely, scrubbing her hands thoroughly just to be on the safe side before going back to the office.

'Here,' the night sister said, putting a cup of tea into her hand, and she took it gratefully and buried her nose in it.

'Oh, gorgeous, Angie, thanks,' she said with a smile. 'It's really chilly out there.'

'Was that the cause, do you think?'

Julia wrinkled her nose. 'Maybe. She might have skidded on a little patch of ice, but I think it's unlikely. Judging from the fact that she reeked of booze, there was probably another reason.'

'Good grief. It's only the first of December! Are they getting into the spirit of Christmas this soon?'

'Some people only need the slightest excuse,' she said grimly, and concentrated on her tea instead of thinking about Andrew and another frosty night nearly four years ago—

'So, how was the weekend?' she asked. 'Lots of admissions?'

'Wouldn't you know? It's been bedlam, apparently. We had six surgical emergencies and three RTAs last night alone. We haven't got them all, but ICU is chocka and they're stacked up in Resus.'

Julia rolled her eyes and sighed. 'Oh, yum. One of those days.'

'Absolutely. And we've got the new boy starting shortly, lord help us all—if he ever gets here. He said he'd be here by seven, and he's late, too. Maybe he came the same way.'

'Well, if he did he'll be stuck in the queue, because the roundabout's blocked solid. I'm only here because I know the back way.'

'Great. We've had a call from A and E to stand by for an RTA victim with a deep incision in the neck— could that be yours? If it is, I hope this Armstrong guy gets here soon, because Nick Sarazin's just phoned in with flu and Armstrong's next in line, so he'd better be up to speed, because she's punctured her carotid,

apparently, and they've just tacked her together in A
and E pending a proper job.'

Just then there was a knock on the door, and she
looked up straight into a pair of familiar rainwashed
eyes. Her heart slammed against her ribs, and he
smiled in recognition and came into the room. He'd
shed his coat and changed his shirt, but his temple still
carried a little streak of blood beneath the floppy dark
hair.

Her eyes scanned him in the second it took him to
cross the room towards her, absorbing the fact that he
looked less chunky without the padded jacket. He was
still broad, but with a lithe muscularity that spoke of
great strength. His broad, capable hand was extended
in greeting, and his voice sent shivers down her spine.

'Hi, there. We meet again. David Armstrong.'

Their new consultant, a man she'd work with on a
daily basis. Her heart gave a little jiggle of delight,
but she ignored it, struggling for a measured response.

'Julia Revell. I'm the ward sister. Welcome aboard.'

She took his hand, the fingers cool and hard, the
palm warm and dry and firm. A confident hand, strong
and yet gentle. She felt a strange kind of helplessness
creep over her, an urge to crawl into his arms and let
him take away all her problems.

Not that she had many problems. Not if you didn't
count the bills that were waiting to be paid, and the
fact that Katie wasn't feeling too well and really, really hadn't wanted to go to the childminder or school
this morning, and the car was overdue for servicing
and her wardrobe was looking distinctly ragged.

Still, there was always the lottery.

She realised she was still holding his hand, the
handshake now extended beyond mere convention,

and with a tiny shake she pulled herself together and released him, stepping back. 'This is Angie Featherstone, our night sister. Angie, Mr Armstrong's the doctor I was telling you about at the RTA—last seen holding a pressure pad to a young woman's neck.'

He gave a wry grimace, his eyes crinkling with humour. 'Yes—in at the deep end. She's coming up to Theatre and guess who's on take all of a sudden? So it looks as if I get to do the follow-through on my good Samaritan act. Can we squeeze her in or shall I tell her it's not convenient?'

Julia laughed and looked at Angie for confirmation. 'Can we?'

'There's always the corridor,' she said drily. 'Anyway, I'm out of here in a minute. I'll leave you to sort it out. I would suggest some rapid shuffling and a little emergency discharge. Talk to Nick Sarazin's registrar—one or two of his are looking pretty bright.'

'Good,' Julia said with feeling. 'We could use freeing up. OK, we'll stand by to take her shortly.'

He grinned. 'Right. I'd better go and get scrubbed up. I'll see you again later.'

He went out and closed the door, and Angie looked at Julia and sighed theatrically. 'Oh, what a luscious man. What did we do to get so lucky? Did you *see* those eyes?'

Oh, yes—and the strong, safe, capable hands, Julia thought, but it was only a thought, and that was all it could ever be. Never again, she'd vowed all those years ago, and it would take more than eyes the colour of an April storm and a touch that made her long for more to undermine that resolve. She straightened her shoulders and arched a brow at her colleague.

'I thought you were married?' she said drily, but Angie just laughed.

'I am—but you'd have to be dead to fail to notice a man like that—and don't tell me you didn't notice him, because I'll know you're lying.'

Julia shrugged, suppressing her interest. 'So he's good-looking,' she said dismissively. 'Lots of men are. I don't mix business and pleasure.'

Angie shot her a curious look. 'Did I suggest you should?'

She felt colour brush her cheeks, and sighed inwardly. 'Just setting the record straight. Let's get this report out of the way and I can start shuffling patients,' she said, clutching at normality. Anyway, she thought, her mind still running on the same track, he was bound to be married. All the decent men were, and most of the indecent ones, too. Not that she was interested, even if he was available.

Busy, that was what she needed to be—too busy to think straight, so there wasn't time to worry about David Armstrong and his broad shoulders and powerful hands and gorgeous eyes...

There was an old saying—be careful what you wish for, you might get it.

By the time she clocked off at three, Julia was deeply regretting her wish to be busy. They'd been rushed off their feet all day, and it was only at three thirty, when she'd done the handover and was in her car on the way to pick Katie up from school, that she realised just how tired she was.

Not just from today, but from every day, from the relentless passage of the days, one after the other, each with their own special problems.

If only she could stop worrying about the money, but there never seemed to be enough, not with Andrew's debts still to clear. Still, another three months and the credit-card bill would be paid, and maybe then things would be easier.

She pulled up outside the school and went in to retrieve Katie from the homework class she joined for the few minutes she had to wait each day. Sometimes it was more than a few minutes, but Julia was very wary about leaving her too long and shaking her confidence.

It had taken enough of a battering when Andrew had died.

'Mummy! Mummy, look what I did!'

'Hello, darling—oh, gorgeous! We'll stick it up on the fridge when it's dry.'

She fielded the wet painting, threw a distracted smile of thanks at the teacher supervising the little group and headed for the cloakroom with Katie to find her coat. It was wet and muddy—she'd been pushed over at lunchtime and had sat in a puddle, but she seemed quite unmoved by it.

'Why didn't you tell the dinner ladies?' Julia asked, wondering about the incident. 'They would have dried it for you.'

'Doesn't matter,' Katie said airily. 'Can we go? I want a drink.'

Was she being evasive? No. Julia told herself not to go into overdrive about bullying. It was probably just a casual bump, more than likely an accident.

'It'll be dry by tomorrow. Here, borrow my jumper so you don't get cold and then you won't have to wear your coat while it's still wet. Are you feeling better now?'

Katie nodded. 'School was fun today. We did sing-ing.'

'That was nice.' She bundled her daughter up in her sweater, put her coat back on and headed for the car, damp coat and damper painting in hand. The sleeves of the jumper were trailing almost to the ground, and Katie skipped along, swinging them and laughing and looking quite unconcerned.

Not bullied, thank God.

Julia sighed with relief. It was sometimes so hard being a single parent and keeping things in perspec-tive. She drove them home, made a simple meal of pasta and vegetables baked in the oven with grated cheese on top, and they sat together and watched chil-dren's TV while it browned, and then read Katie's book for a while after supper.

By seven thirty, when the little girl was tucked up in bed and the house was tidied, Julia was wiped out. She poured herself a small glass of wine from the bot-tle in the fridge, sat down in front of the television for a little relaxation and promptly fell asleep, waking much later with a wet lap and a crick in her neck.

She looked at her watch in disbelief. It was nearly ten, and she'd slept through the only programme she liked. Typical. With a wry grimace she put the now empty wineglass down, turned off the television, had a quick bath and went to bed, expecting to fall into a sound sleep instantly.

Oh, no. Her mind, slightly refreshed by the doze on the sofa, had no intention of letting her escape that easily. Instead it spooled endlessly through the events of the day, starting with the accident in the morning, then her next meeting with David Armstrong on the ward, then his visits later to check on his post-ops.

Every time he'd seen her he'd smiled that eye-crinkling smile, and she'd turned to putty. His shoulders had brushed against hers at someone's bedside and her heart had nearly stopped. He's just a man, she'd told herself, and now, lying in bed, she reminded herself of this again.

He's just a man.

And that, of course, was the root of the problem, because a man was what she wanted, what she needed in her life. Just a man, an ordinary, everyday decent human being to share life's ups and downs.

Or cause them. Every down that had happened to her in the past six years had been caused by Andrew.

No, she didn't want a man. Well, she did, but she didn't *need* a man. What she needed was sleep, so she could get up in the morning and do her job properly and not get the sack!

But her restless mind wouldn't let go, and when it did, it was only so that it could torture her with dreams...

'Hi, there.'

Julia looked up from her computer terminal at the work station, a smile of welcome already on her lips. Oh, heavens, she thought dizzily, the dreams didn't do his eyes justice.

She pulled herself together and tried to look professional instead of like a mesmerised rabbit. 'Morning. You're in bright and early.'

'I wanted to check my post-ops before my clinic at nine, and I need time to read through the notes before then, and I need to meet my secretary and have more than a five-second conversation with her at some time before the clinic, so—'

'You got up at five to make an early start.'

David laughed. 'Something like that. I don't suppose there's a kettle anywhere on the ward, is there? I'd like to chat about a couple of the patients with you. Besides, I only had time for a quick slug of tea before I left home, and I'm parched.'

'Have you had breakfast?' she asked, wondering what his wife thought about him leaving home so early and telling herself it was none of her business.

'You sound just like my mother,' he said with a slow smile that messed up her heart rhythm again, 'and, no, I didn't have time for breakfast either.'

'Better have some toast, then, to go with your tea— or was it coffee?'

'Tea sounds good.'

He followed her into the little kitchen, his broad shoulders and deep chest somehow filling the space and crowding her, but not unpleasantly. She felt...odd, as if his aura was brushing up against hers, chafing softly against it and sending little shivers up and down her spine.

She filled the kettle and switched it on, then turned and bumped into him, and he smiled and moved back a little. 'Sorry,' she said a touch breathlessly. 'It's rather cramped in here.'

'It's a nice cosy little retreat,' he corrected, the smile playing around his mouth and drawing an answering smile to her lips.

'It can be, but not for long. We're too busy usually to take advantage, but yesterday's bedlam seems to have retreated a bit.'

'Just as well, isn't it? You were running at full stretch, I would have thought.'

'We were a bit overcrowded. Still, with Nick off

with flu we should be able to catch up a little. Two slices, or more?'

'Two to start with,' he said, and propped his hips against the units, his hands resting on the worktop each side so that his suit jacket gaped open and displayed his broad chest and lean hips to unfair advantage. She dragged her eyes away from him and put an extra couple of slices of bread in the toaster for herself.

'So, our young lady from the RTA yesterday—I gather she's had a good night and is looking better,' he said, watching her work.

'Yes—apparently. She's finished her transfusions and she's on saline now, and she seems comfortable.'

'She was lucky, you know. She had a stupid, gimmicky necklace on made of old beer cans cut up into triangles and bent onto a leather thong, and one of the triangles had sliced the edge of her carotid artery. If she hadn't had medical attention when she did, she would have bled to death within minutes, certainly before the paramedics got there.'

Julia threw tea bags into two mugs and poured boiling water over them. 'She was over the limit, you know. The police were in last night to talk to her. Her passenger's got spinal injuries, but nothing drastic. His kneecaps have both got starburst fractures, and his head's sore, but he was very lucky she wasn't going faster. Here, your tea. Help yourself to sugar.'

'I don't, thanks. He should have had his seat belt on, of course, then he probably wouldn't have been injured.'

'Whereas ironically her injury was probably caused by the seat belt cutting into her necklace,' Julia pointed out.

'No, it was caused by the stupid, dangerous necklace,' he corrected, plucking the toast from the toaster and dropping it onto the proffered plate. 'Looks good.'

'Butter, or marg?'

He grinned. 'I'll give you three guesses.'

She shook her head and slid the butter towards him along the worktop, together with a knife, and then spent the next few minutes trying not to stare at him as his even white teeth tore into the toast and the muscles in his jaw worked to chew it.

She scraped margarine on her toast and ate it fast, one eye on the time, and she was just swallowing the last bite when the door opened and Sally Kennedy put her head round.

'Ah, Julia, you're hiding in here. New admission—could you come? It's one for Owen Douglas.'

'Sure.'

She drained her tea and threw David a distracted smile. 'Sorry, I'm going to have to cut and run. Take your time—make more, if you want.'

'I'm fine. Thank you. You're a lifesaver.'

That smile again.

Blast.

She found herself spending the day wishing one of his patients would have a problem so she could call him back to the ward, but as luck would have it they were all fine.

Julia left the hospital on time, more or less, chastising herself for dawdling in the corridor just in case David was on his way to the ward, and then just to punish her God decided that her car was going to choose that afternoon to fail to start.

'Great,' she said, slamming her hands down on the steering-wheel and glaring at the bonnet. 'Marvellous.'

With no very real idea of what she might be looking

for, she pulled the bonnet catch and spent several fruitless moments trying to get the safety catch off so she could raise it.

'Here,' a passing stranger said, and slid his hand under the edge, tweaked something and the bonnet came up into his hand. How intensely irritating!

'Thanks,' she said grudgingly, put the stay up to hold it and stuck her head into the engine bay. Not that she had any idea what she was looking at. She knew just enough to know that the engine hadn't been stolen, but beyond that she was stuffed.

A shadow fell over her line of sight, and she glanced up and straightened, bumping her head on the bonnet catch.

She yelped and clutched her head, and David tutted softly.

'You all right?'

'Oh, yeah,' she muttered ungraciously. 'My car won't start, goodness knows why, so I'm going to be late to fetch my daughter from school, and now just to improve things I've got a hole in my head.'

'That would be a no, then,' he said softly, and she laughed in spite of herself.

'In short.'

'Hmm.' He stood beside her and stared down at the engine, and hope dawned.

'I don't suppose you know anything about engines?' she asked him optimistically.

He chuckled. 'Not enough to fix them. I suppose you've got petrol?'

Julia nodded. 'Yes, I've got petrol, I filled it up at the weekend.'

'In which case,' he said, dropping the bonnet with a solid clunk, 'I suggest you get a taxi to your daughter's school and get a garage to come and look at it later. Do you belong to a motoring organisation?'

She shook her head. 'No—and there's no way I can afford a taxi.' Or a garage.

'In which case, can you drive an automatic?'

She stared at him blankly. 'An automatic? Yes, my father's got one, I've driven it a few times. Why?'

'Because you could take my car, get your daughter and go home, and I'll get my rescue service to come out and fix yours and then I'll drive it home for you and pick mine up.'

'But it's not your car! They won't do that.'

'It doesn't need to be mine. I just need to be driving it.'

He dangled his keys in front of her temptingly, and she hesitated.

'Don't you need it? Why aren't you working? And won't your wife or whatever mind if you're late home?'

'I've got the afternoon off. I was doing paperwork. I saw you from my window—and I don't have a wife, or a whatever, so she won't mind in the slightest. Come on, you can't be late for your daughter—unless your husband can pick her up?'

She shook her head. 'No—he's dead,' she said bluntly, not bothering to be subtle. 'Are you sure?'

'Of course. It's just over there—the silver BMW.'

'I'll crash it,' she muttered under her breath, and he winced and laughed.

'I'd rather you didn't,' he said mildly, propelling her gently in its direction. 'I've only had it a short while—not that it's new, but it still cost me enough, and I'm quite fond of it already.'

'What about insurance?'

'You're covered. Any driver over twenty five.'

She nodded. 'Thanks.'

He paused, his hands on the top of the door, just as she was about to drive it away. 'Your address would be useful.'

Julia felt a little rush of colour flood her cheeks. 'How silly. Sorry. Twenty-five Victoria Road. It's near the park.'

'I know it. I'll see you there.'

He shut the door firmly, and she eased out of the parking place and headed for the road, too absorbed in trying to avoid scraping his car against the barriers to worry about the fact that she'd just given him her address. It was only when she pulled up outside her house and took Katie in that she realised she'd broken one of her cardinal rules...

David watched her go, his face thoughtful.

So Julia was a widow with a daughter. That was tough. She couldn't be more than about twenty-seven or -eight, thirty at the outside. He wondered when her husband had died, and if she was over him or if she still cried for him in the small hours of the night.

He didn't know, but suddenly he wanted to find out. He'd spent the last few years moving around from one Special Registrar's post to another, completing his training, and now that he could finally settle down in one place, he was hoping in time to find a woman he could spend his life with.

And maybe, just maybe, that woman might be Julia Revell.

A slow smile nudged the corner of his mouth. He even had her address, thanks to the car. All he needed now was for the recovery people to come up trumps and fix it, and he'd be round there...

CHAPTER TWO

DAVID arrived at eight-thirty, but not in Julia's car.

'It needed a little part and he didn't have it, so he's taken it to the garage for repair,' he told her, not adding that he'd booked it in for a full service because it was clearly desperately in need of one.

Even so, her face fell. 'I wonder how much it'll cost? Oh, well, I have to have it. I can't survive without a car.'

Which was exactly what he'd thought, and why he'd phoned his father and borrowed the runabout they kept at the farm for his younger brothers and sisters when they were home from university.

'I won't ask,' his father had said wisely, and David had been unable to stop the little smile. Now he handed her the keys.

'It's a family runabout. You can have it till your car's ready.'

A tiny frown pleated her brow. 'Are you sure? That seems very generous. Won't someone need it?'

'It's not being used at the moment, they're all away at university still.'

'Oh. Well, if you're really sure...' She hesitated, then seemed to make a decision. 'Can I get you a coffee or something? Or supper? Have you eaten? You must have been hanging around for ages, I'm so sorry.'

He hadn't, in fact. The car had been dealt with by a quarter to six, and he'd been home and had had a

22

meal with his parents and stalled until he'd thought her daughter might be in bed, but it wouldn't hurt to let her think he'd been hard done by.

'A coffee would be great,' he said with just enough enthusiasm. 'I've grabbed something to eat.'

He thought of the wonderful hotpot his mother had given him and waited for God to strike him down for dismissing it so casually, but it was in a good cause after all—and one his mother would be the first to further!

'Come in,' she said belatedly, stepping back and letting him into the hallway of her little Victorian terraced house.

He looked around at the stripped pine doors and pale walls, relieved by the careful placement of a few large, simple prints and colourful fabric hangings, and smiled. 'It's lovely. Have you been here long?'

'Three years. I moved here after Andrew died.'

He filed that information and followed her down the hall past the stairs towards the kitchen. A huge tabby cat was curled up in a sheepskin cat bed that hung from the radiator by the breakfast room door, and it yawned at him as he walked past.

He scratched its head and it purred and jumped out of the bed, trotting behind him into the kitchen.

'Arthur, you've been fed,' she told him, but the cat jumped up on the worktop beside her and nudged her with its big head.

'Horrible cat, get down,' she admonished, putting him on the floor, so he wound himself round David's ankles instead, sniffing them and checking out all the cats and dogs from the farm that had rubbed against his legs that evening.

Satisfied, it arched its back for a caress, and he bent

and stroked it absently while he watched Julia moving around her little kitchen.

The units were dated, but the room was bright and cheerful and spotlessly clean and, like the rest of the house that he'd seen so far, it was welcoming.

Strange, then, that Julia seemed so edgy in a way, and so unlike the capable and efficient nurse he'd seen at work. Her body was like a coiled spring, the tension in her almost palpable. Did no one ever come here? She'd hesitated before inviting him in. Perhaps she was an intensely private person—or perhaps it was just because he was a man.

Instinctively he scooped up the cat and fussed it, and Julia seemed to relax slightly, as if he couldn't be threatening if he was an animal lover. To remove the threat still further he migrated to the breakfast room through the archway and sat down, thus shrinking himself—all the tricks he'd had to learn in paediatrics because of his size. He felt a twinge of guilt at manipulating her emotions, but told himself it was in a good cause. After all, he needed to get to know his colleagues.

She followed him, mugs in hand, and hesitated again. 'Are you all right here, or do you want to go through to the sitting room?'

He wanted to see the sitting room, or indeed anywhere else that would give him more clues to the person she was, but he forced himself to shrug. 'Wherever you're most comfortable,' he told her, figuring that the more relaxed she was, the more chance he'd have of getting to know her better.

She smiled softly. 'Here, then, as the cat's so comfy. He's not really allowed in the sitting room because he trashes the carpet and it's the only decent one in the house, so Katie and I spend a lot of time in here,' she told him, slipping into the chair opposite and settling down, her elbows on the table, her mug cradled between her slender hands.

Her fair hair slithered forwards and screened her face, and he had an almost irresistible urge to reach out and tuck it back behind her ear so he could see her expression better.

Instead he held onto his coffee-mug like a lifeline and concentrated on the silk-like softness of her hair, the tired droop of her shoulders and the little frown plucking at her forehead.

'My car,' she said after a moment. 'Which part did it need?'

David laughed and shrugged. 'I can't remember. Something to do with the ignition. Would it mean anything if I could remember?'

Her mouth kicked up in a wry smile and she shook her head, her hair slipping softly over her face again. She tucked it back out of the way, and he could see the smile still hovering around her lips. 'No. I wouldn't have a clue. I was just curious. It seems awful not to make the effort to understand somehow.'

'I gave up years ago when I moved on to cars with electronic ignition,' he said with a chuckle. 'It all got too complicated for me. I could understand carburettors and timing belts and stuff like that. The modern engine management systems give me the heaves.'

'So which garage is it at?' she asked, worrying her lip with her teeth.

'The one my father's always used. Don't worry, they're cheap and sensible.' And amenable to suggestion about rigging the bill, furthermore, but she didn't need to know that. He leant back in his chair, giving the cat more room to stretch out, and met her eyes over the table.

'This is a nice house,' he said softly. 'Friendly.'

Julia smiled again. 'We like it. The other one was modern and soulless—a detached ''executive''—' she wiggled her fingers in the air to make quotes '—house with an *en suite* bathroom and very little else to commend it. I hated it.'

Her smile had faded, and he pressed her gently for more information. 'Not your kind of thing, then?' he suggested, and she shook her head.

'It was Andrew's choice. I had to sell it when he died because—well, there was a problem with the insurance.' She hesitated. 'I couldn't afford to stay on even if I'd wanted to, but this came on the market, and it's quite handy for the hospital and the school, and, being near the park, it's nice in the summer. So I bought it. It's been a struggle but we're nearly through it now.'

Poor girl. 'It must have been tough, losing him,' he said, fishing again, and she rose to the bait like a charm.

'It was tough being married to him,' she said flatly. 'Losing him was the easy bit. Then...'

'Then?'

Julia looked at him blankly for a moment, as if she'd forgotten he was there, and then she shrugged. 'He had other debts. A card. They caught up with me just after we moved.'

'But surely you weren't responsible for that,' he said, puzzled, and her sad smile tore at his heart.

'It was a joint card,' she said. 'It was my own fault. I should have been more on the ball. Still, you live and learn and, as I said, it's been tough but it's nearly over now, and we'll survive.'

She tucked her hair behind her ear again, her lips pressing together as if she'd said too much, and sure enough she didn't go on.

Still, she'd said more than enough. Unable to help himself, David reached across the table and laid a hand over her wrist, quelling the anger that rose inside him. 'I'm sorry,' he said gently. 'I didn't mean to pry.' He was surprised to find he meant it. He'd obviously strayed into a very private part of her life, and one which, he guessed, she didn't share easily.

She flashed him a quicksilver smile, gone almost before he could register it, and he drained his coffee and stood up. Quit while you're winning, he told himself.

'Right, I'm off. I've got to go back over to my parents' tonight, because my house is without electricity at the moment. I shall be glad when it's done up and I can move in properly.'

'Where is it?' she asked, exhibiting a promising flicker of interest, and he reminded himself that she was probably only being polite.

'Just outside Audley—a village called Little Soham.'

'I know it,' she said, nodding. 'It's nice there.'

'It is. It's got a pub and a village shop and a post office, and a church and a village hall, and enough people to make it all viable. It also has a tumbledown little cottage with wonderful potential but in need of a huge cash injection—or more time than I'm going to be able to find. Probably both, in fact, but that's just my natural optimism leading me astray again.'

Her chuckle warmed him, and as she preceded him

up the hall to the door he could smell the faint drift of perfume or soap or something.

She stopped suddenly and he bumped into her, her hair brushing his nose. Shampoo. That was what it was. She'd washed her hair, and it smelt of flowers and sunshine on a summer's day.

'Keys,' she said, turning to look up at him as he murmured an apology and moved back.

'I gave them to you.'

She patted her pocket and smiled, retrieving two sets of keys. 'So you did—and I forgot to give you yours back, didn't I? Sorry. Brain like a sieve. I can never find the ward keys either.' She paused, then looked up at him, her hand on the door catch. 'Thank you so much for all you've done this afternoon. I really am grateful.'

'My pleasure.' He looked down into her guileless smudge-grey eyes, and wondered if she'd run screaming if he gave in to his instincts and bent and kissed those moist, soft lips.

Probably. He smiled a little crookedly, took the keys of his BMW from her hand and walked down the path, his hand raised in farewell. Wise decision, he thought, because one kiss might not have been enough...

Julia shut the door and leant against the wall, her heart skittering under her ribs. For a crazy moment there she'd thought he was going to kiss her, and she'd felt herself start to sway towards him.

Thank goodness she'd caught herself in time! Imagine the embarrassment if she'd closed her eyes and waited like a lovesick fool for a kiss that hadn't come!

But she hadn't, thank goodness, because if she had and by a miracle he *had* kissed her, she would have had the problem of telling him she didn't get involved in relationships, and then having to work with him afterwards.

Too, too awkward.

Messy.

She shrugged away from the wall and ran upstairs to check on Katie. She was fast asleep, her little arm flung up on her pillow, her hair spread like a golden halo, her face innocent in sleep.

Julia reminded herself of all the reasons why she couldn't afford involvement with another man—and they began and ended with her small, vulnerable daughter. She was far too important to Julia to risk in any kind of emotional entanglement that stood the slightest chance of going wrong, and there were no guarantees with love.

She knew that to her cost, and so did Katie. Fatherless at two years old because of an act of mindless stupidity, and it had taken the best part of the next year to get her back on an even keel. Even now, nearly four years later, she was still a little clingy if Julia went out at night.

So she didn't, because nothing, and most particularly not herself, was more important than her daughter.

She'd do well to remember that.

'New admission with acute cholecystitis, woman of thirty-three, no previous history.'

'OK, Sally, thanks.' Julia perched a hip on the desk and tipped her head on one side. 'Have we got a bed?'

'Yes—Nick Sarazin's registrar just discharged two, so we've even got a spare!'

Julia grinned. 'Wonders will never cease. Right, let's go and get the bed ready.'

'You're too slow. The others have gone home and the beds have been done.'

'You're a love. I was only gone half an hour.'

'You ought to go for longer—just think what we could achieve!'

'I might leave you with the rota.'

Sally held up her hands, two index fingers crossed and held out towards her. 'Not the rota!' she begged theatrically. 'Anything but the rota!'

'It's the one thing I really hate about being ward sister,' Julia said with a grimace. 'I always seem to get it wrong.'

'Well, you know what they say. You can please some of the people some of the time...'

'Tell me about it. So, has David Armstrong seen his new patient?' she asked, going back to the original subject.

'I gather not. She's coming from a GP. She'll be here shortly— Ah, here's a trolley. This looks hopeful.'

It was, indeed, their patient, accompanied by her anxious husband, and Julia got her settled in a bed and started the ball rolling with a urine sample and a set of charts, a NIL BY MOUTH sign over the bed and the woman's first set of observations taken, while Julia soothed and studied her watchfully and took mental notes ready to report to David.

A firm, brisk tread behind her alerted her to his presence, and within the space of a heartbeat her skin was tingling, her breath had jammed in her throat and her legs felt like rubber.

Get a grip, girl, she scolded herself, but it was a

fruitless task. Ever since she'd met him five days ago, her body had decided on its own response to his presence, and she might as well save her energy for more useful tasks—like dredging up what might pass for a smile.

Julia approached him, the smile fixed firmly in place, and quickly ran over the patient's present status.

'She's a bit shocky—seems to be in quite severe pain, her blood pressure's a little elevated, her respiration is light and fast, she's been vomiting and she seems very upset and distressed.'

He nodded. 'OK. Let's have a look at her, and then we'll start her on IV opiates to relieve the pain and see how she is then. I want her fluid balance done, please, and IV antibiotics. Have you got a tube down her?'

Julia shook her head. 'She only just arrived a few minutes ago. I've done a battery of urine tests. The results are written up.'

She handed him the notes, and he scanned them before approaching the patient and speaking gently to her and her husband. While he examined her she was very edgy and finally refused to allow him to touch her. It was a typical response to an acute attack of cholecystitis, and he covered her up again and turned to her husband.

'I don't think there's any doubt that she's got a handful of gallstones making a bid for freedom, but we'll run some tests once she's more comfortable and, depending on the results, I'll operate after the weekend. If the X-rays and tests show what I suspect, then we'll treat her conservatively over the weekend to let it resolve a little, and I'll operate on Monday morning. Pain relief first, though,' he went on, turning to Julia, 'and fluids, and I'll see her again later unless you're worried. OK?'

Julia nodded, avoiding those gorgeous piercing grey eyes, and after a moment he turned back to their patient. 'Right, Mrs James, Sister Revell is going to get you some pain relief, and then everything should start to feel a bit better, OK? We'll talk some more when you're more comfortable.'

The woman nodded slightly and moaned, and Julia quickly set up the intravenous line and gave her the first dose of painkiller. Within minutes she was feeling the benefit, and her breathing eased and she relaxed visibly onto the pillows.

'Better now?' Julia asked gently, and her patient nodded, a weak smile of relief touching her pale face.

'Yes, thanks. Oh, that was awful.'

'I'm sure. Right, we're going to slip a little soft tube down your nose and into your stomach to empty it so you don't have to keep being sick. That'll make you feel much better, too. Mr James, why don't you wait out in the corridor for a moment, and I'll call you back as soon as your wife's more comfortable?'

Sally helped her, and the procedure seemed to bring yet more relief to the beleaguered Mrs James. 'Oh, thanks, that's better,' she said weakly once her stomach had been drained. Her lids fluttered down and, after making her comfortable, Julia and Sally left her for a while to settle, her husband at her side again.

Two hours later David was back on the ward, striding towards Julia and doing silly things to her heart again.

'How's Mrs James?' he asked without preamble, but he made no move towards the woman.

'Settling. Quiet now, but still uncomfortable. Her obs are better.'

'Good. How's the car? Ready yet?'

She nodded. 'I rang them this morning—they said I could take the one you lent me over there and swap them, because they had to service it or something.'

'That's right.'

'I have no idea where the garage is, of course. Can you give me directions? I've only got the phone number.'

'I thought so.' He smiled, sending her off-kilter again. 'I thought I could do it for you this evening, if it helps. Take ours over and pick yours up.'

She chewed her lip doubtfully. 'I have to pay the bill,' she told him, but he shrugged it aside.

'I'll pay it for you—you can give me a cheque later.'

'If you're sure,' she said reluctantly. 'You seem to be going to a lot of trouble. I could do it myself quite easily.'

Except, of course, that Andrew's parents would be arriving to take Katie home with them for the weekend, and so she would have to be at home for that. Rats, she hated being beholden to anyone.

'I'll tell you what,' David went on. 'Take the BMW home, and I'll go straight from here with my parents' car and do the swap then run yours over to you. There'll be less messing around that way, and I'd have to take the runabout in for servicing anyway. Satisfy you?'

Julia smiled, relieved that it was sorted and that she'd get her own car back. She'd been having fits of guilt all week about driving his parents' car, and she'd been worrying about how she could do the swap that night. David's suggestion was the perfect solution—if only she didn't feel so guilty about accepting his help yet again.

And because she did, her guilt prompted a rash and silly suggestion.

'Andrew's parents are taking Katie for the weekend,' she told him. 'They'll pick her up at about six. Why don't you come for supper later when you bring the car back? Nothing exciting, just some pasta or something, just to say thank you.'

His eyes warmed with a smile. 'That would be really nice. What time?'

Julia shrugged. 'Seven?' To make sure that Andrew's parents were right out of the way and not likely to ask any awkward questions. Not that it was any of their business, and not that they would mind, but since there was nothing to know, really, they might as well not start to speculate. 'Is that all right? Or would you rather come later?'

'It's fine. I'll look forward to it. Now I suppose I really ought to go and see Mrs James.' He smiled at her a little crookedly, and she felt herself melting again.

'Do you want me to come?'

'Got time?'

'I can make time,' she said, thinking of all the things she still had to do before she went off duty, and how, if she was going to feed him tonight, she would have to find time to take Katie to the supermarket on the way home, so she couldn't afford to leave late.

They walked down the ward together to Mrs James, and found her asleep, her husband drowsing beside her.

'Mr James. How is she?' David asked him, and he blinked sleepily and straightened.

'Oh, Mr Armstrong. Sorry. She's better, thank God. We had an awful night last night before she'd let me call the doctor.'

'I'm sure.' David scanned the notes and nodded. 'She seems to be improving gradually. I think if we can just get her through this episode, I'll have a better chance of sorting her out on Monday without risk of infection. I don't really want to do it before then.'

'So she'll definitely need an operation, then?'

David nodded slowly at Mr James. 'I'm pretty sure she will, I'm sorry to say, but I'll do it with keyhole surgery if I possibly can, so she'll be up and about again within a couple of days and she should be home by Thursday next week, if all goes well. We'll see after the weekend. All right?'

Julia went with him up the ward, pausing to talk to one or two patients on the way, then he glanced at his watch and sighed. 'Back to the grind,' he said with a grin. 'I've got a clinic now. I'll see you later. Ah. Keys.'

Julia blinked. 'Oh—yes. Idiot me.' She went into her office and fished about in her bag for them. 'There might be one or two things in the car, I'm not sure.'

'I'll take them out and bring them back to you.' They swapped keys, and with a smile and a wave he was gone, leaving her with too much to do and a total lack of concentration to help her to do it...

The Revells were late, of course, but it was just as well because Julia had been held up in the supermarket after dithering over the supper menu.

Not that she had a great deal of choice, on her limited budget, but even though there was nothing between her and David Armstrong, somehow it still seemed important to do it *right,* and so she'd hovered and dithered in the salads, and debated the grossly expensive mange tout for three minutes before common sense had prevailed.

She still didn't know what her car was going to cost, after all, and she had to clear the rest of Andrew's debts. She'd chastised herself, bought ingredients for a simple lasagne and then had had to queue for five minutes, even in the supposedly quicker basket queue.

Then she'd spent another five minutes looking for her car in the car park before remembering that she'd had David's. By the time she'd got home she'd been flustered and panicking, and she'd snapped at Katie for dawdling over the packing of her little case and had then felt racked with guilt.

By the time Andrew's parents arrived, the lasagne was in the oven, the salad was washed and torn up and she and Katie were friends again.

'Hello, dear,' Annette Revell said, kissing Julia's cheek fondly. 'We thought you weren't here—we couldn't see your car.'

'No, it's in the garage. It broke down the other day. I'm getting it back later,' she explained, being frugal with the truth.

'Mummy's borrowed a car,' Katie piped up, dumping her in it, then added, 'from a friend,' just so there was no possibility of pretending it came from the garage.

'How kind,' Annette said distractedly, too preoccupied to take her up on it, thank goodness. 'Darling, we need to hurry,' she said to Katie. 'Grandad's parked on a yellow line—are you all ready?'

Katie nodded cheerfully, kissed her mother goodbye and left without a backward glance for another weekend of being spoiled rotten. Ah, well. Normally Julia would stress about it. Today she had too much else to worry about—like why on earth she'd invited a man to come to supper who did things to her blood pressure!

David parked Julia's car as near as he could to her house, then paused for a moment before going in. For some unaccountable reason he felt nervous, but it wasn't as if this was a date.

A thank you, she'd said, and she'd looked as if the invitation had been squeezed out of her by her conscience. If he'd had any decency, he'd have said no, but he really wanted to spend time with her.

Except that now he was here, he was suffering a little pang of what felt just like stage fright. With a wry chuckle he rammed his hand through his hair, dragged it down the back of his neck and sighed.

'Come on, Armstrong. It's just supper with a colleague. She doesn't have any interest in you. Chill.'

He scooped up the wine and the chocolates, hoped the Italian red would go with the pasta and that she hadn't changed the menu, and headed for the door. The bell rang, echoing through the house, and after a few moments he saw her through the glass running down the stairs.

'Hi,' she said breathlessly, pulling the door open. 'Sorry, the Revells were late taking Katie and I was a bit behind. Come in.'

Julia looked gorgeous, slightly flushed, her eyes wide, her hair flying like strands of silk, and his body leapt to attention. She might not have any interest in him, he thought wryly, but he sure as eggs was interested in her...

'So how often does she go to stay with them?' David asked.

Julia, her fork suspended on the way to her mouth, grimaced. 'Every three weeks. She loves it, but they spoil her dreadfully and I can't afford to— Which reminds me, what do I owe you for the car? I mustn't forget to pay.'

'Leaving the country?' he asked mildly, leaning back against the chair and smiling enigmatically.

'Of course not.' She ate the forkful, then looked at him again. 'So how much was it?'

'Thirty-two pounds,' he said. 'All bar a few pence.'

She sighed with relief. 'Right. I'll give you a cheque after supper.' She eyed his plate and pushed the lasagne dish towards him. 'Have some more. It doesn't keep.'

'I will. It's delicious.' He offered her a scoop, but she shook her head, content to watch him eat. More than content. Too much more. Darn, this had been a really bad idea!

She toyed with a little salad so she didn't sit and stare vacantly at him, and then finally he was finished and she whisked the plates away into the kitchen next door and brought back the pudding. 'Sorry, it's a cheat,' she said, serving up the little choux pastry balls filled with whipped cream and drizzled with chocolate sauce. 'I didn't have time to make profiteroles but these are quite fun and nearly the same. Cream?'

He smiled and took it, pouring on a generous slug and tucking in with enjoyment. 'They're nice,' he said,

made, and they went through to the sitting room. She'd lit the gas fire because it was chilly, and they pulled their chairs up and stretched their feet out to the flames and listened to the gentle hissing of the gas, and Julia found herself wishing it would never end.

It did, though, about an hour later, when their coffee was finished and her eyelids were drooping.

'You're tired,' he said softly. 'Why don't I go and let you get an early night?'

She felt a little pang of regret, but he was right.

'I feel too idle to move,' she told him, and he laughed and pulled her to her feet.

'Come on, lazybones. See me off and lock the door and go up to bed like a good girl.'

But she didn't want to be a good girl. The feel of David's warm hands around hers made her long to feel them elsewhere, touching her, holding her, caressing her...

She slipped her hands out of his and pushed her hair back from her face, tucking it behind her ears. 'You're a nag,' she told him lightly, and he chuckled.

'So I'm told. Never mind, you'll be grateful later when you don't wake up with a crick in your neck and cold feet.'

They went out into the hall, and as her hand reached out to turn on the light, he stilled it, catching her hand in his and easing her against his chest.

'Wait,' he murmured, his voice low, and then his lips brushed hers, just lightly, and her knees sagged so that she swayed against him. His arms came up round her, his mouth locked to hers, and out of nowhere came a heat so intense she thought her body would catch fire.

Just before the flames took hold he eased away,

dropping one last feather-soft kiss on her lips before moving to the door.

'I'll pick you up tomorrow at two,' he said, and his voice was low and gruff and scraped over her nerve endings like rough silk.

Then he was gone, and she went back into the sitting room and curled up in his chair and relived the touch of his mouth against hers until the longing was so great she thought she'd weep with it.

She was seeing him again tomorrow, she thought, and even though her common sense told her it was too dangerous for her status quo, her heart soared with joy.

CHAPTER THREE

DAVID'S cottage was lovely. The roof was low, the walls red brick, and it was set back from the village green behind a little gate and a dense evergreen hedge that gave it privacy. There was no traffic to speak of, because the green was off the main route through the village, and it was peaceful and gloriously romantic.

That spooked Julia. After his kiss last night, she didn't need a romantic setting to make it even harder to keep their relationship in perspective!

Still, the interior did a little to dispel her fears. Far from romantic, it resembled a building site in parts, and she had to use her imagination to the full to picture how it would be when it was finished.

Not that it was cold or unwelcoming, but it was just, well, unfinished, to say the least. The front door opened straight into a large room that ran the width of the cottage, with an inglenook fireplace at one end and old oak beams that spanned the room, supporting the upper floor. Once done it would be lovely, but now it was bare except for an ancient sofa in front of the glowing woodburner and a lonely television sitting on the old brick floor in the corner.

David led her through into the kitchen behind it, which looked over the garden and across fields to the other side of the valley beyond. It was a very pretty view, and she could see why he'd fallen in love with it, but it was going to take years—or thousands of pounds—to put it right.

'I'm going to have a few hand-built pine kitchen units put in around that area,' he told her, indicating an L-shaped section of wall under the windows. 'Then over here I'll have a couple of dressers and things— very simple and unfitted, except for the bit with the sink and the washing machine and dishwasher, but they'll have to be built in so they don't show.'

'And a table?' she said, looking at the space in the middle and wondering if it was big enough. 'A table would be nice. Is there room?'

'Somewhere. I might have to find a little one or put it against the wall but, yes, a table in the kitchen is an absolute must! Come and see the garden while it's light. It's a mess, but it could be pretty.'

Julia looked at the tangled beds and overgrown shrubs with no real understanding. She'd never been much of a gardener—had never really had the time— and now she felt ignorant as he talked about hardy fuchsias and dividing clumps of perennials and the advantages of spring over autumn pruning.

He tipped his head on one side after a minute and looked at her apologetically. 'Sorry. You're not a gardener, are you? I must be boring you to death.'

She laughed, anxious to dispel his worries. 'I wouldn't say I wasn't a gardener. To be honest, I don't know if I am or not. I've never really had the time to find out. My garden in Victoria Road is just a concrete yard and a tiny patch of rather tatty grass with a straggly shrub in the corner. Goodness knows what it is. I plant a few tubs in the spring to brighten it up and cut the grass when I remember.'

He chuckled. 'There's time to learn, if you want to. Your daughter might like it. We all spent hours in the garden with Mum, weeding and edging and hoeing the vegetables. Fruit picking was always the best bit. We never grumbled about having to do that, especially not the raspberries.'

She pictured a mischievous little boy with pink juice running down his chin, and laughed. 'I can imagine. No wonder you wanted to live in the country after a childhood like that. Did you help on the farm, driving tractors and things?'

'When we were older. At first we had to help with the animals. We had stock in those days, and there was always something to do, feeding calves or lambs or collecting eggs. We weren't allowed on the tractors until we were eight, and couldn't drive them till we were ten—our legs weren't long enough. It's all arable now, though, so it's easier. Wheat doesn't get you out of bed at four on a Sunday morning.'

'That would be easier,' she agreed, and his mouth quirked in that wonderful smile again.

'Absolutely. Come and see the rest.'

'The rest' turned out to be a neglected little orchard at the end, with a gnarled old apple tree in the corner with an ancient swing dangling from one branch. 'I'm going to plant daffodils and bluebells around here in clumps,' he told her, 'and have a wild bit—butterfly plants and so on. Do my bit for conservation.'

'Looks like nature's doing that already,' she said with a smile, and he chuckled.

'Let's go in and put the kettle on, and I'll show you the upstairs. It's pretty much as it was. I haven't got round to trashing it yet, but the bathroom's next on the menu. That'll be fun, having the water off. Oh, well.'

'Pioneering spirit, you said.'

David grimaced good-naturedly and shut the back door behind them. 'So I did. Come on up.'

He flicked the button on the kettle in passing, and led Julia back into the main room of the cottage and through a little door at the far end by the fire. It opened to reveal stairs climbing steeply to the next floor, and he led her up them, warning her to mind her head, although she was nothing like as tall as him so it was easier.

'I'm having an extension if the plans are passed— just a single room downstairs and one up, with a proper staircase onto this landing, because getting furniture up these is a nightmare.'

'I can imagine,' she said, looking round as they reached the top. 'Gosh, it's a huge landing.'

'Well, not really. Technically it's a small bedroom,' he told her with a grin, 'and the other one is through there. I'm going to divide this up to make a bathroom, and the bedroom in here...' he ducked through the doorway '...will be split into two again as it used to be. Then the new room at the back overlooking the fields will have its own bathroom as well.'

She looked around and nodded, and wondered if he was good with his hands. He had to be, she decided, because there was a lot of talk of 'I'm going to do this' and 'I'll put this here', as if he intended to do the work himself.

Besides, he was a surgeon, so it wasn't hard to imagine that he'd be practical.

They went back down the twisty staircase to the kitchen, and while he made a pot of tea she sat in the comfy carver and studied him appreciatively.

Odd, how she'd thought he was bulky when she'd first seen him. He wasn't at all, she considered thoughtfully, just broad-shouldered, with a deep chest. At somewhere around six feet tall there was a lot of him, but he was fit and muscled, and in those old jeans that snuggled his lean hips he looked good enough to eat.

'Hungry?' he asked, and she wondered guiltily if her eyes had given her away.

'Pardon?' Lord, did she really sound so breathless?

'I asked if you were hungry. I've got some of my mother's fruit cake. It's good—not too rich, so you don't feel over-indulged, but tasty enough to be a real treat.'

'Sounds lovely,' she said, dredging up a smile that hopefully wasn't too inane and wondering if her thoughts were as clearly written on her face as she imagined them to be.

Apparently not, or, if they were, he was ignoring them. They took their tea and cake through to the sitting room, such as it was, because it was chilly in the kitchen even with the portable gas stove, and David had lit the woodburner in the sitting room in the morning, so it was lovely and cosy.

They sat together on the two-seater sofa in front of the fire because there was nowhere else, and he handed her the tray while he pulled up a bright plastic toolbox to put it on.

'I like your coffee-table,' she teased, and he grinned.

'Good, isn't it? You don't see many like that.'

'Certainly not, although I have to say it's a little colourful for my taste.'

The smile lurked around his mouth as he lay back into the corner of the sofa, his mug balanced on his belt buckle, and sighed contentedly. 'I'm glad you're here. I should be stripping wallpaper.'

'Don't let me stop you,' she advised, her mouth twitching, and he closed his eyes and chuckled.

'Oh, I think I should. Ignoring a guest would be too rude to contemplate.'

'I could help you, when we've finished our tea,' she suggested a moment later. 'I'm good at it—lots of practice. There were six layers in my bedroom.'

He cracked an eye open and peered at her. 'Really?'

'Really. I counted them.'

He sat up. 'No, I mean, really, you'd help me?'

Julia gave a wry laugh. 'Why not? I've got nothing else to do that won't keep, and I hate being in the house when Katie's away. It seems so empty and desolate.'

'So we could look on it as a little therapy for you so I don't have to feel guilty, is that right?'

She chuckled. 'If it makes you feel better. Actually, I just enjoy it. Or I could cook if you'd rather.'

'And get out of the washing-up? Not a chance. No, we'll have our tea and then we'll turn the radio on and strip to music.'

He was only teasing, but she felt her cheeks heat. 'In your dreams,' she retorted, trying not to remember her dreams of the night before or how empty and alone they'd left her feeling.

He pulled a wry face and grinned. 'Worth a try. We'll take some wallpaper off, then, if you insist.'

'I do,' she said firmly, but as he smiled that understanding smile at her, she found she wished she didn't.

Monday morning seemed to take for ever to arrive. He'd dropped her home at ten thirty on Saturday, after a wonderful casserole that she had a sneaking suspicion had come from his mother, and she'd dreamed of him again and woken restless and unsettled. Sunday had been a day of catching up with jobs—the laundry, the cleaning—and then Katie had come home, full of all the things she'd done and all the places she'd been, and Julia had felt inadequate as usual because she didn't have any money to spend on the child in such frivolous ways.

She could, of course, have asked his parents for help with paying off the credit-card debt that Andrew had run up, but her pride forbade her. Julia told herself he'd been her husband at the time, although they'd been separated, and she should have taken steps to close the account. It had, after all, been a joint card, and thus she had still had responsibility for the debts on it when he'd died.

She'd just never thought about it. He'd changed the address, so the statements hadn't come to her, and she'd totally forgotten the card existed.

More fool her. It had been a mistake she wouldn't make again, but in the meantime Katie was being spoilt by his parents and Julia was having to deal with the fallout.

So it was with relief for several reasons that she went into work on Monday morning, and her first job after taking report was to prep Mrs James for surgery. The test results had come back showing a handful of stones obstructing her gall bladder, and she was to have keyhole surgery first thing that morning to remove them.

'Are you sure he'll be able to see well enough through a tiny hole?' Mrs James asked Julia as she explained the procedure again. 'I mean, are you sure it's safe?'

'Yes, I'm sure. He'll fill up the inside of your abdomen with carbon dioxide gas to separate all the bits and pieces, and then he'll use a thing called a laparoscope to see inside you, and the surgical instruments will be pushed through little holes in your side and tummy and he'll guide them using the laparoscope. The gas helps to hold everything apart so he can see more easily.'

'And afterwards I'll feel much better much quicker, is that right?'

'That's right. You won't feel nearly the amount of pain you would with a conventional open operation, and your recovery will be much, much quicker. You should be home in a couple of days if all goes according to plan.'

'And if it doesn't?'

Julia perched on the side of the bed. 'In the unlikely event that he wants a closer look or it's worse than he'd thought, you'll have the conventional operation and you'll be in hospital a week or so longer—but don't bank on having a holiday at our expense,' she added with a reassuring smile. 'I gather he's very good.'

'I'm delighted to hear it,' a deep voice said from behind her, and she turned quickly, her hand flying up to her chest.

'You gave me such a fright,' she said with a laugh, and stood up. 'I was just assuring Mrs James that the likelihood of her staying here longer than a couple of days more is slight.'

David nodded, the warmth in his eyes changing to

professional concern and greeting as he turned to Mrs James and smiled at her.

'Morning. How's my patient?'

'Still very sore, but much better, thank you, Doctor.'

'Good. Well, hopefully by tonight you'll be much more comfortable. I'm planning to do you first, so you'll get a head start post-op and you won't have to hang around now. OK? And I'll come and see you later.'

He turned and gave Julia his professional smile. 'I wonder if we might have a word?'

'Of course.'

Julia walked up the ward with him, wondering what he wanted, but he didn't keep her in suspense long. 'I've got a problem,' he told her quietly. 'The plumber's starting this week, and when we're on take I need to be nearer than I am at my parents'. Is there a room I can use if I reach a critical stage and the water's cut off?'

'Sure, there's a room on the ward and another in the doctors' residence,' she said, simultaneously relieved and disappointed that his question was so mundane. She had hoped for some reference to their weekend.

'Unless, of course, you want to put me up for the odd night?'

Her eyes widened, but then she caught the teasing glint in his and pursed her lips. 'You're dreaming again,' she told him, and he gave a silent huff of laughter.

'No comment,' he said in low voice, and there was a hint of something in there that made her wonder if he, too, was being plagued by sleepless nights and wild dreams.

'You need to make sure your SHO isn't using the room on the night you need it,' she reminded him, refusing to let her mind be sidetracked.

'No. He probably wouldn't appreciate having to sleep with me,' he said with a chuckle, and Julia caught herself just before she said something stupid that would give her clean away.

'Anything else?' she said brightly to cover her al-most-lapse, but he shook his head.

'No, nothing, just the information about the room.'

'While I think about it,' she said, remembering her drive to work that morning, 'thank you so much for getting my car fixed last week. That part must have been going wrong for ages, you know, because it's running like a charm. I don't think it's ever run as sweetly as it is now. I thought it needed servicing re-ally badly, but it must have just been that one bit, which is a real relief because just now I don't have the money to pay for a major service.'

Something flickered in his eyes and was gone. 'Good,' he said heartily. 'I'm glad it's done the trick.' He glanced at his watch. 'Lord, is that the time? I'd better get up to Theatre. I'll see you later.' He paused for a second, then shook his head.

'What?'

'I was going to suggest lunch, but I doubt if I'll be finished in Theatre before two, and you go at three. Never mind. We'll do it another time.'

She agreed without thinking, and then as he walked away she shook her head slowly. Supper here, lunch there, then a real date, then—wham! Involvement.

Unless she kept it all very neutral and didn't let him close to her. She could enjoy his company, couldn't she? Just go out with him from time to time if he asked her, nothing heavy, no commitment, just two friends.

Then she remembered the kisses...

Mrs James had her keyhole surgery as planned, and went home on Wednesday morning, delighted to be feeling so much better and clutching her jar of gall-stones as a trophy.

'I'll put them on the mantelpiece when the in-laws come,' she said mischievously, and Julia chuckled.

'Highly ornamental. Or you could make a candle and suspend them in it like those pretty ones with leaves and things all round the sides, and use it for a table centrepiece on Christmas Day!'

'It might put the others off, but at least I'll get to enjoy lunch,' she said with a grin. 'Better out than in.' Her smile faded, and she took Julia's hand in both of hers. 'Thank you so much for all you've done. I know that to you it was just a simple operation, but to go from what I felt like on Friday morning to how I feel now is nothing short of a miracle for me, and I'm really, really grateful. Thank you.'

She leant forwards and kissed Julia's cheek, hugging her slightly before letting go and laughing a little breathlessly. 'Oh, dear, I'm going to cry in a minute,' she said, and blinked away a sheen of tears.

Julia waved her off, sorry to see her go. She'd been uncomplaining and cheerful, unlike some of the others. Old Mrs Bailey was groaning at the moment, but Julia knew the moment her visitors arrived she'd be sitting up in bed as perky as a parrot.

'My dear, this sheet's creased again,' Mrs Bailey said petulantly as Julia paused beside her. 'It's really most uncomfortable. It's the mattress, I'm sure. Couldn't you find me a better one?'

'It's the plastic covers,' Julia explained. 'The sheets slide around on them. I'm sorry, they're all the same. Let me straighten the sheet for you.'

She whisked the curtains round the bed, turned back the covers and straightened the offending sheet with a swift tug, tucking it firmly back under the mattress. 'Better?' she asked, and Mrs Bailey nodded grudgingly.

'I shall be glad to get home to my own bed,' she said, and Julia could sympathise with that. There was nothing like your own bed, and a plastic-covered mattress in a public ward was certainly nothing like it.

She looked at her patient more closely, and saw the weary lines around her eyes. 'Are you sleeping all right?' she asked, and the woman shook her head.

'No. Of course not. They all cough and fidget and call out, and, besides, I can't get comfortable because I'm in pain.'

Julia could well believe it. She'd had a very tricky resection of her stomach and duodenum following years of supposed indigestion that had turned out to be chronic ulceration and inflammation, and her post-op recovery had been slower than expected. Despite Mrs Bailey's difficult nature, she felt her sympathy aroused. Her sympathy, and her instinct.

'I'll get Mr Armstrong to look at you when he's next on the ward—perhaps he can write you up for something that will make you feel better,' she said gently.

Mrs Bailey sank back against the pillows and closed her eyes. 'Oh, I hope so. I really am very tired of it, and it does seem to be getting worse.'

Julia wondered if the cheerful act with the visitors was just that, an act, and if Mrs Bailey really was suffering more than she was letting on. She paged David, and asked him to call in on the ward when he was passing.

'I was just on my way up anyway,' he said. 'I wanted to check something in some notes before my next case. I'll see you in a minute.'

He appeared shortly, looking somehow even more appealing than ever in blue scrubs, and he smiled that smile and nearly dissolved her bones.

'Right, what's the matter?' he asked, and she told him that she felt Mrs Bailey wasn't progressing and just looked a bit off colour.

'I don't know, it's probably nothing, but my instincts tell me things aren't right. Her bowel sounds haven't come back yet, and she's looking peaky. I don't know—she's just not getting better fast enough.'

He nodded. 'OK. I'll buy that. I'm a great believer in instinct, especially coming from an experienced professional like you.'

It wasn't flattery, it was delivered as a statement of fact, and it made her glow all over.

He went with her and looked at Mrs Bailey, examining her carefully and checking her charts. Because he'd taken over from her consultant when he'd left, he hadn't performed the operation, but she was now in his care and he was clearly going to take Julia seriously.

'I think I'd like a scan of that,' he said. 'I wonder if there's a little abscess forming? We'll do some blood tests as well. If you've got an infection brewing you will be feeling rough. Sister Revell, perhaps we could discuss the tests I'd like done?'

David led Julia up the ward, his fingers rubbing his chin thoughtfully. 'I don't like the look of her,' he said quietly. 'I think you're right, there's something going on in there—I reckon I'm going to have to open her up again. Let's not jump the gun, though. I'd like a thorough look through her notes before I commit myself, and an MRI scan and the bloods. Can you sort that out for me? I'm on call overnight, so I'll be here. If necessary we can take her up to Theatre this evening.'

'I'll get it all organised now—the results should be back by late this afternoon if you're lucky.'

'You mean if I lean hard on the lab?'

She smiled. 'Something like that.'

'I'll bear it in mind. What are you doing at lunchtime?'

She cocked an eyebrow at him. 'Chivvying the lab for you?'

'Wrong. Having lunch with me before I start my afternoon list. Got time?'

She thought of her resolve to keep him out of her daughter's life, but lunch was hardly a threat to Katie's stability and, besides, she had to eat.

'I'll make time,' she promised, and the warm glow in his eyes filled her with anticipation. Good grief, she thought, we're only talking about lunch here, but her heart was singing for the rest of the morning.

She met him in the larger of the two canteens, but before they could get their meal his pager bleeped. He scanned the message, rolled his eyes and dropped it back in his pocket. 'No peace for the wicked. I have to go to A and E. I'm sorry.'

'David?'

He paused in the act of turning away. 'Yes?'

'Tonight,' she said, without allowing herself to think. 'What are you doing all evening, if you aren't needed?'

He shrugged. 'Just hanging around.'

'Want to hang around at my place? I could give you supper—if you want to. It's only five minutes from the hospital in the evening.'

His eyes softened and he smiled slightly. 'Thank you,' he said in a low voice. 'That would be wonderful. What time?'

She laughed. 'You're on take. Whenever you can get away. I'll do a casserole and feed you when you get there. Any time after seven-thirty.'

'After Katie's in bed.'

She refused to feel guilty about that. 'Yes,' she confirmed, and he nodded, his smile wry.

'OK. After seven-thirty it is.'

In fact it was nearer nine, because he had three cases tacked onto the end of his afternoon list and he had only just finished them, he explained when he arrived.

'You look bushed,' she told him, and he grinned tiredly.

'There's a surprise. I'm also starving. I haven't eaten since breakfast.'

'Good. Come on through.'

He followed her down to the kitchen, shedding his coat onto the back of a chair on the way, and then stood behind her, his arms round her waist and his head on her shoulder while she dished up.

'Smells good. You do, too,' he murmured, and she felt shivers run down her spine.

'You smell of hibitane,' she told him bluntly, and he chuckled and let her go, moving away to give her room to move.

Perversely she didn't want that much room, but she could hardly tell him she found the smell of hibitane curiously exciting and would he come back, please, and hold her again!

Julia handed him a plate groaning with mashed potatoes and a steaming chicken casserole, and scooped up her plate and cutlery. 'In here, or in the sitting room on your knees?' she asked.

Arthur was sleeping peacefully in his sling on the radiator, and David looked bushed. 'Sitting room?' she said, making the decision for him, and he nodded.

'Absolutely,' he said. 'Then I don't have to move after I finish.'

He didn't. Not only did he not move, he fell asleep within minutes, and she took the plate carefully off his lap and let him sleep. She probably could have felt offended, but he'd been working hard and who knew what the night might hold?

In fact, he only dozed for a few minutes, then he woke and stretched and smiled apologetically. 'Sorry about that,' he said softly, and she felt a well of tenderness inside her.

'Don't be, you needed it. Coffee?'

He shook his head. 'No. Don't move. Just come here.'

So she went to him, and sat beside him on the sofa, her head on his chest and his arm around her, and he sighed with contentment and pressed his lips to her hair. 'This is nice,' he murmured, and she had to agree. It was something she could grow very used to, and if she could only summon up the resolve, she'd fight it.

But she couldn't, so she didn't, and they sat there

for over an hour before his bleep squawked and he had to return to the hospital.

'All good things come to an end,' he said as he shrugged into his coat. 'Thank you for this evening.'

'My pleasure. Shall I wake you in the morning?'

David laughed. 'If by a miracle I should happen to be asleep. Tea would be nice.'

'Don't push your luck.'

He kissed her, a tender, lingering kiss that held a wealth of promise, and Julia closed the door behind him and went back into the sitting room, watching him cross the road and drive away with a wave of his hand and a flash of headlights.

The house felt extraordinarily empty without him.

CHAPTER FOUR

JULIA tapped gently on the door of the duty room and opened it a crack. It was quiet, the silence broken only by the soft sound of David's breathing. She slipped inside and closed the door behind her, setting the tea down on his bedside table and perching on the edge of the bed.

'Hey, sleepyhead,' she said softly, and he blinked and yawned and grinned sheepishly.

'Hi. Sorry. I meant to be up. What time is it?'

'Ten to seven. I managed to get Katie up a little earlier today. She was excited because they're casting the nativity play today and she wants to be Mary, so she couldn't wait to get to school. How was your night?'

He groaned. 'Grim, and I have to go back to Theatre now with Mrs Bailey, but there's a problem. We're a scrub nurse short. I don't suppose you can lay your hands on anyone with Theatre experience who could do it, do you?'

She thought rapidly. Sally Kennedy was on with her that morning, and while she was quite capable of running the ward, she hadn't worked in Theatre for years. Whereas Julia herself...

'I could do it,' she offered. 'If it's only the one case.'

'It is. Would you?'

She thought of standing hip to hip with David, watching him work, and a little bubble of anticipation rose in her chest. 'Sure,' she said, trying to sound non-chalant. 'When?'

'Soon as you like. I think she's prepped.'

'I don't know. I haven't seen Angie yet. I'd better go and check it's OK before you get excited.'

'Good idea. Is that a cup of tea for me?' he asked hopefully, peering at the bedside table, and she nodded. 'Great.' And without hesitation he lifted himself up on one elbow, reached his arm out of the sheets and picked up the cup, giving her a tantalising display of his bare chest and shoulders.

Oh, lord. Her heart backed up into her throat, her blood pressure rocketed and if anyone had asked her, she probably couldn't have remembered her name.

'I'll go and see Angie,' she mumbled, and headed for sanity.

Not for long, though. Sally appeared and confirmed that she was happy to run the ward for an hour or so, and then David emerged from his room fully dressed a few minutes after she'd woken him and filled her in with the results of the scan.

'It looks like a piece of the stomach wall has died following the resection—maybe the blood vessels were disrupted by the operation and a bit was left without adequate supply. Whatever, we need to open her up and find out, or she'll just continue to deteriorate. She's been on antibiotics since last night, and hopefully it should be straightforward.'

'Hopefully,' Julia commented, eyeing his shoulders in the crisp white shirt and trying not to remember what they'd looked like just a short while ago, the bare skin sleek and warm and tempting. Too tempting. They looked good enough in the shirt to test the resolve of a nun. Anything less was just downright unfair. She forced herself to concentrate on Mrs Bailey.

'Have you explained to her?' she asked, and he nodded.

'She's not surprised. She said she's been feeling worse and worse for the past three days or so.'

'Why didn't she say anything? She just got grumpy with the staff, and all the time she must have been feeling dreadful. Maybe she just didn't register how serious it might have been—perhaps she thought it was just part of the recovery process, like itching of the wound and that kind of thing.'

'Who knows? Anyway, I'm going up to Theatre. Want me to send someone down for her now?'

'You could. I'll have a chat to her and come and scrub.'

And so she went and told Mrs Bailey she was assisting in the operation, and the elderly woman took her hand and squeezed it and said she was glad.

'I trust you, dear,' she said simply. 'You can tell me all about it later.'

'I will,' Julia promised, and then she went up to Theatre, scrubbed and changed and came out of the dressing room to find David sitting with a cup of coffee in his hands, waiting for their patient.

'Hi, there,' he said, and she felt suddenly conscious of the blue pyjamas and whether she looked hippy in them. She was bound to. *Everyone* looked hippy in them—well, everyone except him, of course, because he hardly had any hips, just shoulders and a deep chest and powerful arms.

Oh, heck.

'How's Mrs Bailey?'

'Fine. Wants a blow-by-blow account of the op later.'

He grinned. 'I'll let you do that—especially if we don't find anything and we've opened her up for nothing,' he said, but in the event they found a small black section of stomach wall which had withered and died without a blood supply, as David had suspected, and he removed it, patched and repaired the hole and then closed the wound with neat stitches, leaving healthy pink tissue that would heal quickly and put Mrs Bailey on the road to recovery.

He was a joy to watch, and for a few minutes Julia forgot about the feel of his hip against hers and concentrated on watching the precise and careful movements of his hands as he inserted the fine sutures.

'I've got some mending at home. I think I'll let you have it,' she teased, and his eyes creased over the mask.

'In your dreams,' he murmured, and straightened, flexing his shoulders and rolling his head. 'Right, she'll do. Thank you, everybody.'

They left her with the anaesthetic staff and went into the changing area, and Julia's side felt cold without him next to her. How odd, she thought, because normally she didn't like to be too close to people.

Well, men, anyway, and yet David, for all he was all man and hugely attractive to her, seemed in no way a threat. Instead, being that close to him just seemed...right.

Very right. Worryingly so.

A little late to do anything about it, she realised she'd allowed him to become important to her. Not only that, she'd maybe allowed herself to become important to him, and that was unfair, because there was no way anything permanent would come of their relationship, or even anything more serious than what they were already indulging in.

But what were they indulging in? she wondered. A little light flirtation? Friendship? Nothing overtly sexual—nothing that smacked of an affair about to be embarked upon. There were no suggestive remarks, no forbidden touches, no stolen kisses—just friendship, and the occasional goodnight kiss that didn't even get mildly out of hand.

Maybe she was blowing it up out of all proportion. Maybe it was only her, and he was unmoved.

'Thank God that's over,' he said now, stripping off the top of the blue scrubs, and with one last longing glance at his powerful back and shoulders, she headed for the changing room.

He might be unmoved, but she wasn't. If she'd had the slightest hope that it would work, she would have had a cold shower, but she had a horrible sneaking suspicion that it would take more than a simple dousing in icy water to subdue her feelings for David Armstrong...

'So will I get better now?'

'Oh, yes. I'm glad I had the chance to assist him. He's a very careful, thoughtful surgeon. He'd be a good builder—measure twice, cut once, you know the sort of thing.'

Mrs Bailey smiled faintly and nodded. 'Good. I shall look forward to feeling more my old self, then.'

Julia settled her down comfortably on her pillows and left her to rest. She'd been too groggy yesterday for much of a conversation about her surgery, but today she'd had questions that Julia had been able to answer, and now she seemed content to relax and allow herself to get better.

It was a shame she'd had the setback, but these things sometimes happened. Julia found herself wondering if it would have happened if David had performed the initial operation, and wondered just how biased her answer was.

Very, probably! Oh, dear. She really was losing her perspective on this man, and just to mess her up worse, she could hear his voice in the office. It sounded as if he was on the phone, and he appeared beside her a moment later, a smile warming those astonishing eyes.

'Hi, there. I just borrowed your phone to speak to a GP. I hope you don't mind.'

'Of course I don't mind. It's hardly my phone.'

His smile widened. 'Some people are very territorial about their ward phones.'

'I have better things to worry about,' she said primly, and he chuckled.

'Of course. How's Mrs Bailey?'

'Happy. I told her you were wonderful.'

'Naturally. What else would you tell her?'

'The truth?' she suggested, and then spoilt it by laughing. 'I told her you'd make a good builder.'

He rolled his eyes and laughed. 'Is that supposed to inspire confidence?'

'Yes—her husband was a builder. It's a concept she understands. Talking of builders, how's the house?'

'Oh, coming on. I should have a bathroom by the weekend. Want to come and see?'

She pulled a face. 'I'd love to, but I've got Katie. I'm going to need to spoil her a bit because she didn't get the part of Mary in the nativity play. She's got to be a lamb, and she's disgusted. Maybe another time.'

David's eyes met hers, troubled and a little sad-
dened. 'Am I ever to be allowed to meet your daughter?' he asked gently.

She looked away. 'I don't want her getting caught
in the cross-fire,' she said, all humour banished. 'I
don't think it's a good idea.'

'Nor do I, but what cross-fire, exactly? I don't see
us fighting, and we aren't involved in an intimate relationship that's going to cause questions. I really
don't see the problem. I'm a friend, Julia. I'd like to
be more, but for now I'm just a friend. Surely she's
allowed to meet your friends?'

A flashing light caught her eye, and she latched onto
it like a drowning man to a straw. 'I have to go, someone needs me.'

'No, they need someone. Not necessarily you. Julia,
think about it. I'll talk to you later.'

And he walked away, leaving Julia staring after him
and wondering if, indeed, he really was only a friend
and if she and Katie could spend time with him without harm coming to her daughter. The weekends were
often long, and she had more and more trouble finding
cheap, fun things to do.

Maybe visiting David's cottage and going for a
walk in the country might be rather fun, she thought,
allowing herself to be tempted. After all, with Katie
there he was hardly likely to do anything to threaten
the status quo—even if at times she might rather want
him to, against all common sense.

The flashing light called her still and, putting aside
her personal thoughts and feelings, she went back to
work.

Just friends, he'd promised her, and he spent the whole
of Saturday morning telling himself that as he worked

on the cottage. She and Katie were coming over that afternoon, and he was cleaning it up and trying to make it look less like a bombsite and more like a home.

Fruitless task. He stopped himself picking a bunch of greenery out of the hedge and sticking it in a milk bottle on the kitchen window-sill. Dear me, he thought, you're losing it.

Instead he concentrated on picking up the scattered tools so that Katie wouldn't fall over them and hurt herself, and making sure he had an adequate supply of his mother's biscuits and lots of juice and milk and so on for her to drink.

At a quarter past one, just as he was clearing away the last dustsheet from the sitting room, there was a tap on the door. He opened it, dropping the sheet behind it, to find Julia there, an apologetic smile on her face and a tiny, bright-eyed little girl with blonde curls fizzing round her head staring up at him in obvious excitement.

'Sorry we're early,' Julia began, but Katie cut her off.

''S my fault,' she said. 'I wanted to see your house. Mummy said it was re-e-eally pretty and got a big garden with a swing, and I wanted to come now!'

Julia's smile was apologetic. 'She's been nagging since seven this morning. I hope we aren't too early.'

'Of course not,' he said, unable to help the smile. 'Come in. I was going to change, but you've caught me. You'll have to take me as you find me, I'm afraid.'

A pale wash of colour ran over her skin, interestingly, and David stored that little snippet for later consumption. Suppressing his smile, he led them both into the kitchen and offered them refreshments.

'Juice, please,' Katie said politely, and perched on the edge of a chair, sipping her orange and nibbling a biscuit while he made tea. He noticed her eyes kept sliding to the back door, but she didn't say anything. He was impressed. Julia might have had to bring her up alone, but she'd done a good job, from what he'd seen so far.

'Right, while the tea cools, what would we all like to do?' he asked, and her eyes lit up.

'I want to see the swing,' she said, and Julia was just opening her mouth when he got there first.

'I think that can be arranged. Julia, shall we take our tea up the garden with us?'

'It's freezing,' she pointed out, but he just smiled.

'We can wear coats.'

So they put on their coats, and while Katie swung gently back and forth on the swing with its creaky branch and rusty chains, Julia and David stood nearby in a pool of sunlight and drank their tea and watched her.

'She's enjoying herself,' Julia said softly. 'Thank you so much for suggesting it. The weekends are getting difficult.'

'Because of her grandparents?'

'Partly,' she confessed, unwilling to blame them too much. After all, it wasn't their fault they had money and wanted to spend it on their grandchild. 'Partly because we've done all the obvious things a million times.'

'Well, I'm only too happy to be of service,' he said with a wry smile. 'It's not a lot to ask, letting the kid have a go on the swing.'

'Can we go for a walk round here?' she asked, and he shrugged.

'I don't know. I'm not sure of any of the walks, I haven't had time to try them yet. We could go to my parents'. She'd love it there. She could help pick up the eggs and things, and play with the dogs and cats. There are some puppies at the moment.'

'Puppies?' Julia said, weakening visibly, and he pushed the slight advantage ruthlessly.

'They'll be going soon. They've all got homes but Mum won't let them go so close to Christmas, so they're only there until just afterwards. They need children to play with, to help them socialise.'

She was struggling. 'What sort?' she asked, a tiny thread of yearning in her voice, and he played his ace.

'Golden retrievers. Mum breeds them. They're lovely—like little woolly bears. They're cute,' he added, and watched her crumple.

'Well...maybe for a short while,' she conceded, and David had to restrain himself forcibly so he didn't punch the air.

'We'd better make a move, then. It takes twenty minutes to get there from here, and it's cold and dark so early at the moment.'

She nodded, and called to Katie. 'Would you like to go and see a farm, and some puppies?' she asked, and the child skidded off the swing and ran over, bright eyes shining, curls bouncing.

'Puppies?' she squeaked excitedly. 'Real ones?'

He chuckled and hunkered down. 'Absolutely real. They belong to my parents. Want to go?'

She nodded so fast it was a wonder her head didn't fall off, and they moved her booster seat from Julia's car into the back of the BMW and set off, and all the way there Katie bombarded David with questions about the puppies and the farm until his head was reeling.

Then they pulled up outside, and she skipped up the path to the back door beside him, little face shining up at him, and he lost his heart.

'Stay for supper.'

Julia hesitated, unwilling to overstay their welcome, and Mrs Armstrong smiled understandingly.

'You're more than welcome,' she said firmly. 'The house is just too quiet these days with the youngsters away at university and David moving into his own home. I can't get used to cooking for two and I always overdo it. We've got a big casserole—Jeremy would be delighted if you'd help to eat it up so he doesn't have to have it for days running.'

Julia looked at David for help, but he just shrugged. 'I'll take you home if you like, but I'm coming back for supper. I can't resist Mum's casseroles and she knows it. It's up to you.'

'Please, can we stay?' Katie asked pleadingly from her position in the puppies' playpen in the corner of the kitchen. She had three of them asleep on her lap, sprawled across her like fat furry butterballs, and three more resting against her legs. Extracting her was going to be worse than pulling teeth, Julia realised, and gave in.

'All right—but just for supper. Then we have to go home.'

'Can we take a puppy home?'

She sighed inwardly. She'd known this had been coming since the moment David had first said the word. Fortunately Mrs Armstrong had an answer, because she couldn't bear to have to say no to yet another thing her child had set her heart on.

'I'm afraid they all belong to people already,' she said kindly, pausing beside the playpen to look down at Katie with a smile. 'But they will need someone to play with them and cuddle them from time to time until they can go to their new homes after Christmas. If your mother doesn't mind, you'd be very welcome to come over and do that until they go—and by then we might have some kittens. One of the farm cats is looking suspiciously fat. And in the spring there'll be a couple of lambs to play with and lots of baby chicks.'

Katie's eyes were like saucers, and Julia felt panic rising in her chest. So much for keeping Katie and David apart! His mother was sucking them in relentlessly, giving her daughter a million and one things to look forward to that all depended on her relationship with David—a relationship she wasn't even sure she had or could cope with.

She looked at him in desperation for help, but he was watching Katie and his mother and smiling indulgently. So, no help there, then.

Supper was wonderful, of course, not only because the food was delicious but because they were both made to feel so welcome. Katie was never excluded from the conversation, and Julia only realised later quite how much of herself she'd revealed during the course of the meal.

They were so easy to talk to, though, and the glass of mulled wine beforehand by the drawing-room fire might have had something to do with it. Whatever the reason, she found she'd told them a little of their lives since Andrew had died, all in very neutral terms, of course, because Katie had been there and Julia made it a habit not to discuss Andrew in a derogatory way, but they weren't stupid, and she'd seen the understanding in their eyes.

'What are you doing for Christmas?' Mrs Armstrong asked as they cleared the table. Katie was back in the puppy pen, Mr Armstrong was walking the dogs and David was busy with the washing-up.

Julia shrugged. 'Nothing much. We'll spend it quietly at home. We'll probably go for a walk in the park.'

'What about family?'

She shook her head. 'My parents live in Lancashire, and my brother and sister-in-law and their children are going to them. It's a long way to go just for two days, and I'm working the morning of Christmas Eve and again the day after Boxing Day, so I can't really squeeze it in this year. Katie will spend the weekend before with Andrew's parents, having their own little Christmas while I'm on duty. They'll spoil her to bits—it'll be her real Christmas, I suspect.'

'You could come here,' Mrs Armstrong said softly. 'There's always room, and I know David would love to have you. All the others will be back, so it'll be a bit manic, but we'll still have the puppies and David's sister's children will be here for Katie to play with as well. Why don't you think about it?'

She could picture it—warm and colourful and loud and loving and the most wonderful fun. She ached for it, and a huge lump formed in her throat. 'I couldn't,' she said, the words almost torn from her, but she could feel them being sucked in deeper and deeper, and the desperate longing to be part of it terrified her.

'Think about it,' Mrs Armstrong said again, and Julia nodded blindly.

'We ought to be going soon,' she said, putting the plates down beside David on the draining board.

'Ten minutes,' he promised, and she nodded and picked up a cloth and wiped the cutlery absently and worried about how she could refuse their invitation for Christmas without hurting all their feelings. All three of them had been so kind to her and Katie that day, and she wondered what David had said to his parents about her, if anything.

They hadn't expressed any surprise or untoward interest in her, just an easy acceptance of her as a friend of his, but Julia was afraid they would start expecting more. After all, he was thirty-two, still single, and most men would be seriously thinking of settling down by then, if not before.

Was David? Was that why he was interested in her?

Because, if it was, it really wasn't fair to him to allow him to spend time with her, because she had no intention of allowing their relationship to develop into anything serious and it was only right that he should know that from the outset.

All she had to do was tell him so.

She was quiet on the way home. David watched her out of the corner of his eye, and the child sleeping in the back of the car, and wondered what was on her mind.

He had a feeling he knew. She'd withdrawn from him since supper—well, since his mother had issued the invitation to come for Christmas. She'd done that while he'd been in the kitchen, but he'd heard her, and his heart had sunk.

Too much too soon, he'd thought, and it seemed he might have been right. Could he undo the damage, though?

'Don't let my mother crowd you,' he said now, softly so as not to disturb Katie. 'She's always throwing the door of the house open to anyone who strays within reach. She means well, but sometimes people feel a little overwhelmed.'

'She's lovely,' Julia replied in a low voice. 'Really welcoming. She makes Christmas sound very tempting, but I think it would be better if we don't come.'

'Keeping Katie out of our relationship?' he murmured, and she flashed him a quick, startled glance.

'We don't really have a relationship,' she reminded him, and he sighed inwardly.

'We could.'

'No.'

'We could be very discreet. Katie need never know, if you didn't want her to.'

He glanced across at her and surprised a look of yearning on her face. Ruthlessly he pressed his advantage, and slid a hand across onto her lap, twining their fingers together. 'Julia?'

Her fingers clung to his for a moment, then his hand was placed carefully back in his own lap, and she retreated. 'No.'

'I won't give up. I'm a persistent man,' he told her gently.

She didn't answer, just turned her head away and looked out over the moonlit countryside as he navigated the roads back to Little Soham. He pulled up outside the cottage and turned to her again.

'Do you want me to drive you home and pick you up in the morning to fetch your car? It seems such a shame to wake Katie and put her into a cold car. And besides,' he said, trying to inject a little humour, 'you still haven't seen my new bathroom.'

She sat motionless for a moment, then her shoulders seemed to droop and she turned back to him, a resigned smile on her face. 'I haven't, have I? That was rude of me.'

'I agree. I think you should remedy it.'

She nodded. 'OK.'

'So shall I take you home?'

'Please.'

David tried not to smile too victoriously, but he felt as if he'd won a major concession.

And he'd see her again tomorrow.

Life was suddenly looking up.

She must have been mad. Fancy agreeing to let him bring her home last night so that she had to see him again today! And after all she'd said about them not having a relationship!

What an idiot. It would give him all sorts of false hope and encouragement, and make him even more persistent.

Julia yanked open her sweater drawer and looked in despair at the miserable collection of old knitwear. She had nothing decent to wear. He'd seen her only respectable sweater about three times now, and he must be heartily sick of it, but it was too cold to go without and, anyway, her blouses and shirts weren't much better.

And then she realised what she was doing, and slammed the drawer shut in disgust. 'You're a fool,

Julia Revell,' she told herself crossly. 'You don't want David, so why are you trying to make him want you?'

Because I do want him, and I want him to want me.

It was a sobering thought.

CHAPTER FIVE

Of course, the day didn't start and end with the bathroom inspection. They went for a walk, and then because Katie begged and pleaded they went back to the farm and played with the puppies again, and as Katie seemed happy Julia and David took the dogs and went for a ramble in the woods behind the farm.

'I wasn't doing this,' she told him with as much firmness as she could muster, and he smiled that smile that did incredible things to those gorgeous eyes and crumbled her resolve even further.

'Of course not,' he said soothingly, and took her hand and tucked it into his pocket, their fingers entwined, and the warmth of his hand spread through her entire body and threatened to melt it.

She would have taken her hand back, but she was too weak. It felt good snuggled up with his in the warmth of his jacket, and she could feel the hard pressure of his hipbone against the back of it, shifting rhythmically with his stride. Lean, hard male, focused on her, she thought, and it was giddily intoxicating.

They climbed uphill a little, and then came out through a break in the trees and looked back down towards the farm. They could see the smoke curling from the chimney, and the edge of the roof, but nothing else for miles except a church spire in the distance.

'It's beautiful here,' she said wistfully. 'What a wonderful place to be brought up.'

'It was. I love it. That's why I came back.'

David stood behind her, his arms round her waist and his head resting lightly on her shoulder, and she felt the soft puff of his breath against her cheek as he nuzzled her ear.

'You smell good,' he murmured, and Julia felt his lips move softly over her jaw and down the side of her throat. She tipped her head instinctively to allow him access, and she felt the hot, moist trail of his tongue across her throat, and the icy coolness of his breath as he blew softly on the damp skin, bringing her whole body singing to attention.

'Come here,' he murmured, and without releasing her he turned her into his arms and kissed her.

It was a long, slow, drugging kiss, nothing hasty or hurried, just a leisurely mating of their mouths, a gentle exploration that left her weak and wanting more. Much more.

More than was good for her.

She eased away, looking up at him with eyes that must have held a host of conflicting messages. 'No,' she said, but she didn't sound convinced even to her own ears.

'Yes,' he murmured back, and drew her closer, claiming her mouth again.

She pushed him away, more firmly this time, and he laughed softly and let her go.

'Spoilsport,' he murmured, but he didn't push it, for which she was hugely grateful because she was already missing the contact with his body and for two pins would have gone straight back into his arms and given him anything he asked for.

That was scary.

He took her hand in his again and led her back down to the house. Katie was still in the playpen with the puppies, but it was time for their food so David lifted her out and the puppies were fed and left to sleep.

'One of them weed on me,' Katie announced without any great concern.

'I'm not surprised,' Julia told her. 'Are you very wet?'

She shook her head. 'No. It was only a tiny wee. Here.'

She showed her mother the wet patch on her leg, the size of a large coin, and then told her all about the puppies—that they didn't have names yet, because the people who were going to have them would give them names and so they had to be just called 'puppy' until then, and how they were just five and a half weeks old now and would be going to their new homes at seven weeks, just after Christmas.

'Can we come every day and play with them?' she asked, and Julia stifled the urge to say yes and shook her head.

'No, darling, of course not. Mrs Armstrong doesn't want us here in the way all the time and, anyway, you're at school in the day and I'm at work. There isn't time.'

'Next weekend, then,' she pleaded, but Julia pointed out that next weekend she would be with Granny and Grandpa Revell.

'But I won't see them again, then, because it's nearly Christmas and they're going!' she said, and burst into tears.

Julia looked helplessly at David, who just shrugged. 'You can come every day,' he said under his breath.

'No.'

'Or at least once or twice, in the evening.'

'I don't know the way.'

'I'll bring you.'

'No.'

'Please!' Katie sobbed, and Julia felt as if she'd been put through the wringer.

'Why don't you stay for lunch and let her play with them again after their sleep?' Mrs Armstrong suggested practically, but that was almost worse, because it just seemed as if they were moving in wholesale.

'Did you have any other plans?' David asked, and she shook her head.

'No. Not really. I need to do something with the washing and ironing, and my vacuum cleaner thinks it's been made redundant, but apart from that…'

'Sounds like a good reason to play hookey,' David said with an easy grin.

'What about you?' she asked. 'I've hijacked your day again. You wanted to get on with the cottage.'

'Did I?' he said mildly. 'I'm sure it won't catch fire if I turn my back on it for another day.'

'You could leave Katie here after lunch and go and get on, the two of you, and pick her up later,' Mrs Armstrong suggested. 'I've got nothing else to do today apart from the chickens, and your father's out for the day at a vintage farm fair in Norfolk, so I'd be quite happy with the company.'

Julia could feel herself wavering. On the one hand she had the temptation of David and a happy child, on the other hand she had Katie miserable and the housework to do.

No contest.

'Are you sure?' she asked, despising her weakness and yet tingling at the thought of spending more time with him.

'Absolutely. Let's have a quick lunch and you can go and get on. Ham sandwiches all right?'

'Your mother's very kind.'

'She's just a mum. She misses the others—says it feels odd without children underfoot. That's why she breeds the puppies—it satisfies her maternal instincts. So, what are you going to do for the rest of the afternoon? Do you want to go and do your housework, or do you want to come and dabble in DIY with me?'

'What are you going to be doing?' she asked, not at all drawn to her ironing board.

'Bits of this and that. The bathroom's all plumbed in but I need to fix the bath panel and stick on the tiles and paint the walls.'

'Do you have the tiles?'

He nodded. 'Yes. Why? Fancy sticking them on?'

'I could. I'm quite good at tiling.'

His grin was infectious. 'Excellent, because I seem to have squiffy eyes. I can never get them on straight.'

So Julia spent the afternoon sitting on the side of his bath with her feet in the tub, sticking white tiles all over the walls around the bath and up towards the ceiling at the tap end because he had a shower mixer, while he painted the walls around her.

'There,' she said in satisfaction, sticking the last one in place. 'You can grout them—I hate that job.'

He chuckled. 'You and me both, but at least they're straight. Thanks.' He put the roller in the tray and looked down at her from the top of the stepladder. 'Tea break?'

She looked at her watch. 'Shouldn't we be going back for Katie? It'll be suppertime in an hour.'

'Exactly. If we time it just right, we'll get fed, too.'

'David, that's awful,' she said with a shocked little laugh. 'We can't just eat there all weekend!'

'Why not?' He came down the ladder and tapped the tip of her nose with a blunt forefinger. 'Don't worry. Mum loves company. Anyway, she's expecting us.'

She stared after him as he left the room and headed for the stairs. 'Excuse me?' she said to his retreating back. 'What do you mean, she's expecting us?'

He turned back at the top of the stairs and threw her a smile. 'I said we'd be back then. Come on, wash that adhesive off your hands and come and have some tea. You worry too much.'

Did she? She didn't think so. She was beginning to feel she hadn't worried anything like enough nearly soon enough, because David and his family seemed to have wormed themselves firmly into their lives while she wasn't looking.

Julia washed her hands thoughtfully and went downstairs to find him pouring boiling water into two mugs. 'Cake?' he offered, but she shook her head.

'No. David, this is ridiculous. We're there all the time—'

'Are you bored there?'

'Of course not.'

'Is Katie suffering? Are we doing anything to hurt her?'

'No, of course not—'

'Well, then. Stop worrying. Here's your tea. Going to change your mind and have cake? It's my mother's date and walnut.'

And yet again, for what seemed like the hundredth time in the past two days, she weakened.

*   *   *

'Morning.'

Julia's heart fluttered betrayingly at the sound of David's voice, and she lifted her eyes from the paper-work and feasted them on his face. 'Morning. You're here bright and early.'

'I've got a tricky case. I wanted to go through the notes again.'

'Mr Burrows?'

He nodded. 'How is he? Good night?'

'Seems so. I was just sorting out these discharge papers and then going to see him. I think he's a bit apprehensive.'

David eased a hip onto the corner of her desk and smiled wryly. 'Not surprising. He's got very little to look forward to in the immediate future, and I'm just hoping I'm going to be able to give him some good news after the op, but I'm not optimistic. He's had his symptoms too long, and cancer of the bowel doesn't respond well to neglect. Have you got the notes handy?'

'Sure.'

She stood up and pulled the notes out of the trolley and handed them to him. 'Want a cup of tea? I've got a few minutes before I go and do the drugs, and we've got plenty of staff on this morning for a change.'

'That would be lovely,' he said, lifting his head from the notes for just long enough to flash her a smile.

She made two mugs and took them back into her office, and found him ensconced in the chair beside the radiator, the notes open on his lap. He was staring at X-rays on the light box, and he looked thoughtful.

'Working out how to tackle it?' she said, and he nodded.

'It's going to be tricky. I won't know until I get in there just how bad it is, but I think I'm going to have to remove the first section of his colon and reattach the end of the ileum to the top. Hopefully he won't need a colostomy, but I'll know more when I get in there.'

He slapped the notes shut, dropped them on her desk and picked up his tea with a smile. 'Thanks. I'm ready for this. I'll go and talk to him in a moment.'

He stretched his legs out, feet crossed at the ankle, and dropped his head back against the wall with a sigh. 'So when are you coming to grout my tiles?' he asked with his eyes shut, and she laughed.

'Never. I told you, I don't do grouting. It's a horrible job. It always takes me ages and I never manage to get all the grout off the surface of the tiles, so they always look cloudy and patchy.'

'I think you're just making excuses,' he said lazily, and buried his nose in his mug. 'I think anyone who took pride in their work would want to finish the job.'

'Is that right?' she said, going back to her paperwork and pretending to ignore him.

David placed a large, flat hand in the middle of the form she was filling in, and she looked up into his laughing eyes and felt herself start to smile.

'Did you want something?'

'My grouting.'

'Beggars can't be choosers.'

'I'll swap you.'

'Swap what?'

'I'll take you out for dinner next weekend, while Katie's with her grandparents.'

Julia laughed. 'You must hate it even worse than I do,' she said, and he chuckled.

'You can have no idea. So that's a deal, then.'

'No.'

'What?'

'You heard.' She stopped pretending to work and looked up at him again. 'David, we don't have a relationship,' she said quietly.

For a few seconds he was silent, searching her eyes, then he gave a gentle sigh. 'I disagree. I think we do have a relationship—and I think it would be a tragedy not to explore it and extend it.' He straightened up, taking his hand off the form, and looked down at her with tender and understanding eyes.

'Give us a chance, Julia. I know you're running scared, but we could have something really special here. I feel it, and I'm sure you do, too, or you wouldn't have spent so much time with me already.'

He glanced at his watch and sighed again. 'I have to go and see Mr Burrows, then I have to start my list. I'll see you later—and think about what I said.'

'You just want your grouting done,' she said, trying to lighten the tone, but she sounded nervous and panicky, and he just smiled.

'We'll talk about that later.'

He went out and closed the door softly, and she stared blankly at the form on her desk and wondered if she dared allow him to talk her into this, or if it was just madness.

Her heart was skittering against her ribs, her breath was jamming in her throat and she could feel panic rising like a tide to swamp her.

He's not Andrew, she told herself, but even so she

was afraid. She'd been vulnerable before, and she'd been badly hurt. Did she dare risk it again?

'Mummy, can David and his mummy and daddy come to my nativity play? I want them to see me being a lamb.'

'Oh, darling, I don't know if they can,' Julia said, trying not to dash her daughter's hopes too cruelly. 'David's very busy at work, and his parents have all the puppies and hens and things to look after. What about Granny and Grandpa Revell?'

'I don't want them. I want David. Can you ask him? Please, Mummy!'

She hesitated. 'Well, yes, I can ask, but don't get too excited. When is it?'

'Tomorrow.'

'Tomorrow!' Julia exclaimed, horrified. 'I didn't realise it was so soon! Oh, darling. They might be busy. Anyway, how many people can you take?'

'Don't know—I got a letter. Hang on.' Katie rummaged in her little schoolbag and came out with a crumpled form. Julia smoothed it on the kitchen table and scanned through it.

'You can take two people, it says here.'

'You and David,' she said promptly.

Oh, lord, Julia thought. I can't sit there with him and watch my daughter in a nativity play like real parents! What will the teachers think? What about the other mothers?

'Please, ring him,' Katie said, handing her the phone.

She stared blankly at the instrument. 'I don't have his number,' she said, and realised it was true.

'Is he at the hospital? Ring him at the hospital, Mummy. Please—I really want him to come.'

Oh, lord. She looked at her watch. He might still be there.

'I'll try,' she said, and dialled the number and asked them to page him.

He came on the line a moment later, sounding crisp and efficient.

'David? It's Julia. I'm sorry to trouble you at work, but I don't have your home number, and Katie wanted to ask you something.'

'Look, I'm tied up just now. Can I pop in on my way home?'

He sounded harassed, and it flustered her into agreeing. 'Sure. Sorry. It's not important.'

'Yes, it is!' Katie protested, and she heard him chuckle.

'Don't worry. I'll see you later—about six.'

Which, of course, was just when their supper would be ready. Julie looked at the little cottage pie in the oven and wondered if it would stretch to feed him as well. Not a chance. Oh, blast. Still, she didn't want to invite him. She was busy telling him they didn't have a relationship—she couldn't then invite him for supper with the next breath! She peeled carrots and trimmed sprouts—just enough for the two of them—and by the time he arrived the table was laid for two and the supper was ready.

She opened the door and stood there in the hall, deliberately not inviting him in. 'I'm sorry to drag you out of your way,' she began, 'but Katie wanted to ask you to come to her school nativity play. Please, feel free to say no.'

He laughed softly and leant against the doorframe.

'I wouldn't dream of disappointing the child. Just tell me when and where.'

Just then Katie realised he was there and came flying down the stairs, curls bouncing, and skidded up to him with a sparkling smile.

'It's my nativity play tomorrow night at school—can you come? I can have two people, and Mummy's one of them, and I want you to be the other one. Please, say you can—please, please, *please!*'

'Tomorrow?' he said, hunkering down and pulling out his diary. 'Let's see—Tuesday. OK. What time?'

'Six-thirty,' Julia said. 'At the school on Northgate Avenue, but parking's a bit hit and miss.'

'How will you get there?' David asked her.

'I'll walk from here with her, a little early. You could park here and walk with us, but it might mean hanging around for a while, or you could meet us there—if you really can spare the time?'

He looked up at her, his eyes laughing. 'Wild horses wouldn't keep me away,' he told her firmly, and any hope she'd harboured that he'd back out fizzled and died on the spot.

'Have you come for supper?' Katie asked, taking him by the hand and dragging him into the hall.

'No—I haven't been invited,' he said, looking at Julia with teasing eyes over Katie's head.

She felt colour sweep her cheeks, carried on the tide of a little rush of guilt. 'Do you have plans for tonight?' she asked, and he shook his head.

Her heart was in her mouth, but she forced herself to smile at him. 'Would you like to spend the evening with us? It's nothing special, but you're welcome to join us, if you'd like. I can do some extra vegetables.'

David searched her eyes, seeing probably far too

much, and then he smiled. 'You're trying to get out of the grouting,' he said softly, and she laughed a little breathlessly.

'You guessed. Well?'

'I'll stay—whatever the reason,' he said quietly. 'Thank you.'

'It's more or less ready. I just need to do the veg,' she said, dragging her eyes from his and telling her heart to behave. 'Come on through. Katie, go and wash your hands ready for supper, darling.' And I'll just spend the next twenty-four hours wondering how to introduce this gorgeous hunk to the other mothers without inspiring a whole host of searching questions!

The gorgeous hunk in question followed her down the hall to the kitchen, hanging his coat on the banisters on the way past and propping himself up against the worktop while she opened a tin of sweetcorn and heated it in the microwave. There was an apple pie lurking in the back of the freezer, and she gave that a whirl in the microwave, too, and put it into the oven to warm and crisp as she dished up, all under David's watchful eye. 'So why the change of heart?' he asked softly, and she dolloped shepherd's pie on the worktop instead of the plate.

'Change of heart?' she said, scraping it up and putting it onto her plate. 'What makes you think I've had a change of heart?'

'The fact that I'm in here having supper and not talking to you through the letterbox? The fact that earlier today you weren't having anything to do with me, and tonight you ask me to your daughter's nativity play?'

'No,' she corrected. 'Katie asked you to her nativity play. It was her idea—and it's just the sort of thing I was worried about. But it's too late, because you're coming now and I'm just going to have to deal with the fallout.'

'Fallout?'

'Fallout—as in, who was that man with you on Tuesday night?'

'Ah. That sort of fallout.'

'Mmm. Got any good ideas?'

He shrugged. 'Tell them I'm a friend of the family. It's not a lie.'

It was a definite thought, and a huge improvement on any of the things she'd come up with. Anyway, it was impossible to continue the conversation because Katie came bouncing in, hands still damp, and turned them palms up for inspection.

'Lovely. Go and sit down, and take David with you and lay another place. I'll bring the supper in a minute.'

Katie towed him away, and Julia sank back against the wall and sighed. Maybe letting him join them for supper had been a mistake, but it would have been impossible to retract Katie's invitation without being unpardonably rude.

Damn.

Oh, well, the damage, if there was any, was done. Julia finished dishing up, took the plates through and put them down and drew up her chair.

'I'm afraid there isn't much,' she said, patting hers down to spread it so it didn't look so small, and he looked from plate to plate and smiled slightly.

'It looks a lot better than whatever I would have had at home. Thank you,' he said quietly, and he ate his small portion without a word of complaint.

'I'm still hungry. What's for pudding?' Katie asked,

and Julia produced the now warmed apple pie, put a dollop of ice cream on each slice and watched them wolf it down.

'More?' she asked, and two sets of hungry eyes met hers.

'If you can spare it.'

'Of course I can spare it,' she said. 'Anything to get out of the grouting.' David laughed.

'What's grouting?' Katie asked.

'The white stuff in between all the tiles. You have to squash it in with a rubber thing called a squeegee, and your mother hates doing it,' David explained.

'It's boring—and, anyway, they aren't my tiles.'

'Whose tiles are they, then?' Katie asked, looking puzzled, so Julia explained about finishing off the tiling in the bathroom at the cottage.

'I'll do it!' Katie offered enthusiastically. 'I like squidgy things.'

'I think it's a bit too difficult for you, my darling,' Julia told her, 'and, anyway, you're too busy with your play and everything.'

'I'm a lamb,' she told David, looking disgusted. 'It's a stupid part. I wanted to be Mary, but they said I was too little, and one of the big girls got it, but I wanted it.'

'Maybe next year,' David said reasonably. 'You'll be bigger then—and, anyway, being a lamb is very important. Each part is important. Without the lambs the shepherds wouldn't have a job, and without the shepherds who would have followed the star and visited the baby Jesus?'

Katie thought about that for a moment, then perked up. 'I'm the smallest lamb,' she told him. 'Just so you know.'

'I'll look out for you.'

'Right, young lady, bathtime and then bed,' Julia said, and Katie pulled a face, but she wasn't letting her get away with it just because David was there. Maybe he'd take the hint and go, Julia thought, but he just stretched out at the table and relaxed.

'I won't be long,' she told him, and by the time she came down he'd washed up and dried all the dishes and left them stacked on the side. The kettle had boiled, mugs were on standby beside it and he was reading a magazine at the table in the breakfast room.

'Good grief,' she said faintly. 'Ever thought of taking a job as an au pair?'

He chuckled and came up behind her, sliding his arms round her and nuzzling her neck. It was something she could get rather used to, she thought, shifting her head slightly to give him access.

'Tea or coffee?' she asked dreamily, but he turned her into his arms and kissed her, and she forgot that she was supposed to be keeping their relationship cool and kissed him right back.

After a moment he lifted his head and looked down at her with eyes that blazed with heat. 'Wow. Where did that come from?' he murmured, and moved away from her fractionally. 'Just remind me that your daughter's in the house and we can't do this,' he added, and retreated to the next room and the safety of the magazine.

'Um—tea or coffee?' she asked again, and he gave a strangled laugh.

'I don't care. Just put a hefty sedative in it.'

She bit her lip to stop the smile, and took the tea through to the breakfast room, putting it down on the table in front of him with a hand that shook slightly.

'Tea,' she said. 'Unfortunately I'm right out of sedatives. I'll pick some up next time I go shopping.'

He chuckled, but his eyes were still heated and there was a tautness to his jaw that hadn't been there before. He didn't say anything, though, just picked up the tea and sipped it thoughtfully in silence.

It wasn't a companionable silence. It was charged with emotion, with need recognised but not fulfilled, and Julia wanted nothing more than to put her tea down and go into his arms and finish what they'd started.

Instead she changed the subject. 'How's Mr Burrows?' she asked, and he arched a disbelieving brow.

'You want to talk about Mr Burrows? OK. Well, he's not wonderful. The tumour was more widespread than the scan suggested, and it had tracked to the lymph glands, so the prognosis is pretty dismal, I'm afraid. I've done all I can do for now, and I'm discharging him to the oncologist once he's healed from the surgery. All they can do is keep him comfortable, I'm afraid, and slow the progression maybe.'

'What a shame.'

'It is. He's a nice man. Very stoic. That's the trouble. He should have pressed the panic button a bit sooner.'

'How long do you think he's got?' Julia asked, knowing full well that any answer would be wildly inaccurate but just seeking to extend the conversation a little longer—anything rather than go back to that charged silence!

David gave her a level look that spoke volumes. 'You know better than to ask me that,' he said with a wry smile. 'Three months? A year? Who can tell?'

'Does he know?'

He shook his head. 'No. He was too ill yesterday after his surgery to discuss it. I want to get him a day or so down the line before I broach it.'

He put his mug down, looking at her with those clear rainwashed eyes, and she felt as if he could see deep into the innermost recesses of her soul. She looked away, but he was undeterred.

'Julia.'

She drank her tea, ignoring him, but he reached across the table and took the mug out of her hands, and tilted her chin up so she was facing him.

'Look at me,' he said softly, and she met those wonderful eyes and felt sick with anticipation. 'We have to talk about this,' he went on, his voice gentle but implacable. 'There's something simmering just under the surface, and we both know it, but you keep trying to deny its existence, and I want to know why.'

Because of Andrew.

She moved away, standing up and going back into the kitchen, fiddling with the kettle. He followed her, but he didn't touch her or crowd her, just stood nearby, watching her silently.

'My husband left us,' she began, her voice flat as she remembered that awful day. 'Katie was eighteen months old. I'd moved down here with him the year before, leaving my family and friends, because he wanted to be near his parents.

'I made a few friends, but not many. He was a bit possessive, and he used to flirt with my friends—it was embarrassing. We had the odd dinner party that ended in disaster because he couldn't manage to restrain his hands and the husbands got upset. He blamed it on me—said I'd gone off sex since Katie and what was a man to do? Anyway, one day we had a blazing row because I'd been out for coffee with a friend and he'd come home from work expecting to find me there, and I wasn't.'

She paused, remembering his temper and frustration, and shook her head. 'He waited for me, and went berserk when we got back. He told me I was a waste of space and he didn't want any more to do with me, and he wanted a divorce. He packed a bag and left, and came back at the weekend and took all the rest of his things. He was living with his parents, and they took his side, of course, while I had no one.'

'Why didn't you go home to your parents and friends?' he asked, and she laughed a hollow little laugh.

'Because I was married. I'd made vows that I believed in, and I kept hoping he'd come back. I thought it was my fault, and it was years before I realised that it was him and not me that had had the problem.'

David shook his head slowly, his eyes full of understanding. 'So what happened then?'

'He died. That winter, just before Christmas, he had an accident one night, going home drunk from an office party, and managed to kill himself. Fortunately he had nobody in the car with him, and he hit a tree. Then I found out he'd cancelled the endowment policies and the mortgage wasn't cleared, so I had to sell the house and look for somewhere with the small amount of equity that was left. Then, just after I bought this house with the money I managed to scrape up, the credit card company caught up with me and gave me a bill for ten thousand pounds that he'd run up on a joint card.'

David muttered something derogatory under his

breath, and she gave a tiny laugh. 'Oh, yes. He really was a piece of work. So now I don't trust anyone but myself, and I've always sworn I'll never give anyone else the power to hurt us or threaten our home in any way. So…I'm sorry, but that's why.'

'So even in death, he's still got the power to ruin your life.'

Julia tilted her chin. 'My life isn't ruined. I have my daughter, and I love her more than you can imagine. I have a good job, and a lovely home. I have everything I need.'

'Not quite,' he said softly. 'You're still denying yourself the right to an adult relationship.'

'I have to,' she said, desperation echoing in her voice. 'I have to, David. I can't allow myself to get close to anyone because it makes me vulnerable, and I can't let that happen. Not again.'

For a long time he stood there looking at her, then he drew her into his arms and hugged her gently. 'I won't hurt you. Either of you. I promise that. We can take this as slowly as you want, be as discreet as you like. You can back off at any time. But, please, give us a chance. We could have something so special here, Julia. Something lasting. Don't close the door on it without knowing what it is you're walking away from.'

He kissed her, just a feathering of his lips across her forehead, and then he turned and strode down the hall, picking up his coat on the way, and she heard the soft click of the front door behind him.

It was the loneliest sound in the world.

CHAPTER SIX

JULIA went onto the ward in the morning in a dither of nervous anticipation. She wanted to see David but, although she'd spent the whole night thinking about it, she still wasn't sure she dared to test their relationship.

There just seemed to be too much at stake, although the urge to trust him was sometimes overwhelming. If she could only hand over her responsibilities, just for a while, or share them, even—just to take the pressure off. It was so, so tempting—but then she'd remember Andrew, and how she'd trusted him, and how he'd changed after Katie's birth, and then she'd realise the stakes were too high.

It was just hormones leading her astray again, she thought, like they had with Andrew. He'd been charming to her at first, flirtatious and teasing, then putting the pressure on more and more, but so skilfully that she'd tumbled into bed with him without a second thought.

He'd taught her more about her body than she could have imagined, but his heart had never seemed to be involved, and after a while she'd found it mechanical and unsatisfying. Then she'd had Katie, and his demands had seemed to increase and become even less sensitive to her needs.

And now David was pushing the same buttons, and awakening feelings she'd all but forgotten, and she was afraid to get back on the merry-go-round in case the same thing happened.

It didn't stop her heart from reacting every time she heard his voice, though, or her skin from shivering every time he was near. Common sense seemed to have deserted her where he was concerned, and she had to struggle to keep her mind on the job that morning.

What would he say when he saw her? Would he bring the subject up again, or leave it for her to make the next move?

And if so, what move would she make?

She went to see Mr Burrows, who'd been fretting in the night according to the report, and he was anxious to see David.

'I'd like to talk to him,' he said. 'Will he be round today?'

'I'm sure he will,' she told him. 'I know he intended to talk to you as soon as you were feeling a little brighter. I'll contact him if he doesn't come down in the next hour, all right?'

Mr Burrows nodded. 'I just want the uncertainty to end,' he said frankly. 'I just need to know, one way or the other.'

'I'll make sure he comes,' Julia assured him. She made him comfortable, tried not to think about David and went back to the work station to see who was on the list for Nick Sarazin that day.

'Morning, gorgeous.'

She jumped, caught unawares by David's quiet footsteps, drowned out by the hubbub of the ward. 'Morning,' she said, turning round with a smile coming naturally to her lips. 'And it's Sister Revell to you.'

'Sorry, Sister.' He smiled, but he looked preoccupied, she thought, cocking her head on one side.

'What's the matter?' she asked softly.

He sighed, his smile fleeting and a little sad. 'Mr Burrows. He's been fretting in the night, apparently. My SHO didn't know what to tell him. I need to talk to him now and let him know the score—could you come, too?'

'Sure. He was asking for you a minute ago. I was going to page you, actually, but I was fairly sure you'd be here soon.'

'Is he over the anaesthetic?'

She shrugged. 'Ish. It was quite a long op, wasn't it? He's still feeling a little groggy, but that could be the pain relief. Whatever, he wants to know what you found.'

David dragged a hand through his hair and sighed again. 'I hate doing this. It doesn't matter how many times I have to do it, it never gets any easier. In fact, I think it gets harder, because you're more than ever aware of just what you're telling them.'

'I think he knows.'

He nodded. 'So do I—but thinking you know and being told are two different things. Until I talk to him, he'll still have a lingering glimmer of hope. My words will extinguish it, and he'll have to start the grieving process. Still, it has to be done. Let's see how gently I can do it.'

Very, Julia was to discover. He was kind and patient and answered all Mr Burrows's questions about the surgery and what he'd found. And then he asked the final question.

'I'm going to die, aren't I?' he said, and David nodded slowly.

'Yes. I'm afraid, ultimately, you are. The oncologist will talk to you about the palliative care he can give you—that's treatment to hold the cancer at bay for as long as possible and keep you comfortable, but at the end of the day that's all we can do now. I'm very, very sorry.'

Mr Burrows nodded pensively. 'I thought as much. Well, thank you for being honest. I need to know—things to do at home, you know? Preparing. Don't want to leave a muddle for the family to sort out. Still, at least the pension's taken care of and my wife won't have to worry about money or the house, and my children are all taken care of— I don't have to feel guilty for letting them down, at least.'

He cracked then, his face crumpling and his shoulders heaving, and Julia perched on the edge of the bed and put her arms round him and held him while he cried. He didn't indulge himself for long, just a few moments to release his pent-up emotions, and then he pulled himself together and apologised. He scrubbed away the tears on his cheeks with the back of his hand, and Julia gave him a tissue and they left him alone for a while to come to terms with his news.

Julia found herself tearing up a little as they left the room, and David shot her an understanding look, propelled her gently into her office and hugged her. 'OK?' he murmured after a moment, and she nodded into his shoulder.

'Yes. It just seems so hard—he's such a nice man, all he's worried about is that his family don't have to suffer or worry.'

Unlike Andrew, who had never given that a moment's thought. Odd, how men could be so different.

'Death, or impending death, tends to bring out the

real person, I've found,' David said quietly. 'It's amazing how the silliest people seem to have huge inner strength, and the ones you'd expect to cope go completely to pieces.'

'I wonder how his wife will be.'

'I don't know. I'll come back and talk to him again later. He's bound to have more questions. Perhaps you'll keep an eye on him and talk to him if he needs reassurance.'

'Of course. Do you want to see his wife?'

He shrugged. 'We'll play it by ear. He may have definite views on what he wants her told. We have to respect that.' He eased away from her and looked down into her face, his eyes searching hers. 'You OK now?'

She nodded, smiling self-consciously. 'I'm just a softie.'

'I noticed. That's fine by me. There aren't nearly enough softies in the world. Everyone's busy being hard and tough and independent. We need to lean on each other.'

'That's fine until you lean on someone and they aren't there any more,' Julia pointed out.

'I'm here—and I'm going nowhere,' he said softly. 'Actually, that's a lie. I'm going to my clinic. I'll see you later. Ring me if you need me.'

She nearly laughed out loud at that, but stopped herself in time and produced what she hoped was a sensible smile. 'Will do.'

She watched him go, his long stride eating up the corridor as he headed towards Outpatients, and she turned back to her work with her heart in turmoil again.

'I'm here—and I'm going nowhere,' he'd said. Could she dare to believe him?

'Mummy, it's time to go! I'm going to be late!'

'No, you aren't. David said he'd drive us there and then park his car somewhere and come back. He'll be here,' Julia promised, trying to inject confidence into her voice, but it was hard. Andrew had always been late, arriving with a cheerful excuse and brushing aside her concerns.

She checked her watch. David was late—only three minutes, but they were cutting it fine as it was. If they left now, they could just about walk there in time. Any later—

The peal of the doorbell cut across her fretting, and she whisked the door open to find David there, looking apologetic. 'Sorry I'm on the drag—I had to go back and talk to Mr and Mrs Burrows. Are you both ready?'

She nodded, hating herself for having doubted him. 'Yes. Are you all right for tonight, or do you need to go back to the hospital?'

'No, not tonight. I'm OK.' He smiled past her at Katie. 'All ready, littlest lamb?'

She nodded and giggled. 'Yup.'

'Let's go, then.'

He bundled them into his car, settled Katie on the new booster seat that seemed to have appeared as if by magic in the back of it, and slid behind the wheel. Three minutes later they were at the school, and Julia pointed out the entrance he should come through when he came back.

'I'll go and get her ready and come back to meet you,' she promised, and they left him on the kerb and ran inside. There was a fine drizzle falling, and they

arrived in the hall slightly damp and breathless, just
as the year-one teacher was calling for her lambs and
shepherds.

'Anything I can do?' Julia asked, but she was cheerfully dismissed and sent off to enjoy herself, so she
kissed Katie for good luck and went back out to wait
for David, arriving at the door just as he did.

'That was quick!' she exclaimed, and he chuckled.

'I had a stroke of luck. There was a space just
around the corner, so I nabbed it. Thought it would be
easier for afterwards.'

'Absolutely. Come on in, we need to find a seat.'

They were just settling themselves down, and she
was wondering if she'd get away without having to
see anyone she knew, when Nick and Ronnie Sarazin
appeared and waved. Nick did a mild double-take at
David, and they squeezed into the row behind them.

'Hello, David,' Nick said, eyeing him assessingly.
'I didn't know you had children here.'

'I don't. I'm here with Julia,' he said, deadpan, and
Julia's heart sank. Of all the people to meet, it had to
be them! Now there was no chance of keeping it quiet
in the hospital.

Nick eyed her thoughtfully, then smiled. 'Good.
About time. Ronnie, I don't believe you've met David
Armstrong. David, my wife Veronica.'

'Ronnie, please,' she said with a grin, and shook his
hand. 'Nice to meet you.'

'So, how did Julia talk you into coming to this
dreadful thing?' Nick asked, *sotto voce,* and David
chuckled while Ronnie told him off.

'It's not dreadful! It'll be lovely.'

'You're just a softie. They'll all forget their lines.'

'And you'll get pink-eye like you always do.'

Nick coloured slightly and gave a rueful grin. 'Very likely. So?' he added, looking pointedly at David.

'So I'm a sucker,' David said with a smile. 'Katie asked me. I couldn't refuse a beautiful girl, could I, now?'

'Evidently not,' Nick murmured, and his eyes met Julia's and twinkled.

'We're just friends,' she said firmly, and Nick snorted softly and sat back in his seat.

'If you say so.'

They were spared any further discussion by the dimming of the lights and the arrival on stage of one of the older pupils reading the usual passage from the Bible about the decree from Caesar Augustus that all the world should be taxed.

Then the curtains opened and there were children milling around on the stage, making preparations for the journey.

It was a colourful little pageant, with all the usual mishaps. A headdress skidded sideways and fell off, one of the shepherds wet himself, a lamb cried and had to leave the stage, and the innkeeper forgot his only line, but apart from that it was perfect, and at the end David clapped as loudly as any of the fathers.

There were refreshments in the back of the hall while they waited for the children to change and come out. They stood with Nick and Ronnie, and Julia tried to avoid the interested looks of the other mothers.

Not that she'd escape for long, she knew that. The next time they were waiting to pick up the children at the end of the day, Julia knew the questions would start. In fact, she was surprised they were holding back now, some of them!

Then Katie came skipping out and threw herself at

David, and with the reflexes of a tried and tested uncle he scooped her up into his arms and plonked a kiss on her cheek. 'Well done, lambkin,' he said, and hugged her.

'Did you see me?' she asked, holding herself away from him so she could see his face.

'Yes, I saw you. You were near the front.'

'Next to Daniel—he cried.' She said it with all the disgust of a five-year-old, and Julia saw David's lips twitch.

The two Sarazin children came running up then, a boy and a girl with Nick's laughing eyes, and he put an arm around each and hugged them. 'Well done, kids,' he said, and then the party broke up and they headed for the door.

The drizzle had turned to mist, and their breath fogged on the cold air. The streetlights made orange haloes high above them, and Julia was glad David was there with them. It was a little creepy, like something out of a Sherlock Holmes film, and she found herself moving closer to him, Katie between them.

'Here's the car,' he said, flicking the remote control and lighting up the interior with a welcoming glow. Moments later they were on their way home, and as they pulled up outside Julia looked across at him, her heart in her mouth.

'Coffee?' she said, and he smiled slightly.

'I'm starving, I haven't eaten yet. I was going to go and get something. Have you had supper?'

She nodded. 'I had scrambled eggs with Katie at five.'

'Could you force anything else down?'

She smiled. 'Possibly. What did you have in mind?'

'A Chinese take-away?'

Her mouth watered. 'I can always find room for a Chinese,' she confessed, and he grinned.

'I'll see you in a few minutes, then. Any preferences?'

She shook her head. 'None—just lots of fried rice. I love it.'

'OK.'

She took Katie in and put her straight to bed, still excited but almost asleep on her feet. 'Was I all right?' she asked her mother as she snuggled under the quilt.

'You were lovely,' Julia said honestly. 'I was very proud of you. You were the best lamb.' That last was probably poetic licence and maternal pride, but Julia didn't care. She kissed the baby-soft cheek and went downstairs, lit the fire in the sitting room and put the kettle on.

If she'd had a bottle of wine she would have opened it, but she didn't, and anyway David was driving. She found a bottle of mineral water in the cupboard and put it in the fridge in the ice compartment, and then found herself looking in the mirror and finger-combing her hair.

Her heart was pattering in her throat, and when the doorbell rang a moment later she felt it stop for a second.

She closed her eyes for a moment and drew a steadying breath, then walked down the hall and opened the door.

'Here we are,' he said, holding a carrier bag up for her inspection. 'Special fried rice, sweet and sour king prawns, beef in ginger and spring onions, pancake rolls and prawn crackers. Oh, and banana fritters for pudding.'

She laughed in astonishment. 'Good grief, we'll be huge!'

'Speak for yourself. I'm ravenous. Where's the little one?'

'In bed. She was bushed.'

He followed her down to the kitchen, and they put the dishes out on a tray and took them through to the breakfast room with the still tepid mineral water. She'd laid the table with cutlery, but he produced chopsticks from the bag and insisted they use them.

'Everything will be frozen by the time I can eat it!' she wailed, but he just laughed and showed her how to hold them, and then came round behind her and held her fingers in the right position and fed her a prawn. She felt the heat of his body against her shoulders and a deep ache started inside her.

'I think I can manage,' she said breathlessly, and for a second he didn't move. Then he dropped his hand to her shoulder and squeezed it gently before going round to the other side.

He sat opposite her, watching her and laughingly teasing her when she dropped things, and she had more fun eating that meal than she'd had in years. She laughed so much she could hardly pick anything up, and in the end David took pity on her and fed her, and the atmosphere changed, becoming charged with the most incredible tension.

He fed her the banana fritter from a spoon, and when the syrup dribbled down her chin he wiped it up with a fingertip and then put it in her mouth. Her eyes closed on a moan, and she curled her tongue around his fingertip and suckled it gently.

He gave a low groan, and she opened her eyes and

met his in a blaze of heat, and her breath jammed in her throat.

She lifted her hand and took his in it, their fingers meshing, and she looked at him and said unsteadily, 'What's happening to us, David?'

'Nothing you don't want,' he murmured, but that didn't help her, because she wanted him, even though she was afraid it might turn into another dreadful mistake. . .

'I don't know what I want,' she said honestly.

'I know.' His hand turned and cupped her cheek, and he brushed his thumb gently over her cheek in a soothing, rhythmical gesture that slowed her heart and steadied her trembling limbs. 'OK now?' he murmured, and she nodded.

'How about a cup of coffee before I go?' he said, and she nodded again wordlessly and went through into the kitchen and put the kettle on.

'I lit the fire,' she told him in a strained voice. 'I thought we could go into the sitting room.'

'OK.'

He helped her clear up while the kettle boiled, and then they took their mugs through to the sitting room and she looked at the sofa and the chairs and hesitated.

'Sit here with me,' he said, taking the initiative and settling himself into one end of the sofa.

Julia sat at the other end, tucking her feet under her bottom and hunching over her mug, and he put out a hand and caressed her toes where they peeped out from under her thigh. Gradually she relaxed and wriggled down a little, so that his hand rested across her foot and the backs of his fingers touched her thigh, the heat of them scorching her.

'Thank you for letting me come to the nativity play,' he said softly after a while. 'It was fun.'

'You must be a masochist,' she said with a little laugh. 'But thanks for coming. Katie was delighted to have you there. I think she misses having a father figure to parade on these occasions.'

She wondered as she said it if he'd think she was hinting, but it was highly unlikely in view of her reluctance to get involved with him. In fact, it was the first time she'd thought of it herself, and she wondered suddenly how much of Katie's invitation had, in fact, stemmed from that. Surely not.

'Don't worry about it,' he said, reading her mind. 'It was just a nativity play. I'm sure lots of children's parents brought guests.'

But male guests—eligible, single, personable male guests? 'I don't want her building up her hopes,' she said worriedly. 'If she gets some ridiculous idea into her head that we're about to get married and starts telling her friends you're her new daddy—'

'Would it be so ridiculous?' he said softly, and her jaw dropped.

'Don't be daft—I hardly know you!'

David shrugged, and for an instant she thought she saw a vulnerability in his eyes that frightened her. Oh, no. Was he taking this more seriously than she'd realised?

'Whatever,' he said evenly. 'I shouldn't worry about Katie. You're borrowing trouble. Tell her we're just friends, if she says anything.'

She nodded and turned her attention back to her coffee, but it was cold. She put the mug down, and as she straightened up again he reached out and caught her hand.

'Come here,' he coaxed, and she was helpless against the gruff appeal of his voice.

She went into his arms, and he kissed her slowly, lingeringly, moving her so that she lay across his lap, her head cradled on his arm and his head bent over her. His lips were gentle but thorough, and she felt heat building in her.

I shouldn't be doing this, she thought, but she couldn't help herself. Her fingers threaded through his hair, drawing him down against her, and he shifted so that his chest lay against hers and she could feel the ragged rise and fall of his ribs and the thunder of his heart on hers.

'You taste amazing,' he murmured, plundering her mouth again, and she almost wept with need.

Touch me, she wanted to cry, and as if he'd heard her, his hand came up and cupped her breast, the fingers firm but gentle. 'Oh, lord, Julia, stop me,' he whispered, but she couldn't. His hand slid under her blouse, finding the edge of her bra and working its way underneath, so that his hot, hard palm cupped the tender mound.

His breath scorched her face, his eyes burning into hers, and with a ragged groan he took her mouth again in a kiss that threatened to rage out of control.

I want him, she thought with the last coherent remnant of her mind. I want him…

Julia forgot about Katie upstairs, forgot about Andrew, forgot about caution and all the reasons why it was such a bad idea. All she could think of was David and getting closer to him.

And then he lifted his head and eased his hand away, and cradled her against his heaving chest, and as the heat cooled slightly, so common sense returned and she realised what she was doing.

Mortified, she struggled out of his arms and stood up, hugging her arms around her waist. She would have given him anything—anything! What had happened to her?

'Julia, don't,' he said softly. He had moved to stand behind her, and his hands cupped her shoulders and drew her back against him. 'It's all right.'

'I'm behaving like a desperate widow,' she said in a high, cracked voice. 'That is *so* awful.'

'No, you're not. You're behaving like a woman. A real, live, hot-blooded woman. You've done nothing wrong, nothing to be ashamed of.'

'Only because you stopped,' she said, horrified at herself. 'I was—'

'What? Aroused? That's not a sin.'

She turned and forced herself to meet his eyes. 'Oh, yes, it is. I've got a daughter upstairs. I forgot that.'

'I didn't.'

'We could have—oh, lord.'

'No, we couldn't. I wouldn't have done that. Not with Katie in the house.'

Julia moved out of his arms and went to the window, parting the curtains and staring out into the night. 'I think you should go,' she said in a strangled voice. 'Please. I didn't mean this to happen.'

'Julia, stop torturing yourself,' he said softly. 'I'll go, but not because anything will happen if I stay. It won't. I promise you. Not until you decide in the cold light of day that you want it to.'

David drew her into his arms and kissed her tenderly, then he went out into the hall. She heard him putting on his coat and collecting his keys, then the soft click of the front door, and she watched through the gap in the curtains as he went down her path and away from her.

She could still feel the heated throb of her body, the gnawing ache of frustration. There was only one thing that would take it away, and it was the one thing she couldn't allow herself to have. She'd decided long ago that love was a luxury she couldn't afford, and nothing had happened to change that.

It was just that now, it seemed a harder sacrifice to make...

So near, and yet so far.

David drove around the block and pulled up a short distance down the road, and watched as the sitting-room light went out and Julia's bedroom light came on a few moments later.

He tried not to think about what she was doing, or what she'd look like without her clothes, but it was next to impossible.

'You're turning into a peeping Tom,' he growled at himself, but he couldn't drive away until that light was off and he knew she was settled for the night.

It was about five minutes before she switched it off, leaving the house almost in darkness. He could just see the slight glow of a light through the front door, probably the landing light reflecting down the stairs, and after a minute or two he started the car and drove slowly home to the cottage.

He made himself a cup of tea, but he didn't want it. What he wanted was Julia, and he couldn't have her.

Not yet, and maybe not ever.

He was frustrated, unhappy and totally at a loss to

know how to proceed. He was falling for her, hard. He'd hoped when he'd met her that she was the right woman for him, and he knew now that she was, just as he knew the sun would rise in the east. He also knew that she was still running scared, and if he could have got his hands on that husband of hers, he would have killed him.

Fortunately the bastard had saved him the effort, probably the only decent thing he'd done in his whole life.

'Oh, Julia,' he said softly in despair, and dropped his head back against the sofa. He could smell her perfume on his sweater, just a light touch of fragrance that seemed uniquely her, and it tormented his already tortured body.

If only he could convince her that he was different, but he couldn't. It would just take time, and he was going to have to tough it out.

There was no way he was going to sleep, he realised. It wasn't even worth trying, so he changed into his work clothes, got out the grouting compound and the squeegee and went into the bathroom. A bit of hard work might settle his libido, if nothing else—and once it was done he could start using the shower.

Cold.

Oh, rats.

CHAPTER SEVEN

'MUMMY, can we see the puppies again soon?'

Julia's heart sank. It was all she needed after her restless night, but Katie had talked about almost nothing else since the weekend, and she knew just how much the little girl would have loved a dog of her own.

If their circumstances had been different, Julia would have loved one as well, but as it was, it just wouldn't be fair, and anyway, Arthur would no doubt object violently.

'Maybe we can go and see them in a day or two,' she stalled, but Katie understood that for what it was and her optimistic little face fell.

'I knew you wouldn't let me go back,' she said, 'and I've got to go to Granny and Grandpa Revell this weekend, so I can't see them then, and after that it's Christmas and the puppies are going—'

'What about my morning off?' Julia suggested, weakening. 'You break up tomorrow, and on Friday I don't have to be at work until twelve, so we could go before you go to Granny and Grandpa, if you like— if Mrs Armstrong doesn't mind.' And David will be at work, she thought, so it'll be safe.

'Ring her,' Katie pleaded, but Julia shook her head. 'Darling, it's only twenty to seven in the morning, and we have to go now, anyway, or I'll be late for work. I'll ring her tonight.'

'Promise,' Katie said, and her mother promised.

She dropped her at the childminder who looked af-

ter her before school, and then pulled up in the car
park at the hospital just as David was getting out of
his car.

'Hi,' he said soberly, and she looked at him, at the
shadows round his eyes and the tiredness on his face,
and thought he'd possibly had an even worse night
than her.

'Hi,' she said, and tried for a smile.

He didn't smile back. Instead he came over to her
and stood in silence for a moment, then rammed a
hand through his hair. 'Look, about last night—things
got out of hand. I didn't mean to push you. I know
you wanted to take things slowly, and I rushed you.
I'm sorry.'

Her silly heart ached for him. 'Don't be sorry. You
didn't do anything I didn't want you to do. That's the
problem. I just think—oh, I don't know. It would be
so easy to go too far, too fast, and I don't want Katie
hurt.'

'I know. I realise that.'

'She wants to see the puppies again,' she told him.
'I don't suppose your mother would let us go over on
Friday morning, would she? I don't have to be in until
late, and Katie's on holiday from tomorrow.'

He grinned a little lopsidedly. 'I'm sure she'd love
it. I was wondering, actually, if you want to go over
there this afternoon, after I finish. I thought maybe
Mum could babysit and we could go out for a drink
and talk.'

'Is there anything to talk about?' she asked, trying
not to let herself get excited at the thought.

David's smile was wry. 'I don't know. I hope so. I
thought we should go somewhere safe and chaper-
oned, and just talk a bit. We only seem to see each

other at work, or in front of Katie, or when we're alone and then we get distracted. That's making it difficult for us to do the normal getting-to-know-each-other things, and I'd like to find out more about you—find out what makes you tick.'

'There's not much to know,' she said, thinking of what a narrow life she led, but he shook his head reprovingly.

'Nonsense. Will you? Would Katie like that?'

'Katie would be ecstatic,' she said drily.

'And you?'

I'd be ecstatic, too, Julia thought, but she wasn't telling him that! 'I dare say I could tolerate it,' she said with a smile, and he winked at her.

'Good girl,' he said approvingly.

She stood there for a second, just enjoying the smile in his eyes, and then collected herself with a start.

'What am I thinking about? I'll be late—I can't stand here chatting!'

'Any chance of a cup of tea?'

'What—now you've made me late?' She laughed, running towards the door. 'What do you think?'

He followed her, going into the kitchen and putting the kettle on while she took report from Angie Featherstone, and then he came into the office and handed her a mug of tea, settling himself down on the other side of the desk with his own mug and a lazy smile.

'So, anything exciting happen in the night?' he asked.

'Not really. You've got something white on your eyebrow, by the way. It looks like paint.'

He stood up and went over to the little mirror behind the door, and picked at the white mark.

'Grout,' he said in disgust, and she stifled a laugh.

'Grout?' she echoed, and he gave her a black look in the mirror.

'You heard.'

She couldn't hold back the smile, but neither could he, and they ended up laughing together. It felt good, she thought in surprise. Natural.

Wonderful, actually.

'What time tonight?' she asked, suddenly looking forward to their drink.

'I should be able to get away about six. We shouldn't be too late really, because of Katie, I suppose. Mum could feed her, and we could have a meal in the pub. Does that sound OK?'

'It sounds good.'

'I'll pick you up after I finish, then. I must go. I've got some paperwork to do with my secretary this morning and I want to look through the notes again. Do I need to see anyone on the ward while I'm here?'

Julia shook her head. 'Not that I know of. Your registrar or SHO should be able to cope today. I'll see if Mr Burrows is all right—he's the only one I'm worried about. Do you think he should be talking to the oncologist now?'

He nodded. 'Probably. He'll take over treatment as soon as Mr Burrows has healed from the surgery. I'll ring him and have a word—perhaps we'll talk to him together. Whatever. I'll see you later. Ring me if you want me.'

That again, she thought, but this time she smiled. They were going out together somewhere safe, where they could just talk, and perhaps that was just what they needed. A chance to get to know each other without being distracted by their hormones. And maybe, just maybe, she might learn to trust him.

The phone rang, distracting her from her thoughts. It was A and E, to say that an elderly lady suffering from a perforated bowel had been admitted directly to Theatre, and to stand by to expect her.

She put the phone down and was on her way to shuffle beds to make room when Nick Sarazin came onto the ward.

'Ah, Julia,' he said, and her heart sank. He was the last person she needed to see after bumping into him last night at the nativity play. Judging by the sparkle in his eyes, he wasn't about to allow her to get away with it.

'I gather you've got an admission from A and E,' she said, trying to head him off, but he wouldn't be deflected.

'Yes, I'm going up now. I was just coming to warn you but someone's done it. I'll fit her in first, obviously.' He cocked his head on one side and smiled at her inquisitively. 'So, you and David—what's the story?'

'No story. He's a friend,' she said firmly, but one brow shot up into a disbelieving arch and he snorted under his breath.

'Pull the other. He couldn't take his eyes off you.'

'Really?' she said lightly. 'I didn't notice.'

'Then you must be more dead than alive,' he retorted, but he seemed to relent, his tone gentling. 'He's a nice guy, Julia. You might do worse than to give him a chance.'

'We know very little about him,' she pointed out.

'That's rubbish. He went to a nativity play, for heaven's sake, because your daughter asked him to.

He comes in early to talk to patients, and stays late if necessary. He likes children and animals. He's kind. What more could you want to know?'

'How do you know he likes animals?' she said sharply, and Nick laughed.

'I don't. I'm just guessing. Am I right?'

She coloured and laughed despite herself. 'Yes, dammit, you are.'

'So there. I rest my case—and now I'm off to Theatre. See you later.'

He left the ward and she went on her bed hunt, running her conversation with Nick through her mind. Had David really been unable to take his eyes off her? She'd thought he'd been watching the play, but she'd been so busy watching it herself she couldn't be sure. And Nick was right—David was a kind person.

Which was more than could ever have been said about Andrew!

Still, it was a big step to take, and she'd need more than kindness to convince her to take it.

Her bed-shuffling done, she went to see Mr Burrows and found him propped up on his pillows, writing something on a spiral-bound notepad. She perched on the edge of the bed and smiled at him.

'Hi, there. How are you doing?' she asked, and he smiled back tiredly and shrugged.

'Oh, so-so. Just making lists of things to do. I don't want to forget something important.'

'I think you are forgetting something important,' she said gently. 'You're forgetting to rest.'

'I can't rest—not until I'm sure I've done everything. I have to talk to my solicitor.'

'The oncologist is going to be coming to see you soon about your treatment,' she told him. 'You need to rest and get well enough for that, and it will give you more time to do things afterwards. There's no desperate rush.'

He smiled fretfully at her. 'I know, but I just feel useless lying here, and it takes my mind off it.'

'Can I get you something to do? Maybe the occupational therapist has got something simple you could be doing in a day or two to keep your mind busy. Shall I ask her to come and see you?'

'OK.'

'And you are remembering to do your leg exercises every hour to keep your blood moving in your legs, aren't you?'

'Yes. Well, mostly.'

'Try and remember. Let me check your stockings are up properly,' she said, and straightened the top of one that was threatening to roll down. All the patients wore graduated pressure stockings to prevent the blood pooling and clotting in their legs during and after surgery, and keeping them smooth was one of the banes of her life.

'That's better,' she said, and listened to his abdomen with a stethoscope. 'No bowel sounds yet, are there? Are you feeling any movement? Any wind?'

'I can feel wind inside, but it's not shifting.'

'You'll feel better when it does,' she assured him. 'Your wound's healing nicely, anyway.'

'I suppose I should be grateful for small mercies,' he said with a fleeting smile, and she wondered what it was like to be handed a death sentence at fifty-eight.

Grim.

'I'll get the OT lady to see you when she's next on the ward—and in the meantime you rest, please.'

He put the pad down and sighed. 'I am tired, actually.'

'And in pain. Don't overdo it, it's only your second day post-op and it was major surgery. I'll get one of the health care assistants to come and give you a mouthwash, then I want you to settle down for a sleep, otherwise I'll get Mr Armstrong to write you up for a sedative and we'll make sure you rest.'

He smiled wearily, and she left him with his eyes shut and found someone to go and make him comfortable, because Nick's lady from A and E had come back from Theatre and was needing her attention.

She put Mrs Harrison into the other single room opposite the nursing station, next to Mr Burrows. That way she could keep an eye on her from the nursing station once she didn't need such intensive attention, but in the meantime she'd need specialist nursing from someone designated to the task.

In view of her general frailty, Julia decided to do it herself, and handed the running of the ward over to Sally, her staff nurse.

There were lots of machines to monitor. The intravenous analgesic pump that delivered painkillers at a steady rate, the heart and oxygen monitors, the automatic blood pressure monitor—all had to be watched and checked to make sure they were working properly, and the results noted at regular intervals. Mrs Harrison's temperature was high and needed a constant eye kept on it to make sure it didn't rise.

Then the wound drain, the urinary catheter and IV line all had to be watched for potential problems, and the patient had to be turned and repositioned at regular intervals even though she was on a low air loss bed to prevent pressure sores.

She'd had a temporary colostomy to allow her bowel to recover, and the stoma had to be cared for very carefully until it had healed. There was a stoma nurse who would come and deal with it after the immediate post-op period, but for now it was Julia's job.

Nick came down at lunchtime after his list was finished to check on his patient, and he gave Julia a run-down on her operation.

'She's had diverticular disease for years, apparently, and she'd been feeling rough for a while but hadn't said anything. A neighbour raised the alarm this morning and they found her collapsed in bed. She's lucky to be alive, but she's got raging peritonitis. We may lose her yet. I hope not. I flushed her out with anti-biotic solution, and she's got antibiotics IV, but she's pretty weak.'

'She seems to be holding at the moment,' Julia said thoughtfully. 'Some of these elderly ladies are as tough as old boots. They seem indestructible.'

'I know. Well, we can only hope she's one of them. Her daughter's on her way from the Midlands—she should be here any time. I'll come and talk to her if you give me a call when she arrives.'

'OK. Thanks.'

Nick looked out of the door and grinned, then popped his head back inside. 'Lover-boy's here,' he whispered teasingly, and ducked out of the way before she could summon a reply.

She heard him talking to David outside, and her heart fluttered betrayingly. Seconds later David came into the room and smiled, and her heart flipped right over.

Anatomically impossible, but that was what it felt like.

'Hi,' he said softly, and she found herself grinning inanely.

'Hi, yourself. How was your paperwork?'

'Boring. I've left my secretary to deal with it. How are you?'

'Oh, pretty busy. I'm specialling Mrs Harrison here. She had a perforated bowel.'

He nodded. 'I heard. I rang my mother—she's happy for us to drop Katie over there this evening.'

'Oh—right. Thanks.'

'Don't thank me,' he said with a lazy, sexy smile. 'I have a vested interest in this evening.'

'So you do,' she said, her heart skittering again, and she wondered if he'd ever be able to smile at her without doing things to her insides.

'I'll see you later—I'm just going down to my clinic. If it's nice and straightforward, I might even get away early, but don't hold your breath.'

'I won't,' she promised, but in the end she did, of course, haunting the front window from five thirty onwards.

A watched kettle and all that, she thought at five past six, and went into the kitchen to feed the importuning cat again and make sure he had fresh water. 'You're getting fat, Arthur,' she told him, and he mewed tragically at her until she put his dish down. He dived headlong into it and crunched up the food with great enthusiasm. 'Perhaps you've got worms,' she said drily. 'Or maybe you're just a pig.'

Nevertheless, she got David to hold him when he arrived a few minutes later so she could stuff a worming tablet down his throat, just to be on the safe side. She was always very fussy because of Katie, even though she knew she was probably worrying unnecessarily. She wormed Arthur regularly every month after all, which according to the vet should be enough for even the most voracious hunter.

'He's just a big cat,' David reassured her. 'We've got one on the farm that looks like him.'

'Leo,' Katie said authoritatively. 'I've met him. He's even bigger.'

'I think he might be. Right, are we ready?'

Katie hopped excitedly from foot to foot. 'I am, I am. Can we go?'

Julia laughed and ruffled her hair. 'All right, pumpkin. Come on.'

She reached for her coat and found it taken out of her hands and held for her, David's hands snuggling it round her neck before releasing it. Just another of the thoughtful little things he did instinctively, she thought, and stored it away in her mental filing cabinet.

By the time she'd buttoned it he'd got Katie wrapped up in her coat, and he ushered them out to his car and whisked them through the traffic and out into the country on the back roads.

They called in at the cottage so he could change into something less formal and, true to his word, he left them in the car for only two minutes, reappearing in casual cotton trousers and a rugby shirt with a thick sweater over the top.

'That's better. I hate ties,' he said with a grin, and they set off again for the farm.

'Oh, they've grown!' Katie exclaimed as they entered the kitchen and saw the puppies.

'They do. They grow really fast at this age,' Mrs Armstrong said. 'You're just in time to help me feed them, and then you can have supper with us.'

David's father came out of his study to say hello, and Julia couldn't help but notice the natural and friendly way he greeted both her and Katie.

'So, young 'un, how was the nativity play? I gather you were a very wonderful lamb,' he said, and Katie giggled.

'Did David tell you?' she asked, and he nodded.

'Certainly did. I hope we get to see a photo.'

'Oh, they take lots of photos,' Julia assured him. 'No doubt I'll have to buy them all.'

'Of course,' Mrs Armstrong said with a laugh. 'We've got hundreds of such photos—some of them of David. Remind me to show you the baby photos one day.'

'I think not,' David said, colouring slightly, and he ushered Julia towards the door. 'If you two are quite happy for us to go, I think we'll make a move. I feel a steak calling me.'

'Bye, darling,' Julia said, but Katie was in the playpen with the puppies already and hardly spared her a glance.

'So, where are we going?' she asked to break the silence in the car.

'The village pub. It's excellent, and they have a log fire. At this time of night we'll probably be able to get a seat near it in the corner—unless you want to eat in the restaurant?'

'Not really,' she said. 'Well, I don't mind, but I'm not really dressed for formal dining.'

'Nor am I, not now,' he said with what sounded like relief. 'We'll eat in the bar.'

He was right, it was a lovely pub, and the food was wonderful. They tucked themselves away in the corner by the fire, and they talked. David told her about himself—about his training in London, his various jobs around the country, his yearning to be back in his native Suffolk—and he asked Julia about herself.

'You've hardly told me anything about yourself,' he said with gentle reproach. 'You've told me about Andrew, and Katie, but almost nothing about you.'

She shrugged diffidently. 'I'm not that interesting.'

'You are to me.'

He seemed to mean it, so she told him about her childhood in Hampshire, and her parents' move to Lancashire when she was sixteen, a social disaster for her and very unsettling.

'I had to leave all my friends, and it really was very hard, breaking into a new group in the sixth form. I didn't do as well in my A-levels as I'd been expected to and, instead of doing physiotherapy, I ended up on a nursing course, which actually in the end has probably suited me better.'

'So how did you meet Andrew?' he asked quietly, and she sighed.

'Oh, after I'd qualified and got a job nearer home. He was on a fast track to the top, and he'd been posted to Blackburn to run a new branch of the company he worked for. I met him at a friend's house, at a party, and he was funny and charming and he made me feel special.'

Julia fell silent, remembering how easy it had been for him to seduce the almost innocent girl she'd been, and she sighed.

'I take it that didn't last.'

'Only until I had Katie. He changed. Well, no, maybe he didn't, but I did. I was a mother. I was tired, and my priorities shifted. He didn't like that.'

'Men often don't. They feel neglected.'

'So I found out.' She stopped, not wanting to go on. There were things she didn't want to talk about—the demands he'd made on her, the way he'd expected her to welcome his advances so soon after the birth, the impatience with which he'd greeted her slow recovery.

Andrew had been insatiable, jealous and ever more critical of her figure and performance, both in bed and out of it, and then he'd left her, her confidence in rags, her self-image devastated.

Julia shook her head, remembering, and David squeezed her knee. She glanced up at him and he smiled gently. 'Tell me about you,' he coaxed. 'What's your favourite colour?'

'Silver,' she said, thinking of his eyes, and he smiled again.

'So you like my car, then.'

'Amongst other things. Moonlight. Water. Your eyes.'

'My eyes?'

'They're silver,' she said, and his mouth quirked fleetingly.

'Really?'

'Really.'

'I always thought they were grey.'

'No,' she corrected. 'Mine are grey. Yours are silver.'

'OK. What's your favourite sort of music?'

'Oh, easy. I like cheesy pop music.'

'Good grief,' he said, looking shocked.

'Don't tell me, you're a classical fan,' she teased, and he nodded.

'Absolutely. I like quiet, pure music, like plainsong

and church music. Choristers, piano, the flute—simple sounds. Nothing brash.'

She nodded. 'I could probably tolerate that.'

'Big of you.'

She chuckled. 'So, what about you. What's your favourite colour?'

'Green. Soft, willow green, shivering in the breeze. The brilliant acid green of opening leaves in the spring, and rich long grass, and glossy holly leaves—'

'That's about four different greens.'

'Very likely. It's the one colour that was lacking in London, except in the parks, and I didn't have very much time to go and sit in them when I was training. And I hate hospital green with a passion.'

'Ditto,' she said, laughing, and he leant over and kissed her cheek.

'There, we agree on something,' he said, and their eyes meshed and held.

'So, what about films?' he asked.

'*The Horse Whisperer*—and *Elizabeth*.'

'Not *Armageddon?*'

'No. I hate sad films.'

'*The Horse Whisperer* is sad.'

'Well, yes, but it's sort of right.'

'So is *Armageddon*.'

Julia laughed. 'We'll have to agree to differ again.'

Their conversation moved on, touching on medical things and ending with a deep and fundamental disagreement on embryo research. In the end she fell silent, and David cocked his head on one side and looked at her.

'What's the matter?'

She shrugged. 'Nothing.' But it wasn't nothing.

They seemed to be differing on a lot of things, she thought, her earlier cheerfulness dwindling. Oh, dear.

She looked up at him and shook her head, dredging up a smile again. 'It's nothing,' she said again, but he seemed to understand.

'It is nothing. Don't worry about it,' he murmured, reading her mind. 'We're allowed to be different. That's what makes the world go round.'

'Thought that was love.'

'Well, that, too,' he said with a grin. 'But I was trying to steer clear of the subject—like sex and politics. Always dangerous.' He glanced at his watch. 'We ought to be going. It's nearly nine, and Katie's got school tomorrow, hasn't she?'

Guilt swamped her. 'Yes—oh, lord, I had no idea it was so late.'

'She'll live. They won't do anything very much at school tomorrow anyway. You never do at the end of term, and particularly not when you're five.'

'Nearly six,' she reminded him. 'She's six in January.'

'I'd better start saving,' he murmured, helping her into her coat. 'No doubt it will cost a fortune to distract her from the idea of a puppy.'

Julia rolled her eyes. 'Well, I'll let you deal with that one,' she said, 'since it's your fault, but I'd be grateful if you didn't spend a fortune on her, as I can't afford to match it.'

David paused in the act of shrugging on his coat, and frowned slightly. 'I was joking,' he said mildly. 'I don't believe in spoiling children—well, not like that, anyway.'

She let out a little sigh. 'Another thing we agree on,

then,' she said lightly. 'Come on, let's go while we're winning.'

But it didn't feel like they were winning, and when he dropped her off at the house with a chaste peck on the cheek in deference to Katie's presence, she was if anything more confused than ever...

CHAPTER EIGHT

FORTUNATELY for Julia, Mrs Harrison was still very poorly the following day and so she was able to tuck herself away with the frail patient and watch her closely.

She was still on quarter-hourly observations, and Julia felt she should really have been in ICU, but it wasn't possible because as usual they were full. Besides, she was quite happy to have the opportunity to do a little intensive nursing for a change instead of admin, which seemed to be the way her job was going these days.

Mrs Harrison's daughter was with her, and they talked through her operation and the expected programme of her recovery in between Julia's checking and noting. She didn't really have a minute to herself, which suited her. She had too much time to think these days, and she just wanted some time out. Being closeted with Mrs H. and her daughter was a good way of doing it.

And, she thought, it had the added advantage of taking her out of circulation, so she could avoid cosy little chats with David.

Or so she hoped, at least. At lunchtime, Sally stuck her head round the door and told her to go for lunch.

'I'll take over. You can't have all the fun—and Mr Armstrong wants you to join him. Said something about a patient conference.'

Julia muttered something disbelieving under her

breath and went out to find David lounging against the wall looking expectant.

'Ready? Get your coat.'

'Where are we going and why?' she asked, but he just smiled.

'Secret. Come on.'

'I thought this was a patient conference?' she said mildly, allowing him to engineer her down to the car park entrance.

'Just a ruse to get you into my clutches,' he said with an unrepentant grin. Feeling highly dubious but intrigued for all that, she let him put her into his car, and they drove out into the countryside just minutes away.

There he parked, on a rise looking over a pretty river valley, and with a flourish like a magician he produced a cardboard box from the back seat and put it on the space between their seats.

'*Voilà!*' he said, and she laughed softly.

'What is that?' she asked.

'Lunch. I hate canteen food, and I wanted to talk to you after last night. You looked worried.'

She felt her smile slip. 'We disagreed on so many things.'

'Not that many—and, anyway, we're allowed to disagree. It makes life more interesting.' He opened the carton and peered in. 'Here—prawn salad sandwiches, chicken legs, cherry tomatoes—what's in this little pot? Pasta salad—and plastic forks. We'll have to share. Think we can manage that?'

'I expect so,' she said, peering into the box and suddenly realising how hungry she was.

David picked up a chicken leg and gestured at the box with it as she hesitated. 'Come on, it's not a spectator sport,' he teased, and she helped herself to a sandwich bursting with fat, juicy prawns and crisp shreds of salad.

'So where did this lot come from?' she mumbled with her mouth full.

'A sandwich firm in town. I got them to deliver it.'

That shocked her a little, even though she knew he earned good money and only had himself to spend it on. 'How extravagant,' she scolded mildly, but he shook his head.

'Not really. We have to eat, and they deliver to the hospital anyway. Besides, you aren't supposed to look a gift horse in the mouth and all that. Now eat.'

Julia did, and it was wonderful. She didn't buy his story that it wasn't extravagant, but she was too hungry to care and it was nice to be alone with him, although she'd been trying to forget about him all morning.

Unsuccessfully, she realised.

'You've been hiding from me,' he said, reading her mind again.

'I know. I just wanted some thinking time.'

'And?'

She smiled ruefully. 'I'm still thinking.'

'Want to think out loud?'

She shook her head. 'You won't want to hear it.'

'Andrew again?'

'We had nothing in common,' she told him heavily. 'We differed in so many respects, and I was never allowed an opinion. If I disagreed with him, I was an idiot.'

'Arrogant bastard.'

'You and I disagreed,' she reminded him. 'Last

night, about embryo research. We disagreed really quite fundamentally.'

'That doesn't mean you aren't allowed your opinion,' he pointed out, and put a chicken leg in her hand. 'Eat.'

She ate, wondering if he really meant it or if, given time, he'd start to erode her personality as Andrew had done. It was so insidious, that was the trouble. It had taken ages before she'd realised what had been happening to her.

They shared the pasta salad, David feeding them alternate forkfuls, and he opened the bottle of spring water and poured her some into a plastic cup before sitting back with a sigh and looking out over the gently rolling landscape.

'I love this part of Suffolk,' he said softly. 'I really missed it.'

'I missed Hampshire when we moved—the downs near Winchester, the New Forest. It seemed very wet and cold and forbidding in Lancashire after that.'

'I'm sure.' He tilted his head and looked at her searchingly. 'Do you want to go back to Hampshire?'

She shook her head. 'Only to visit. This is my home now, and Katie's home. We've got roots here, even if they are a little damaged from being transplanted so many times.'

'Is that gardening talk?' he teased laughingly, and she smiled.

'You know, I'd love to learn a bit about gardening,' she said wistfully.

'I'll teach you. You can help me at the cottage, if you like, and we can sort your garden out and make it pretty for you.'

She snorted. 'That won't take long, it's only tiny.'

'It could still be lovely, I'm sure. I'll have a look next time I'm there—if you like.'

Yet another thread that would weave them together, she thought, but she found herself agreeing anyway. It was only the garden, after all.

'We ought to get back,' she said, looking at her watch, and David nodded.

'I know, but there's something I want to do first,' he said. Taking the carton, he put it into the back of the car and then drew her into his arms and kissed her.

It was a gentle kiss, almost without passion, but then he lifted his head and looked down into her eyes, and kissed her again.

This kiss was far from gentle. It was a deep, searching kiss, a yearning kiss, and it started an ache inside her that hadn't really gone away since the last time. And this time, when he lifted his head, it wasn't sunshine that gleamed through his quicksilver eyes but desire, hard and hot and urgent, and it turned her to jelly.

'Hell's teeth,' he muttered, and dragged himself back behind the wheel, closing his eyes and dropping his head back against the headrest. 'I have to go back to work. I have a clinic. I have to talk to patients, and all I'm going to be able to think about is you. I'll disgrace myself.'

'It's your fault,' she pointed out, wondering if her heart would slow down before it gave up the unequal struggle and just stopped permanently. 'You didn't have to do that.'

He rolled his head towards her and gave a strangled laugh. 'Oh, yes, I did,' he said softly and, sitting up, he started the engine, clipped on his seat belt and

backed out of the gateway, turning back towards
Audley and reality.

And not before time, Julia thought with a little bubble of panic.

She almost ran back to the ward, and as she went
into Mrs Harrison's room, Sally looked up and her
eyes widened.

'Good lunch?' she asked, and Julia nodded.

'You might like to go and sort your hair out—it's
falling down,' Sally pointed out, and Julia looked in
the mirror over the basin and groaned inwardly. It was
a good job Mrs Harrison's daughter was having a
lunch break, she thought, because she looked thoroughly and comprehensively kissed.

She pulled the band out of her hair, scraped it back
again and twisted it up into a bun, securing it again
with another twist of the scrunchie. Better.

She turned and gave Sally a level look. 'I'll take
over again now,' she said, and Sally shut her mouth,
handed over the charts and left without a word.

Julia said goodbye to Katie the following morning
with reluctance. They'd spent a little while at the farm
with the puppies, and she'd had coffee with Mrs
Armstrong and had tried hard not to get dragged into
conversation about David.

When they were leaving, his mother drew her to
one side and said softly, 'Think about Christmas. You
don't have to decide beforehand. Just come—even if
you wake up on Christmas morning and want to come
over, you'd be welcome. Or even on Christmas Eve,
if you just want to come for a drink in the evening.
We'll all be here.'

'Thank you,' Julia murmured, knowing full well she

had no intention of joining them at any time but wishing that she could. She removed Katie yet again from the puppies and took her back to the house to wash and change before she left. The Revells picked her up at eleven-thirty, on time for once, and Julia arrived at work for twelve with the knowledge that the weekend stretched ahead of her emptily. She was working on Sunday, but Saturday was a yawning void and she wondered if anyone wanted to swap shifts.

No. She had to do some Christmas shopping with the few pounds she had available. Should she buy David something? If so, she had no idea what. She didn't have enough money to get anything worthwhile, and she couldn't imagine he'd want anything she could make.

Even a cake would be heartily outdone by his mother's everyday offerings.

Oh, rats.

She found Mr Burrows restless and unsettled, and impatient to get on with the remaining months of his life. 'I don't have time to lie here,' he fretted, and she had to talk to him again about resting to speed his recovery.

'If you don't rest, it will take longer, so you'll just have to be patient,' she reminded him, and took his notepad away again. 'Now, lie back and count sheep or something.'

'I'll count bullying nurses,' he said with a smile, and Julia squeezed his hand and left him to it, going into the room next door to see Nick's patient with the perforated bowel.

Mrs Harrison seemed to have turned the corner with her peritonitis, and Julia was pleased to see her daughter sitting with her again. She was waking up more now and talking, and her daughter sat beside her with her knitting and chatted to her when she was awake. The rhythmic clicking of the needles seemed to comfort the elderly woman when she had her eyes closed, because she knew her daughter was still there by her side.

She didn't need observing so closely now, but she still needed checking every half hour and turning and, of course, she had to have the physio to keep her chest and legs moving.

'Wiggle your feet for me,' Julia would say every half-hour when she turned her, and Mrs Harrison would move her feet a little to help pump the blood back from her calves.

She got the daughter in on the act, and she proved to be a most useful helper, and reliable enough for some of the routine tasks to be handed over to her.

'How long are you here for?' Julia asked.

'Till Christmas. She was coming to us, but I don't suppose she can now. I've got the children coming with their other halves and the grandchildren, so I have to go back home, but I'll be back again afterwards if she needs me, and she can come to us to convalesce.'

'I won't need to come to you, I'll be going home,' Mrs Harrison said confidently, but Julia wasn't so sure. Her recovery was going to be long and slow. She was nearly eighty, after all, and she'd been extremely ill. Still, time would tell.

The end of her shift came with the arrival of Angie Featherstone, and she handed over and went home to a house that seemed empty and bleak. She'd need to buy a tree ready to put up with Katie on Christmas Eve, and she had to go shopping for food for Christmas and also presents.

She'd done the presents from Katie to her grandparents, and presents to her own parents and siblings had been posted ages ago, but she still hadn't got anything for Katie.

Or David.

She tried to watch television, but there was nothing on that caught her attention, so she made a hot drink and went to bed, and early the next morning she got up and walked down into town to do her Christmas shopping. It was Saturday, two and a half shopping days to Christmas, and already by nine o'clock it was heaving.

It was a horrible day, cold and damp with a blustery wind that cut right through her, and she ducked from shop to shop, fruitlessly searching for anything to give either Katie or David. Time after time she drew a blank, and just when she was despairing of ever finding anything, she saw an old print of Little Soham, with David's cottage in it, in the window of an art shop in the middle of town.

It was perfect, and she was just going through the door to ask for it when a sudden gust of wind caught her and pushed her against the wall. People laughed and leant into the wind, hats and scarves flying, and then suddenly there was a grinding, tearing noise and the laughter turned to screams of terror as the tarpaulin-clad scaffolding on the front of a shop toppled slowly outwards and crashed down onto the packed precinct.

There was the sound of splintering plate-glass windows, and flying glass hurtled through the air in all directions, slashing through the panicked crowd and cutting them down like ninepins.

For a moment there was shocked silence, and then the screams started.

'Oh, my God,' Julia whispered, her skin crawling with horror, and as she looked around she saw blood everywhere.

'Call the emergency services!' she snapped. 'Tell them it's a major incident and they'll need medical teams out here fast.'

'Right,' the man behind the counter said, startled, and she ran out into the street. Oh, lord, where to start?

People were running round in panic, crawling on the ground and cutting themselves trying to find their relatives, and the screaming was horrendous.

Then a deep, authoritative voice cut through the panic and silenced them.

'Everybody keep still! Stop moving and wait for help to come to you. If anyone has any first-aid experience, please come over here.'

'David,' she said, relief flooding through her, and she picked her way across to him. 'I'm here,' she said, and he closed his eyes for a moment, then opened them again and gave her a shaky smile.

'Good,' he said, and he sounded stunned for a moment, then pulled himself together. 'Start with triage. There are some hideous injuries—and mind the blood. Remember the risks.'

'I'm a nurse,' someone said, and another woman ran up and said she was a GP. Someone from a pharmacy brought out a box of latex gloves, and the first aid volunteers helped themselves, then looked to David for further instructions.

'Come with me,' Julia said, and they waded into the sobbing crowd, scanning for priority cases.

'Help me,' people were saying, but they could only

do so much, and when the sirens sounded just moments later, Julia heaved a sigh of relief.

David and a group of strong men had lifted the scaffolding off the people trapped under it, propping it up on things dragged from shops to support the poles so rescue workers could get underneath and assess the injuries.

Now she could see him working on someone just a few feet away, and he lifted his head and hailed the paramedics.

'Major arterial bleed here,' he said, and they ran over to him and relieved him so that he could continue with his triage.

He scanned the area and beckoned Julia, who had just tied a scarf tightly round a bleeding arm to staunch the flow.

'What is it?' she asked, and he drew her into the shop immediately opposite the scaffolding, where they picked their way carefully over the shattered glass.

The shop had been packed, and as the ends of the poles had come through the window the glass had flown in and caused mayhem.

'This isn't going to be nice,' he warned, and she looked around and her hand came up to cover her mouth.

'Oh, lord,' she said, gagging slightly.

'Come on,' he said bracingly. 'You've seen worse.'

She wasn't sure that she had. Following him and trying to scrape together her professionalism, she stepped over the decapitated body of a woman and followed him into the devastated interior.

They worked for nearly an hour, and then David decided they'd be more use at the hospital. 'They'll need emergency surgical teams,' he told her. 'We could open up a theatre—will you scrub for me? Have you got time?'

'Sure,' she said, all too ready to get back to the clinical order of the hospital instead of the pandemonium of the shattered street.

Within half an hour they were in Theatre, repairing the damage done by flying glass and shattered shop-fittings. Some of the injuries were straightforward, others much more complicated and life-threatening.

Pregnant women, terrified children, old men who'd lost their wives in the chaos and were worried to death—all came through their hands and were repaired and sent off to be slotted into corridors and odd nooks and crannies and sorted out by the police and medical social workers so they could be reunited with their loved ones.

They were working until nearly six that night with only a short break between cases while the theatre was cleaned, and by the time the last casualty was stitched up and put to bed they were dropping with exhaustion.

'Come on,' David said firmly to her as she slumped in the changing room. 'I'm taking you home.'

'My clothes are covered in blood,' she told him, almost in a trance.

'Stay in your scrubs. My car'll warm up fast.'

She nodded. 'I need to have a shower, but I just want to get out of here.'

'Me, too. Let's go to your place and pick up some clothes, and then go over to the cottage and wash and change and have something to eat. You don't need to be alone this evening and neither do I.'

She nodded again and went with him, content to let him take over. She felt too tired and shocked to argue, and her house was too empty without Katie. She grabbed a few things from her bedroom and ran back down, fed Arthur and went back out to David's warm car with a feeling of relief.

It was cosy and safe and there was something hugely comforting about his presence.

The cottage when they got there was warm, because the woodburner had been alight earlier and the embers were still glowing.

'You go and shower,' he told her firmly, 'I'll get the fire going and start supper.'

Julia ran upstairs and went into the bathroom and turned on the taps, but the water ran with blood and she stared at it and started to cry helplessly, great shaking sobs that racked her body and ripped through her, tearing her apart.

'Julia? Let me in. Julia!'

She stumbled to the door and opened it, falling into David's arms, and he held her tight and rocked her wordlessly.

'It's the blood,' she wept. 'All I can see is the blood.'

'It's all right,' he soothed, and, leading her back into the bathroom, he perched on the side of the bath and turned off the taps, then pulled her down onto his lap, cradling her against his chest. 'Shh. It's all right. I've got you.'

She shuddered in his arms, and his hands came up and rubbed her shoulders soothingly.

'It was just so awful,' she said emptily. 'Just before Christmas. Those poor people.'

'I thought you were under it,' he said. 'I'd seen you a moment before, and then I lost you in the crowd. When it came down…'

He broke off, his arms tightening, and she slid her

arms around his chest and hugged him back. 'I'm fine. I'm here.'

'I know.'

He lifted her to her feet and stood up, then peeled the top of her scrubs off. Her bra followed, then her trousers and shoes and pants, until she was standing naked in front of him.

He turned on the shower, stripped off his clothes and lifted her into the bath with him, pulling the curtain round them and holding her against him under the stream of hot water. After a moment she relaxed, and he reached for the shampoo, washed her hair and rinsed it and then soaped her, scrubbing her arms and hands to get rid of the memory of the blood.

She did the same for him, her fingers working through his scalp, running over his body, lathering him until he was so clean he nearly squeaked.

And then suddenly something changed, and they stood face to face under the stinging spray and their eyes locked.

'Oh, lord, Julia, forgive me,' he said raggedly, and his mouth came down over hers and he kissed her with all the pent-up yearning of the last few weeks.

She kissed him back, pressing herself against him, winding her limbs around his and sobbing his name, and then he lifted her against him, propping her against the tiles and driving into her until she screamed his name and fell apart, her body convulsing around him, and she felt the heavy, pulsing throb of his climax as he spilled deep inside her with a shuddering cry.

For a long moment they stayed there, motionless under the stream of the shower, and then David lowered her gently to her feet and wrapped her hard against his chest, his lips pressed to her head.

'Are you all right?' he said gruffly, and she nodded against his chest.

In fact, she wasn't sure. Her legs felt like jelly, her heart was still racing and in the back of her mind was a nagging thought that wouldn't quite come into focus.

He turned off the water, stepped out of the bath and wrapped himself in a towel, then swathed her in another one and lifted her out like a child, settling her on his lap as he perched on the loo seat and rubbed her gently dry.

'I didn't mean that to happen,' he said softly. 'I'm sorry. And we didn't think about contraception.'

The thought focused.

'Ah,' she said. 'No.'

'I'm sorry. It didn't seem like a priority at the time. Are you likely to get pregnant?'

She shook her head. 'No. I've got a coil. I had it put in after Katie, and I've never done anything about it. I suppose it's still all right.'

She felt the tension go out of him, and he hugged her gently against his chest.

'Good,' he said. 'And just in case you're worried, you won't catch anything from me. I've always been very careful.'

She stared at him, shocked. It had never occurred to her to think otherwise, and she realised how long she'd been out of circulation. 'David, I never even thought of it,' she said honestly.

'You should.'

'I've never needed to.'

He sighed and stroked her wet hair back from her face. 'Come on, let's get you dried and dressed and downstairs by the fire,' he murmured. Lifting her to her feet, he towelled her briskly and propelled her into the bedroom. It was chilly and she dressed quickly, suddenly shy of being naked in front of him.

Ridiculous after what had just happened, but nevertheless. Her body was nothing to write home about, her breasts changed by pregnancy and lactation, her abdomen still slightly curved below the waist from childbirth and lined here and there with stretch marks.

Andrew had been shocked at the change in her, and no amount of exercise or skin care had been able to eradicate the damage. David obviously hadn't seen it, but now suddenly Julia was desperately conscious of it and dragged her clothes on hastily before he could notice.

'I forgot socks,' she said in dismay, looking down at her cold feet.

'No problem.' He pulled open a drawer, fished out a pair of soft, thick socks and threw them at her. 'Right, let's get downstairs by that fire,' he said, tugging a jumper over his head and picking up another pair of socks for himself. He ushered her down to the sitting room, tucked her up by the fire and poured her a glass of wine, then pulled on his socks, went out to the kitchen and came back with a tray of bread and cheese and fruit cake.

'It's a bit scratch, but it'll fill a hole,' he said, and set it down on the toolbox. 'Tuck in.'

She did, suddenly starving, and when they'd eaten their fill and finished the wine he looked across at her and held out his hand.

'Come to bed with me,' he said, and the need she'd thought was slaked rose up again so that the breath jammed in her lungs and her heart skidded against her ribs. Putting her hand in his, she stood up with him and followed him up the stairs to his room.

Then the shyness came back, and when he'd stripped off his clothes she was still standing there fully dressed, her arms wrapped around her waist, her confidence fading by the second.

'Julia?' he murmured.

'Can we turn off the lights?'

He laughed softly. 'Why? You're lovely. I want to see you.'

'I'm not lovely,' she protested. 'My boobs droop and my stomach sags and I've got stretch marks...'

He laughed at her, just for a moment, then he realised she was serious and he drew her stiff, unyielding body into his arms and rocked her hard against his chest.

'Oh, you silly girl. That isn't what it's all about. Come on.'

'Please. I want the light off.'

'OK.'

He turned the top light off, but left the landing light on and the door open slightly, so they could see to move around the room. She turned away and removed her clothes, then slid between the chilly sheets with a shiver.

'Are you OK?' he asked, but she shook her head.

'It's been such an awful day,' she said, the memories suddenly crowding back in the dark so that she wished she'd braved it and left the light on.

'You're freezing. Come here,' he said, and tucked her up against his powerful body. His leg wedged between hers, his lips tracked over her face and throat and down over her breasts, leaving a trail of fire in their wake, and by the time he returned to her mouth she was shuddering with need.

David moved over her, his body trembling with passion held in check, and then they were moving together, driving out the memories of the day and replacing them with warmth and life and strength.

Julia felt the first ripples of release wash over her and cried out, and his body shuddered in response, driving into her until the sensation swamped her and she sobbed his name over and over again as he arched against her with a wild cry.

Then he slumped onto her, shifting his weight so he lay slightly to one side, his chest heaving against hers and his heart thundering in the aftermath of release.

Still locked together, they lay silent as their bodies calmed and slowed, and then, still together, drifted into sleep.

CHAPTER NINE

JULIA woke to the warmth of David's body and the firm, solid weight of his thigh between hers. They were sprawled together in his bed, face to face, and his hand lay by her breast, the back of it just grazing the sensitive skin as she breathed in and out.

As if he'd been waiting, his eyes opened and his lips quirked into a contented smile.

'Hi, gorgeous,' he murmured, and his voice was gruff with sleep and tantalised her.

'I have to go to work,' she told him, and he groaned and pulled her into his arms.

'No,' he grumbled gently.

'Yes.'

His sigh was deep, the breath teasing her hair. 'What time is it?'

'I don't know.'

He shifted, just far enough to turn his head and look at the clock. 'Oh, hell. It's only five-thirty. Ten more minutes.'

He nuzzled into the side of her neck, and she felt the familiar stirrings of desire deep inside her.

'No,' she said, pushing him away with a breathless little laugh.

'Yes.'

'I need a shower.'

He gave a gusty sigh and rolled away from her onto his back, his arm flopping above his head. 'Go on, then. I'll follow you.'

She slid out of the bed into the morning chill and went through to the bathroom. There was no lock, but it didn't worry her. She didn't think there was any way he was going to stir for at least another half-hour.

The bathroom was warm, courtesy of the heated towel rail, and she turned on the shower and stepped into the stinging spray. Wonderful. She turned her face up to the water and stood there for a moment, and then let out a tiny shriek of surprise as David's arms slid round her from behind.

She relaxed against him, relishing the feeling of his warm, hard body against her back. 'This is becoming a habit,' she scolded softly, and he chuckled and buried his lips in her hair.

She tried to turn round but he wouldn't let her. Instead he picked up the soap and lathered her, his hands tracing her body intimately until she was whimpering with need and her legs were giving way. She felt the first shock waves start to wash over her, and then he turned her, lifting her against him and driving into her as the climax ripped through her.

He staggered, his body shuddering in release, and then lowered her gently to her feet, his arms wrapped round her, her head tucked under his chin so she could hear the pounding of his heart and feel the rise and fall of his deep chest as his breathing slowed and he recovered.

Then he eased away from her and bent his head, taking her lips in a lingering kiss under the pelting water of the shower. It streamed over them but they ignored it until they couldn't breathe, then they broke apart, laughing, and he smoothed the rivers of hair from her face and kissed her again, just lightly.

'I love you,' he said, and the water seemed to turn to ice.

Julia backed away, his words echoing in her head, and reality slammed home.

What was she *doing?* She'd never meant to let things go so far, and now here they were, in the shower again, and David was telling her he loved her—

'No,' she said, her voice hollow with shock and panic. 'No, you don't.'

'Yes, I do.'

'No. No, really, you don't. It's just sex, David. That's all. Just sex.'

He stared at her for a moment, stunned, then shut off the water and stepped out of the shower, throwing her a towel.

'Don't be stupid. It's far more than that.'

'No,' she said, shaking her head again in denial. 'You're wrong. It's just hormones—just a basic human urge. Believe me, I know.'

'Really?' he said, and his voice was hard and cold. 'Surely, if it was *just sex* I'd go for a nubile, pert eighteen-year-old, not a widowed mother of nearly thirty who's got droopy boobs and a sagging stomach and stretch marks.'

She recoiled, her hand flying up to cover her mouth, and he shook his head in disgust.

'Your words, not mine,' he said, jabbing a finger at her. 'But you might want to think about it.'

'You bastard,' she whispered, pain ripping through her, tearing her apart. It was Andrew all over again, pouring scorn on her body, shredding her confidence, using her—

'No, I'm not the bastard,' he said, his voice still

harsh, but then he let out his breath on a ragged sigh. 'I'm not here for sex, Julia, I'm here for love, because I love you, not your body—not that there's anything wrong with your body—'

'Liar,' she cut in savagely. 'Don't backtrack. You said what you meant.'

'No, I said what you said. And anyway, it's irrelevant. Whatever your body might or might not be like, did you notice me having trouble finding you attractive last night? Or again this morning?'

'You couldn't see me last night.'

'I didn't need to—I just needed to feel you, and you felt fine. You felt wonderful. You felt like you—and I love you.'

Her hands flew up to cover her ears. 'No!' she wept, not daring to believe him and be led once again into that tangled web of lies. 'I don't want to hear it!'

'Tough. It's not my fault. And don't blame me for loving you, it's not something I have any control over. But I do love you, and it's real. I won't lie and pretend otherwise just because you feel threatened by it. I'm sorry.'

She sank down onto the edge of the bath, the horror of what they'd done washing over her again and again. 'I didn't want this,' she said in a strangled whisper. 'I knew it was wrong. I knew this would happen.'

David flung the towel at the rail and turned to her, hands on hips, his beautiful body rigid with tension. 'You should have thought of that before, then, instead of encouraging it and leading me on and allowing it to happen,' he said savagely. 'You're not the only one that can get hurt, you know. I'm vulnerable too—just like anyone else.'

His eyes were locked with hers, the anger in them

terrifying her. She felt tears spill down her cheeks, and dashed them away. 'I never meant to do this,' she said brokenly. 'I really didn't.'

'No,' he said, his voice deadly quiet, 'nor did I. It's a pity I didn't listen to you—a pity we ever met—but don't worry. The lesson's well learnt.'

He yanked open the door, letting in a stream of frigid air. 'Get dressed. I'm taking you home.'

They were mercifully busy at work. Ridiculously busy for a weekend, but extra staff had been called in to deal with the aftermath of the scaffolding collapse, and they could just about cope.

There was no time, though, for idle chat. No time for anyone to look closely at Julia and think anything other than that she looked tired and shocked. They knew she'd been at the scene of the collapse and had helped all day in Theatre, and any doubts anyone might have had about her cheerfulness could easily be blamed on that.

It was just as well. She felt as if the slightest word, the merest glance would reduce her to tears. All day she waited to hear David's voice, convinced he'd come in to see his patients of the day before, but he didn't. He stayed resolutely away, and she told herself she was glad.

She lied. She ached for him, on this day of all days, the anniversary of Andrew's death. It had been just as dawn had broken on the morning of the twenty-third of December four years ago that the police had come to tell her he was dead.

And as dawn had broken today, so her heart had shattered all over again.

Fool, she thought. It's taken you four years to put

your life back together, four years to get things on track, and you have to go and do this!

She'd have to change her job, of course. She couldn't work with David, not now. It wouldn't be fair on either of them. Perhaps she'd move back towards her parents, she thought, or maybe down to Hampshire. No, not Hampshire. She couldn't afford the house prices.

She thought of Katie's school friends, of Andrew's parents who for all their faults loved their little granddaughter to bits, and she thought of her friends and colleagues. She couldn't leave them all behind. Not again.

And now he wouldn't teach her about the garden, she thought, and that last silly little thing was the straw that broke the camel's back.

Sally Kennedy found Julia sobbing in the sluice and, assuming it was because of the strain of the day before, she sent her home early. Not very. It was nearly two, only just over an hour before the end of her shift, but she was all in.

The day before had taken its toll and, coupled with a lack of sleep and the emotional parting from David that morning, it was enough to send her straight to bed the moment she got home.

She found three messages on her answering machine from the Revells who had heard about the accident in the shopping precinct, and rang them to assure them she was all right.

'Could you keep Katie until tomorrow for me, though?' she asked. 'I know it's a nuisance, but I have to work in the morning and I had a horrendous day yesterday—I didn't get my day off at all. I'd really appreciate the rest.'

'Of course,' Mrs Revell said. 'Today, of all days, we'll keep her with us.'

Julia closed her eyes. They were grieving, of course, for their son, the apple of their eye, the man who in their eyes had done no wrong.

Well, maybe he hadn't. Maybe it had been her all along, in which case David would thank her in the end.

She hung up and crawled into bed, waking in the night to an unidentified hollow ache. Then she remembered, and the pain crashed over her again and nearly swamped her.

She rose early next morning and bathed, put on make-up to cover the ravages of her tears and went to work absurdly early.

Angie was pleased to see her. They were still running flat out and had been all night, and she joined in with the morning drug round and the taking of the obs. She took report, Angie handed her the keys and went off duty, and she carried on with all the million and one things that still needed doing, dispensing brittle little smiles right and left and hanging on by a thread.

And then David appeared.

She was just coming out of Mr Burrows's room, and her stride faltered for a second. His mouth was tight and he looked straight through her.

'Good morning, Sister,' he said quietly, his voice devoid of emotion.

She swallowed the obstruction in her throat. 'Good morning,' she managed, amazed that she managed to speak at all.

'How is Mr Burrows?'

Mr Burrows. Oh, lord. How was he? She made herself concentrate. 'Improving. His bowel sounds have returned. He's had sips of water and he's tolerating it well.'

He nodded. 'We can try him on something bland today. Nothing much—low residue liquid feed, I think.'

'Right. I'll sort that out.'

'And you can remove the catheter—see if we can get his bladder working properly again. Is he walking yet?'

Walking? Oh, lord. 'Um—yes. With assistance. He's walked round the room.'

'Good. Right, I'd better have a word.'

He stood in front of her, and after an agonised second she collected herself and moved out of his way so he could go through the door. She took another second to compose her face before following him, and conjured up a smile for Mr Burrows.

While David talked to him and examined him, she stood motionless, hanging onto her control by a thread. She'd known he'd be cool to her. She'd expected it, and she'd expected it to hurt. She'd just had no idea it could hurt so much.

She forced herself to concentrate.

'I don't suppose there's any chance I could go home for Christmas?' Mr Burrows was saying.

David glanced at his watch, his face expressionless. 'Christmas—that's tomorrow.' He sounded almost bemused, and after a second he seemed to shake himself slightly. 'Um, I don't know if that would be a good idea. You aren't well enough to be discharged.'

'Oh, I know that,' Mr Burrows said quickly. 'I just wondered, well, if I could go home for the day, or part of it.' He hesitated, then added in a low voice, 'It might be my last Christmas.'

David nodded slowly. 'Yes. I'm sorry. Yes, I think you could. I think you should. Go in the morning— about ten or so. Have a very quiet day, and come back before six. We'll give you the special diet and any pills you'll need during the day, but so long as your bladder's working and your bowel is comfortable, I don't see why not.'

The man's face crumpled with relief. 'Thank you,' he said with sincerity. 'Thank you so much. I was dreading tomorrow.'

David straightened his shoulders, stiffening slightly, and Julia felt another arrow of pain. Mr Burrows wasn't the only one dreading it.

'Right. Well, have a good Christmas. I'll see you on Boxing Day—and don't overdo it.'

'I won't. And Merry Christmas to you, too.'

'Thank you.' David turned on his heel and nearly fell over Julia. His hands came up instinctively to steady them both, but then he dropped her like a hot brick and exited the room with a muttered apology.

'He seems a bit preoccupied today,' Mr Burrows said thoughtfully, looking after him with a puzzled frown.

'I expect he's just busy,' Julia said. 'A lot to do before the holiday period.'

She straightened the sheets, flashed Mr Burrows what she hoped would pass for a smile and shot into the kitchen. She was trembling from top to toe, her cheeks were chalk white and she looked as if she'd seen a ghost.

The Ghost of Christmas Past? Or Christmas Present?

Which reminded her, she still hadn't got anything for Katie. Damn. And she was coming home at one, just after Julia got home from work, so there would be no time to shop for her before then.

They'd have to go to town that afternoon, and she'd have to let Katie choose her own present, unless she could lose her for a moment and do it surreptitiously.

She looked at her watch. Nine-thirty. Just two and a half hours to go before she was off duty and could escape.

Well, she couldn't hide in the kitchen for the entire morning, no matter how much she might want to. She drank a glass of cold water, straightened her shoulders and walked out of the door—slap into David.

'I was looking for you,' he said. His voice was strained and his eyes were fixed somewhere in her hairline. Far from looking *for* her, she thought, he was hardly even looking *at* her. Then he held something out to her, something hard and square, wrapped in Christmas paper with a little shiny red bow on top. 'This is for Katie,' he said. 'It's a mug with retriever puppies on it. Perhaps you could give it to her for me—and, ah, say goodbye.'

He thrust it into her hands and turned on his heel, striding away, his shoulders rigid, his hands rammed down into the pockets of his coat.

She stared after him, her throat aching, and then her eyes dropped to the parcel in her hands. He'd bought her daughter a present, and not just any present. Not a plastic toy or an inappropriate book or a jumper that didn't fit, but a mug with her beloved puppies on it.

A tear slipped down her cheek, and she stared down at her feet and blinked hard. Don't cry, she told herself. Not here. Don't start, you won't be able to stop. Just hang on.

'Julia?'

A pair of feet appeared beside hers, and she looked up at Sally.

'Oh, love, is it David?' she asked, and Julia nodded.

'Don't be nice to me. Whatever you do, don't be nice to me.'

Sally gave a crooked little grin. 'OK, I won't. Mrs Harrison's bowel appears to be working again—she's just had explosive diarrhoea through her stoma and overflowed the bag. Want to give me a hand?'

Julia laughed a little unsteadily. 'Oh, wow, I can hardly wait. Yes, I'll give you a hand. Let me put this in my locker.'

She rejoined Sally at Mrs Harrison's bedside, and together they tidied her up and comforted her. The poor woman was acutely embarrassed and upset, and Julia put her problems aside and concentrated on convincing her that it didn't matter and nobody minded and once her tummy settled down it wouldn't be a regular feature of having a colostomy.

'Anyway,' she said, 'it's probably only for a short while until your bowel's healed, and then you can have it reversed.'

'Oh, I can't wait,' Mrs Harrison said miserably. 'I just hate this so much. I can't believe it's happening to me.' She started to cry again, and Julia hugged her and settled her down again for a rest.

Then she phoned Nick Sarazin and told him about the return of bowel function, and he said he'd come and talk to her as she was so unhappy, and see if he could cheer her up before Christmas.

He appeared a few moments later, chatted to Mrs Harrison for a few minutes and then came and found Julia.

'I've said I'll reverse the colostomy before Easter

at the latest. I just hope I don't get struck down for lying to her, but hopefully the timescale will be all right.' He paused and peered at Julia closely. 'Hell, you look a bit rough. I gather you were caught up in the chaos on Saturday—are you all right?'

She nodded, glad that he'd taken the obvious line and not enquired more closely. 'I'll be OK after a couple of days off.'

'Hmm. David's looking pretty grim as well. It must have been a hell of a day. Are you spending Christmas together?'

She busied herself at the desk. 'No—he's got a big family do on. Katie and I are having a quiet Christmas on our own.'

'You can't!' he exclaimed. 'Oh, Julia! If we weren't going away I'd say come to us for the day. Isn't there anywhere you can go?'

She dredged up a smile. 'We'll be fine. Don't worry about us, we're OK. We're used to it.'

'Well, if you're sure,' he said doubtfully, but she was saved by his bleep going off. She handed him the phone and made herself scarce before his searching eyes delved a little deeper and came up trumps.

Then, finally, it was twelve o'clock and she could go off duty. She left the ward in a hail of Christmas greetings, and made her way home through the busy traffic. Everyone, it seemed, was knocking off early.

She showered and changed when she got home, and then at a quarter past one the doorbell rang and Katie skipped in, laden with presents and smiling from ear to ear.

'Thank you so much for keeping her the extra night,' Julia said to Mrs Revell. 'Have you had a lovely time, Katie?'

Her daughter nodded furiously. 'We did so many things! We went to see Father Christmas, and we had tea in town, and we put the presents under the tree and opened them yesterday morning— Have we got a tree yet, Mummy? Can we do it later?'

'We're going to get one this afternoon,' Julia promised. 'We have to go to town—I didn't get my shopping done on Saturday.'

'You won't get anything now, dear,' Mrs Revell said, looking disapproving. 'You should have started earlier. I'd done mine by October.'

'Well, I hadn't,' Julia said as evenly as she could manage. 'So, if you don't mind, we need to get on because time is now very short, as you've pointed out. Thank you so much. Katie, say thank you, darling.'

The child hugged her grandmother, kissed her goodbye and turned to Julia expectantly. 'Are we going now?'

'Yes—right this minute. Have you had lunch?'

She nodded, and so Julia put her coat on, scooped up her bag and keys and they headed down into town on foot. There was no point trying to take the car, and it was only a short walk.

The precinct was nearly deserted today, the scaffolding all cleared away and the shopfronts boarded up where the glass had been broken. It seemed like a ghost town, Julia thought. The blood had all been washed away, but she could still hear the screams and the weeping, and propped up against the shop that had been most badly affected were several bouquets of flowers.

Three people had died in there, two others under the scaffolding, and the tragedy seemed to hang in the air.

People fell silent as they passed the site, and in the surrounding shops business was far from brisk.

They went into a big department store that seemed to have escaped from the sombre atmosphere of the street. 'So, what did Granny and Grandpa get you for Christmas?' she asked Katie as they wandered round through the last-minute crowds.

'Oh, lots,' she said, and rattled off a list of things, several of which had been on Julia's list of possibles and many more too expensive to be in reach of her budget.

Her heart sank. They walked out into the street again, to find that the Salvation Army band and choir were standing outside. They were singing 'In the Bleak Midwinter,' and as Julia and Katie went past, the choir sang the words, 'What can I give Him, poor as I am?'

The words struck a chord with Julia in her desperation. What can I give my daughter? she thought. Not my heart—she has that already and, anyway, just at the moment it's not really worth having. Oh, David...

They passed the shop with the print of Little Soham in it, and she hesitated outside. She still wanted to buy it for him—and they had another picture, too, of puppies playing in the snow. It was only a modern print, nothing special, but the puppies looked just like the ones at the Armstrongs' farm, and she knew Katie would love it.

'Oh, look, there's Father Christmas!' Julia said, pointing to a jolly man in the usual red garb with a flowing cotton-wool beard and red cheeks and a wonderfully padded stomach. 'I tell you what. I want to go into this shop for a minute. Why don't you stand here in the doorway and watch him, just for a second, all right?'

Katie nodded, and followed her into the shop, standing just inside the doorway while Julia had a murmured conversation with the man behind the counter.

One eye on her daughter, she pointed out the old print of Little Soham and the one of the puppies.

'Could you wrap them for me, please?' she asked, rummaging for her cheque book. 'My daughter's just standing over there, I don't want her to see.'

'Sure.' The man whipped the puppy picture down behind the counter, and then wrapped the two together in bubble wrap and brown paper.

'Thank you so much,' Julia said, hugely relieved that she'd found something suitable. She wrote out the cheque, told herself not to think about the cost and turned, pictures under her arm, Katie's name on her lips, but the doorway was empty.

'Katie?' Pushing past the people in the shop, she went out into the street and looked up and down, but there was no sign of her.

'Katie?' she called, telling herself to be calm, but the panic was starting to rise and she ran back into the shop, frantically calling and searching amongst the racks of prints.

'Are you looking for a little girl?' a woman asked her. 'The one with blonde curly hair?'

'Yes—she's five. Nearly six. She's got a blue coat on.'

'She went out, just a minute ago, while you were at the counter.'

Oh, God. Oh, please, God, no.

Julia ran back out into the street, calling Katie at the top of her voice, but there was nothing.

A policeman heard her calling and came over to her. 'Have you lost someone, madam?' he asked, and she looked up at him and started to shake.

'My daughter,' she said. 'I can't find my daughter. One minute she was there, the next she was gone. I told her to stand there. She was looking at Father Christmas—'

'Small girl, blonde hair, blue coat?'

She nodded in relief. 'Yes. Yes, that's her. Where is she?'

The policeman's face creased in a frown. 'She went with the man—Father Christmas. She was talking to him, and they went off together. I assumed she knew him.'

Julia stared at him in horror. 'She went with him? But she didn't know him! She'd never seen him before! Where did they go?'

But the policeman was already on the radio, calling for help to locate them. 'Don't worry, madam, we'll have her found in an instant,' he assured her, but she didn't believe him.

Her legs were trembling, her heart was pounding and there was a roaring in her ears. 'Katie,' she whispered desperately, her eyes still scanning the street. 'Katie, come back. Where are you?'

But there was no sign of her, or of the man dressed as Father Christmas who'd used the disguise to prey on her innocence and lead her goodness knows where. As the significance of her disappearance started to sink in, Julia's terror threatened to choke her. She could hardly breathe, bile was rising in her throat and the trembling spread to her whole body so she was racked with violent shudders.

Police were arriving, asking her questions, putting

her in a patrol car and driving slowly along the precinct in the direction the pair had been seen to take.

Still no sign, no word, nothing. No one had seen them, nobody knew anything. Then a Father Christmas outfit was reported abandoned in a litter bin in the multi-storey car park, and Julia's world fell apart.

'We'll take you back to the station, madam, and start looking through the security videos from the CCTV cameras around the town,' the policeman sitting in the front of the patrol car suggested. 'Maybe we can pick something up. If you wouldn't mind coming to help us, we can probably pick her out easier with your assistance.'

'Oh, no,' she said, her hand over her mouth. 'I need to be in the town in case she comes back, looking for me.'

'Don't worry about the town—we've got people on the lookout for anyone answering her description. Do you have a picture of her?'

A picture? 'Yes—yes, I do, her school photo. It's in my bag.' She unzipped the little back pocket in her bag and pulled out the picture. Katie's bright, smiling face was shining up at her, and the happy image was more than she could stand. Would she ever see her again?

Julia started to cry, huge racking sobs that tore through her body, and the WPC next to her put her arms round her and held her tight.

'Don't worry, we'll find her,' she promised, but they were just empty words, and everyone knew it.

They pulled up at the police station and went inside, and someone asked for tea. 'Is there anyone we can call for you?' the policeman from the car asked, and she replied without thinking.

'David,' she said. 'I need David.'

They handed her a phone, and she phoned the hospital and asked them to page him. When he answered, he sounded wary. 'What is it?' he asked, his voice tight, and her courage almost failed her, but then she thought of Katie, and she knew she couldn't do this alone.

'Are you finished there?' she asked him.

'Just about. Why? Changed your mind? I can't deal with this, Julia. Not now. Not here. Besides, I didn't think there was anything left to say—'

'It's not me,' she said hurriedly, terrified that he'd hang up. 'Please, David, listen to me. It's Katie. She's gone missing, in town. David, someone's taken her, and I don't think I'll ever get her back!'

CHAPTER TEN

THERE was silence for a moment, then David said, 'Where are you?'

'The police station. David, hurry.'

'Stay there. I'm coming,' he told her, and the phone went dead.

Julia didn't know how she got through the next few minutes. Somehow saying it out loud had made it all much more real, and a terror she'd never imagined swept over her. She remembered thinking that if she could just lose Katie for a minute, she might be able to buy her a surprise present, but she'd never meant this—

'We need to look through this video first,' someone was saying to her. 'Tell us if you recognise her.'

She tried to focus, but her eyes were dry and unblinking and she could hardly see. People milled about in front of the camera, but because of the angle it was difficult to work out what she was seeing anyway. A great feeling of helplessness threatened to swamp her—helplessness and guilt, because if she hadn't taken her eyes off her...

'This is the shop you were in,' the man told her, pointing out a doorway, and gradually it began to make sense. 'Now, we had the call from PC Oswald about ten minutes after this, so it should be possible to see you go into the shop. How long do you think you were in there?'

She shook her head numbly. 'I don't know. Not

long. I knew what I wanted and there wasn't a queue. I just bought two pictures.'

'So we might see you on this piece of film—there. Is that you?'

Was it? Possibly. 'I think so—and there's the Father Christmas that we saw.'

'Excellent. So, we're in the right place on the tape. All we have to do is keep watching.'

There were voices behind her, and she turned just as David came into the room.

'Julia,' he said, and his face looked so dear and familiar that she burst into tears.

His arms were round her, holding her up against his firm, solid chest, and his hands were rubbing her shoulders soothingly and holding her close.

'I didn't think you'd come,' she wept. 'Oh, David, help me. We have to find her.'

'We'll find her,' he said, but although she wanted to believe him, in a town the size of Audley, what hope did they have of finding one small girl before it was too late?

'What can we do?' he asked the police over her head.

'Not much, at the moment. We're screening video footage from the CCTV cameras around the area and in the car park where the costume was found.'

'Costume?' he asked.

'Father Christmas. The man dressed up as Father Christmas.'

'And so she trusted him,' he said slowly. 'Oh, my love.' His arms tightened, and she clung to him and dragged him down onto the seats.

'We have to look for her,' she said, her voice brittle

with desperation. 'On the videos. We've just found the bit where we go into the shop.'

They watched impatiently as the Father Christmas stooped to talk to the little children that passed, and then suddenly there she was, her Katie, her little face turned up trustingly to the cheerful figure in red.

'That's her,' Julia said. 'That's Katie.' She had a death-like grip on David's hand, and he put his other arm round her and held her tight. They watched in silence as the man held out his hand, and Katie slipped her little hand into it and went with him without question.

The police team worked on the images, refining them as much as possible, but it wasn't good enough to get any idea of the identity of the abductor. With the heavy disguise it was impossible to see more than just the eyes, and they were too indistinct to be of any use.

Then David stiffened and leant forwards to get a better view.

'Look,' he said. 'That hand—it doesn't look like a man's hand, and that person's not very big, you know. Katie's deceptively small—you compare them to the other people around them. I don't think it's a man at all. I think it's a woman.'

They looked again, studying the film over and over, and Julia nodded slowly. 'You're right. That person doesn't walk like a man. There's too much sway of the hips. Men don't walk like that, and Katie would look smaller beside a man, anyway, unless it was a very small man.'

'Right. I want the women checked,' Tony Palmer, the detective in charge, snapped. 'Any woman with a record of abduction or anything similar, anyone with a psychiatric record—anything that might be even slightly relevant. Let's look through the car park footage again. We were looking for a man—we might have overlooked something.'

Please, Julia thought, let it be a woman. A woman might not hurt her—not so much. Not in that way. Oh, God, please, let it be a woman.

And then they found her. An ordinary woman, slim, dressed in jeans and a jumper, was ushering a child in front of her, stooping to talk to her. As she turned to unlock the car, they could just make out that the child was Katie. She seemed quite happy, and there was certainly no struggling. She got into the car without protest, and a moment later they drove away.

'Get that registration,' Tony Palmer snapped, and for the first time, Julia felt the first tiny stirrings of hope.

They had the number of the car, and with that number they could trace her.

They zoomed in on the video image and managed to get all but one letter of the registration. Julia's hope faded again, but David squeezed her hand. 'They'll get it. They know the make and colour of the car. That's enough.'

Did she dare to believe him? 'Please, hurry,' she said under her breath. 'Please, please, hurry.'

'Right, got it,' someone said a couple of minutes later. 'The car's registered to an Avril Brown— 84 St Anne's Drive.'

'Right, let's go,' the team leader said, and held a hand out to them. 'You'd better come. If she's there, Katie will need you.'

The drive was a nightmare of sirens and flashing

lights, but as they approached the house the sirens were turned off and they approached carefully.

Men ran round the back, others surrounded the front of the modest little semi-detached house, and then Tony Palmer rang the doorbell.

For a moment there was no response and Julia felt her hope draining away again, but then the door opened and a sad, mousy woman with hopeless eyes stood there on the step.

'She's here,' she said woodenly, and then Katie appeared at her side, a bedraggled teddy tucked under one arm, and beamed up at them, and Julia's thrashing heart nearly stopped dead with relief.

'Hello, Mummy,' Katie said excitedly. 'I've been watching telly and playing. Avril's one of Father Christmas's helpers—she has to dress up and talk to the children to help him, but she'd finished work today so we came back here, and she let me play with all sorts of toys. I said we should tell you, but she said you wouldn't mind. Did you mind, Mummy?'

Julia thought she'd fall apart, but David had a vice-like grip on her hand and from somewhere deep inside her came the strength to hang on.

'I was a bit worried,' she said, wondering how it was possible to make such a massive understatement without giving herself away. 'You should have stayed where I told you, you know.'

Her little face fell. 'I'm sorry,' she said. 'Mummy, come and see the toys. They were Jenny's. They're really nice.'

Jenny's? 'Not now, darling,' she said as steadily as she could manage. 'We have to go and decorate the tree—remember? And anyway, Avril's busy. The police need to talk to her.'

Katie looked around at all the police standing there, and her face creased in a little puzzled frown. 'Did she do something wrong?' she said, and beside her Avril started to cry.

'I never meant to hurt her,' she sobbed. 'I only wanted to talk to the children, but she was so like Jenny…'

'Jenny died,' Katie explained innocently. 'This was her teddy. Here…'

She pressed the teddy worriedly into Avril's hands, then reached up her little arms and pulled the woman down to kiss her. 'Bye,' she said. 'I have to go now. Thank you for having me.'

For a second the woman clung to her, then she let her go, and Katie ran down the path to Julia and took her hand. 'Can we go and do the tree now?' she said innocently, her guileless little face shining up at her mother.

'I think that's a good idea,' Julia said, trying not to give in to the urge to sweep her up into her arms. She couldn't believe Katie was back with her and unharmed. It was like waking from a nightmare, but finding you were still in the place you'd dreamed of.

They sat in the back of the police car, her and David with Katie in between them, and drove back to the police station while Katie chatted happily about Avril and Jenny and the toys, and all Julia could think was that Katie was alive and poor little Jenny was dead, and how sad Avril had looked.

'That poor woman,' she murmured, and David squeezed her arm supportively.

'Are you all right?' he mouthed, and she nodded.

Yes. Yes, she was all right. Katie was alive and unharmed. Nothing else mattered.

At the police station it was agreed that they should go home and that a WPC with special training with children should come and talk to them on Boxing Day to get Katie's story, although it seemed fairly cut and dried from the video evidence and what she'd already said.

'It's just a formality, really,' Tony Palmer explained, 'and with it being Christmas, we don't need to do it now.'

'I'll be at home,' Julia said, but David cut in.

'No. She'll be with me at my family home for the next few days. I'll give you the address and the phone number.'

'Really?' Katie said, bouncing on the spot. 'Are we going there for Christmas?'

'Would you like that?' he asked, and she nodded vigorously.

'Will the puppies still be there? Can I still play with them?'

'Of course you can, half-pint. They'll be expecting you.' He ruffled her hair, and she giggled and put her arms around his hips and hugged him as he jotted down the details of the farm.

Julia stared at him, torn between wanting to be near him and the need to maintain her independence at all cost. 'But—David—you don't want us—'

'Don't tell me what I feel,' he said, his voice deathly quiet. 'And anyway, it's irrelevant. You aren't spending Christmas alone, and that's that. Besides, they'd have my guts for garters if I didn't take you there.'

She didn't bother to protest. She didn't want to be alone with Katie, her feelings were too fragile, and she didn't want to turn what seemed to have been a pleasant experience into one of horror for the child by over-reacting.

And Christmas with David's warm and loving family would be just what they all needed.

If only things hadn't gone so badly wrong at the weekend, she thought. If only things hadn't got out of hand and propelled them into that wild and tempestuous physical relationship, then they could still have been friends, instead of hurting each other and making the situation impossible.

Still, their feelings didn't matter at the moment. It was Katie she was concerned about, and she and David were both old enough to put their relationship on one side for the sake of the child.

'Don't forget your parcel, Mrs Revell,' the WPC said as they were leaving, and handed her the pictures that had caused all the trouble. 'Have a good Christmas. I'm so glad everything worked out all right.'

Julia hugged her, grateful for her support during the ordeal. 'Thank you. You've given me the best present in the world,' she said emotionally, looking round at them all. 'Thank you all so much.'

'Our pleasure. You take care, now,' Tony Palmer said.

She hesitated. 'About Avril—she needs help.'

He nodded. 'We'll see to it. She'll be all right, don't worry about her. You get on home now and have your Christmas. We'll see you afterwards.'

David ushered them out into the car and strapped Katie into the car seat, while Julia tried to fasten her own seat belt with fingers that trembled with reaction.

'Let me,' he said, sliding in beside her. 'Are you all right?'

She nodded. She didn't dare speak for a moment, and he squeezed her hand in understanding and started the car.

'Right, let's go to your house and pick up some things for you on the way,' he said briskly.

She hadn't even thought of it. There were a million things she hadn't thought of, but none of them mattered. She dropped her head back against the headrest and let him take over.

'Here we are,' he said, dredging up a smile for Katie's benefit. 'Have you got your keys?'

She nodded. 'Do your parents know what's happening?'

He cut the engine. 'I rang them on the way to the police station and told them what had happened. I need to phone them and tell them we've found her.'

'Call them from my house while I pack,' she suggested, and he nodded.

As she ran upstairs with Katie to gather their things together, he went into the kitchen, picked up the phone and dialled the number. His fingers were trembling slightly, and at the sound of his mother's voice he had to swallow hard before he could speak.

'She's all right, we've got her back and we're coming over,' he said gruffly.

'Oh, darling,' his mother said, and burst into tears. His father came on the line, more controlled but no less anxious, and David appealed to them for calm at the house.

'Katie's fine, but she's totally unaware of the havoc she's caused. I'll tell you all about it when we get there, but just don't say anything, all right? All she can talk about is playing with the puppies.'

'Fine. I'll prime them all. We'll expect you soon.'

He put the phone down and closed his eyes, breathing slowly and deeply and struggling for control. He had to be strong for Julia and for Katie—and if she could do it, so could he.

He couldn't believe how controlled she'd been when Katie had come out of the door. He would have grabbed her and run, and as for her attitude to Avril—where did she find so much compassion? He would have killed the woman for taking his daughter, and if Katie had been harmed, his daughter or not, he probably would have done so.

But she hadn't been harmed, and it was all going to be all right, and all he had to do was get through the next few days without falling apart.

They arrived at the farm shortly before six, only three hours after Katie had disappeared. It had been the longest three hours of Julia's life, and nothing could have prepared her for the agony of that wait.

Still, it was over, and all she wanted was to put it behind her. She walked slowly down the path to the front door, Katie running ahead and throwing herself into Mrs Armstrong's waiting arms, and she looked at Julia over the child's head and smiled tearfully.

'Hello, my dear,' she said, and putting Katie down she drew Julia into a warm and motherly embrace. 'I'm so glad everything's all right,' she murmured, hugging her hard, and Julia hugged her back.

'Thank you.'

Mrs Armstrong held her at arm's length and studied her closely. 'Are you all right? You poor child, it must have been awful. Come inside—I expect Katie's in with the puppies already. She'll have to share them today, because David's sister's children are here. Jeremy, open a bottle of wine, we need to celebrate.'

And just like that they were absorbed into the warmth of the family. They all crowded round the big kitchen table for supper, with the three children sitting together across one end and the adults all squeezed up on odd chairs, and Julia was sandwiched between David and his mother and plied with food and drink.

She could see Katie bubbling with excitement, and gradually she felt the tension in her start to ease.

'She's fine,' David said, intercepting an anxious look, and she laughed unsteadily and nodded.

'Yes, she is. I know. Thank you—it wouldn't have been nearly so easy at home. You were quite right.'

'You ought to learn to trust me,' he said softly, and she looked into his beautiful quicksilver eyes and wished she could dare to believe in him.

Supper finally came to an end, and they all helped to clear the table and do the dishes. David's sister's husband washed, and his brothers and younger sister dried and put away and cleared the table. David went into the drawing room and put logs on the woodburner and went out to fill the log basket.

Julia found herself with Mrs Armstrong and David's sister, supervising the children so that the puppies didn't get too exhausted, and while they watched over them Mrs Armstrong said, 'Shall we put Katie in with the other two for the night? I'm sure they'd love to bunk up together, if you're both happy with that?'

'Sure, fine,' David's sister said, but Julia felt a moment of panic.

'Oh. I thought— Can't she share with me?'

David paused beside them. 'I thought you could have my room,' he said to Julia. 'There's a day-bed in the study. I'll sleep on that. The kids are just next to my room, so she wouldn't be far away, and she'll have more fun in with them. It'll keep her mind occupied, as well.'

Julia nodded. He was right, of course, but the thought of her being out of sight—

'She'll be safe,' Mrs Armstrong said softly. 'No harm will come to her in this house.'

She felt the tension ebb out of her. 'You're right. Of course you are. Yes, let her sleep with the others, she'll love it.'

And she herself would be in David's room. What sweet irony.

The children were packed off to bed by nine, protesting through their yawns, and then the Christmas stocking fillers came out.

'I wasn't sure if Katie would be here, so I got her a few things,' Mrs Armstrong explained. 'I don't know if you do the Christmas stocking thing, or if after today—well, maybe you don't want references to Father Christmas.'

But Katie had been happily telling everyone of her adventure with one of his helpers, so Julia didn't think it would do any harm.

Not to the child, at least, and nothing would remind Julia herself of the events of the day because there was no way they were out of her mind for more than an instant.

'I'm sure she'd love a stocking, she always has one at home,' Julia agreed, touched that Mrs Armstrong had thought of Katie in the midst of all her family preparations. And so had her son, of course. 'David gave me a present for her the other day,' she told them. 'Should I put it under the tree with all the others?'

'That would be nice for her.'

'And I need some wrapping paper—I don't suppose you've got any, have you? I've just got a couple of things to do.'

They found her some paper and tape and pretty bows, and she sat at the kitchen table and wrapped David's picture while Mrs Armstrong stood guard and made sure he didn't come in.

'Oh, it's perfect—how appropriate!' she said, looking over Julia's shoulder at the print of Little Soham. 'Oh, Julia, you clever girl, he'll love it.'

'I hope so,' she said wistfully. She wasn't convinced. She thought of all the terrible things they'd said to each other at the weekend, and wondered how he'd managed to be so kind to her today.

Still, maybe it was appropriate, as it had been his picture she'd been buying when Katie had disappeared. Well, his and Katie's, to be fair.

She finished wrapping it, did Katie's puppy picture and managed to slip them both under the tree ready for the morning while no one was looking. She just hoped no one else had given Katie anything, because she felt very guilty about having nothing to give any of the others after all their kindness.

Still, under the circumstances it was unlikely, she thought.

They spent the rest of the evening by the fire in the drawing room, with all the usual banter of a large family surrounding Julia and wrapping her in its warm friendliness, and then at eleven the party broke up and they started to drift off to bed. Mr Armstrong took the dogs out, Mrs Armstrong gave the puppies a last feed and cleared up after them, and the others all disappeared upstairs.

David's sister went off with the three Christmas stockings in hand to put on the children's beds, and David took Julia up to his room.

Her case was on the bed, and he showed her the switch for the bedside light, and asked if she wanted the window open or closed, and then he stopped talking and looked at her for a long, considering moment.

'Are you all right?' he asked gently, and she nodded.

Actually it was a lie. She suddenly felt very emotional and raw all over again, and as if he realised that, he took her hand and led her out onto the landing and opened the children's bedroom door.

'She's fine. Look—fast asleep.'

Katie was, absolutely out for the count, exhausted by all the fun she'd had that evening with the other two and all the puppies. Julia bent over her and pressed a gentle kiss to her cheek, and she sighed softly and rolled onto her side.

For a long moment she stared at her daughter, and then everything seemed to blur, and she stood up and stumbled blindly towards the door.

David's arm came round her shoulders and he led her back into his room, turning her into his arms and holding her while the scalding tears fell. Then he mopped her up and gave her a slightly strained smile.

'Better now?'

She nodded. 'I'm sorry. It's just been one of those awful days.' She bit her lip, and he cupped her face in his hands and brushed her tears away with his thumbs.

'I don't know how you've been so brave,' he said gruffly.

'I couldn't have done it without you,' she told him

with painful honesty. She looked away, unable to meet his eyes after all the dreadful things she'd said. If only she could undo them, go back to the beginning of the end and stop them before everything had gone so horribly wrong—but she couldn't.

'Will you be all right?' he asked quietly.

She nodded. 'I think so. I'll have to be, won't I?'

'I'll say goodnight, then.'

She nodded again, and he opened the door and took one step through it before her courage deserted her.

'David?'

He stopped. 'What is it?' he asked softly.

'Stay with me,' she said in a rush. 'I know it's too much to ask, but I really can't face being alone. I'm sorry…'

He was motionless for a minute, then he let out his breath on a ragged sigh. 'Don't be sorry. I'll be back in a minute. You get ready for bed.'

He left her, and she changed quickly into her night-shirt. It was a little tired and washed out, but it was the only one she'd been able to find and anyway, it didn't matter. She wasn't trying to dress up for him.

She cleaned her teeth at the basin in the corner of the room, and then there was a knock on the door and David came in. He was dressed in pyjamas, and he hardly looked at her.

'All right?' he asked.

She nodded. 'I just need the bathroom.'

'It's next door,' he reminded her, and she slipped out of the room and glanced along the corridor. Would his parents object to them being together, she wondered, or would they be pleased? Not that it was significant. She'd dealt a death blow to any hopes she might have had in his direction.

David was sitting on the edge of the bed when she got back, and he looked up at her unsmilingly.

'Which side do you want?' he asked.

She shrugged. It didn't matter. She was so used to sleeping alone that either side would feel odd. 'I don't mind.'

'Then I'll have the left,' he said, and turned back the quilt for her. 'Get in—I'll put out the light.'

She slid between the cold sheets and lay down as he flicked off the light, then she felt the mattress dip as he got in beside her. For a moment all she could hear was her own heartbeat, loud in the silence, and the even, quiet sound of his breathing, then the bed shifted as he turned towards her and he reached out his arms.

'Come here,' he said gruffly, and she found herself enfolded in a warm and undemanding embrace. 'That's better. Now, go to sleep.'

'I can't. I keep thinking about today.'

'It's over, Julia. Let it go. She's safe.'

He was right, and she was suddenly exhausted. She let herself relax into his arms, and after a few seconds she felt sleep claim her.

It didn't last. She woke at some time in the middle of the night with a start, and slipped out of bed to check Katie. She stubbed her toe in the dark, and hobbled next door as quietly as she could, feeling relieved and yet foolish to find her daughter exactly as she'd left her.

'Is she all right?' David asked as she came back in.

'She's fine. I'm just being silly.'

'I don't think so. You've had a hell of a day.'

She slid back into bed and lay there, a few inches away from him, afraid to move closer in case he thought she assumed too much. She hoped he'd take her in his arms again, but he made no move towards her. Strangely dispirited, she fell asleep, but when she next woke it was to find herself in his arms once more, her head pillowed on his chest and their legs entangled.

'Are you OK?' he asked, and she realised he must have been awake. Watching over her? She didn't know, but it felt like it, and it was wonderful.

More than she deserved.

She thought of his kindness to her that afternoon, the way he'd dropped everything and come straight to her, giving her unquestioning support and never once telling her what she'd known, that she'd failed Katie by not watching her.

Andrew would have told her.

No. What was she thinking about? Andrew wouldn't have come near her, a widow with a child! No, he would have gone for the pert eighteen-year-old that David had talked about, like the girl he'd been with the night he'd died. There was certainly no way he would have come anywhere near her if she'd spoken to him the way she'd spoken to David on Sunday morning. His pride would have prevented it, but there was no sign of David's pride.

Just his compassion, and caring, and loyalty.

She swallowed hard. He wasn't anything like Andrew. She'd thought he was, because the sex had been so good and Andrew had always prided himself on his performance, but there had been no pride about David on Saturday night, just generosity and passion and honesty.

Maybe he really did love her? It seemed impossible that he could, but even more impossible that he didn't, given the way he'd behaved since. Not only did he love her, she realised, but he'd been there for her when she'd needed him in a way Andrew would never have been.

So, so different. How could she possibly have confused them? Fear, of course. Fear of another failure, of more pain and humiliation, fear for Katie, but there was nothing to fear from David.

She realised that, now it was too late.

But not too late to apologise.

'David?' she whispered.

'Mmm?'

'I'm sorry,' she said softly. 'I said some dreadful things to you the other day, and I was wrong about you—appallingly, horribly wrong. Can you forgive me?'

He was silent for a moment, then turned towards her, his hand coming up and cradling her cheek. 'There's nothing to forgive,' he said, his voice raw. 'You were frightened. I pushed you too hard—you weren't ready. And talking of forgiveness and saying dreadful things, I don't know why I was so cruel to you. I can't believe I said what I did about your body. It was totally uncalled for, even if they were your own words. I was just angry and hurt and I lashed out. I'm sorry.'

Her hand covered his in comfort. 'Don't be. And don't lie to me about it. I know it's no great shakes—'

'It's beautiful.'

She felt tears fill her eyes. 'Don't lie, please, David, don't lie,' she begged him, but he drew her closer into his arms and kissed her.

'I'm not lying. You're a wonderful woman, Julia. Brave and beautiful and strong and funny and sexy and tender, and if I wanted you any more than I do it would be dangerous for my health.' He kissed her again, then said quietly, 'Maybe it's just because I love you.'

Her heart sang with joy. She'd thought she'd never hear him say those words again, and they gave her the courage she needed. She lifted her hand and stroked his cheek, revelling in the rasp of his beard against her palm.

'I love you, too,' she said unsteadily. 'I have done almost from the moment we met. I didn't mean to. I didn't want to, because I didn't think you could ever return my love and I was afraid of hurting Katie, but I couldn't resist you. Now, though—I can understand if you don't want to know, I've been a bit slow on the uptake, but today I realised I can trust you. I just hope it's not too late for us. I want to be with you, share my life with you, have your children.'

She took a deep, steadying breath and went on, 'Marry me, David. Please?'

For an endless moment she thought he was going to refuse, then he took her lips in a searing kiss that erased any last shred of doubt she might have had.

'Oh, my sweet love, of course I'll marry you,' he said raggedly, and drew her back into his arms. 'I thought I'd lost you—thought it was all over and I'd blown it—but now we've got another chance. I didn't think we'd get that lucky. Let's not blow it this time, please?'

He made love to her then, not like the wild and passionate mating of the weekend, but slow and tender and infinitely gentle, and at the end she wept in his arms, and their tears mingled on her cheeks.

They fell asleep with their limbs still entwined, and

awoke to the sound of the children giggling with delight and bouncing on the beds next door.

'Good grief, whatever time is it?' he mumbled gently.

'Time to get up?' she suggested, and he gave a strangled laugh and turned on the bedside light.

'It's not even six!'

'It's Christmas.'

He dropped back onto the pillow and groaned. 'Do we have to go down?'

She sat up and looked down at him, no longer worried about her nakedness. 'I think so. We've got something to tell them, haven't we?'

He smiled slowly. 'Absolutely.' He threw off the covers, retrieved his pyjamas from the foot of the bed and pulled them on, lobbing her nightshirt to her. 'Come on, stick that on with your dressing gown and let's go and tell them the news.'

They followed the sound of excited voices down the stairs, and found all the family gathered in the drawing room, trying to stall the children from opening the presents.

At the threshold David stopped her and drew Julia into his arms, glancing up at the mistletoe pinned to the beam above before kissing her lingeringly. 'Happy Christmas,' he said softly.

She thought of yesterday, and how she'd nearly lost everything that mattered to her in the world, and how now she had it all, and her lips softened in a smile of utter joy. 'Happy Christmas,' she echoed.

They turned towards the drawing room and found everyone had fallen silent, their eyes fixed on them with identical expressions of curious fascination.

'I hope that kiss means what I think it means,' Mrs

Armstrong said searchingly, and David looked down at Julia for confirmation.

Over to you, he seemed to be saying. She looked at Katie, watching them with her head tilted to one side and a puzzled and slightly hopeful expression on her face.

'How do you fancy a new daddy?' Julia said, and Katie scrambled to her feet and ran over, looking up at them with shining eyes.

'Do you mean David?' she asked, and when he nodded, she squealed with delight and threw herself into his arms.

'I take it that's a yes,' he said with a chuckle, scooping her up against his chest. Julia looked up at him, at his laughing eyes and tender smile, and her daughter hugging him and raining kisses on his early morning stubble, and felt her heart swell.

The others were hugging them and pumping David's hand, his mother was in tears again, and Julia knew if she lived to be a hundred, there could never be a more perfect Christmas...

Christmas at His Command

HELEN BROOKS

Helen Brooks lives in Northamptonshire and is married with three children. As she is a committed Christian, busy housewife and mother, her spare time is at a premium but her hobbies include reading, swimming, gardening and walking her old, faithful dog. Her long-cherished aspiration to write became a reality when she put pen to paper on reaching the age of forty, and sent the result off to Mills & Boon®.

Look for a marvellous new novel from Helen Brooks, **The Billionaire's Marriage Mission**, in December from Mills & Boon Modern Romance®.

CHAPTER ONE

'OH, NO, please, *please* don't do this to me.' Marigold shut her eyes, thick dark lashes falling briefly on honey-smooth skin before she raised them again to glare at the dashboard in front of her. 'What are you doing to me, Myrtle? We're miles from anywhere and the weather's foul. You can't have a tantrum now. I didn't mean it a mile or two back when I called you crabby.'

The ancient little car didn't reply by so much as a cough or a splutter, but Marigold suspected there was a distinctly smug air of 'You should think before you speak' to Myrtle's demeanour as the car's four wheels settled themselves more comfortably into the two inches of snow coating the road in front of them. The old engine had been hiccuping for the last half an hour or so before dying completely.

Great. Just great. Marigold peered out into the driving snow that was already coating the windscreen now the wipers had ceased their labouring. In another hour it would be dark, and here she was, stuck in the middle of nowhere and with what looked like a very cold walk in front of her. She couldn't stay in the car—she'd freeze to death out here if no one came along—and for the last little while there hadn't been sight of a house or any dwelling place on the road.

She reached out and unhooked the piece of paper with the directions to Sugar Cottage off the dashboard, wondering if she had taken a wrong turning somewhere. But she hadn't, she assured herself in the next moment. She

5

knew she hadn't. And Emma had warned her the cottage
was remote, but that had been exactly what she wanted.
It still was, if only she could get to the flipping place!

She studied the directions again, frowning slightly as
she concentrated on working out how far she still had to
go along the country track, her fine curved brows drawing together over eyes which were of a vivid violet-blue.
The last building had been that 'olde-worlde' thatched
pub she'd passed about ten miles back, and then she'd
driven on for—she consulted the directions again—probably another mile or two before turning off the main road
into a country lane. And then it had been just a rough
track for the last few miles. Perhaps it wasn't so far now
to Sugar Cottage? Whatever, she had no choice but to
start walking.

She allowed herself one last heartfelt sigh before turning and surveying the laden back seat. Right. Her wellington boots were in her old university knapsack along
with an all-enveloping cagoule that nearly came down
to her toes! She had packed her torch in there too after
Emma had emphasised umpteen times how isolated and
off the beaten track the cottage was. Mind you, Emma
had been more concerned about the electricity failing—
a common occurrence in winter apparently—or
Marigold having to dig her way to the car from the front
door. They'd both assumed she'd actually *reach* the cottage before any dramas reared their heads.

There was a large manor house across the other side
of the valley, Emma had said, but basically the small
cottage in Shropshire she had inherited from her grandmother in the spring was secluded enough for one to feel
insulated from the outside world.

And right now, Marigold told herself firmly as she
struggled into her thick, warm fleece before pulling on

the cagoule, that was worth braving a snowstorm for. No telephone and no TV, Emma had continued when she'd offered Marigold the use of the cottage over Christmas— her grandmother had refused to allow any such suspect modern inventions over the threshold! And the old lady had baked all her own bread, kept chickens and a cow in the paddock next to the house, and after her husband died had remained by herself in her home until passing away peacefully in her sleep aged ninety-two. Marigold thought she'd have liked to meet Emma's grandmother.

The cagoule and wellington boots on, Marigold quickly repacked the knapsack with a few necessary provisions from the bags of groceries piled high on the front passenger seat. She would have to leave her suitcase and everything else for now, she decided regretfully. If she could just reach the cottage tonight she'd sort everything out tomorrow somehow. Of course, it would have helped if she hadn't left her mobile phone in the flat back in London, but she'd been three-quarters of the way here when she'd remembered it was still sitting by her bed at home and it had been far too late then to go back for it.

The last thing she did before leaving the warm sanctuary of Myrtle's metal bosom was to stuff the directions to Sugar Cottage in her cagoule pocket. Then she climbed out of the car, locked the door and squared her shoulders.

Finding the cottage in a snowstorm was nothing, not after what she'd been through in the last few months, she told herself stoutly. And if nothing else it would be a different sort of Christmas, certainly different to the one she'd had planned with Dean. No doubt right now he and Tamara were sunning themselves on the Caribbean beach *she'd* chosen out of the glossy travel brochures they'd pored over for hours when they'd still been together. She couldn't believe he was actually taking Tamara on the holiday which was to have been their honeymoon. On top of all the lies and deceit, that had been the ultimate betrayal, and when one of their mutual friends—awkward and embarrassed—had tipped her the wink about it she'd felt like going straight round to Dean's flat and socking him on the jaw.

She hadn't, of course. No, she had maintained the aloof, dignified silence she'd adopted since that first white-hot outburst when she'd found out about the other woman and told Dean what a low-down, slimy, no-good creep he was as she'd thrown her engagement ring in his blustering face.

The familiar welling of tears made itself felt deep in her chest and she gritted her teeth resolutely. No more crying. No more wailing after what was dead and finished. She had made herself that promise a couple of weeks ago and she'd die before she went back on it. She wanted nothing to do with the opposite sex for the foreseeable future, and if this cottage was really as far away in the backwoods as Emma had suggested she might just make her an offer for it now. Emma had confided she was thinking of putting it on the market in the new year.

Marigold began walking, hardly aware of the snowflakes swimming about her as her thoughts sped on. She'd been thinking for some time, ever since the split with Dean at the end of the summer, in fact, that she needed a complete change of direction and lifestyle.

She had been born and bred in London, gone to university there, where she'd started dating Dean in the last year of her art and design degree, and after her course ended had found a well-paid job in a small firm specialising in graphic design. She had worked mainly on posters and similar projects to start with, but when the firm had decided to diversify into all manner of greetings cards her extensive portfolio of work—accumulated throughout her training years—had come into its own, and she had found herself in the happy position of working solely on the new venture. Dean had proposed about the same time—twelve months ago now—and she had thought her future was all set. Until Tamara Jaimeson came on the scene.

'Ow!' As though the thought of the other girl had conjured up an evil genie, Marigold suddenly found herself falling full length as her foot caught in what was obviously a pothole in the rough road. The snow cushioned her landing to a certain extent but when she tried to stand again she found she'd wrenched her ankle enough to make her grimace with pain, and now all thoughts of a remote little studio, somewhere where she could freelance both to her present firm—who had already expressed interest in such a proposition—and others, couldn't have been further from Marigold's mind.

She could only have been limping along for ten minutes before she heard the magical sound of a car's engine behind her, but it had seemed like ten hours, such was the pain in her foot.

It was still quite light but she dug into her knapsack and brought out the torch nevertheless, moving to the edge of the road by the snow-covered hedgerow. She couldn't risk the driver of the approaching vehicle missing her in the atrocious weather conditions.

The massive 4x4 was cutting through the snow with an imperious regality which highlighted its noble birth and also underlined poor Myrtle's less exalted beginnings, but the driver had already seen her and was slowing down, even before she switched on the torch and waved it frantically.

'Oh, thank you, thank you.' She almost went headlong again as she stumbled over to the open window on the driver's side. 'My car's broken down and I don't know how far I've got to go, and I fell over and I've twisted my ankle—'

'OK, slow down, slow down.'

It wasn't so much the cold, impatient tone of his voice which stopped Marigold in full flow, but her first sight of the big dark man sitting behind the steering wheel. He was handsome in a rather tough, rugged way, but it was the cool grey eyes which could have been formed in a block of hard granite that caused her to be momentarily lost for words.

'I take it that's your car back there, which means you could only be making for Sugar Cottage.'

'Does it?' Marigold stared at him stupidly. 'Why?'

'Because it's the only other house in the valley apart from mine,' he replied—obviously, Marigold's mind emphasised a second too late.

'So you must be Emma Jones; Maggie's granddaughter,' the chilly voice continued flatly.

'I—'

'I understand you came once before to look over the cottage when I was abroad. I was sorry to have missed you then.'

The words themselves could have been friendly, however, the tone in which they were spoken made them anything but, and Marigold blinked at the quiet enmity coming her way.

'I promised myself after that occasion that if I ever had the chance to give you a piece of my mind, I would,' he said with soft venom.

'Look, Mr...?'

'Moreau,' he provided icily.

'Look, Mr Moreau, I think I ought to explain—'

'Explain?'

Marigold had heard of incidents where one person could freeze another into silence and she hadn't actually experienced it until now, but in the last moment or two he had shifted slightly in his seat and now the grey eyes had taken on a silver hue which turned them into two flares of cold white light.

'Explain what?' he continued curtly. 'The reason why not one of your family, you included, saw fit to visit an old lady in the last twelve months before her death? The odd letter or two, the occasional phone call to the village shop that delivered her groceries every week was supposed to suffice, was it? Messages delivered secondhand can't compare to flesh and blood reality, Miss Jones. Oh, I know she could be difficult, recalcitrant and obstinate to a point where you could cheerfully have strangled her, but didn't any of you understand the fierce plea for independence and the pride behind it? She was an old lady, for crying out loud. Ninety-two years old! Didn't *any* of you have the imagination and the sensitivity to realise that behind her awkwardness and perversity she was crying out to be told she was still loved and wanted for the woman she was?'

'Mr Moreau—'

'But it was simpler and easier to write her off as bigoted and impossible,' he bit out savagely. 'That way you could all get on with your nice, orderly lives with your consciences clean and unsmirched.'

Anger was beginning to surface inside Marigold, not least because of this man's arrogant refusal to allow her to get a word in edgeways. He had clearly been seething about what he saw as the neglect of Emma's family towards the old lady for a long time, but he wasn't giving her a chance to explain who she was or what she was doing here!

'You don't understand. I'm not—'

'Responsible?' Again he cut her off, his eyes like polished crystal. 'That's too easy a get-out clause, Miss Jones. It might suit you to give out the air of helpless femininity in the present situation in which you find yourself, but it doesn't fool me. Not for a second! And while you are considering how much you can make on selling your grandmother's home—a home she fought tooth and nail to keep going, I might add—you could consider the blood, sweat and tears that went into her remaining here all her life. And there were tears, don't fool yourself about that. And caused by you and the rest of your miserable family.'

'You have absolutely no right to talk to me like this.' Marigold was at the point of hitting him.

'No?' His voice was softer now but curiously more deep and disturbing than its previous harsh tone. 'So you aren't looking to sell the old lady's pride and joy, then? The home she fought so hard to keep?'

Marigold opened her mouth to fire back a rejoinder but then, in the next instant, it dawned on her that that was exactly what Emma was planning to do and for a moment the realisation floored her.

'I thought so.' She was at the receiving end of that deadly stare again. 'How someone like you can have the same blood as that courageous old lady flowing through their veins beats me, I tell you straight. You and the rest of your family aren't worthy to lick her boots.'

Marigold stared at him through the snowflakes that had settled on her eyelashes. She was about to tell him she *didn't* have the same blood, that she was in fact no relation at all to Emma's grandmother, when the hot rage which was bubbling checked her words. Let him think what he liked, the arrogant swine! She would rather struggle on all night than ask him for help or explain he'd got it all wrong. The man was a bully, whatever the facts behind all he had said. He knew she'd had to abandon her car and that she had hurt herself, yet he'd still been determined to browbeat her and have his say. Well, he could take a running jump! She wasn't going to explain a thing and he could drive off in his nice warm car, knowing that he had had his pound of flesh. The rotten, stinking—

'Lost for words, Miss Jones?' he enquired softly, the tone of his voice making the icy air around Marigold strike warm.

'Not at all.' She drew herself up to her full five feet four inches and never had she wished so hard she was half a foot or so taller. 'I was just wondering whether it was worth wasting any breath on such an unsavoury individual as you, that's all.'

'Really?' He smiled, but it was just a twist of the hard carved lips. 'And what have you decided?'

She glared at him for one moment more, her blue eyes sparking with the force of her emotion, and then turned and began walking up the road, trying not to limp in spite of the excruciating pain in her ankle, which seemed worse now she had rested it for a few moments.

She heard the engine rev behind her and fully expected the big vehicle to roar past her in a flurry of snow, so when it drew up beside her, keeping pace with her limping gait, she bit her lip hard but didn't turn her head from the white landscape in front of her.

'You said you fell over and twisted your ankle,' the hateful voice said flatly at the side of her.

She ignored it, along with the urge to burst into tears as waves of self-pity made themselves known.

'Get in.' This time the touch of raw impatience was very obvious, but again Marigold ignored him, struggling on, her face set resolutely ahead.

'Miss Jones, I think I ought to point out that you are extremely lucky I had an appointment elsewhere today which necessitated my leaving this morning. There is absolutely no chance of anyone else using this road and the cottage is at least another mile. Need I say more?' he added condescendingly.

'Get lost,' she bit out through gritted teeth.

There was a moment's pause and then his voice drawled, with disparaging amusement, 'Out of the two of us I would say that's a more likely occurrence for you. Get in the car, Miss Jones, and let's cut out the drama. It might be unpleasant for you to be told the truth for once, but you are old enough, and I'm sure tough enough, to survive.'

'I would rather freeze to death than accept a lift from you.' She turned for just an instant to meet the silver-grey eyes and her face spoke for itself.

'Now you are being ridiculous.'

'Well, that's just one more thing you can add to my list of crimes, then, isn't it?' she returned tartly.

'Get in the car.'

At this point Marigold so far forgot herself as to come out with an expletive she had never used in her life before. He thought he could order her about, tell her what to do after he had spoken to her the way he had? OK, so he might think she was Emma, and Marigold had to admit she didn't know all the ins and outs of this matter, but he had known she was asking for help and that she was hurt, and he had just left her standing in the snow while he'd given her a lecture on family responsibility. Nothing, but *nothing* would induce her to accept any form of assistance from this arrogant swine.

'Don't force me to make you get into the car, Miss Jones.'

'You think you could?' she spat derisively.

'Oh, yes.' It was cool and even and more than a little menacing, but the rage caused by his previous misplaced contempt and male arrogance was still hot enough to keep Marigold walking on, her head held high under its covering of wet plastic and the bottom of the cagoule flapping round her knees.

If he laid one finger on her, just one, he'd get a darn sight more than he'd bargained for, Marigold promised herself with silent fury as the vehicle drew level with her once again.

'Your grandmother was a woman in a million.'

Marigold ignored him completely.

'For her sake I don't intend to leave the only child of her son to freeze out here, even if it is exactly what you deserve.'

'How dare you?' She glared at him again, her eyes narrowed and shooting blue sparks but her lips were bloodless with the pain she was trying to conceal and her face was as white as a sheet. He stared at her for a second, the piercing eyes taking everything in, and then he sighed irritably before springing out of the vehicle with an abruptness which took Marigold by surprise. One moment she was standing glowering at him, the next she found herself whisked right off her feet as he lifted her up into his arms as though she weighed nothing at all.

'What on earth do you think you're playing at? Put

me down this instant!' she hissed furiously, struggling violently as she pushed at the solid male chest.

'Keep still,' he muttered exasperatedly, striding round the vehicle and depositing her in the passenger seat none too gently. She immediately tried to scramble out again, catching her injured foot as she did so and crying out with pain before she could check the yelp.

'Miss Jones, I have a length of rope in the back and I warn you I will have absolutely no compunction about securing you in your seat, all right?' he ground out tightly. 'You will sit there until we reach Maggie's cottage and then as far as I am concerned it'll be good riddance to bad rubbish, and I'll have done my duty.'

'You're despicable!' It was all she could manage with the pain now excruciating, but added to the physical discomfort was the shock which had gripped her in the last few moments. This man must be all of six feet four, and his tall, lean height and powerfully muscled body had convinced her she didn't have a hope of fighting him, but close to—and she had been close, how close she didn't dare dwell on right at this moment—he was aggressively and compellingly handsome with no sign of softness about him at all.

His face above the massive, thick oatmeal sweater he wore was darkly tanned and finely chiselled, his eyes of silver-grey ice set under black brows thrown into more startling prominence when taken with the jet-black hair falling over his forehead. He was…well, he was quite amazing, Marigold thought weakly after he had slammed the passenger door shut.

She watched him walk round the bonnet before he climbed in the open driver's door, unconsciously shrinking away slightly as he slid into the vehicle. If he noticed the instinctive withdrawal he made no sign of it, merely easing the car forward—the engine of which he had kept running—as he said, his voice curt, 'Did you arrange for food and fuel to be delivered to the cottage beforehand?'

No, because she hadn't known she could. Emma hadn't mentioned it when she'd offered her the use of the place over Christmas when Marigold had confided, a couple of weeks ago, that she was dreading the big family Christmas her parents always enjoyed. Their enormous, sprawling semi was always full of friends and relations over the holiday period right up until the new year—a kind of open house—which was great normally, but in view of her broken engagement and cancelled wedding was not so good. Everyone would be trying to be tactful and treading on eggshells. Poor, *poor* Marigold—that sort of thing.

'Why don't you tell them you've got the chance of a super little cottage with log fires and the full Christmas thing?' Emma had suggested after she'd offered the cottage and Marigold had said her parents would expect her to go home. 'I can understand they'd hate the thought of you staying in your flat by yourself, but if you say you and a friend are going away... And anyway, I'll be coming up a couple of days after Boxing Day to make a list of the furniture and one or two things, so it won't actually be a lie.'

Marigold thrust the reminder of her duplicity out of her thoughts as she answered the man at the side of her in as curt a tone as he had used, 'No, I didn't.'

'And when was the cottage used last?'

She didn't know that either. She thought quickly and then said airily, 'Recently.'

'Recently as in months or weeks?' he persisted coldly.

She wanted to tell him to mind his own business but in view of the present circumstances it seemed somewhat inappropriate. She remembered Emma had said the cottage might strike a bit cold and damp in the winter because she had only ever visited it in the warmer months, and guessed, 'Months.'

He nodded but said nothing more, concentrating on the road ahead, which was nothing but a cloud of whirling snowflakes in a landscape that was now a winter wonderland when viewed from the comforting warmth and security of the powerful car. Marigold privately admitted to a feeling of overpowering relief that she wasn't still battling through what was fast becoming a blizzard, and along with the acknowledgement came a few pangs of guilt at her churlishness before she reminded herself that *she* shouldn't feel guilty! He had been way, *way* out of line to talk to her as he had—even if he did believe she was Emma, and however much he had liked and respected the old lady. Rushing in and assuming this and that!

She risked a sidelong glance under her long lashes, aware she was dripping water all over the seat and that the melted snow from her boots had created a pool at her feet.

His face was hard, as though it had been carved from solid rock; he didn't seem quite human. Marigold suddenly became aware she was completely at this fierce stranger's mercy and she swallowed deeply. Somehow the idea of a noisy, crowded Christmas ensconced in the womb of her parents' home didn't seem so bad.

'Don't look so nervous; I wouldn't touch Maggie's granddaughter with a bargepole in case you're harbouring thoughts of rape and pillage.'

The deep voice had a thread of amusement running through it and immediately it put steel in Marigold's backbone. She reared up in her seat, her face, which had been pale a moment ago, now flushed with high colour, and her voice sharp as she lied, 'Nothing was further from my thoughts.'

'Hmm.' It was just one low grunt but carried a wealth of disbelief.

Loathsome man! Marigold drew her usually soft, full lips into a tight line and warned herself not to respond to the taunt. In a little while she would be at the cottage and he would be gone. She could see about bathing her ankle and strapping it up, and then she would sort herself out for the night. This snowstorm wouldn't last forever, and come morning she could make her way back to Myrtle and see if the little car could be persuaded to start. If not…well, she'd just have to carry everything to the cottage herself somehow. She didn't dwell on the thought of how she was going to lug her suitcase and the bags of food, let alone the sack of coal and other things she'd brought with her, through deep snow with an ankle that was hurting more every minute and now so swollen she wondered how she was going to get her boot off.

Nor did she linger on the fact that if the snow continued to fall as it was doing, two inches could rapidly become two feet. Coping with this angry, aggressive individual at the side of her was more than enough for the moment.

The ground had been dipping downwards almost from the spot where she'd first heard the car, and now, as they turned a corner on the winding road, Marigold saw they were in a wooded valley and that to their left in the distance was what must be Emma's cottage. It was set back some fifty yards from the track in its own garden, complete with neat picket fence and small gate. The cottage itself was painted white, from what Marigold could see, and it was the slate roof which was most clearly visible through the swirling snow.

She breathed a silent sigh of relief and gingerly flexed her injured ankle, knowing she had to climb out of the vehicle and walk to the cottage door in a few moments. The immediate stab of white-hot pain was worrying, but again she told herself it would be all right once she could strap it up.

'Your inheritance.' It was caustic.

She turned her head and looked at the granite profile. 'What makes you think it might be put on the market?' she asked evenly.

'Well, apart from the fact that you and the rest of your family have already shown you have no soul, you were heard talking about it in the pub down the road when you came up before,' he said shortly.

'People *eavesdropped* on a private conversation and then had the gall to repeat it?' Marigold asked with genuine disgust.

Her tone evidently rattled him. 'From what I heard, this "private" conversation was all but yelled to the rafters after you and your partner had consumed a bottle of wine each. If you don't want people to overhear what you say, don't get drunk. You can perhaps moderate your voice better that way. And the comments about the "yokels" didn't win you any friends in these parts either,' he added scathingly.

Oh, Emma, Marigold winced inwardly. She'd known Emma for a little while, but since she had met her current boyfriend—a high-flier with a sports car and a big opinion of himself—she'd changed.

Fortunately the car had just pulled up outside the little garden gate and Marigold was saved the effort of having to think of a reply. She took a deep breath and prayed

this could end right now and that she would never set
eyes on this man again in the whole of her life. 'Thank
you for giving me a lift,' she said stiffly, conscious of
the drips of water trickling off the cagoule hood and
hitting her nose.

'A pleasure,' he drawled with heavy sarcasm, un-
hooking her knapsack, which had somehow managed to
jam itself to one side of the controls, after which he
opened his door and walked round the bonnet to open
her door for her.

The courtesy surprised her, especially in view of the
content of their conversation to date, and flustered her
still more, highlighting, as it did, the dark attractiveness
she had been trying to ignore for the last few minutes.
She would have liked to ignore the outstretched hand,
too, but in view of the pain in her ankle and the height
of the car she decided to err on the side of caution as
she rose, putting her weight onto her good foot.

She had stripped off her wet gloves in the car, stuffing
them in her pocket, and now as she put one small naked
paw into his large fingers the contact of skin on skin
brought an unwelcome little tingle of awareness in her
flesh. She hesitated for a second, wondering how she
was going to land on her injured ankle and whether she
should try and shift her weight onto it now so she could
land on her good foot.

'How bad is the ankle feeling?' he asked flatly.

He had obviously noticed her uncertainty and guessed
the reason for it, and, in her immediate desire to convince this brute of a man that she was *perfectly* all right
and didn't need his assistance a second longer, Marigold
did what she later admitted to herself was a very silly
thing. She stepped down from the vehicle, hoping her

ankle would support her for the brief time it took for her to bring her other foot to bear. It didn't, of course.

She lunged sideways, the pain unbearable for a few sickening moments, and because he still had hold of her hand she swung like a plastic-wrapped rag doll on the end of his arm, her hood falling off her hair as she twisted against him. He almost overbalanced, too, saving himself just in time and gathering her against him in seconds as he half lifted her against his hard male frame.

Marigold had always bewailed the straight, sleek silkiness of her hair, which utterly refused to allow itself to be curled or put up in elegant, sophisticated styles, but now as the rich chestnut veil swung over her hot face she was immensely glad of the thick, concealing screen. Her reluctant good Samaritan was swearing under his breath, but then, as the world steadied and righted itself and his voice died away, she nerved herself to flick back her tousled hair and look at him.

He was looking at her too and his face was just inches away. Close to, his lips appeared more sensuous than hard, she found herself thinking—totally inappropriately—and the lines carved into the tanned skin radiating from his eyes and his mouth added a depth to the good looks he wouldn't have had in his teens and early manhood. And his eyelashes; she hadn't realised how long and thick they were—utterly wasted on a man.

Marigold felt her nerve-ends begin to prickle and it was the subtle sexual warning that enabled her to draw back in his arms, forcing more space between them, as she said breathlessly, 'I'm all right now, really. I'm sorry, I just lost my footing…'

'Can you walk?' His eyes had moved to her hair and then back to the wide violet eyes, and there was a smoky quality to his voice which hadn't been there before. It caused the most peculiar sensations to flutter down every nerve and sinew.

'Yes, yes...' She tried to prove it by pulling free and hobbling a step, but found to her dismay that the brief period of inactivity in the car had made the ankle feel ten times worse, not better.

As her lips went white with the pain he swore again, lifting her right off her feet with the same effortless strength he had shown on the road. She was being held close to the broad masculine chest for the second time in as many minutes, and she found it more than a little surreal as he strode over to the gate, kicking it open with scant regard for Emma's property and striding up the snow-covered path towards the front door.

He didn't glance down at her again until they reached the door, and then he said crisply, 'Key?'

'What?' She had seen his lips move and heard the sound but somehow the word hadn't registered in her brain. She was conscious of being held by him, of the leashed power in the hard male frame next to her and the subtle and delicious smell of his aftershave, and everything else seemed to have faded to the perimeter of her awareness.

'The key. For the door.' It was said with a derisive patience that brought her out of the stupor more effectively than a bucket of cold water.

'Oh, yes, of course.' She knew she was as red as a beetroot. 'You...you'll have to put me down. It's in my pocket and I can't reach it.'

'Stand on one foot; I'll hold you. And don't try to walk until we've taken a look at that ankle.'

We? We? If her pulse hadn't been thudding so crazily and her throat hadn't been so strangely dry she might have challenged him on the 'we', but as it was she assumed a pose she had seen the pink flamingos adopt in a recent wildlife documentary as he lowered her gently down, and fumbled for the key. She was horribly conscious of his hands round her waist, and although she told herself he was only steadying her it didn't help.

The trouble was he was too *male* a man, she thought distractedly. It wasn't just that he was big, very big, but he was larger than life somehow. Very tall, very hard and handsome and muscled, very everything in fact. In the most disturbing and unnerving way.

'Here it is.'

He adjusted his stance slightly, sliding one arm round her, positioning her against his masculine thigh as he took the key from her nerveless fingers. It was ridiculous, truly ridiculous, she told herself feverishly, in view of all the layers of clothing between them, but it felt shatteringly intimate.

As the door swung open he picked her up again and stepped into a small square hall, clicking on a light switch to one side of the door as he did so. He obviously knew his way around the cottage, Marigold thought, and this was borne out in the next moment when he opened a door to their right and entered what was clearly the sitting room, turning on the light again as he did so. The room was crowded with old, heavy furniture, smelt fusty and damp and had an unlived-in air which was chilling in itself as he placed her on a sofa in front of an empty fireplace.

It was awful. Marigold cast despairing eyes over her temporary home. Absolutely awful. And so *cold*. And no doubt the bedroom was just as damp and chilly. Whatever was she going to do? She looked sideways at the man standing to one side of the sofa and saw he was looking at her in an uncomfortably speculative way.

'Lovely,' she said brightly. 'Well, I think I can manage perfectly well now, thank you, and I'm sure you want to get home—'

'Sit still while I light a fire; the place is like a damn fridge. We'll attend to the ankle in a moment.'

He had disappeared out of the door before she could bring her startled mind to order, and as she heard another door open and close she called desperately, 'Mr Moreau? Please, I can manage now. I would much prefer to be left alone. Mr Moreau? Can you hear me?'

It was a minute or two before he returned, and then with a face as black as thunder. 'There's no coal or wood in the storehouse,' he said accusingly. 'Did you know?'

She could have told him it was because Emma and Oliver had had coal fires every night when they'd been here—despite it having been high summer. 'So romantic, darling,' Emma had cooed. 'And Oliver just loves to enter into the whole country thing.'

Instead she just nodded before saying, 'There's some in my car.'

'But your car isn't here,' he ground out slowly.

'I can see to it in the morning.'

He shut his eyes for a moment as though he couldn't believe his ears, before opening them and pinning her with his gaze as he said, 'Ye gods, woman! This isn't the centre of London, you know. There's not a garage on every other corner.'

'I'm well aware of that,' Marigold said as haughtily as she could; the effect being ruined somewhat by her chattering teeth. 'I'm hoping Myrtle will be all right tomorrow.'

The eagle eyes narrowed, a slightly bemused expression coming over his dark face. 'One of us is losing the

plot here,' he murmured in a rather self-derisory tone.
'Who the hell is Myrtle?'

Marigold could feel her face flooding with colour.
'My car.'

'Your car. Right.' He took a long, deep and very visible pull of air, letting it out slowly before he said, in
an insultingly long-suffering voice, 'And if...Myrtle de-
cides not to fall in with your plans, what then? And how
are you going to walk on that foot? And what are you
going to do for heat tonight?'

Marigold decided to just answer the last question; of
the three he'd posed it seemed the safest. 'Tonight I'm
just planning on a hot drink and then bed,' she said
stoutly.

'I see.' He was standing with his legs slightly apart
and his arms crossed, a pose which emphasised his
brooding masculinity, and from her perch on the sofa he
seemed bigger than ever in the crowded little room. 'Let
me show you something.'

Before she could object he'd bent down and picked
her up again—it was getting to be a habit to be in his
arms, Marigold thought a trifle hysterically as he
marched out of the sitting room and into the room next
to it. This was clearly the bedroom and boasted its own
share of clutter in the way of a huge old wardrobe, ancient dressing table and chest of drawers, two dilapidated
large cane chairs with darned cushions and a stout and
substantial bed with a carved wooden headboard. If anything this struck damper and chillier than the sitting
room.

'That mattress will need airing for hours even if you
use your own sheets and blankets,' he said grimly. 'Did
you bring your own?'

He looked down at her as he spoke and she felt the

impact of the beautiful silver-grey eyes in a way that took her breath away.

This man was dangerous, she thought suddenly. Dangerous to any woman's peace of mind. He had a sexual magnetism that was stronger than the earth's magnetic field, and she'd sensed it even when he was being absolutely horrible on the road earlier. And he was ruthless; it was there in the harshly sculpted mouth and classic cheekbones, along with the square, determined thrust to his chin and the piercing intensity of his eyes. The sooner he left the more comfortable she'd feel.

'Well?'

Too late Marigold realised she'd been staring up at him like a mesmerised rabbit, and now she shook her head quickly, her cheeks flushing. 'No, Em—I mean, I didn't think I'd need any with there being bedding here,' she said quickly as he turned abruptly, striding through to the sitting room, whereupon he deposited her on the sofa again.

'Your grandmother kept a fire burning in the sitting room and bedroom day and night from October to May,' he said flatly, 'and the cottage was always as warm as toast when she was alive. But this is an old place with solid walls; not a centrally heated, cavity-walled little city box.'

He was being nasty again; his tone was caustic. Marigold tried to summon up the requisite resentment and anger but it was hard with her body still registering the feel and smell of him. 'Be that as it may, I'll be fine, Mr Moreau,' she managed fairly firmly. 'I noticed one of those old stone bed warmers on the chest of drawers in the other room; I'll air the bed with that tonight and—'

'There's nothing else for it. You'll have to come back

home with me.' He didn't seem to be aware she'd been talking.

As a gracious invitation it was a non-starter; his voice couldn't have been more irritated, but it wasn't his obvious distaste of the thought of having her as a guest which made Marigold say, and quickly, 'Thank you but I wouldn't dream of it,' but the lingering, traitorous response of her body to his closeness.

'This is not a polite social suggestion, Miss Jones, but a necessity,' he bit out coldly. 'Now personally I'd be happy to leave you here to freeze to death or worse, but I know Maggie wouldn't have wanted that.'

'I shan't freeze to death,' she snapped back.

'You have no heat, no food—'

'I've a couple of tins of baked beans and a loaf of bread in my knapsack,' she interrupted triumphantly.

The expression in the crystal eyes spoke volumes. 'No heat and no food,' he repeated sternly, 'and you can't even walk on two feet. You've obviously damaged your ankle severely enough for it to be a problem for a few days, and without fuel and food your stay here is untenable.'

'It is *not* untenable!' She couldn't believe the way he was riding roughshod over her. 'I've told you—'

'That you have two tins of baked beans and a loaf of bread. Yes, I know.' It was the height of sarcasm and she could have cheerfully hit him. 'Let me make one thing clear, Miss Jones. You are coming with me, willingly or unwillingly; of your own volition or tied up like a sack of potatoes. It's all the same to me. I shall send someone see to the car and also to start getting the cottage warm and aired; believe me, I have as little wish for your company as you seem to have for mine. Once we've ascertained the extent of the damage to your ankle we can consider when you can return here.'

And it couldn't be soon enough for him. Marigold stared up into the cold, angry face in front of her, reminding herself it was Emma he was furious at—Emma and her family. And if they had neglected the old lady as he suggested he probably had good cause for his disgust, she admitted, but he was a hateful, *hateful* pig of a man and she loathed him. Oh, how she loathed him.

'So, what's it to be? With your consent or trussed up like a Christmas turkey?' he asked in such a way she just knew he was hoping for the latter.

She glared at him, almost speechless. Almost. 'You are easily the most unpleasant individual I have ever come across in my life,' she said furiously.

Her smouldering expression seemed to amuse him if anything. 'I repeat, Miss Jones, are you coming quietly and at least pretending to be a lady or—?'

'I'll come,' she spat with soft venom.

'And very gratefully accepted,' he drawled pleasantly, his good humour apparently fully restored.

She eyed him balefully as she struggled to her feet, pushing aside his hand when he reached out to help her. 'I can manage, thank you, and don't you dare try and manhandle me again,' she snapped testily.

'Manhandle you? I thought I was assisting a…lady in distress,' he said mockingly, the deliberate pause before the word 'lady' bringing new colour surging into Marigold's cheeks. 'How are you going to walk out to my car?'

'I'll hop,' she determined darkly.

And she did.

CHAPTER TWO

'SO, MISS JONES, or can I call you Emma, as you have so graciously consented to be a house guest?' They had just driven away from the cottage and the snow was coming down thicker than ever, Marigold noted despairingly. She nodded abruptly to his enquiry, earning herself a wry sidelong glance. 'And you must call me Flynn.'

Must she? She didn't think so. And there was a perverse satisfaction in knowing he didn't have a clue who she really was.

'So why, Emma, have you decided to spend Christmas at your grandmother's cottage and all alone by the look of it? From what I've heard from your grandmother and more especially from the ''yokels'' after your last visit, it just isn't your style. What's happened to the yuppie boyfriend?'

Oliver *was* a yuppie, and Marigold couldn't stand him, but hearing Flynn Moreau refer to the other man in a supercilious tone suddenly made Oliver a dear friend!

Marigold forced a disdainful shrug. 'My reasons are my own, surely?' she said coolly.

He nodded cheerfully, not at all taken aback by the none-too subtle rebuke. 'Sure, and hey, there'll be no objections from anyone hereabouts that lover boy's not with you,' he added with charming malice. 'He didn't exactly win any friends when he swore at the landlord and then argued about the bill for your meal.'

30

Oh, wonderful. Emma and Oliver had certainly made an impression all right, a bad one! Marigold sighed inwardly. Her ankle was throbbing unbearably, she didn't have so much as a nightie with her, and it was Christmas Eve the day after tomorrow; a Christmas Eve which Dean and Tamara would spend under a hot Caribbean sky, locked in each other's arms most likely.

She wasn't aware her mouth had drooped, or that she appeared very small and very vulnerable, buried in the enormous cagoule with her shoulder-length hair slightly damp and her hands tightly clasped in her lap, so it came as something of a surprise when a quiet voice said, 'Don't worry. My housekeeper will look after you once we reach Oaklands and her husband can take a load of logs and coal to the cottage tonight and begin drying it out. He's something of an expert with cars, too, so Myrtle might respond to his tender touch.'

Marigold glanced at Flynn warily. The sudden transformation from avenging angel breathing fire and brimstone to understanding human being was suspect, and her face must have spoken for itself because he gave a small laugh, low in his throat. 'I don't bite,' he said softly. 'Well, not little girls anyway.'

'I'm a grown woman of twenty-five, thank you,' she responded quickly, although her voice wasn't as sharp as she would have liked. Hateful and argumentative he had been disturbing; quiet and comforting he was doubly so. When she had been fighting him she had felt safer; now she was on shifting ground and the chemical reaction he had started in her body before was even stronger.

'Twenty-five?' Dark brows frowned. 'I thought Maggie sent you a present for your twenty-first just before she died?'

Oops. Marigold decided to bluff it out. 'I can assure

you, I know how old I am,' she answered tartly, and then, seeing he was about to say more, she added quickly, 'Is Oaklands your house?'

He didn't reply for a moment, and then he nodded. 'I bought it from a friend of mine who decided to emigrate to Canada a couple of years ago,' he said shortly. 'Your grandmother might have spoken of him; apparently they were great friends. Peter Lyndon?'

Marigold nodded vaguely and hoped that would do.

'She missed him when he left,' Flynn continued quietly. 'His children used to come across the valley and visit her often and they were a substitute for her real family, I suppose.' The accusing note was back but Marigold chose to ignore it. 'Certainly when I called to see her it was photographs of Peter's family that she showed me. She never showed me any of yours—too painful probably.'

Marigold felt she ought to object here. 'How can you say that when you have just admitted you didn't know her very long?' she asked in as piqued a voice as she could manage, considering all her sympathies—had he but known it—were with Emma's poor grandmother. The family seemed to have behaved appallingly to the old woman, and although as a work acquaintance Emma was perfectly pleasant it wasn't beyond the bounds of possibility to imagine her disregarding the fact she'd got a grandmother if it suited her to do so.

'Peter was a good deal older than me and he'd known Maggie for a long time,' Flynn said evenly. 'I think he knew your father, too. They didn't get on.' There was a pregnant pause.

Again Marigold felt she ought to say something. 'I don't know anything about that,' she said truthfully, and then she stopped abruptly, aware they were passing through large open gates set in a six-foot dry-stone wall which had appeared suddenly out of the thick cloud of snow in front of them. This must be the grounds of his home.

The car was travelling along a drive flanked by enormous oak trees, stark and beautiful in their winter mantle of feathery white, and she could just make out a house in the distance. A very large, very grand house. Marigold swallowed hard as Emma's casual comment about the other dwelling in the valley came back to her—a manor house. And this was a manor house all right.

She glanced speculatively at Flynn under her eyelashes; the expensive and clearly nearly new vehicle, the thick, beautifully cut leather jacket she'd noticed slung in the back seat, the overall quality of his clothes suddenly making an impression on her buzzing senses. Her eyes moved to the large tanned hands on the steering wheel—was that a designer watch on one wrist? It was. A beauty. Oh, boy... Marigold stifled a groan. This guy was *loaded*.

A couple of enormous long-haired German shepherd dogs suddenly appeared from nowhere, barking madly and making Marigold jump. 'Sorry, I should have warned you.' Flynn was looking straight ahead but he must have noticed her involuntary movement. 'That's Jake and Max; they pretend to be guard dogs.'

'Pretend?' Marigold looked out of the window at the enormous faces with even more enormous teeth staring up at her, and shivered. 'They've convinced me.'

Flynn turned and grinned at her as he brought the car to a halt, the dogs still leaping about the vehicle. 'Don't tell anyone but they sleep in front of the range in the kitchen,' he said softly, 'and they're scared stiff of my housekeeper's cats.'

Marigold managed a smile of her own but it was a weak one. Did he know what sort of effect the softening of the hard planes and angles of his face produced? she asked herself silently. It was dynamite. Sheer dynamite. 'I...I've never had much to do with dogs,' she said weakly.

And then his face changed. 'I'd gathered that,' he said shortly.

Now what had she said? Marigold stared at him uncomprehendingly. 'I'm sorry...?'

'It was made plain through the solicitors that any animals Maggie had were to be got rid of, but then you're aware of that,' Flynn said coldly, 'aren't you? Sold if anything could be got for them; put down if not. Of course, there weren't too many buyers for a few scruffy chickens and an ancient cow, nor for her dog and cat.'

Oh, no. Emma hadn't...

'Don't tell me that was something else your father kept from you?' Flynn asked flatly, his eyes smoky dark now in the muted twilight.

'I...I didn't know.'

'No?' His eyes were holding hers and she couldn't look away. 'I don't know if I believe that.'

Marigold had suddenly decided she didn't like Emma's family at all and was heartily wishing she hadn't taken the cottage for Christmas, even if she was paying Emma well for the privilege. 'I didn't know,' she repeated weakly, her tone unconvincing even to herself, but she was still thinking of poor Maggie's pets.

He surveyed her for a moment more, and Marigold was just about to tell him everything—that she wasn't Emma, that she had taken the cottage on impulse when it was offered and only knew the barest facts about Emma and her grandmother and the family—when he shrugged coolly. 'It's history now,' he said evenly. 'Let's get you inside.'

As she watched him walk round the bonnet of the car the fate of the animals was lost in the panic that he was going to hold her again. She'd felt faintness wash over her a couple of times when she had hopped out to the car, the movement jarring her injured ankle unbearably, but right now that was preferable to being held next to that muscled body again. Being nestled close to his chest had caused a reaction inside she still couldn't come to terms with.

She had never responded to a man's body or presence like this before, not with Dean, not with anyone, and her brain was still reeling from the unwelcome knowledge that underneath the panic and alarm was forbidden pleasure. Pleasure and excitement.

She would tell him she could hop into the house, she decided as he came towards the door. It wasn't quite the entrance she would have wished for, what with his housekeeper and her husband watching—not to mention the two dogs with their slavering jaws—but it couldn't be helped. What did it matter about a little lost dignity or the dogs thinking her dangling leg was a new toy?

As it happened, Flynn didn't give her the chance to make her feelings known one way or the other. The car door was pulled open and she was in his arms in the next moment and being carried towards the front door of the house, which was now open, the dogs gambolling about them and barking madly at this new game and Flynn swearing at them under his breath.

The lady who had opened the front door met them on the second step, her plump, plain face concerned as she said, 'Oh, Mr Moreau, whatever's happened?'

'I'll explain inside.'

And what an inside. As the warmth of the house hit Marigold, so did the opulence of the surroundings. The entrance hall was all wooden floors and expensive rugs and a wide, gracious staircase that went up and up into infinity, passing galleried landings as it did so.

However, she only had time for one bemused glance before she was carried into what was obviously the drawing room, and placed on a deep, soft sofa which had been pulled close to the blazing log fire. One arm had been round Flynn's neck, and although he had held her quite impersonally every nerve in her body was vitally and painfully alive and for a crazy second—a ridiculous, *insane* second—she had wondered what he'd do if she'd tightened her hold on him and pulled his mouth down to hers. It had been enough to keep her as rigid as a plank of wood when he'd lowered her carefully onto the sofa.

'This is Miss Jones, Bertha.' Flynn turned to the housekeeper, who had been right behind them. 'Maggie's granddaughter. Her car broke down a mile or so from the cottage and she's hurt her ankle. Take care of her, would you, while I find Wilf and tell him to go and take a look at the car? He can take John with him; I'd like them to get it back here if possible. And we've got a few spare electric heaters dotted about the place, haven't we? They can take those and start warming the cottage. And get John to deliver a load of logs and a few sacks of coal tomorrow morning.'

'Please, it's not necessary…' She had to tell them she wasn't Emma. She didn't know now why she hadn't told Flynn before, except that it had suited something deep inside to let him make a fool of himself when he had been so obnoxious on the road at first. And then she'd felt backed into a corner somehow, and there had never seemed to be a suitable moment to confess the truth. But this was getting more embarrassing, more awful, by the minute.

Flynn was already walking towards the door when Marigold said urgently, 'Mr Moreau? Please, I need to explain—'

'First things first.' He turned in the doorway, his face unsmiling and his voice cool. 'I need to get Wilf and John along to the car before it's completely dark, and you need that foot seen to. And the name's Flynn, as I told you before.'

'But you don't understand...' Her voice stopped abruptly. He had gone. Marigold looked up at the house-keeper, who was peering down at her over her apron, and said dazedly, 'I need to talk to him.'

'All in good time, lovey. You look like you've been in the wars, if I may say so. Now, let's get your things off and then we'll try and ease that boot off your poorly foot, all right? I'll be as careful as I can but I reckon we might have a bit of a job with it if your ankle's swollen.'

At least there was *someone* who didn't think she was horrible, Marigold thought gratefully as she returned the older woman's friendly smile. And after the last hour or so that felt wonderful.

In the event they had to cut the wellington boot off her foot, and when her ankle was displayed in all its glory the housekeeper drew the air in between her teeth in a soft hiss before saying, 'Oh, dear. Oh, dear, oh, dear, oh, dear. You've done a job on that, lovey.'

'It will be all right.' Nothing was going to keep Marigold in the house a second longer than was absolutely necessary. 'Once it's strapped up and after a good night's rest I'll be fine.'

The housekeeper shook her grey head doubtfully as

she looked at the puffy red and blue flesh, and then bustled off to get two bowls of hot and cold water—'to bring the bruise out', she informed Marigold before she left.

Marigold thought it was coming out pretty well all on its own. She lay back on the sofa, her foot now propped on a leather pouffe, and shut her eyes, trying to ignore the sickening pain in her foot. What a pickle, she thought despairingly. She was an unwelcome guest in the home of a man who loathed her—or loathed the person he thought she was at least—and if she wasn't careful she'd impose on him over Christmas. But she wouldn't, no matter how her ankle was tomorrow, she promised herself fervently. She'd make sure she went to the cottage tomorrow if she had to crawl every inch of the way. But it was going to be a pretty miserable Christmas by the look of it. At least she'd had the foresight to call her parents from a big old-fashioned red phone box at the side of the road just after the pub, and let them know she was within a few miles of the cottage and that she was all right but that she wouldn't be calling them again.

Once she'd got herself sorted at the cottage she could sit in front of the fire and read Christmas away while she nursed her ankle. There were people in much worse situations than she was in, and she had plenty of food in the car, and now she was going to have an excess of fuel by the sound of it. She'd pay him for the logs and coal, and his trouble, she thought firmly. If nothing else she could do that. And thank him. She twisted uncomfortably on the sofa, more with the realisation that she hadn't even acknowledged his—albeit reluctant and grudging—kindness in offering her sanctuary for the night.

'When Bertha said it was bad, she meant it was bad.'

Marigold's eyes shot open as she jerked upright. Flynn had reappeared as quietly as a cat and was now standing surveying her through narrowed silver eyes. For a moment she thought he was going to be sympathetic or at least compliment her on her stoicism, but she was swiftly disabused of this pleasant notion when he continued, his tone irate, 'What the hell were you thinking of, trying to walk on it once you'd hurt yourself so badly? Didn't you realise you were making it a hundred times worse with each step, you stupid girl?'

'Now, look—' a moment ago she'd been feeling weak and pathetic; now there was fire running through her veins '—I didn't know you were going to come along, did I? What was I supposed to do? Hobble back to the car and freeze to death or try and reach the cottage where there was—?'

'Absolutely no heat or food,' he cut in nastily. 'And why didn't you try phoning someone anyway? Anyone! The emergency services, for example. Do you have emergency insurance?'

'Yes.' It was a snap.

'But you didn't think of asking for help? It was easier to march off into the blizzard like Scott in the Antarctic?'

She bit hard on her lip. He was just going to love this! 'I'd left my mobile at home,' she admitted woodenly.

He said nothing at all to this—he didn't have to. His face spoke volumes.

'And my ankle's not that bad anyway,' she added tightly.

'It's going to be twice the size it is now in the morning and all the colours of the rainbow,' he said quietly.

The cool diagnosis irritated her. 'How do you know?' she returned churlishly. 'You're not a doctor.'

'Actually I am.' She blinked at him, utterly taken aback, and the carved lips twitched a little at her amazement.

The knowledge that he was laughing at her brought out the worst in Marigold, and now she said, in a tone which even she recognised as petulant, 'Oh, really? A brain surgeon or something, I suppose?'

'Right.'

Her eyes widened to blue saucers. Oh, he wasn't, was he? Not a neurosurgeon? He couldn't be!

She said as much, but when he still continued to survey her steadily and his face didn't change expression she knew he wasn't joking. And of course he couldn't have been a normal doctor, could he? she asked herself acidly. A nice, friendly GP dealing with all the trials and tribulations that the average man, woman and child brought his way. Someone who was overworked and underpaid and who had a vast list of patients demanding his attention.

She knew she was being massively unfair. She knew it, but where this particular individual was concerned she just couldn't *help* it.

She forced herself to say, and pleasantly, 'Not your average nine-to-five, then?'

'Not quite.' He was still watching her intently.

'Do you work from a hospital near here or—?'

'London. I have a flat there.'

Well, he would have, wouldn't he? Marigold nodded in what she hoped appeared an informed sort of way. 'It must be very rewarding to help people...' Her words were cut off in a soft gasp as he knelt down in front of her, taking her foot in his large hands—hands with long, slim fingers and clean fingernails, she noted faintly, surgeon's hands—and gently rotating it in his grasp as he felt the bruised flesh. How gently she wouldn't have believed if she hadn't felt it. Suddenly his occupation was perfectly feasible.

She wanted to snatch her foot away but in the state it was in that wasn't an option. She glanced down at the thick, jet-black hair which shone with blue lights and found herself saying, 'Moreau... That's not English, is it?'

'French.' He raised his eyes from her foot and Marigold's heart hammered in her chest. 'My father was French-Italian and my mother was American-Irish but they settled in England before I was born.'

'Quite a mixture,' she managed fairly lucidly because he had now placed her foot back on the pouffe and stood to his feet again and wasn't actually touching her any more.

Bertha bustled in with the basins of water and a towel draped over one arm, and Flynn glanced at his housekeeper as he turned and walked to the door. 'Five minutes alternating hot and cold, Bertha, and then I'll be back to strap it.'

He was as good as his word. Bertha had been making small talk while she bathed the ankle and Marigold had been relaxed and chatting quite easily, but the moment the big, tall figure appeared in the doorway she felt her stomach muscles form themselves into a giant knot and her voice become stilted as she thanked the housekeeper for her efforts.

As Bertha bustled away with the bowls of water Flynn walked across to the sofa. 'Take these.' He held out two small white tablets with a glass of water.

'What are they?' she asked tentatively.

'Poison.' And at her frown he added irritably, 'What do you think they are, for crying out loud? Pain relief.'

'I don't like taking tablets,' she said firmly.

'I don't like having to prescribe them but this is not a perfect world and sometimes they're necessary. Like now. Take them.'

'I'd rather not if you don't mind.'

'I do mind. You are going to be in considerable pain tonight with that foot and you won't get any sleep at all if you don't help yourself.'

'But—'

'Just take the damn tablets!'

He'd shouted, he'd actually shouted, Marigold thought with shocked surprise. He didn't have much of a bedside manner. She took the tablets.

Along with the tablets and water, the tray he was holding contained ointment and bandages, and she steeled herself for his touch as he kneeled down in front of her again. His fingers were deft and sure and sent flickering *frissons* radiating all over her body which made her as tight and tense as piano wire. And angry with herself. She couldn't understand how someone she had disliked on sight, and who was the last word in arrogance, could affect her so radically. It was humiliating.

'You should start to feel better in a minute or two,' Flynn said dispassionately as he rose to his feet, having completed his task.

'What?' For an awful minute she thought he had read her mind and was referring to the fact that he wasn't touching her any more, before common sense kicked in and she realised his words had been referring to the pain-killers and the support now easing her ankle. 'Oh, yes, thank you,' she said quickly.

'I'll get Bertha to bring you a hot drink and a snack.' He was standing in front of the sofa, looking at her steadily, and she could read nothing from his face. 'Then

I suggest you lie back and have a doze until dinner at
eight. You must be exhausted,' he added impersonally.

She stared at him. He seemed to have gone into ice-
man mode again after shouting at her and she rather
thought she preferred it when he was yelling. Like this
he was extremely intimidating. 'Thank you,' she said
again, as there was really nothing else to say.

'You're welcome.'

She rather doubted that but she didn't say so. In truth
she was feeling none too good and the thought of a nap
was very appealing.

Flynn turned and walked to the door, stopping at the
threshold to say, 'You've got severe bruising on the ankle, by the way; you'll be lucky to be walking normally
within a couple of weeks.'

'A couple of weeks!' Marigold stared at him, horrified.

'You were very fortunate not to break a bone.'

Fortunate was not the word she would have used to
describe her present circumstances, Marigold thought
hotly as she protested, 'I'll be able to hobble about if
I'm careful tomorrow, I'm sure. It feels better already
now you've strapped it up.'

He said nothing for a moment although her remark
had brought a twisted smile to his strong, sensual mouth.
Then he drawled, 'Fortunately I think we have a pair of
crutches somewhere or other; a legacy of last summer,
when Bertha was unfortunate enough to have a nasty fall
and dislocate her knee.'

Oh, right. So when Bertha hurt herself it was just an
unfortunate accident; when *she* hurt herself it was because she was stupid! Marigold breathed deeply and then
said sweetly, 'And I could borrow them for a while?'

'No problem.'

'Thank you.'

He nodded and walked out, shutting the door behind him, and it was only at that moment that Marigold realised she'd missed the perfect opportunity to set the record straight and explain who she really was.

CHAPTER THREE

AFTER eating the toasted sandwich and drinking the mug of hot chocolate Bertha brought her a few minutes after Flynn had left, Marigold must have fallen immediately asleep; her consuming tiredness due, no doubt, in part to the strong painkillers Flynn had given her.

She surfaced some time later to the sound of voices just outside the room, and for a moment, as she opened dazed eyes, she didn't know where she was. She stared into the glowing red and gold flames licking round the logs on the fire in the enormous stone fireplace vacantly, before a twinge in her ankle reminded her what had happened.

She pulled herself into a sitting position on the sofa, adjusting her foot on the pouffe as she did so, which brought forth more sharp stabs of pain, and she had just pulled down her waist-length cashmere jumper and adjusted the belt in her jeans, which had been sticking into her waist, when the door opened again.

The room was in semi-darkness, with just a large standard lamp in one corner competing with the glow from the huge fire, so when the main light was switched on Marigold blinked like a small, startled owl at Flynn and the other man. 'You'll be glad to know Myrtle is safe and snug and tucked up in one of the garages for the night,' Flynn said evenly as the two men walked across to the sofa. 'This is Wilf, by the way. Wilf, meet Miss Jones, Maggie's granddaughter.'

'But she isn't.' Bertha's husband was a small man

with a ruddy complexion and bright black robin eyes, and these same eyes were now staring at Marigold in evident confusion.

'What?'

'This isn't the same woman who was in the pub that day; the one who was all over that yuppie type and then made such a song and dance about being charged too much when Arthur gave them the bill,' Wilf said bewilderedly, totally unaware he was giving Marigold one of the worst moments of her entire life.

'I can explain—'

Flynn cut across Marigold's feverish voice, his own like ice as he said, 'Perhaps you would like to introduce yourself, Miss…?'

Marigold took a hard pull of air, reflecting if she didn't love her parents so much she would hate them for giving her a name which had always been an acute embarrassment to her. 'My name's Marigold,' she said a little unsteadily. 'Marigold Flower.'

'You're joking.'

She wished she were. She wished she could have announced a name like Tamara Jaimeson. 'No,' she assured Flynn miserably as he looked down at her, his expression utterly cold. 'My name really is Marigold Flower. My mother…well, she's a little eccentric, I guess, and when she married a Flower and then had a little girl she thought it was too good a chance to miss. My father was just relieved I wasn't a son. She was going to call a boy Gromwell. They're lovely pure blue flowers that my mother had in her rock garden at the time…'

Marigold's voice trailed away. She had been gabbling; Wilf's slightly glassy-eyed stare told her so. Flynn's eyes, on the other hand, were rapier-sharp and boring into her head like twin lasers.

'I'm pleased to meet you and thank you for dealing with the car.' She extended a hand to Wilf, who bent down and shook it before moving a step backwards as though he was frightened she would bite.

'Perhaps you would be good enough to leave Miss...Flower and myself alone for a few minutes, Wilf, and inform Bertha we don't want to be interrupted?' Flynn said grimly, his gaze not leaving Marigold's hot face.

Wilf needed no second bidding; he was out of the room like a shot and Marigold envied him with all her heart. She watched the door close and then looked up at Flynn, who was still standing quite still and looking at her steadily; the sort of look that made her feel she'd just crawled out from under a stone. 'I did try to tell you,' she muttered quickly before he said anything. 'Several times.'

'The hell you did.'

'I did!' She glared at him. Attack might not always be the best line of defence but it was all she had right now. 'But you blazed in, all guns firing, on the road before I even had a chance to open my mouth and wouldn't let me get a word in edgeways.'

'You're saying this is *my* fault?' he snarled in obvious amazement. 'You tell me a pack of lies, pretend to be someone else and inveigle your way into my home under false pretences—'

'I did not inveigle my way into your home,' she stormed furiously. 'I didn't want to come if you remember but you wouldn't take no for an answer, and I'll pay you for tonight and for the coal and logs. I can go to the cottage right now—'

She tried to rise too quickly and then fell back on the sofa with a shocked little cry, her face twisting with pain.

'For crying out loud, lie still!' He was shouting again and he seemed to realise this himself in the next instant. She watched him shut his eyes for an infinitesimal second before taking a great pull of air and letting it out harshly between his lips in a loud hiss. 'Lie still,' he said more quietly, the silver-grey eyes narrowed and cold and the muscles in his face clenching as he fought to gain control of himself.

Marigold had the feeling he didn't lose his temper all that often and that the fact that he had with her was another black mark against her. 'I *did* try to explain,' she said shakily, willing herself not to break down in front of this…this *monster*. 'But you wouldn't listen.'

He continued to survey her for what seemed like an eternity, before walking over to an exquisitely carved cocktail cabinet on the other side of the room near the massive bay windows, and pouring himself a stiff brandy. 'I would offer you one but you can't drink with those pills,' he said shortly. 'Would you like grapejuice, bitter lemon, tonic…?'

'A bitter lemon would be fine, thank you.' Marigold hoped the shaking in her stomach hadn't communicated itself in her voice, and whilst he was seeing to her drink she glanced round the room again. It was gorgeous, absolutely gorgeous, and everything in it just shouted wealth and influence and prestige. The ankle-deep cream carpet; the beautiful sofas and chairs in the palest of lavender mint, the colour reflected in a deeper shade in the long drapes at the windows; the rich dark wood of the bookcase and cocktail cabinet and occasional tables… Everything was beautiful.

'Here.' As Flynn handed her the drink she could read

nothing in his expressionless face, and after he had seated himself in an easy chair a few feet away he took a long swallow of the brandy before crossing one knee over the other and leaning back in his seat. 'I take it you *do* have permission to use the cottage?' he asked evenly.

'Of course,' she said indignantly, appalled he could think otherwise. 'I work with Emma.'

He nodded slowly, settling further back in the chair and continuing to look at her, obviously waiting for her to explain herself.

Marigold stared at him, wishing he wasn't so big, so male, so *irritatingly* sure of himself. But she *did* owe him an explanation, she admitted to herself silently. He had rescued her when all was said and done, and then brought her here, to his home. She took a deep breath and said steadily, 'I work with Emma, as I said, and she—'

'Doing what?' Flynn interrupted coolly.

'I beg your pardon?'

'You said you worked with her,' he said impatiently. 'In what capacity?'

'I'm a designer.' Marigold hesitated and then said quietly, 'Emma's the company's secretary. It's a small firm, just eight of us altogether, counting Patricia and Jeff, the two partners.'

'You enjoy your work?'

'Yes; yes, I do.'

At some point when she had been asleep Flynn had exchanged his thick sweater for a casual silk shirt in midnight-blue. It was buttoned to just below his collar-bone, and in spite of herself Marigold's eyes were drawn to the smidgen of dark curling body hair just visible above the soft material. That, along with the very mas-

culine way he was sitting, made his aura of virile masculinity impossible to ignore.

Marigold gulped twice and went on, 'Anyway, Emma
offered me the cottage over Christmas a few days ago
and I accepted. It…it was all decided in a bit of a hurry,
I suppose.'

'Why?'

'Why?' She stared at him. 'Why what?'

'Why is someone as attractive as you spending
Christmas all alone? You can't tell me you didn't have
plenty of offers to the contrary,' he said expressionlessly.

It was a compliment of sorts, she supposed, although
his voice and his face were so cool and remote it didn't
feel like one. She didn't know quite how to answer for
a moment, and then she said carefully, 'Personal reasons.' She was grateful to him, she was really, but there
was no way she was going to give this arrogant, authoritative stranger her life history.

'Ah…' He inclined his head and took a pull at the
brandy. The one word was incredibly irritating.

'Ah?' Marigold challenged immediately. 'What does
"ah" mean?'

He uncoiled his body, stretching lazily and finishing
the brandy in one gulp before saying, '"Ah" means you
are running away from a man.'

She had been having some trouble preventing her eyes
from following the line of his tight black jeans, but the
cynical and—more to the point—totally inaccurate statement was like a dose of icy water on her overwrought
nerves. 'I am *not*,' she declared angrily. How dared he
make such an assumption?

'No?'

'No.'

'But a man is at the bottom of this seclusion some-where.'

It was so arrogantly smooth she could have hit him, as much for being right as anything else. She could feel the hot colour in her cheeks, which had nothing to do with the roaring fire in the grate and everything to do with Flynn Moreau, and now her back was ramrod-straight as she glared at him, her mind frantically search-ing for an adequate put-down.

'You have a very expressive face.' Flynn stood up, not at all concerned about her fury. 'I should have known back there on the road you couldn't possibly be old Maggie's granddaughter.'

She didn't want to give Flynn the satisfaction of her asking the obvious but she found she couldn't help it. 'Why couldn't I be?' she asked tightly.

'Because from what Peter told me Maggie's family are a cold lot,' Flynn stated impassively, 'whereas you're all fire and passion.'

The last word hung in the air although he seemed unaware of it as he walked across and casually refilled his glass, returning a few moments later and settling himself in the chair again, in the same disturbing male pose.

It wasn't ethical for a venerable brain surgeon to be so sexy, surely? Marigold asked herself waspishly. Weren't men in Flynn's position supposed to be past middle age, preferably balding, married, with children and grandchildren? Reassuring father or grandfather fig-ures who were slightly portly and about as sexually at-tractive as a block of wood. She could just imagine the furore he created when he walked on to a ward, espe-cially with the cool, remote and somewhat cynical air he had about him. An air that said he'd seen and done everything and nothing could surprise him. Although she had!

The thought, silly as it was, was immensely gratifying, but after the comment about her expressive face she should have been on her guard, because in the next moment Flynn said, 'OK, let's have it. What's amused you?'

'Amused me?' she prevaricated weakly, hastily wiping all satisfaction from her face. 'I don't know what you mean.'

He shrugged easily. 'Have it your own way. So, who's the guy and is he still in the background somewhere?'

'I didn't say there was a man,' she objected sharply, any lingering smugness gone in an instant.

'Ah, but you didn't say there wasn't, which is more to the point.'

One more 'ah' and she'd throw her glass at his arrogant head, Marigold promised herself, before thinking, Oh, what the heck? She was never going to see him again once she was out of here, so she might as well humour him.

'The man was my fiancé,' she said abruptly, 'and at present he is on what was supposed to be our honeymoon with his new lady friend. OK? Does that satisfy you?'

If nothing else she had surprised him again but somehow it gave her no pleasure this time.

Flynn had sat up in his seat as she had spoken, expelling a quiet breath as he looked at her taut face. 'I'm sorry,' he said very softly, astonishing her with the deep sincerity in his voice, which was smoky warm. 'The guy is a moron but of course you are already aware of that.'

She blinked at him. She'd received various words of

comfort and condolence since she'd thrown Dean's ring
at him and sent him packing, but not quite like this.

She relaxed a little, her voice steady as she said, 'Apparently, if one or two mutual friends are to be believed,
she probably wasn't the first. We were together for three
years and I never suspected a thing.' She gave a mirthless smile. 'What does that make me?'

'Lucky.' It was very dry. 'That you're now rid of him,
I mean. You could wait around all your life for him to
grow up and die waiting. Let someone else have the job
of babysitting him while you have a life instead.'

She'd never heard it put so succinctly before but
Marigold realised he was absolutely right. Even when
they had still been together, she thought suddenly, she
had carried Dean and been the source of strength for
them both. She had never been the sort of girl who
couldn't say boo to a goose and expected the man in her
life to make all the decisions, mind you, but with Dean
she had found herself constantly making the decisions
for both of them simply because he wouldn't. It had been
a flawed relationship in every sense of the word, and the
main problem had been—as this stranger had just
pointed out—that Dean hadn't grown up. He was still a
Jack the lad and not ready for a permanent relationship.
Perhaps he never would be; some men were like that.

She raised her head now and looked at Flynn, and the
mercurial eyes were waiting for her, their depths as
smoky as his voice had been. 'Her name is Tamara, the
resident babysitter,' she said with a small smile. 'Apparently she's five feet ten, blonde and blue-eyed, and
has legs that go right up to her neck—so I've heard.'

'The mutual friends again?' he asked quietly.

Marigold nodded.

'Seems to me you could do with some new friends, too.'

She'd been thinking along the same lines; hence the increasing urge for a change. She was still too closely linked with Dean in London. They had had the same group of friends for years, went to the same restaurants and pubs, even their places of work were within a mile of each other. As yet she hadn't bumped into him but it was only a matter of time, and this whole thing—Tamara and the broken engagement—had brought about some deep introspection. And as she had examined her mental and emotional processes she'd discovered several things.

One, she could survive quite well in a world in which Dean wasn't the be-all and end-all. Two, there were only a handful of their so-called friends who were what she would *really* term friends. Three, if it wasn't for Dean and their marriage plans she would have spread her wings and gone self-employed ages ago, and probably moved away from the big city now she had enough contacts within the business world to have a healthy shot at working for herself. Four, she needed to do something for *herself* right now, and, whether she succeeded or failed in the world's eyes, the doing would be enough for her. It was time to move on.

Marigold's thoughts had only taken a few moments but when her eyes focused on Flynn again she saw that his gaze had narrowed. 'About to tell me to mind my own business?' he asked mildly, surprising her.

'Not at all.' She hesitated a moment, and then told him exactly what she had been thinking, including the change in her working lifestyle. The whole evening had taken on something of a surreal quality by now; whether this was due to the painkillers making her light-headed or the fact that somehow she'd found herself in this palatial house with this extraordinary man, Marigold wasn't sure. Whatever, she could talk quite frankly and he was a good listener—probably partly due to his line of work, she supposed.

He had folded his arms over his chest and settled himself more comfortably in the chair as he studied her earnest face, and when she had finished he nodded slowly. 'Do it,' he said softly, just as the housekeeper opened the door, holding a pair of metal crutches.

'Here we are,' Bertha said brightly. 'These will do the trick. And dinner's ready, if you'd like to come through to the dining room.'

Marigold found it a bit of a struggle as she made her way out of the drawing room and into a room at the end of the hall. Like the magnificent drawing room, this room was a mix of modern and traditional but done in such a way the overall effect was striking. Pale cream voile curtains hung on antique gold poles. The maplewood floor complemented the intricately carved table and chairs, which were upholstered in a pale cream and beige, with a splash of vibrant colour here and there in the form of a bowl of scarlet hot-house roses and a magnificent five-foot vase in swirling cinnamon, coral and vermilion hues.

The table was large enough to accommodate ten diners with ease, but two places had been laid close to the roaring fire set in a magnificent fireplace of pale cream marble. Marigold eyed the two places with trepidation as it suddenly dawned on her she would be eating alone with Flynn. 'This really wasn't necessary...'

'I always eat in here when I'm home.' Flynn's voice was just behind her. 'Bertha has merely set another place.'

Did that mean he normally ate alone? Marigold didn't

like to ask outright but it appeared that was what he had meant, and she found it curiously disturbing. This massive house and all the luxury that went with it, and yet he ate alone. But she hadn't for a moment assumed he was married, she realised suddenly. Why was that? She frowned to herself as she carefully sank down onto the chair Flynn had pulled out for her.

'You are allowed just one glass of wine with those pills.' Flynn indicated the bottle of red and the bottle of white wine in front of them. 'Which would you prefer?'

'Red, please.' Marigold answered automatically because her brain had just informed her why she'd sensed Flynn was a bachelor. There was an innate aloofness about him, a cool detachment that spoke of autocratic autonomy, of non-involvement. He would have women, of course, she told herself as she looked into the dark, handsome face. His need for sexual satisfaction was evident in the sensuous mouth and virile body. But he was the sort of man who always kept something back; who gave just enough to keep his lovers satisfied physically but that was all.

And then she caught her errant thoughts self-consciously, telling herself not to be so ridiculous. How on earth did she know anything at all about this man? She had never set eyes on him before today, and she wasn't exactly the greatest authority on men! She had had the odd boyfriend before Dean but they had never got beyond a little fumbling and the odd passionate goodnight kiss, and even with Dean she had insisted they keep full intimacy as something special for their wedding night. She was enormously glad about that with hindsight. Even the degree of intimacy they *had* shared made her flesh creep now when she knew he had been making love to other women whilst they were engaged.

'To chance encounters.' Flynn had filled her glass and then his own, and now he raised the dark red liquid in a toast, a wry smile on his face as he added, 'And mistaken identity.'

It was the first time he had referred to her deception since his initial outburst, and Marigold's cheeks were pink as she responded in like fashion, glad he seemed to be taking things so well.

He turned out to be a charming dinner companion; attentive, amusing, with a dry, slightly wicked sense of humour she wouldn't have suspected at their initial meeting.

Bertha served a rich vegetable soup to start with, which was accompanied by delicious home-made crusty rolls, followed by honey and mustard lamb with celeriac stuffing, and for dessert a perfectly luxurious, smooth and velvety chocolate terrine topped with whipped cream and strawberries. Beans on toast couldn't even begin to compete with Bertha's cooking, Marigold thought dreamily as she licked the last of the chocolate off her spoon.

At the coffee stage her ankle was beginning to hurt again, and she didn't demur when Flynn insisted on her taking another pill—a sleeping tablet this time, he informed her. She was soon more tired than she had ever felt in the whole of her life, the accumulation of the exhausting day, the week or so before when she had worked her socks off to get away a couple of days before Christmas Eve when the roads would be horrendous, and not least the emotional turmoil of the last few months catching up with her in a big way.

Whether it was Flynn's professional eye or the fact that he had had enough of her company for one day, Marigold didn't know, but as she finished the last of the dregs of her coffee-cup he said quietly, 'You need to go straight to bed and sleep for at least nine hours, young lady. Bertha will show you to your room; it's on the ground floor so you haven't got any stairs to negotiate.'

He rose as he spoke and as though by magic Bertha appeared in the next instant. As Flynn helped her to her feet and positioned the crutches under her arms Marigold was terribly aware of his touch in a way that made her jittery and cross with herself. She was a grown woman, for goodness' sake, she told herself irritably as she stitched a bright smile on her face and thanked him for the meal and his hospitality very politely.

'You are welcome,' he said drily, his face unreadable.

She stared at him for a moment, aware she had never really apologised for misleading him about who she was. And it must have made him feel a fool in front of Bertha's husband. Although...somehow she couldn't imagine Flynn Moreau ever feeling a fool. She spoke quickly before she lost her nerve, conscious of Bertha waiting to lead her to her room. 'I...I'm sorry about earlier,' she said quietly, feeling her cheeks beginning to burn. 'I should have explained the situation properly rather than letting you assume I was Emma.'

He smiled the devastating smile she'd seen once before, stopping her breath, before saying lazily, 'I should have known better.'

'Better?' she asked, puzzled.

'Than to let my brain tell my senses that what they were saying was untrue.'

She still didn't understand and her expression spoke for itself.

'The Emma I've heard about is a pert, brash, modern miss with about as much soul as the average Barbie doll,' Flynn said coolly. 'The girl I met on the road didn't tie up with that description at all.'

Marigold stared at him, utterly taken aback by the unexpected compliment. She tried to think of something to say but her brain had put itself on hold, and all she managed was a fairly breathless, 'Thank you.'

'Goodnight, Marigold.' His eyes were unreadable and his voice wasn't particularly warm, but she was conscious of tiny little flickers of sensation racing along every nerve and sinew in a way that was alarming.

'Goodnight.' She began to hobble to the door Bertha was now holding open for her, finding the crutches were a lot more difficult to manipulate than she'd imagined. She turned in the doorway, glancing back at Flynn, who was standing by the fireplace, looking at her. He appeared very dark and still in the dim light from the wall-lights and with the glow from the fire silhouetting his powerful frame. She swallowed hard, not understanding the racing of her pulse as she said, 'I'm sure I'll be all right to go to the cottage tomorrow if you wouldn't mind Wilf driving me there? I don't want to intrude, and you must have plans for Christmas.'

He shrugged easily. 'A few house guests are arriving on Christmas Eve, but one more makes no difference,' he assured her quietly. 'We always bring in the tree and dress it in the afternoon and decorate the house; perhaps you'd like to join in if you're still here then?'

He didn't sound as if he was bothered either way and Marigold said again, her voice firmer, 'I'm sure I'll be fine to go tomorrow, but thank you anyway,' before turning and following Bertha along the hall.

Marigold was conscious of a faint and inexplicable feeling of flatness as Bertha led her to the far end of the house. She would leave tomorrow no matter how her ankle was, she told herself fiercely. She just wanted to get to the cottage and be alone; to read, to rest, to eat and sleep and drink when *she* wanted to.

'Here's your rooms, lovey. You'll see it's more of a little flat,' Bertha said cheerfully as she pushed open a door which had been ajar and stood aside for Marigold to precede her. 'I understand the previous owner had it built on for his old mother, who lived with them for a time before she died, but it's handy for any guests who don't like the stairs. I've lit a fire and— *Oh, you!*'

The change in tone made Marigold jump and nearly lose her control of the crutches, and she raised her head to see Bertha scooping a big tabby cat up in her arms who had been lying on a thick rug in front of a blazing fire in what was clearly a small sitting room.

Bertha continued to scold the cat as she picked it up from in front of the fire and put it outside in the small corridor which led into the main hall of the house.

'My cats wouldn't dream of sneaking in here,' the housekeeper said fussily as she bustled back into the room and put another log on the fire while Marigold sank down onto a comfy chair. 'But that one has an eye for the main chance all right. He's straight upstairs if you don't watch him, looking for an open door so he can lie in comfort on one of the beds.'

Bertha's tone was full of self-righteous disapproval, and Marigold said, a touch bewilderedly, 'Whose cat is he?'

'Oh, he was Maggie's,' Bertha said, 'Emma's grand-mother, you know? Mr Moreau heard the animals were all going to be put down so they came here.'

'All of them?' Marigold asked in astonishment, re-membering something about chickens and an old cow.

Bertha nodded, bringing her chin down into her neck

as she looked at Marigold. 'All of them. Old Flossie,
Maggie's collie dog, is no trouble—she's taken to Wilf
and goes everywhere with him—and the chickens and
cow are outside in the paddock with the barn for when
it snows, but that cat!' She shook her head, making her
double chin wobble. 'He takes liberties, he does. Rascal,
Maggie called him, and it's Rascal by name and Rascal
by nature.'

Bertha continued to bustle about as she opened a door
and showed Marigold the attractive double bedroom and
en suite, a tiny cloakroom containing just a loo and minute corner handbasin and a small but compact kitchen.
All the other rooms led directly off the sitting room in
a fan layout. It was an extremely comfortable and charming little home in itself and overall was about the size
of Marigold's flat in London.

After Bertha had left her, Marigold stood for a moment just glancing around her. This huge house *and* a
flat in London! Talk about how the other half lived! But
there was clearly a softer side to Flynn, as his taking in
Emma's grandmother's waifs and strays had proved.

She tottered into the bedroom, which was beautifully
decorated in soft creamy shades of lilac and lemon, and
sank down on the broderie-anglaise bed cover.

Did he have a girlfriend? Had he ever been married
even? She realised she knew practically nothing about
him at all, whereas he had drawn out quite a lot about
her during the delicious and leisurely meal. She didn't
even know how old he was, and although doing what he
did for a living must put him over thirty he had the sort
of face and muscled physique that could put him anywhere between his late twenties to early forties.

Marigold suddenly frowned to herself. What on earth
was she doing, thinking like this, anyway? Flynn's love

life was absolutely no concern of hers. Once she left here tomorrow she would never see him again.

She reminded herself of that several times as she got ready for bed when she found her mind wandering again, but once she had snuggled under the covers all thoughts of Flynn and anything else were gone. She was asleep almost immediately; a deep, dreamless slumber that even her swollen ankle couldn't disturb.

CHAPTER FOUR

THE next day dawned clear and bright, and when Marigold limped to the window and looked out into the crystal-white world beyond she was relieved to see the snow was only three or four inches deep. Nevertheless, the feathery mantle on the trees and bushes beyond the window had turned the small garden—which was obviously the flat's own private domain—into a scene from a Christmas card.

Someone, probably Wilf, had brought her suitcase in from the car the night before and placed it in a corner of the bedroom, but the box she had packed her toiletries and make-up in was still on Myrtle's back seat.

The dressing-table mirror told her she resembled a small, white-faced panda, and she groaned slightly as she looked at her reflection. She had only worn a little mascara and foundation the day before, but a little mascara went a long way when it wasn't removed properly and she had only washed her face with soap and water before climbing into bed.

Her injured ankle was throbbing with enough force to make her grit her teeth as she contemplated hopping into the *en suite*, but just as she rose from the dressing-table stool the door opened and Bertha stood there with a breakfast tray. 'Oh, my, you're up bright and early,' the housekeeper said cheerfully as she walked further into the room. 'I thought you'd sleep till I woke you after that pill Mr Moreau gave you—when I dislocated my knee he gave me one, and I nearly slept round the clock. How is the ankle feeling this morning?'

'Not too bad,' Marigold lied firmly, determined she wouldn't stretch Flynn's hospitality another day.

'That's good. Well, you nip back into bed and eat your breakfast,' Bertha said, for all the world as though Marigold was five years of age instead of twenty-five. 'And when you've eaten there's two more of the pain-killers on the tray. I think Mr Moreau thought you'd need them.'

She certainly did, Marigold thought wryly, once she was back in bed again. Even the light duvet seemed like a ten-ton weight on her foot.

However, a good breakfast, followed by the painkill-ers, and then a somewhat wobbly hot shower helped Marigold's sense of well-being, and to her delight she found a gentle facial cleanser in the bathroom cabinet, which took care of the last of the mascara. After cream-ing her face, again courtesy of the bathroom cabinet, she hobbled into the bedroom and blow-dried her hair, and by the time she had delved into her suitcase and donned fresh underwear, jeans and jumper, she felt a hundred times better than when she had first woken.

At least her face had a little natural colour again, she thought critically as she surveyed herself from head to toe before leaving the room an hour or so later, but there was no way she could manage to wear a shoe, or even one of the socks she had packed, on her bad foot. But it didn't matter. She would manage somehow, she de-termined as she wound the bandage in place.

She found she could manage the crutches much better as she made her way out of the little annexe and into the main hall of the house, but then she nearly went sprawling when Flynn suddenly appeared in the doorway of a room to the right of the drawing room where she was making for.

'Good morning.' He smiled at her, a polite smile, and Marigold forced herself to return it as she grappled for control of her brain, which had decided to scramble itself. She had been unconsciously preparing herself for this moment ever since she had first opened her eyes this morning, but it didn't make it any easier when it was actually happening. He was wearing a black denim shirt and jeans, the shirt open at the neck and the sleeves rolled up to his elbows, revealing muscled arms dusted with soft black hair, and he seemed to fill the doorway with his dark, flagrant masculinity.

He probably didn't mean to be so intimidating, Marigold told herself silently, but there was a magnetic quality to his good looks which drew even as it repelled. His whole persona gave off an air of remoteness and cool detachment, yet there was a seductiveness there that would make any woman worth her salt wonder what it would be like to be made love to by this man.

She killed the last thought stone dead as she replied very formally, 'Good morning. I must thank you again for all your kindness yesterday.'

'Not necessary.' His gaze moved over her steadily as he said, 'How are you feeling?'

'Fine.' She had noticed the smoky quality to his voice yesterday, she remembered, but today it was more obvious. Probably because at this moment in time he wasn't angry with her! 'There's really no need for me to impose upon you any longer,' she said quickly, 'but if Wilf could help me take everything to the cottage that would be an enormous help.'

'I'm sure something can be arranged.'

Marigold was cross to find she felt hot and flustered,

and it didn't help that Flynn, in stark contrast, was the epitome of contained coolness. 'Thank you.' She forced another smile. 'I'll wait for him in my rooms, then, shall I?'

'I know we got off to an unfortunate start yesterday, Marigold, but I don't actually bite, you know.'

'What?' For a moment she wondered if she had heard right. Her eyes shot to his face and she saw there was a disturbing gleam at the backs of his eyes. 'I don't know what you mean.'

'You're like a cat on a hot tin roof as soon as you set eyes on me,' he said coolly, 'and I know for a certainty that the ankle is not at all "fine". In fact it must be giving you hell.'

'Not at all.' It wasn't so bad, in truth, now the pills had dampened down the worst of the pain.

'Even if you were Maggie's granddaughter you would be welcome to stay until you felt better,' Flynn continued, his gaze tight on her flushed face. 'As it is, there is absolutely no need for you to scurry away like a nervous little mouse.'

Marigold stiffened, instantly furious. As an only child she had learnt at an early age to stand up for herself— there were no siblings to run to or to ask for help. Likewise she had realised that if she wanted friends for company after school and in the holidays she had to make them herself. She had never run away from a situation or a person, and had *always* taken the proverbial bull by the horns, and now this…this arrogant, self-opinionated, high-and-mighty stranger had had the cheek to think he could make a sweeping judgement like that!

'Forgive me, Mr Moreau,' she said icily, 'but I thought your qualifications were in the realm of brain surgery, not psychology. That being the case, I'd keep the amateur psychoanalysis to yourself if I were you.'

He hadn't liked the tone of her voice; it was there in the narrowing of his eyes and the hard line of his mouth, but his voice was soft when he said, 'So you are not afraid of me?'

'I'm not afraid of anyone!'

'This is very good.' There was the slightest of accents to his voice at times, or perhaps not even an accent but a certain way of putting things that made his mixed and somewhat volatile parentage very obvious. 'Then perhaps you would like to have coffee with me?' he suggested silkily. 'Bertha always brings me a tray at about this time.'

She stared at him warily. She couldn't think of anything she would like less but she couldn't very well say so, and so she nodded stiffly, still very much on the defensive as he stood aside for her to enter the room.

It was clearly his study. Books lined two of the walls and a third was taken up by a huge full-length window, which opened out on to a rolling lawn. A fire was burning in a black marble fireplace, and in front of it— stretched out comfortably on a thick rug as though it was a place he was very familiar with—was the big tabby cat. Flynn gestured to a large, plump leather chair in front of the big mahogany desk strewn with papers. 'Make yourself comfortable.'

Comfortable was not an option around this man, Marigold thought ruefully as she duly seated herself, expecting Flynn to take the massive chair behind the desk, where he had clearly been working. Instead he stood looking down at her for a moment, his eyes wandering over the clear oval face and creamy skin and lingering on the delicate bone-structure, before he perched himself easily on the edge of the desk in front of her.

'I would like you to spend Christmas here,' he said coolly without any lead-up at all. 'OK?'

Not OK. Definitely, definitely *not* OK. Rascal was now purring as he rolled on his back for a moment in the warmth from the fire, fanning the air with plump paws for a moment or two before he sank back into contented immobility.

Flynn probably viewed her like Emma's grand-mother's waifs and strays, Marigold thought ignomini-ously, especially after she had revealed her reason for deciding to spend Christmas at the cottage all alone. Why, oh, why had she told him about Dean? Did he think she was playing for the sympathy vote? She steeled her humiliation not to come through in her voice as she said politely, 'I really couldn't do that. You've said you already have guests coming to stay.'

'I also said that one more won't make any difference,' he reminded her smoothly.

'Nevertheless…'

'You're not fit enough to be in that cottage alone and you know it,' he challenged quietly.

She'd been right. He *did* view her as poor little orphan Annie. 'I disagree.' She smiled brightly. 'I've food, warmth—and I intend to just veg out for a few days. Emma's coming at some point anyway.' She wished he'd move off the desk and into his chair; somehow he seemed twice as intimidating than usual in his present position, and she was uncomfortably aware of hard, powerful male thighs just a few inches away from her face.

'So I can't persuade you?' the deep, dark voice asked silkily.

'No, you can't.'

It was so definite the dark brows rose slowly in disparaging amusement. 'Pity.'

Bertha tapped on the door at that moment and then entered with a steaming tray holding a coffee-pot, cup and saucer and a plate of what looked like home-made shortcake. 'Another cup and saucer, please, Bertha, and milk and sugar. You do take milk and sugar?' he asked Marigold, who nodded quickly, and then felt herself deflate with relief when he slid off the desk and walked round to his chair as Bertha disappeared.

She searched her mind for something reasonably impersonal to say. 'So you've lived here for a couple of years?' she said carefully. 'Isn't it a little remote and far from London?'

He shrugged powerful shoulders and for a moment her senses went into hyperdrive before she got them under control again. 'That's what made it so attractive when Peter decided to sell. I had a place in London at the time and although it was very comfortable in its own grounds—' she could imagine, Marigold thought waspishly '—I was always on top of the job, so to speak. I'd been looking for somewhere like this for some time but the right location hadn't presented itself. Peter and I did the deal in weeks, which suited his circumstances, and after buying the flat in London I moved most of the furniture here. The only stipulation from Peter was that I'd keep an eye on Maggie for him; he was very fond of the old lady and within a few minutes of meeting her I could understand why.'

'I'm sure Emma's family didn't mean to be neglectful—' Marigold began, only to be interrupted by an abrupt wave of his hand.

'Spare me any platitudes.'

She glared at him. He was the rudest man she had ever met by far! She had heard it said that medical consultants and such considered themselves one step down from the Almighty, and now she was beginning to believe it.

Bertha returned with the other cup and saucer before Marigold could think of an adequately scathing retort, and while they drank the coffee and ate the shortbread Flynn kept the conversation pleasant and easy. Marigold had briefly considered sulking, but in view of the fact that he had opened up his home to her she decided a few more minutes of tolerance weren't completely beyond her.

As soon as she'd finished, however, she launched herself a little awkwardly to her feet. 'I'll be off, then,' she said quietly as Flynn rose in his turn. 'Thank you very much indeed for all you've done.'

'Flynn.'

'What?' He'd said his name very softly.

'The name is Flynn,' he persisted irascibly. 'You've avoided calling me anything at all rather than say my name, haven't you?'

She'd call him lots of things if only he did but know it. 'Not at all,' she lied quickly, knowing he was absolutely right. Somehow calling him Flynn took this situation to another dimension, and once she'd said it if they met again in the future—heaven forbid—she couldn't very well go back to Mr Moreau. And she needed to keep a distance between herself and this man; emotionally and mentally as well as physically. She didn't dwell on the thought; she didn't dare, not with Flynn right in front of her. She would examine it later when she was alone.

'Not at all,' he repeated with velvety sarcasm. 'That's

twice you've said those words this morning and each time you've been lying through your pretty white teeth.'

'How dare you?' Marigold stared at him, her face flushed with guilty annoyance. 'You've got no right to talk to me like that.'

'Rights are something to be taken, not given,' he said with silky emphasis. 'Did you call the tune with your fiancé all the time? Train him to walk to heel, that sort of thing?'

'I don't believe I'm hearing this—'

'Because it wouldn't do with a real man, my sweet little warrior,' he drawled coolly, his tone in direct contrast to her outraged voice.

'And you're a real man, are you?' she shot back with furious indignation.

'Oh, yes.' He had walked round the other side of the desk to stand just in front of her, the crystal eyes vivid in the dark tanned face and his mouth twisted in a sardonic smile as he viewed her shocked rage. 'And a real man is what you need, Marigold. Fire needs to be met with fire if it isn't to gradually die and turn to ashes or, worse still, burn up itself and everything around it. For every woman who's an out-and-out shrew there's a weak man somewhere in the background.'

For the first time in Marigold's life she was so furious that words failed her. Her eyes shooting blue sparks and her cheeks burning with angry, violent colour, she silently railed at the need to hold on to the crutches. She would have given everything she owned in that moment to be able to smack him hard across his arrogant, self-satisfied face, big as he was. However, there was absolutely no way she was going to risk falling flat on her face for the privilege!

She turned in one angry, sweeping movement and

made for the door, but Flynn was there before her, opening it with a flourish as he said calmly, 'I'll get Wilf to
bring your things down, shall I?'

'Thank you!' It was a bark, which made his lips
twitch. Marigold saw the amusement he couldn't hide
and willed herself to ignore it, pattering down the hall
as fast as she could and into the little corridor leading
to her rooms. She opened the door to the sitting room
with trembling fingers, so upset she didn't know if she
wanted to cry or scream and nearly losing her balance
in the process.

In the event she neither screamed nor cried, but sat
waiting for Wilf with a straight back and a burning face
once she had closed the suitcase and slipped on her thick
fleece. Impossible man! Utterly, utterly impossible man!
And she hadn't asked him for help in the first place.
Well, reason interrupted, she *had* hoped for a lift to
Emma's cottage when she'd flagged him down on the
road, but that was all. She hadn't asked to come here.
She hadn't asked to spend the night. And she definitely
hadn't asked for his opinion on her, or her life.

It was a further ten minutes before Wilf knocked on
the outer door, and by then Marigold was calmer, at least
outwardly. Inwardly she still wanted to kick something—or someone to be exact. That someone was waiting in the hall when she followed Wilf into the main
house, and as the other man continued outside with the
suitcase Marigold said very stiffly to Flynn, 'Would you
thank Bertha for me for all her kindness?'

'Certainly.' He reached for a leather jacket on a chair
near by and pulled open the front door—which had
swung partially closed—to enable her to pass through.

'And I'll get Emma to pop the crutches back when

she arrives,' Marigold added tightly, hating the fact that
he was coming outside to watch her depart.

Only he wasn't.

The massive 4x4 was parked on the drive with the
suitcase on the back seats, but Wilf was nowhere to be
seen. Marigold reached the vehicle with Flynn just behind her, and as he said, 'Here, let me help you,' she
found herself lifted into the passenger seat before she
could utter any protest. He then proceeded to walk round
the bonnet and climb into the driver's seat, as cool as a
cucumber.

'What are you doing?' She knew her voice was too
shrill but she couldn't help it.

'I thought you wanted to go to the cottage? Have you
changed your mind?' he asked helpfully.

'No, I have not changed my mind,' Marigold snapped
testily. 'I thought Wilf was taking me.'

'I don't know who told you that. As far as I recall, I
said nothing beyond Wilf would bring your case to the
car.'

'But I told you—'

'Ah, but I won't be told, Marigold, as I thought we'd
already ascertained,' Flynn said with unforgivable satisfaction. 'I wouldn't dream of delegating the responsibility of seeing one of my guests to her new accommodation to Wilf, not when I'm available,' he added as
the powerful engine kicked into life. 'Wilf will drive
your car over at some point in the next couple of days
but, as you can't possibly drive with that foot, there is
no hurry, is there?'

It was so reasonable that Marigold felt like a recalcitrant child, which no doubt was *exactly* how Flynn
wanted her to feel, she thought irritably.

The 4x4 ate up the short distance across the valley to

the cottage before Marigold could blink, or at least that was what it felt like. She wouldn't have admitted to a living soul that her spirit shrank at having to enter the damp, dark little house again, but the pale winter sunshine did light up the outside of the cottage beautifully, she thought as Flynn parked at the small gate and then walked round the car to help her descend.

She steeled herself for the rush of damp air and chilliness as Flynn opened the front door with the key she had given him the day before so Wilf could get some heat into the cottage, but instead of the dank, dismal air she remembered the tiny hall was warm and welcoming.

He opened the door to the sitting room for her, and the fusty, damp room of yesterday had been transformed into a still undeniably crowded but bright, warm and charming room. A crackling fire was burning in the grate, two bowls of sweetly perfumed, colourful flowers added a real homely touch, and, with the drapes at the windows pulled back to disclose the white wonderland outside, the cottage couldn't have been more different from her memory.

'We've kept the heaters on night and day so I'm afraid the electricity might be a bit heavy,' Flynn said quietly at her side. 'But it was necessary. Wilf took them away today; now it's warmed through the fires in here and the bedroom will be enough to keep it up to temperature.'

'It's lovely.' She couldn't believe how a bright log fire and bowls of flowers could bring such enchantment to a place, but they had. Everything seemed different. She was suddenly seeing the cottage through the eyes of Emma's grandmother, and her heart went out to the old lady who had fought so hard to remain in her home.

She limped through to the bedroom, where another glowing fire met her, along with fresh sheets and an exquisite broderie-anglaise bed cover in cream linen. Marigold recognised the design. 'This is one of your bedspreads from the house, isn't it?' she said slowly, her eyes taking in more flowers on the dressing table and chest of drawers.

Flynn gave the nonchalant shrug she was beginning to recognise. 'Spares, apparently, which Bertha had in one of her cupboards,' he said dismissively.

'And the flowers?'

'Wilf has a couple of greenhouses in the grounds. He keeps Bertha supplied with flowers for the house and there are always more than we can use.'

Marigold wasn't fooled by the casual words. Flynn had organised all this and she was grateful, she really was, but she was frightened of how pleased she felt. He'd do the same for any foundling he discovered lost in the storm, she reminded herself with wry, caustic humour; this didn't mean anything. And that was fine, just fine, because she didn't *want* it to mean anything. She had just come out of one disastrous relationship—she didn't need anymore emotional turmoil.

'It's so different.' He was right behind her, standing in the bedroom doorway as she turned, and when he didn't move she said quickly, 'You shouldn't have gone to so much trouble but I do appreciate it. What do I owe you for the fuel?'

'Don't be so ridiculous,' he said softly.

Marigold could feel her heart racing, a frantic, fast thud that made her unable to think coherently. She stared up at him, vitally aware of the broad male bulk of him and of her own fragility. 'But I must pay you,' she insisted faintly. 'I couldn't possibly—'

His head lowered as his hands gently gripped her upper arms and the kiss was everything she knew it would be. It was gentle and exploring at first, his mouth caressing and warm and firm, and when she made no effort to push him away it deepened subtly into a sensual invasion that had her making small female sounds of pleasure low in her throat.

'Your hair feels like spun silk,' he murmured against her soft lips, one hand entangled in the chestnut veil as he pulled her head back to allow himself greater access to her mouth. 'And the colours in it are enchanting. I've never seen anyone with such beautiful hair; do you know that?'

Marigold didn't answer him; she *couldn't* answer him. She was dazed and shaking, utterly bewildered by the desire he had aroused with just a kiss. A *kiss*. She had never felt like this once in all her time with Dean.

He took her mouth again, biting gently and expertly at her bottom lip in between kissing her with increasing passion. He had drawn her onto the hardness of his male frame now, their bodies so close she could feel what the kiss was doing for him. One hand was warm and firm against the small of her back and the other was stroking her face, throat and shoulder, soft, sensuous, light caresses that were sending her nerve-endings into quivering delight.

He was so *good* at this; his mouth first languorous and then fierce, teasing and then demanding as it moved against hers with complete mastery. He was ravaging her inner sweetness now and dimly Marigold realised she was kissing him right back, just as passionately.

His fingers brushed against one full breast and then the other before exploring the slender width of her tiny waist, and then, with a low sound of protest deep in his throat, his mouth lifted from hers and he eased her away from him very slowly, still taking care to hold her upright.

'You see?' he said very softly. 'Fire with fire.'

Marigold stared at him, her eyes slowly losing their dazed, fluid expression as reality dawned in all its chilling horror now he wasn't kissing her any more. This man was someone she didn't like; they had barely said more than two civil words to each other since they'd first met, and she had allowed him… She didn't like to think what she had allowed.

He must have sensed something of what she was feeling because his voice was dry when he spoke again, carrying the hidden amusement she'd heard several times before as he said, 'It's all right, Marigold. It was just a kiss.'

No, it wasn't just a kiss, she thought with blinding humiliation, at least not to her. It was easily the most mind-blowing experience of her life and had taught her more about herself in a few moments than in the last twenty-five years; the most important thing being—she didn't have a clue who she really was. If anyone had told her she could lose her head like this she would have laughed in their face, but it had happened. It had happened. And it mustn't happen again.

'Please let go of me.' Her voice was small but clear, and he complied immediately.

What must he be thinking? Marigold asked herself with silent desperation. One day she was telling him how she'd come to Emma's cottage to nurse a broken heart—the next she'd practically eaten him alive! She made no apology for exaggerating on both counts.

'I'm not going to say I'm sorry for kissing you because I wanted to do so even from that first moment on the road,' Flynn said with careful flatness. 'Neither will I pretend not to notice that you enjoyed it.'

She didn't deny this—there would have been no point and Marigold had never been one for dodging the consequences of her actions. Instead she raised her small chin and slanted her eyes—her body language speaking volumes to the tall, dark man watching her so closely—and said tightly, 'I would like you to leave now but first I must pay you for the logs and coal.'

'It was a kiss, for crying out loud!' Flynn rasped irritably, raking a hand through his dark hair in a manner that spoke of extreme frustration. 'Between two consenting adults, I might add. Now, if we had ended up in bed I might be able to understand you feeling slightly…manoeuvred.'

'There was absolutely no question of that,' Marigold snapped angrily. He'd be telling her she was anybody's next! 'I barely know you.'

Dark eyebrows rose mockingly as he crossed powerful arms over his chest. 'Flynn Moreau, thirty-eight, single, and of sound mind,' he offered lazily. 'Anything else you'd deem important?'

'Plenty.'

'Then we'll have to see to that in due course,' he said very softly, and suddenly he wasn't smiling.

'I don't think so.' She tried very hard to make her voice sound firm in spite of the fact her stomach had turned to jelly. He was *interested* in her? She couldn't quite believe it. Men like him—successful, wealthy, charismatic and powerful—went for the tall, leggy blonde model types; Tamara types. Worldly women who knew all the right gossip and wore the right clothes, and who had a list of friends that ran like the current *Who's Who*. She was five-feet-four with straight chestnut-brown hair and a skin that sprouted freckles in the summer, and even her mother couldn't call her a ravishing beauty. Perhaps he thought a little dalliance over the holiday period might be entertaining? Especially as she was on the doorstep, so to speak.

'No?' His voice held the softest edge of irony and he didn't seem at all put out at her refusal to play ball. It confirmed her theory more than anything else could have done. 'Still pining after what might have been?'

For a moment she didn't understand to what he was referring, and then she remembered Dean. Dean. Who hadn't stirred her senses or aroused her body remotely when compared to this man, and who now seemed a very distant memory indeed. Which was frightening, scary, when taking into account that but for Tamara she would now be Mrs Dean Barker. 'Not at...' She stopped abruptly when the silver eyes glittered a challenge. 'No, I am not pining for what might have been,' she said instead, very slowly and very firmly. 'In fact, for some time now I've felt I had a lucky escape.' The time in question being since Flynn had kissed her and she'd known, for the first time, what it was like to actually meet a man passion for passion. She would never have felt like that about Dean, not in a million years.

'But he's shaken your trust in the male of the species,' Flynn said intuitively. 'Hasn't he?'

Yes, he had, and it was annoying that she hadn't realised that till now either, Marigold thought irritably. Mr He-Who-Knows-All-Things here would just love it if she admitted that little golden nugget. 'I'm sorry if that's the only way you can accept that I don't want to get to know you any further,' she said primly.

'So I'm not right?'

She took a deep hidden breath and lied through the pretty white teeth again. 'No, you are not.'

He smiled; a predatory, shark-like smile if she thought about it, Marigold noticed uneasily. 'I'm pleased you're not an accomplished liar, Marigold,' he said charmingly. 'I really don't like that in a woman. Now, there is a small lean-to and hut just outside the kitchen door; Maggie used to keep the chickens in there when the weather was bad. Wilf's stocked it with logs and coal—more than enough for a couple of weeks' fuel—and you must keep the fires going day and night. You know how to bank a fire, I suppose?'

She didn't have a clue, but she nodded stiffly. 'Of course I do,' she said haughtily.

He eyed her mockingly. 'Plenty of damp slack does the trick, along with tea leaves or vegetable peelings; that sort of thing. Pile it on thick just before you turn in and make sure as little air as possible is getting to the fire. That way you should still have enough glowing embers to get it going nicely in the morning once you've scooped the ash into a bucket.'

Quite the little downstairs maid, wasn't he? Marigold thought nastily, and then felt immediately ashamed of herself when Flynn added, 'Your groceries are all packed away in the cupboards and the fridge is stocked. There's no freezer, I'm afraid.'

'Right, thank you. Now, what do I—?'

'If you mention payment once more I'll take it,' Flynn warned with a glint in his eye, 'but it won't be of the financial kind. Do you understand?'

She opened her mouth to protest, looked into his eyes and knew he meant it. Her mouth closed again. She was just eternally grateful he'd never know the way his

words had made her flesh tingle and the blood sing
through her veins.

'Take these every six hours; no more than eight in
twenty-four hours,' he warned quietly, suddenly very
much the professional as he brought a small bottle of
the painkillers out of his pocket. 'And no more than the
odd glass of wine whilst you're taking them.'

She nodded, wishing he'd just go. She needed time to
sort out her whirling thoughts and utter confusion, and
whilst he was here in front of her there was no chance
of her racing emotions being brought under control.

He stepped closer again, lifting a hand to cup her chin
as he said, 'Goodbye, Marigold.'

'Goodbye.' Suddenly, and with an irrationality that
surprised her, she wanted to beg him to stay. Which was
crazy, she warned herself, wondering if he was going to
kiss her again.

He didn't.

What was wrong with her? Marigold asked herself
crossly as she watched Flynn turn and walk to the door.
She couldn't be attracted to him; she wouldn't let herself
be. Her life was difficult enough at the moment and she
had some major changes in view for the new year and
the last thing she needed was a complication like Flynn!

She followed him to the front door and watched the
tall, dark figure stride across the snow where the path
should have been. The blue sky above him was pierc-
ingly clear, and a white winter sun had turned the snow
into a mass of glittering diamonds in which the inden-
tation of his large footsteps stood out with stark severity.
They were like him—utterly larger than life.

Marigold narrowed her eyes against the sunlight as
her thoughts sped on. Flynn was one of those characters
you came across just a few times in a lifetime; the sort

of person who created atmosphere and life wherever they went, sweeping lesser mortals into their orbit for a short time until they moved on to pastures new. It would be fatal to get involved in any way with a man like that.

He had talked about meeting fire with fire, but he didn't know her, not really. She was just ordinary—she wanted a home and family eventually, with the right man. Most of all she wanted someone who loved her, who was completely hers. Someone who thought she was wonderful just as she was and who would never look at a tall, beautiful blonde with legs that went right up to her armpits.

She watched the 4x4 move away, lifting her hand briefly in acknowledgement of Flynn's wave, and it wasn't until she hobbled back into the cottage and made her way into the kitchen, intending to make a reviving cup of coffee, that she even realised she was crying.

CHAPTER FIVE

WITH a determination Marigold didn't know she was capable of, she put all thoughts of Flynn Moreau out of her mind for the rest of the day and evening. Admittedly he did have an annoying habit of invading her mind if she let her guard down even for a second, but, with the radio kept on pretty loudly and a book in front of her nose which she'd been promising herself she'd read for ages, she managed fairly well.

Once Flynn had gone she'd hobbled out to the kitchen and found the cupboards and fridge stocked with masses of stuff she hadn't bought, along with several little luxuries that brought her eyes opening wide. Several bottles of a particular red wine that she knew cost the earth; an enormous box of chocolates; a mouth-watering dessert that was all meringue and whipped cream and fresh strawberries and raspberries, and which would easily have served eight people... The list went on.

Marigold viewed it all with a mixture of disquiet and pleasure, and when she poked her head out of the back door she saw there were enough logs and coal for two months, let alone two weeks. You couldn't fault him on generosity. She bit on her lip hard as, the clock on the mantelpiece chiming eleven o'clock, she found her thoughts had returned to Flynn once more.

She had allowed herself one glass of the wonderful wine with her evening meal—a succulent steak grilled with mushrooms and tomatoes—and the taste of it was still on her tongue as she rose to prepare for bed. It was as different from the cheap wine she normally indulged in as chalk from cheese, and accentuated the difference in their ways of life more distinctly than anything else so far. He must have a cellar stocked with expensive wine, she thought dismally as she climbed into bed a few minutes later—a bed with crisp, scented sheets and the beautiful broderie-anglaise cover. From her brief glance in the bedroom the day before she remembered the bed had been piled with old, unattractive blankets and what had appeared to be a moth-eaten eiderdown in faded pink satin.

She had followed Flynn's advice and banked down the fires as he'd instructed, and now the tiny blue and orange flames licking carefully round the base of the damp slack caused the shadows in the room to dance slightly, the odd crackle and spit from the fire immensely comforting. It was gorgeous having a real fire to look at whilst you were all cuddled up and snug in bed, Marigold thought sleepily. She could understand why Emma's grandmother had fought to stay here for so long. With a certain amount of elbow grease to get things looking spick and span, a few tins of paint and a clearing out of some of the more dilapidated items of furniture, to give more space and to show off some of what Marigold recognised were really very nice pieces in the sitting room, the cottage could be transformed.

This bedroom was really very large, although packed as it was it didn't seem so. With just the bed and perhaps a new, smaller wardrobe there would be heaps of room for a good working area by the window. She'd easily fit a chair and drawing board and everything else in…

Marigold stopped abruptly, sitting up in bed and flicking back her curtain of hair as she realised where her musing had led. Was she still seriously considering making an offer to Emma for her grandmother's old home? What about all the inconveniences? What about the isolation? *What about Flynn Moreau?*

She sat for some minutes, staring into space, before sliding down into the warm cocoon again. No, it was an impossible idea. Even if she forgot about all the practical difficulties there was still Flynn. Her heart began to pound with reckless speed at the thought of Flynn as her nearest neighbour, and she spoke to it sternly, telling it to behave.

She wasn't going to think about this any more tonight. She turned over onto her side, adjusting her legs so that her good foot protected her aching ankle, and shut her eyes determinedly. It was Christmas Eve tomorrow, she was in a snug little cottage with snow all around her and masses of food and drink, and it was nice to be on her own for once. It *was*. She'd enjoy her Christmas—quietly perhaps, but she'd still enjoy it—and she wasn't going to think about anything more challenging than when the next glass of wine or meal was due. She probably wouldn't even see Flynn Moreau again anyway...

She was asleep within minutes, and it didn't occur to her, as she drifted away into a deep, dreamless slumber, that she hadn't given a single thought to Dean and Tamara for hours.

It was about ten o'clock the next morning when the sound of someone banging on the front door of the cottage brought Marigold jerking awake. For a moment or two she didn't know where she was and then, as it all flooded back, she pushed the covers aside and reached for the new thick, fleecy white robe she had treated herself to as an early Christmas present. It was the sort of thing she'd seen some of the stars of the silver screen wear in fashionable magazines, and although it had cost an arm and a leg it made her feel wonderfully feminine and expensive. And since Tamara she'd needed to feel feminine.

She tested her weight gingerly on her poorly foot and when it felt bearable she limped carefully to the door without bothering to use the crutches, wondering if Wilf was outside with Myrtle. She brushed her cloud of hair from her eyes and opened the door.

'Good morning.'

It was snowing again, she thought dazedly as she stared into a pair of crystal eyes above which jet-black hair was coated with a feathery covering of white, before forcing herself to answer, 'Good morning.'

'I got you out of bed.' He didn't sound at all sorry; in fact his eyes were inspecting her with a relish that made Marigold feel positively undressed rather than wrapped round in an armour of fluffy white towelling.

'Yes,' she agreed vaguely, wondering how any one man had the right to look so sexy when she hadn't even brushed her teeth. 'I didn't bother to set my alarm.'

'I've brought you something.' He indicated with his hand at the side of him and she looked down to see a cute little Christmas tree sitting on the step. 'We've just brought in the one for the house and this was close by and it seemed the right size for the cottage. Bertha's sorted out a few decorations and what have you. It's in a tub and you'll need to keep it damp so it can go back outside after Christmas.'

'Right.' She knew she wasn't sounding very grateful but she was acutely conscious of her tousled hair and make-up-free face.

'How's the foot?'

'The foot?' Marigold made an effort to pull herself

together. 'Oh, the foot. It seems a bit better, thank you,'
she managed fairly coherently.

'Good.' He paused, looking down at her with glittering eyes. 'There's not any coffee going, is there?'

Marigold flushed. After his open-handed generosity
she could hardly refuse him a cup of coffee, but he
looked so immaculately groomed, with every hair in
place, and she... Well, she wasn't, she reflected hotly.
Although he had nicked himself shaving. Her eyes focused on a tiny cut on the square male chin and she
found herself suddenly short of breath.

'Marigold?'

'What?' She blinked, realising he had said something
else and she hadn't heard a word.

'I said, if it's too much trouble...'

Marigold's flush deepened. 'Of course not,' she said
crossly, and then moderated her tone as she added,
'Please come in, and you can put the tree in the sitting
room by the fireplace if you don't mind. It...it's very
nice.'

'Yes, it is, isn't it?' he agreed meekly, but she had
glanced into the silver eyes again and they were laughing
at her.

Once in the sitting room, Flynn looked somewhat accusingly at the faint glow from the embers of the fire.
'It's nearly out. You see to the coffee and I'll see to the
fire,' he offered, shrugging off his leather jacket and
slinging it onto the sofa as he spoke. 'Have you come
across the old bucket Maggie used for the hot ashes?'

'It's in the broom cupboard; I'll get it,' Marigold said
hastily. She'd discovered the broom cupboard in an alcove in the kitchen the day before. 'You wait here.' The
kitchen was old-fashioned and with barely enough room

to swing a cat; the thought of herself and Flynn enclosed in such a small space was daunting to say the least.

She hobbled her way into the kitchen and opened the cupboard door, grabbing the bucket and swinging round, and then she gave a surprised squeak to find Flynn right behind her.

'You shouldn't be walking on that ankle yet; where are the crutches?'

He was wearing a pair of faded blue jeans and a big Aran jumper which was clearly an old favourite today; he'd obviously dressed down for the expedition in the snow to bring in the Christmas trees. The clothes were clean but faintly shabby if anything, and didn't have the designer cut and flair of the others she had seen him in. So why, Marigold asked herself weakly, did they enhance his dark masculinity even more than the others had done?

She forced herself to concentrate on what she was saying as she replied, 'The crutches are by the bed, I suppose, but I'd rather manage without them if I can. The narrow doorways here are not conducive to an extra pair of legs.'

'Nor anyone above the height of five feet six,' Flynn agreed easily. 'It took me a few visits to see Maggie before I learnt to duck.'

Marigold swallowed and tried a smile. His body was so close it was forcing her to acknowledge her awareness of his male warmth, and the faint scent emanating from the tanned skin—a subtle, spicy fragrance—was causing a reaction in her lower stomach she could well have done without. The trouble was, Flynn was such a *disturbing* man that just being around him was enough to make her all fingers and thumbs, Marigold admitted to herself crossly. Even when he was just being friendly and helpful, like now.

She held up the bucket, unconsciously using it as a defence against his nearness. 'I'll…I'll put the kettle on,' she said a little breathlessly. 'There's only instant coffee, I'm afraid; Maggie clearly didn't run to a coffee maker.'

'No, Maggie was the proverbial cup of tea and hot buttered scones type.' A black eyebrow quirked. 'There *are* some croissants in the bread bin, though, along with one of Bertha's home-made loaves, if you're offering?'

She hadn't been aware she was. She didn't answer immediately. 'Breakfast seems like years ago when you've been working in the fresh air for a while,' he murmured with blatant scheming.

'Oh, I'm sorry; I thought you'd brought in a couple of Christmas trees,' Marigold said severely, 'not a whole forest.'

He grinned at her, utterly unrepentant at his persistence, and Marigold floundered. 'Croissants it is, then,' she agreed quickly, just wishing he would move and put a little more space between them. 'And I suppose you know where the preserves are, too?'

'Left-hand cupboard above the sink,' Flynn answered meekly. 'And I prefer blackcurrant.'

'You'll get what you're given.'

'Promises, promises…'

But he had taken the bucket and was walking out of the kitchen and she could breathe again.

'And don't try to carry a tray or anything,' he called over his shoulder. 'I'll come and see to it once the fire's blazing.'

By half-past ten Marigold was seated in front of a roaring fire which contrasted beautifully with the swirling snowflakes outside the sitting-room window, eating croissants warmed in the kitchen's big old oven. Flynn demolished five to her two—his liberally covered with blackcurrant preserve—after which he said pensively, 'Ever tried toast made over an open fire?'

'You can't still be hungry!'

'I burn off a lot of energy.' He eyed her over his coffee mug and she didn't ask how.

They found a toasting fork among the instruments hanging on a black iron stand on the hearth, and once Flynn had cut the bread and begun toasting it over the fire the smell was so wonderful that Marigold found herself eating a piece dripping with melting butter even though she was full up.

This was too cosy by half. She slanted a glance at Flynn under her eyelashes. He was busy toasting his second doorstep, crouched down in front of the fire in a manner which stretched the denim tight over lean, strong hips and muscled thighs. He had a magnificent body... The thought came from nowhere and shocked her into choking on an errant crumb.

How on earth had she come to be sitting here in her dressing gown, sharing breakfast with a man she had only known for a couple of days? Marigold asked herself faintly. But she knew the answer—because the man in question went by the name of Flynn Moreau. He was like a human bulldozer, she thought with a touch of desperate bewilderment—riding roughshod over any objections or difficulties in his path to get what he wanted.

Did he want her? She risked another glance and then stiffened as she met his eyes. 'What's the matter?' he asked softly.

'The matter?'

'You were frowning.'

'Was I?' she prevaricated feebly. She managed to divert him by making some excuse about twinges in her foot, before she quickly moved on to the fact she needed a hot bath and to get dressed.

'Go ahead,' he offered blandly. 'I'll wash up and then set up the Christmas tree.'

'No, it's all right really.' The thought of Flynn in the cottage while she lay naked in the bath was unthinkable. 'You must have lots to do back at the house, and didn't you say you had guests arriving today?'

'Later,' he agreed smoothly.

'Well, I'd like to have a really long, hot soak,' she persisted firmly, 'and I shan't feel comfortable doing that if I know I'm keeping you waiting. It…it'll be good for my ankle,' she added.

He stared at her but the doctor in him won. 'OK.' He stood up in one lithe, graceful male movement and she blinked. 'I don't suppose it's any good my offering to wash your back?' he suggested softly.

'No good at all.'

'Shame.'

Yes, it was rather. Marigold smiled brightly. 'Thank you very much for the Christmas tree, and thank Bertha for the decorations for me, would you?' she said evenly.

'You can thank her yourself later,' Flynn returned just as evenly as he walked to the door.

'I'm sorry?'

'Oh, didn't I mention it?' He opened the sitting-room door, passing through to the hall, and she heard his voice in the moments before he shut the door after him say coolly, 'I'm picking you up at six tonight for the party at my house.'

Marigold wouldn't have believed she could move so quickly but she was at the front door within moments, yanking it open and calling to the dark figure making his way to the 4x4 parked at the end of the garden. 'Flynn? *Flynn!*'

'You bellowed, ma'am?' He turned, shrugging on the leather jacket as he did so, and she tried to ignore how good he looked as she said, 'I can't possibly come to your party; you know I can't.'

'I know nothing of the sort,' he returned mildly.

'I can hardly walk, for one thing.'

'You said your ankle was a little better.'

'Not better enough for a party,' Marigold objected.

'You don't have to dance if you don't want to.'

They were having dancing. Dancing meant dance dresses. 'I can't possibly come,' she said again, her voice even firmer. 'I've absolutely nothing to wear. I came here just to crash out for a few days if you remember, and anyway, I was looking forward to a quiet Christmas Eve at the cottage in front of the fire.'

He tilted his head. 'You're twenty-five, right?'

Marigold nodded warily, big, fat, starry flakes of snow drifting idly onto the hall mat.

'Beautiful twenty-five-year-olds don't look forward to sitting all alone in front of a fire like old women on Christmas Eve,' Flynn stated silkily, but she'd caught the metallic chink of steel under the velvety softness of his tone.

She felt the 'beautiful' melting her resistance and fought the weakness with all her might. 'This one does,' she said flatly.

'You're coming, Marigold. As to the clothes, you needn't worry. The bunch who are coming tonight could be dressed in anything from jeans to Dior.' He had walked back to the cottage door as he'd been speaking and now he reached out for her, his firm, slightly stern and very sensuous mouth smiling.

What were the odds on it being the Dior, Marigold asked herself wryly, but with his fingertips against her lower ribs, and the warmth of his palms cupping her sides sending pulsing sensation through her body, it was hard to concentrate on anything but his closeness.

Nevertheless, she opened her mouth to object but before she could say a word his lips had snatched it away, plunging swiftly into the undefended territory as he took full advantage of her momentary uncertainty. This time there was no gentle persuasion; the kiss was hot and potent and dangerous, feeding a heady rush of wild sensation that had her gasping against his mouth. He pulled her hard into him until she felt she was branded against his maleness; the sensation more intimate than all the caresses she had shared with Dean.

This was what it should be like, she thought headily as her senses swam. This need, this desire, this overwhelming, driving urge to get closer and closer. For the first time in her life she was revelling in the knowledge that she was a woman, one half of a perfect whole.

She could feel his heart pounding like a sledgehammer against the solid wall of his chest, and then, as his hands moved beneath the thick towelling and found the warm, soft silk of her nightie, the flesh beneath firm and taut, she trembled helplessly.

She felt this man was an alien being, a dark, powerful stranger who could sweep her into another world without even trying, and yet at the same time she felt she had known him since the world began, that he had always been part of her. She shivered, the extent of her need frightening, and immediately she felt him move away. 'You're cold.' His voice was rueful, and she hated him that he could even formulate words when she was feeling so utterly devastated. 'Go and have that hot bath and I'll see you tonight.'

She didn't say anything for the simple reason she couldn't, but after he had left, in a swirl of snow as he drove the big vehicle hard towards the house on the other side of the valley, she berated herself a hundred times as she lay soaking in the warm, bubbly water.

She must be mad, stark, staring mad, to agree to go to this party tonight! Not that she had actually agreed, she comforted herself vainly, not in so many words. But he'd come for her at six and he wouldn't take no for an answer, she argued dismally. She'd committed herself to an evening with a host of strangers, all of whom would know each other and be decked up to the nines, and there she'd be—the proverbial Cinderella!

She stayed in the water until it was almost cold and she was beginning to resemble a shrivelled white prune, and then towelled herself dry too vigorously. Her ankle was turning all sorts of interesting shades, she noted with a detachment borne of thoughts of the evening, but at least it wasn't hurting so much and the swelling was beginning to slowly subside. She'd have to wear the bandage tonight, of course, but she just might be able to force a shoe on her foot.

She blow-dried her hair to the accompaniment of 'Hark, the Herald Angels Sing', courtesy of the radio, and then creamed herself all over to 'God Rest Ye Merry Gentlemen'. She had expected to feel abjectly miserable on this special day, or at least heartily melancholy, but with mouth-drying apprehension and quivering excitement vying for first place in her breast there was no room for anything else.

Creamed and dry, and still in her bathrobe, Marigold inspected the contents of the wardrobe and groaned weakly. She had packed with a view to a week or so in a remote cottage where warmth and comfort might be at a premium if there were power cuts or any other winter problems; not a top-drawer party!

She had brought her expensive tight black jeans—just in case everything else had got soaked through some catastrophe, not because she had thought she would actually wear them—but the only way they would look right for a party was teamed with a flamboyant top of some kind. And that she definitely did not have.

She frowned to herself, wondering if the cottage boasted a brown paper bag which would fit over her head and at least hide her mortification!

And then her eyes fell on the grubby lace curtain at the bedroom window. It might be dusty, she acknowledged as a dart of excitement shot into her mind, but if she wasn't mistaken it was the most beautiful antique lace in a soft cream. Dared she take it down and use it for tonight? She'd inherited her mother's flair with a needle and she always brought an emergency kit of needle and thread away with her; she could do this. She would buy the most fabulous replacement in the world after Christmas—not that Emma would probably even notice she had used the curtain in the first place. She had been talking about paying someone to come and clear the house—furniture, carpets, curtains and all—the last time they'd met when Emma had given her the key.

Marigold limped over to the window, reaching out a tentative hand and touching the lovely old material reverently. Funnily enough it wasn't Emma's reaction to her using the curtain which bothered Marigold, but her grandmother's. Her eyes moved to the faded wallpaper above the fireplace where a wedding photograph of a young couple was hung. Emma's grandparents, she'd be bound. She hobbled over to the fire, gazing long and hard at the young, smiling girl resplendent in the old-fashioned dress and veil, and deep, dark eyes set in a lovely, sweet face stared back at her.

Take it, they were saying. Use it, enjoy it. Hold your head high and let everyone know you are as good as them. You're your own woman, aren't you? You would have fought to stay where you wanted to be, wouldn't you? *Wouldn't you?*

'I would.' Marigold breathed the words out loud.

So we are sisters, separated only by time. Take the lace and make it into something beautiful…

Marigold had the most absorbing Christmas Eve afternoon.

After gently removing the curtain from its hooks, she washed it tenderly. It dried within minutes by the fire, and then, very carefully, she cut the lace to a pattern she'd drawn out on an old newspaper, humming along to a Christmas carol concert as she worked.

Several hundred tiny, neat stitches later the top was ready, and even to Marigold's critical eyes it looked like a million dollars. She pulled it over her head for the final fit and then sat, flushed with success, as she looked at her reflection in the ancient mirror on the back of one of the wardrobe doors. It could be a Dior, she told herself firmly. Or an Armani or a Versace. It had a real touch of class. And the simple black pumps she had stuffed into her case at the last minute wouldn't look amiss either. Of course, black strappy sandals would have looked better, but no one would have expected that with her ankle the way it was.

It was getting dark outside by the time she dressed the little tree Flynn had brought, but once festooned in the tinsel and glittering baubles Bertha had sent it looked delightful.

Marigold was so pleased with the top and the tree she had a glass of Flynn's wicked red wine with a calorie-loaded pizza at five o'clock, but, owing to the fact that she had resisted taking any of the painkillers with the party in mind that day, she felt she could indulge.

Once she'd eaten, she concentrated on her make-up and her hair. After two attempts to put her hair up she stopped fighting and allowed it its freedom. It fell, shining, swinging and glossy, to her shoulders, its subtle shades complimenting her creamy skin and deep blue eyes, although Marigold herself was oblivious to its beauty. She stared anxiously into the mirror, wishing she could twirl and pin it high on her head to give the illusion of an extra inch or two to her height, but it was so fine and silky it defied pins and restraints.

After applying the lightest of foundations to her clear, smooth skin, Marigold brushed a little indigo-blue shadow on her eyelids and a couple of coatings of mascara on her lashes. A touch of creamy plum lipstick and she was nearly ready. She bit fretfully on her full lower lip as she surveyed her reflection, and then clicked her tongue in annoyance as lipstick coated her two front teeth.

After a tissue had removed the offending colour Marigold tried again, her heart fluttering like the wings of a bird. The top looked great, but what she would give for another five or six inches on her height was nobody's business!

Calm, girl, calm. She fixed tiny silver studs in her ears—the only earrings she had brought with her—as she wondered what on earth she was doing. This was as far removed from the cosy, quiet Christmas Eve she'd had in mind a few days ago as a trip to the moon! But it was happening... She breathed deeply and prayed for serenity. It was happening and all she could do was to get through the next few hours with as much poise and dignity as she could muster.

Why had Flynn asked her to the party? Was he really interested in her or was she just a novelty; worse, did he feel sorry for her? But those kisses hadn't been borne of pity, had they? No, they hadn't, she reassured herself feverishly. She might not be as experienced and worldly wise as Flynn Moreau, but even she knew the difference between sympathy and a far stronger emotion—that of desire.

But she didn't *want* him to desire her! The girl looking back at her from out of the mirror's misty depths challenged that thought with her bright eyes and flushed cheeks, and now Marigold's face showed a touch of panic. She had to get a grip on herself, for goodness' sake. A man like Flynn could have any woman he wanted with a click of his fingers; he wasn't about to lose any sleep over her one way or the other. All she had to do was to make it clear she wasn't on for a little Christmas hanky-panky and she wouldn't see him for dust. Simple really.

The firm, loud knock on the front door of the cottage interrupted this rational line of thought and brought Marigold's eyes snapping open to their fullest extent. He was here! She cast one last, frantic glance at the mirror and then shut her eyes tightly for a moment, before opening them and bringing back her shoulders in a stance which would have been more appropriate for going to war than to a Christmas Eve party.

She had rested her ankle all day and she felt the benefit of this as she walked to meet Flynn, although it had still been a slight struggle to force her shoe over her swollen foot.

'Hi.' His voice was lazy as she opened the door; his eyes were anything but.

Marigold flushed slightly at the male appreciation the grey gaze was making no effort to conceal, and knew every second of the hours it had taken to make the lacy top was worthwhile. 'Hello.' She was pleased how composed her voice sounded.

'You look beautiful,' he said very softly, his height and breadth accentuated by the dusky-grey silk shirt and black trousers he was wearing.

Marigold was overwhelmingly relieved he wasn't in a dinner jacket. Her top with the expensive black jeans came nicely within smart-casual category. Nevertheless, his clothes screamed an exclusive designer label. For a moment she had the slightly hysterical thought—borne of nerves—as to what he would say if he knew she was wearing an old curtain, but then she thrust it to one side and answered politely, 'Thank you.'

'Here.' He had been holding one hand behind his back and now he brought out a small box in which reposed the most exquisite corsage of two pale cream orchids. 'I must have sixth sense or something; it's just the right colour.'

'Oh, how lovely.' She was entranced at the delicate beauty of the flowers, the pink in her cheeks deepening at the unexpected gift. 'But you really shouldn't have.'

He smiled slowly, extracting the corsage from its snug box and bending forward to fix it on her top as he said quietly, his eyes on the flowers, 'Wilf's prepared one for each of the female guests tonight, courtesy of his greenhouse.'

His fingers were warm against her skin as he fixed the

orchids in place and Marigold was glad he was concentrating on the corsage for two reasons. One, his touch was doing the strangest things to her insides, and two, *ridiculously* the fact that every woman at the party was receiving the same gift had hurt for a moment.

'But I chose this one myself.' His voice smoky warm, he added, 'There was something about the delicate beauty on the outside of the flower married to the fierce, passionate colour within which reminded me of you.'

That suggestion again that she was passionate, fiery... Marigold wrenched her eyes from his as she looked down at the orchids, their scent heady and the rich, vibrant scarlet inside the graceful blooms a magnificent contrast to the cool loveliness of the exterior.

'That's very flattering,' she managed fairly lightly, 'especially for someone called Marigold Flower. I've never imagined myself being likened to an orchid.'

'Oh, I'm not underestimating the beauty of the marigold, I assure you.'

He was still very close, too close, and she didn't like how her nerves tingled but found her body's response was quite outside of her control.

'I think they're exquisite flowers, as it happens,' he continued silkily, his eyes intent on her flushed face. 'The French marigold with its yellow and chestnut-red flowers and the full, delicate African variety are just as lovely as the dwarf with its small single orange flowers, and they are all fighters, did you know that? Hardy and determined to survive as well as beautiful. Of course, they prefer sunny, tranquil places and a trouble-free existence, but when adversity and storms arrive they find they can grow almost anywhere.'

Marigold was quite aware Flynn was talking about more than garden plants. She stared at him, wondering how it was that the veiled compliments should give her such enormous pleasure when she had only known him for forty-eight hours or so. And then she took hold of the feeling of excitement and gratification as a little warning voice deep in her mind spoke cold reason. As a chat-up line it was pretty good and he had obviously done his homework on marigolds, she thought wryly, but all this didn't mean anything beyond a brief flirtation.

'You certainly know your flowers,' she said as off-handedly as she could manage.

'No, just marigolds.' He was watching her closely, seriously, and a little trickle of something she couldn't name shivered down her spine. And then the firm, stern mouth relaxed, a smile twisting along his lips. 'Come on, everyone will be wondering where we've got to,' he said evenly. 'Have you got a wrap or coat or something?'

She had only brought her fleece and cagoule with her and neither was remotely suitable for this evening, Marigold thought distractedly as she hurried back to the bedroom. But other than freeze she had no choice but the fleece; she hadn't even brought a cardigan with her—just several chunky jumpers.

She reached for her black purse, which she'd emptied of money a few minutes earlier and replaced with a lipstick and comb, and caught a glimpse of herself in the mirror as she did so. The tight black jeans, waist-length lacy top and black pumps *did* look good.

She glanced at her faithful old fleece, which had seen better days, and decided to freeze.

Flynn was using the snowboard that had been propped against the wall of the cottage to clear the path when she locked the front door and popped the key into her purse, so the walk to the big 4x4 parked just outside the garden gate was problem-free.

Marigold paused before climbing into the vehicle, glancing up at the sky, which was now clear of snow clouds. A host of twinkling diamonds set in black velvet stretched endlessly in the heavens, timeless and enchanting, and below the frost had already formed crystals on the surface of the snow like a carpet of diamond dust. It was a beautiful, *beautiful* Christmas Eve, Marigold thought wonderingly. And she was going to spend it in the company of this commanding, enigmatic man, Flynn Moreau.

And the strange thing, the really fanciful thing was that she'd been fighting a feeling all day that somehow this was meant to be. Fighting it because she knew, in the heart of her, that a man like Flynn would be treating this as a pleasant interlude, no more. And because every instinct she possessed was screaming the warning that he was a dark threat to her peace of mind, her well-being, and if she let just the tiniest chink in her armour fail she would regret it for the rest of her life.

CHAPTER SIX

IT WAS halfway through the evening—when Marigold admitted to herself that she was having the time of her life—that she found she could actually smile at her ridiculous notions concerning Flynn. Of course, by then she had downed several glasses of the champagne that seemed to be flowing as freely as water, but that had only relaxed her a little, she told herself firmly. Flynn's friends were a great bunch and they had welcomed her as if they had known her all their lives, and Flynn himself was a charming host.

The house was a Christmas dream, decorated with traditional holly and ivy and deep-red velvet ribbons, and the enormous Christmas tree standing in the hall was a vision of red and gold, tiny flickering candles and shimmering baubles vying with streams of glittering tinsel and fairy lights.

Marigold found she was never alone, even though she had refused several offers to dance because of her ankle. Somehow she'd been drawn quite naturally into a group of Flynn's colleagues who were about her age or a little older. As the evening progressed she found they were wonderful company, funny and often outrageous, teasing each other with a naturalness that declared they all knew each other very well.

Flynn seemed to be near by even when he wasn't actually with her most of the night, but his attentiveness—if that was what it was—was merely the kind that a good host would display to a guest who didn't really know anyone else, Marigold reminded herself umpteen times during the evening.

At midnight there were howls of excited laughter and little shrieks when Father Christmas, complete in red suit and white beard, appeared, delving into his enormous sack for presents for everyone. All the women had items of jewellery and the men gold cuff-links, and as Marigold unwrapped her gift—a pair of tiny gold hoops with a single red stone enclosed in a teardrop hanging from them—she happened to glance at Flynn, intending to mouth 'thank you' across the heads between them.

He was leaning back against the wall close to where she was sitting, arms crossed over his chest and a faintly brooding expression on his dark face, and for a disquieting moment she got the impression he was viewing them all from a distance, like a scientist forced to inspect some rather uninteresting bugs under his microscope.

Marigold felt the impact of the thought like a shower of cold water and lowered her eyes quickly, making an excuse about visiting the cloakroom in the next moment and escaping from the noisy throng.

Once in the cloakroom, which had been designated for use by the ladies only, the gentlemen having to use one on the floor above, Marigold went into one of the two cubicles and closed the door, needing some privacy to marshall her whirling thoughts. Flynn's whole charming, amenable-host act had been nothing more than that—an act, she told herself flatly. None of them had seen what the real man was thinking or feeling tonight. That look on his face; it had been unnerving, disturbing.

Marigold glanced down at her ankle, which was beginning to remind her it was still around, and breathed deeply several times to control her racing heartbeat. It was what she had sensed in him all along, this autonomy. The women had been flocking around him tonight and even the men searched out his company, obviously enjoying his companionship, but all along he had been... What? she asked herself. And the answer came, absent from them. Flynn was here in the physical but mentally a million miles away.

She sat in the cubicle for a few moments more, angry with herself that the revelation had bothered her so much. All this would seem like a dream when she got back to the reality of her life in London; none of it mattered, not really.

And then, as though to call her bluff, she heard the door to the cloakroom open and the sound of voices.

'But who *is* she? Surely someone knows?'

'Darling, you know as much as me. According to Flynn she's a friend, that's all. She's staying in that dear little cottage we pass to get to the house apparently.'

Marigold had intended to rise and leave her hidey-hole but had frozen at the first words, knowing they were talking about her.

'Friend? Well, there are friends and friends!' The other woman giggled, not nastily but in a way that brought a pink tinge to Marigold's cheeks.

'Janet! You're terrible. You don't know anything's going on, now then. Anyway, don't forget there's always Celine in the background,' the other woman warned in a much more sober fashion. 'Whoever this girl is and whatever the relationship between her and Flynn, she'll go the same way as the rest.'

'He's such a dreamboat, though, isn't he?' Janet sighed, long and lustily. 'One night with Flynn and I bet you'd be ruined for any other man.'

'Janet!' Now Marigold could tell the other woman was definitely shocked although she was half laughing when she said, 'You've only been married six months; you should still be in the first throes of married bliss and thinking only of Henry! Right, that's my face repaired; are you coming?'

'Yes, all right. Let me just put on a bit more lipstick…'

There was a brief pause before the sound of the door opening and closing again, and then silence.

Marigold sat absolutely still for a full minute. Celine. Whoever this other woman was, she would have to be called something like that; something more ordinary just wouldn't fit the bill. Celine, Tamara… Were they born with names like that or did they choose them themselves when they decided to turn into *femmes fatales*? So, Flynn had a Celine in his life, did he? A Celine who he always returned to, by the sound of it.

Marigold stood up slowly, anger beginning to replace the sick feeling of disappointment. He'd had no right to kiss her when he was involved with someone else. 'Whoever this girl is and whatever the relationship between her and Flynn, she'll go the same way as the rest.' The woman's words burnt in Marigold's mind.

Clearly Flynn and Celine had one of these open relationships, or perhaps the other woman just put up with the status quo because she knew she was different to a casual affair? That she had his heart if not exclusive rights to his body?

Marigold looked down at her hands and realised her fingers were curled into her palms so tightly they were hurting. She forced herself to relax them finger by finger, took a deep breath and then opened the door of the cubicle, stepping out into the carpeted area where the two washbasins reposed against a mirrored wall. It was quite empty.

She splashed her wrists with cold water for a few moments before dabbing some on the back of her neck. She had no reason to feel angry and let down, she told herself miserably, but she did. He had only kissed her a couple of times when all was said and done.

And then she frowned. No, this line of reasoning was flawed, she declared militantly to herself. Flynn had told her he was a single man, and maybe he was—technically. But with Celine around, in her book he was definitely not up for grabs. Not that she would have grabbed him anyway, Marigold reassured herself fiercely. But the fact remained he had not been totally honest with her, even if he *had* told everyone she was just a friend. At least those gossipy women hadn't been sure if there was anything between her and Flynn. Which, of course, there wasn't, never had been and never would be, Celine or no Celine, she added vehemently.

So...she would go back out there and behave just as she had been doing all evening. She'd laugh and joke and be friendly, and when Flynn took her home—*if* he took her home; he might well get Wilf to do the honours, for all she knew—she would thank him politely for a wonderful party and make a graceful exit out of his life. And that—*most definitely*—would be that. She would be quietly dignified and decorous, and would never intimate she knew anything at all about Celine. He was entitled to live his life exactly as he chose, but as far as she was concerned she thought it stank!

She stood a moment or two more, staring at herself in the mirrors. She would make it abundantly clear she did not fancy him or want anything at all to do with him; if nothing else he would remember her a little differently from *the rest*. Those words had got right under her skin, she admitted ruefully. There was something terribly humiliating in being herded under such a heading.

She applied fresh lipstick, ran her comb through her hair so it fell in shimmering wings against her soft skin, and then squared her shoulders.

Right, Flynn, she thought with a trace of dark amusement. This is where you start having to face the fact that you are not God's gift to the whole female race!

Couples were dancing to a popular Christmas hit in the hall as she made her way back to the drawing room, edging carefully round gyrating bodies. Still more were jigging about on the perimeter of the drawing room and the buzz of conversation and laughter was deafening. Everyone was having a wonderful time.

'I missed you.' Flynn must have been waiting for her because no sooner had she put her nose through the door than he was at her side, the intensity of his gaze making her skin burn in spite of herself.

'Oh, I doubt that.' She forced a light laugh she was inordinately proud of.

'Then I'll have to convince you somehow,' he murmured softly, smiling his slow smile. 'Let's find a quiet corner.'

Oh, no, she wasn't having any of this. If he wanted a Christmas intrigue—Celine obviously being elsewhere—he had picked the wrong girl, Marigold told herself tightly. She flashed him a brilliant smile. 'I wouldn't dream of taking you away from your other guests,' she said brightly, turning away from him in the same instant and making her way over to the group she had left earlier, inwardly seething.

Those two women had known about Celine and no doubt the existence of the other woman was common knowledge among the rest of the folk here, or a certain number of them at any rate. How *dared* he come on to her in front of everyone?

She had half expected Flynn to follow her and press his cause, but when there was no firm male hand on her shoulder or soft voice in her ear she assumed he hadn't thought it was worth the effort—that *she* wasn't worth the effort.

The talk within the group had shifted to medical matters when she rejoined them, several of the party being doctors and nurses. One of the other women—married to a young surgeon who was just relating the complications he'd encountered when he took the appendix out of some unfortunate soul—leant across to Marigold as she sat down. 'It always turns to work,' she murmured conspiratorially. 'If I've heard about one operation at a dinner party or some function or other, I've heard about hundreds! It's so boring. Oh, sorry, I never thought— you're not in the profession, are you?'

'Not me.' Marigold smiled back into the rosy face topped by blonde curls. She had noticed this particular couple earlier; the wife was about seven months pregnant and always laughing and cuddling her doctor husband, and he was blatantly besotted with his pretty wife. Marigold had found herself envying them with all her heart, which had surprised her at the time. Even when she had been engaged to Dean she had been in no particular rush to settle down and have babies, and now that was definitely on the back burner. But something about this couple had made her terribly broody. It must be wonderful to be pregnant by the man you love, she thought with a sudden painfulness which amazed her afresh.

'Good, I'm glad you're not a doctor or nurse. We can talk fashion and hairstyles and soaps—*anything* but hospitals and operations!' The pretty face smiled at her and Marigold smiled back, forcing herself to concentrate on the conversation rather than do what every nerve in her body was willing her to do and to turn round and see where Flynn was.

At one o'clock Bertha appeared with hot mulled wine and a stack of mince pies and a Christmas cake which would have fed a small army, and at half-past one the first of the guests began to leave—some to their rooms within the house, and others to the village inn some miles away where Flynn had apparently booked rooms. According to Marigold's new friend, those guests staying at the inn were returning in the morning for Christmas lunch and tea.

Flynn had joined the group some fifteen minutes or so after Marigold but he hadn't singled her out for any special attention, keeping everyone amused with a dry, wicked wit that could be slightly caustic, and which had everyone—Marigold noted with acid cynicism—hanging on his every word. He was clearly the big fish in this particular pond, and the other guests' adulation—which bordered on reverence in Marigold's jaded opinion—grated unbearably.

'The offer's still open for you to use the annexe tonight.' Marigold had walked across to the laden trolley at one side of the room to leave her glass and empty plate with the others deposited there, and she hadn't been aware Flynn had followed her until his deep voice stroked across the back of her neck.

'No, thank you.' She tried, she *really* tried to keep her voice light and friendly, but even to her own ears it sounded strained.

'OK, out with it, Marigold,' Flynn said coolly. 'What's the matter?'

'The matter?' She nerved herself to turn and face him, wiping her face of all expression. 'Sorry, I don't understand. I thought I'd made it clear yesterday I intended to sleep at the cottage?' And definitely, *definitely* not in his bed. If he thought he could use her as a bed warmer till Celine turned up, he'd got another think coming.

'Forget where you're sleeping. I asked you what was the matter.'

She stared up at him, at the stern mouth and firm jaw, and it was with deep self-disgust that Marigold realised she envied Celine more than she would have thought possible. 'Nothing is the matter,' she lied steadily.

'Marigold, part of the job of being a good surgeon— and I am a damn good surgeon—is to know when people are tense and worried, when they're keeping something back,' he said evenly. 'Something has happened tonight and I want to know what it is.'

The arrogance was outstanding. Marigold looked him squarely in the eye. 'Just because I don't want to stay in your house—' or sleep in your bed '—doesn't mean there's anything the matter,' she said firmly, hidden desperation helping the lie to trip more easily off her tongue. 'I'm tired, that's all, and I want to go back to the cottage, but I've had a lovely time and thank you for asking me.'

She sounded for all the world like a small child primed by her mother to thank the hostess at the end of a birthday party. Flynn's eyes narrowed as they moved over her uplifted face. 'So you'll be joining us for lunch tomorrow?' he asked silkily.

'Thank you but no. The ankle's really sore tonight so I'll probably spend most of the day in bed.' Lying the second time was easier, she realised detachedly.

Flynn nodded, his face holding all the warmth of a block of cold granite. 'I'll take you back to the cottage.'

'Oh, right.' Somehow she hadn't expected him to capitulate so swiftly. She'd won, she told herself silently as she said goodbye to everyone and made her way with Flynn to the front door, so why did it feel as if she'd lost?

Once they were sitting in the big vehicle she knew it was because she *had* lost. One or two couples who were obviously staying at the inn had followed them outside into the clear, icy air, and now their cars roared off into the freezing night, but Flynn made no effort to drive away after starting the engine.

Marigold turned to him after a few seconds had ticked by with excruciating slowness.

'We aren't budging until I get the truth,' he said pleasantly. 'There's a full tank of petrol and we can sit here all night with the engine running to keep us warm. *Are* you warm enough?' he added.

She was absolutely frozen but would sooner have walked on red-hot coals than admit it. 'I'm fine.'

He didn't actually call her a liar—reaching into the back seat and lifting over a thick car rug was eloquent enough—but Marigold didn't put up a protest when he wrapped it round her; her teeth were chattering too much.

It was a full five minutes before anyone spoke again, and the silence had got so loud it was deafening, when Marigold—warm again, buried as she was in the soft folds of the rug—said tightly, 'This is perfectly ridiculous, you know that, don't you? People will wonder what on earth we're doing out here.'

'I've lived for thirty-eight years without caring what people thought; I don't intend to start now.' He'd shifted in his seat to face her when she had spoken and his voice was perfectly calm.

Now, that was probably the most honest thing he had said to her since they'd met, Marigold thought bitterly. 'So you live by your own codes and values, regardless of anyone else, do you?' she flung back, goaded into saying more than she had intended.

'I wasn't aware I'd said that.'

'But it's the truth,' she stated fiercely. 'Well, I'm sorry but I happen to believe in monogamy within a relationship for as long as it lasts.'

His eyes narrowed. 'Meaning, I presume, that I don't?'

'Are you saying you do?'

'Whoa, lady.' He had been affable up until a moment ago; now the handsome male face was as cold as the scene outside the window and his eyes were steely. 'I'm getting the distinct impression I'm being set up for a fall here, and I don't intend to defend myself to you or anyone else.'

What a very convenient attitude, Marigold thought hotly.

'Now, I don't know what's going on in that pretty head of yours, but for the record I think fidelity is the foundation for any man-woman relationship, whether the parties intend it to be a permanent one or not. Does that answer your question?'

Oh, the *hypocrisy* of it! Marigold was so mad she forgot all her noble intentions. 'And Celine?' she asked icily. 'Does she hold to your views and still kiss every man in sight? Or perhaps fidelity in your book is something different to the dictionary definition?'

For a moment there was absolute stillness within the vehicle, her words seeming to hover in the air and echo all about them, and even before Flynn replied Marigold knew something was desperately wrong. She'd made a terrible mistake.

She braced herself for the explosion that was sure to come if the look on his face was anything to go by, her stomach muscles knotting and her mouth suddenly dry.

'Celine?' His voice was quiet, expressionless. 'Who spoke to you about Celine and what was said?' His very quietness was more intimidating than any outward show of rage.

'No one; it wasn't like that. They didn't know I was there. In the cloakroom…' Her voice trailed away; she was making a mess of this. But he hadn't denied there was a Celine. She took a deep breath and said quickly, 'I was in the cloakroom and two women were talking. They said…' She stopped abruptly, trying to remember the exact words.

'Yes?' One word but painfully chilling.

'They said Celine was always in the background, even when you…when you were with someone else,' she faltered uncomfortably, wishing with all her heart she had never started this.

'What else?'

'Nothing, not really. Just that it sounded as though there had…well, been quite a few…'

'Affairs?' he put in ruthlessly.

'Yes.' Well, it *had* sounded like that. 'All the rest'. How else could she take that?

'So you assumed from this snippet which you over-heard that I have a lover but indulge in brief affairs with other women when the fancy takes me. Is that it? And you did not think it pertinent to ask me about it? You preferred to freeze me out all night?' he grated softly, looking as though he would like to shake her or worse.

Marigold stared at him. What had she done? Oh, what had she done? 'I...I didn't freeze you out—'

'The hell you didn't,' he said grimly, starting the engine as he spoke and then swinging the large vehicle so violently round the drive in a semicircle that Marigold nearly screamed.

The set of his jaw warned her to say nothing more as he drove—far too fast in view of the treacherous conditions—back to the cottage. Marigold sat hunched in her seat, her mind numb and all her senses concentrated on getting out of the vehicle in one piece.

By the time they drew up outside the garden gate Marigold felt weak with relief that they weren't in a ditch or wrapped round a tree, and as Flynn left the car she just managed to pull herself together sufficiently to shrug off the rug before he opened the door, holding out his hand to help her down.

She glanced at his coldly impassive face. 'Thank you.' Her voice was very small but as she descended he said nothing, merely holding her arm as she limped along the path, which was now a sheet of ice.

She had to have two tries at sliding the key in the lock before her trembling hands could negotiate the point of contact, and once the door swung open he turned and began to walk away. Marigold stared after him, her heart racing, and knew she had to say something, *anything*. She couldn't just let him go like this. 'Flynn?' Her voice was shaking.

He stopped but didn't turn round. 'Yes?'

'If I got it wrong, I'm sorry. Truly. But they made it sound...' Her voice trailed away. 'I'm sorry,' she said again.

'You believed what you wanted to believe,' he said flatly.

Marigold opened her mouth to deny it but the words hung on her tongue unsaid. He was right. She stared at the big figure in front of her, appalled. He was absolutely right. There could have been all manner of explanations for what she'd overheard, but she'd jumped to the obvious one because she had needed to distance herself from this man. From the moment she had met him he had been a threat somehow.

When she remained silent he swung to face her, and now a mirthless smile twisted the hard mouth briefly as he read the truth on her face. 'Don't worry, I won't bother you again; you can have your quiet Christmas,' he said wearily, turning and walking on down the path again.

'Flynn?' She had no right to ask and it was probably the height of presumption in view of all that had been said, but she would never sleep again if she didn't *know*. 'Who is Celine?'

For a second she thought he was going to ignore her but then he halted again, his back to her as his voice said flatly, 'Celine was my fiancée; you may have heard of her—Celine Jenet?'

Marigold *had* heard of her; there probably wasn't a woman in the western world who hadn't heard of the beautiful French model.

'We were together for a while some years ago but we parted a week before the wedding. It caused a great deal of interest at the time; probably, in view of what you heard tonight, it still does.' There was a biting note of cynicism running through the cold voice now. 'It deeply disappointed the media, and to a lesser extent our friends and families, that we didn't choose to tell all or rip each other apart, but at the risk of sounding tedious we were friends. We still are, but that's all we are.'

Marigold didn't know what to say but in the event it didn't matter because Flynn obviously considered the conversation finished. He walked on, climbing into the vehicle without even a nod of his head or a wave of his hand.

Long after the lights of the 4x4 had disappeared Marigold continued to stand on the doorstep, only entering the house when she became aware she was chilled to the bone.

Celine Jenet. She sank down onto the rug in front of the glowing fire in the sitting room, removing the guard she had put in place before she left for the party and placing several small logs on the red embers, which leapt into immediate, crackling life. *Celine Jenet.* She was gorgeous. Six feet of sultry, large-eyed, tousled sex-kitten appeal, and she had been his fiancée. No wonder those women had said no one else could match up to Celine. Why had she left him? For another man? Because of her career maybe?

Marigold stared into the flames, her heart thudding. Whatever the reason, it had not caused Flynn to hate Celine, but did he still love her? He had said they were only friends but that didn't mean he didn't secretly wish for more, perhaps even hoped they might get back together some day.

She held out her cold hands to the fire but found the chill came from within rather than without. Flynn might not hate his ex-fiancée but it was a sure-fire bet he hated her, Marigold thought miserably. And now she thought about it, especially in view of his explanation about the Frenchwoman, she didn't understand why she had behaved so badly. She didn't normally jump to erroneous assumptions about people; in fact she was just the opposite. If she hadn't given Dean the benefit of the doubt on various occasions she would have realised what he was up to long before she had. But with Flynn...

With Flynn it was different. For some reason this man affected her like no other human being she had ever met.

Marigold bit hard on her lip, hating the way she was feeling but unable to conquer the utter desolation that had swept over her. So much for a quiet, peaceful Christmas by herself to recharge her batteries and get strength to face the changes she intended to make in the future. She wished she'd never set eyes on this cottage, or Flynn, or—

The knock at the door startled her so much that for a second she was in very real danger of overbalancing into the fire. She put a hand to her thudding heart, rising quickly and limping across the room and into the hall. She went right up to the front door, her voice small and cautious as she said nervously, 'Who is it?'

'Father Christmas, who else?' Flynn's voice said sardonically.

Flynn! Marigold opened the door with a certain amount of embarrassment, her head whirling. She hadn't expected to see him again and she'd been amazed how badly that had made her feel, but now he was here she was warning herself, This doesn't mean anything, not a thing. After Celine Jenet, how could it?

As the door swung open Flynn just stood and looked at her steadily for a moment or two before saying, 'Hello, Marigold. Can I come in?'

'Oh, yes, of course.' She was so flustered she hardly knew what she was doing and was quite unaware she'd kept him standing on the doorstep.

Once they were standing in the sitting room she had the presence of mind to say quickly, 'Can I get you a drink? A glass of wine, or coffee or hot chocolate?'

'Coffee would be great.'

'Right.' She could feel her cheeks burning and desperately needed a few minutes to compose herself away from his searching gaze.

'Can I help?' he asked softly, for all the world as though the last caustic hour hadn't happened.

'No, you sit down,' she said a little weakly. 'I won't be a minute.'

By the time she'd prepared a tray with the coffee-cups and a plate of biscuits, Marigold's colour had subsided though the secret excitement and nervous agitation bubbling away in the depths of her hadn't.

Flynn was sitting on the sofa in front of the fire when she walked back into the room with the tray, and he appeared perfectly relaxed, one knee crossed over the other and his arms stretched along the back of the cushions. It was a very male pose, but she had noticed that about him—every movement, every gesture was overwhelmingly masculine. If Flynn was a man who was in touch with his feminine side, he hid it very well.

'I just want to say I really am very sorry for jumping to conclusions about...about what I heard,' Marigold said before she lost her nerve, setting the tray down on the little table Flynn had obviously placed in front of the sofa before he sat down.

'You believe me, then?'

'Of course I do.' He looked incredibly sexy sitting there, his eyes veiled and his countenance expressionless, and a shiver trickled hotly down Marigold's spine, curling its way into the core of her.

'There's no "of course" about it,' he said evenly. 'But I realised once I'd left that I'd expected a hell of a lot. You were in a crowd of people, none of whom you knew, and you hear a little idle talk from people who should have known better. The thing is—' he paused abruptly, his jaw clenching, before he continued '—my private life is just that—private—and I don't appreciate it being under discussion. It's of no interest to anyone but me surely?'

Now, that was expecting too much, especially of the female of the species, Marigold thought as she stared back into the handsome face. Looking as he did and with the air of remote detachment he had about him, let alone the sort of work he did, where his skill and expertise was the difference between life and death, gave him a fascinating power and magnetic appeal which was irresistible to any hot-blooded woman.

The thought sent a wave of unease trembling through her as it hammered home her own attraction to Flynn. She didn't want to be attracted to him; she didn't want to be attracted to anyone for years and years until she had worked through the Dean and Tamara thing in her mind. But Flynn, with his abundance of male aggression and sexual appeal—he was the last man on earth to get involved with, however fleetingly.

Marigold plunged in before she had time to weigh her words and chicken out of what she knew she had to make clear. It still seemed incredible that Flynn might be interested in her, albeit mildly, but just in case... 'Flynn, what you said earlier, about me believing what I wanted to believe? Well, you were right in a way,' she said feverishly, standing just in front of him with her hands clasped tightly together. 'It's just that after Dean I don't feel I can cope with...with a new friendship,' she finished weakly, aware the last few words sounded ridiculous.

'I think we are both aware it wasn't altogether friendship I had on my mind.'

His voice was quiet but carried the velvet, smoky undertones she'd heard before and brought the colour which had recently subsided back to her cheeks again.

He was offering her an affair, a brief relationship, and probably from his point of view that was perfectly OK—certainly from what she'd overheard in the cloakroom he'd gone the same route many times before since Celine. But how did a woman bounce back after Flynn Moreau? Marigold asked herself silently as she looked into the rueful eyes fixed on her face. The others must have managed somehow, but she wouldn't. It would be a case of going from Dean's frying-pan into Flynn's fire, and she'd have no excuse with Flynn. She'd be walking into this relationship with her eyes wide open.

'The thing is…' She stopped, wondering how she could make him *see*. 'The thing is…'

'What is the thing?'

'Those…those women said you'd had other relationships since Celine, all temporary,' she managed at last. 'And that's fine,' she added quickly, 'if it's what you and your girlfriends wanted. But I don't think I'm like that, and it's too soon after Dean to even start thinking about… And you're wealthy and successful and always meeting new people and everything, and I'm—'

'Delightful.' He'd stood up, and as strong arms caught her against him she looked up into a hard male face that appeared mildly amused.

'Flynn—'

He cut off her voice by the simple expedient of taking her lips and as she stiffened, determined not to give in to the thrill of being in his arms again, the smell and feel of him surrounded her and she knew she was lost. The thing was, he kissed so *well*, she told herself helplessly. She had never met anyone who kissed like Flynn.

She sighed against his mouth and immediately, as he sensed her submission, the kiss deepened with masterful intent, his lips moving against hers and bringing forth a response she was unable to control.

She felt herself beginning to melt as before, and although his power over her senses was frightening it was so exhilarating she curved into him, hungrily searching for more. She had never considered herself a particularly cold person, but before Flynn lovemaking had been a mildly pleasurable experience at best, an irritation at worst when she hadn't really been in the mood.

But this, *this* was like something you read about in novels—mind-blowing, dazzling, and in spite of herself Marigold admitted to a feeling of excitement and satisfaction that she could actually experience such passion. Being in Flynn's arms like this made her feel desirable and wholly feminine, one half of a two-piece, flesh and blood jigsaw.

His mouth moved to the honey-tinted skin of her throat, nuzzling, caressing as she shivered with delight, her body arched backwards as he leant over her. He kissed her ears, her eyelids, tracing a scorching path back to her mouth, which opened obediently at his touch. His hands had moved under the lacy top, his fingers firm and warm as they stroked the silky skin of her narrow waist before moving upwards to run over the soft swell of the top of her breasts beneath her lacy white bra.

Her hands had splayed up into his thick black hair, her fingertips softly massaging his scalp in a sensual abandon which would have shocked her if she had been able to think coherently.

His mouth had parted her lips and he was tasting the inner sweetness with tiny darting movements, causing electric vibrations that had her trembling against him.

Marigold was enchanted, enchanted and beguiled, avidly searching for something she had never had but which she now sensed was within her grasp.

Flynn's breathing was heavy when he at last lifted his head, his lips releasing her mouth, but his arms still holding her close to him.

Marigold opened dazed eyes to find the silvery gaze fixed on her face, and for a moment she had the insane impulse to beg him to *really* make love to her; to follow her into the bedroom next door where they could lie on the big, soft bed with the glowing fire illuminating their naked bodies and all thoughts of the outside world banished.

It was enough to bring her out of the stupor and back down to earth with a bump. And he knew, instantly; the hungry, watchful expression on the hard male face changing to one of wry regret. 'You're doing it again,' he murmured softly.

'What?'

'Thinking instead of feeling.'

She moved back a little in his arms, pushing at the broad, muscled chest and he let go of her immediately. 'You don't approve of rational thought?' she asked in as light a voice as she could manage, considering she was feeling utterly bereft. 'I would have thought it was a necessity in your line of work.'

'There's a time and place for everything.' He smiled a slow, sexy smile and her heartbeat went haywire.

'Flynn—'

'I know, I know.' He interrupted her softly, tilting her chin to look into the deep violet-blue of her eyes. 'You aren't ready for a relationship. It's too soon. We're miles apart in lifestyles. Right?'

Marigold nodded shakily. 'Right.' In the space of

three days this man had turned her world upside-down. How had he done that? And in spite of all she had said if there hadn't been the mental image of Celine in the background, she wasn't at all sure that she wouldn't have thrown caution to the wind and just gone with the flow.

'Marigold, we both know that if I hadn't stopped a minute ago we'd be making love on the rug in front of the fire right now,' Flynn said in such a conversational tone of voice that for a moment she didn't take it in.

She stiffened, angry with him for telling the truth. 'If you believe that, why *did* you stop?' she challenged tightly.

'Because this is not the right time or the right place,' he returned silkily, 'and contrary to what you might think I consider that important. There's something between us you can't deny; it's been there from the first moment we laid eyes on each other and there can only be one possible conclusion to such raw physical attraction. But you have to accept me into your life before you accept me into your body, I can understand that, otherwise, being the sort of woman you are, you'd tear yourself apart.'

She stared at him, utterly bemused by the straight talking and the fact that he clearly considered an affair between them was just a matter of time. 'I can't believe you're saying this,' she said weakly.

'Why?' he asked casually, turning away and pouring them both a cup of coffee, before he added, 'Cream and sugar?'

Cream and sugar? Was he mad or was it her? He had just calmly stated that regardless of all she had said he intended to make sure he slept with her at some point in the immediate future, hadn't he? 'Flynn, you can't ride roughshod over all I've said,' she stated more firmly, ignoring the coffee tray.

'I wasn't aware I was,' he said mildly. 'I have taken into account all your objections but I have a predilection for the truth, Marigold, and it's the truth that you're really objecting to.'

Marigold looked at him in exasperation. He had an answer for everything! She opened her mouth to argue some more but then shut it abruptly. She'd never win in a war of words with Flynn, but then she didn't have to, not really. He had said he'd wait until she had accepted him into her life before pressing his case—at least that was what she thought he had said—and so it was quite simple really. She would be on her guard for the next few days while she was here in Shropshire, and then when she left, that would be that. No contact, no telephone calls or anything else. She'd be ruthless; she would have to be because Flynn was right about one thing. This physical attraction between them *was* raw and powerful, and far too compelling to play about with. For her at least.

'Cream and two sugars, please,' she said sweetly.

'What?' Marigold had the satisfaction of seeing him blink before he said, 'Oh, yeah, the coffee.'

And the coffee was all he was going to get, this night or any other, Marigold told herself firmly, even as a little voice in her mind reminded her nastily, until he chose to kiss her again...

CHAPTER SEVEN

WHEN Marigold awoke on Christmas Day it was to the realisation she had promised to have lunch and tea with Flynn and his friends, and she rolled over onto her stomach, pulling a pillow on top of her head as she groaned loudly. She was mad, quite mad!

Flynn had behaved perfectly for the rest of the time in the cottage the night before. He had drunk two cups of coffee, eaten most of the biscuits and made small talk, which had the advantage of being amusing and interesting. After inveigling her agreement regarding the next day he had given her a brief peck on her forehead and left immediately, leaving Marigold with the unwelcome—but faintly exciting—thought that Flynn was a man who would always get what he wanted.

After a long, hot soak in the bath Marigold inspected the meagre contents of her limited wardrobe. The black jeans would have to be utilised again, and a long, thick cream sweater with a large rolled neck would fit the bill for today. She felt a thrill of anticipation and elation shoot through her, and it was enough for her to spend the next hour or two warning herself she couldn't afford to let her guard down for a moment.

Flynn was the type of man who would whisk her into his orbit and keep her there for as long as it took for the attraction between them to burn itself out. And then? Then she'd be left floating in the middle of nowhere. It had been stupid to agree to go the house today, but this would be the last time she would concur with what he demanded. And there *was* a houseful of guests around. It wasn't as though they were there alone, she comforted herself briskly as she put the last touches to her make-up. It would be fine, just fine.

And it was. He came for her just after eleven o'clock and Marigold was ready and waiting, determined to give him no excuse to be alone with her in the cottage.

She hastily shut the front door as the big vehicle drew up outside the garden gate, her ankle allowing her to walk almost normally as she hurried down the snow-covered path.

Flynn had climbed out of the 4x4 and opened the passenger door as she reached him, her senses registering six foot plus of gorgeous manhood encased in black jeans and a black leather jacket. 'Hi.' His voice was soft and he grinned, dropping a quick kiss on her lips before he helped her up and closed the door behind her.

It took Marigold all of the drive to the house to get her racing heart under control, but his manner once they were there—warm and friendly and not at all threatening—relaxed her sufficiently to allow her to have a wonderful day.

Bertha, along with Wilf—whom the housekeeper had commandeered to help her—excelled herself with Christmas lunch, her pièce de résistance in the form of two enormous Christmas puddings, flaming with brandy and accompanied by lashings of whipped cream, bringing forth a round of applause from everyone at the dining table.

Replete, everyone played silly games all afternoon, although again Marigold noticed Flynn was more of a benevolent spectator than participator, and after a magnificent buffet tea they all gathered in the drawing room, where Flynn played the grand piano and everyone sang carols before the party broke up, and people began to leave for the drive home.

'I didn't know you could play the piano.' Flynn had tucked Marigold's hand in his arm, thereby conscripting her to stand with him on the doorstep, where he was watching his guests leave, and she spoke primly, trying to put things on a less intimate footing. With ninety-nine out of a hundred men, standing close like this would present no problems at all, but Flynn was the hundredth, as her racing pulse testified.

'There are a lot of things you don't know about me, Marigold,' he answered evenly, but with the smoky inflexion in his voice which gave it a sensual kick that was pure dynamite. 'Something I would be only too pleased to rectify, given half a chance.'

His eyes stroked her face for a moment before he looked down the drive again. 'I enjoy playing the piano and I'm told I can make a half-reasonable noise on the trombone. I like parasailing and scuba-diving; I prefer American football to English football or rugby and I loathe golf. But of course there are other…activities which give me more pleasure than all the rest put together.'

She didn't ask what they were, keeping her gaze on the car in front of them, from which the passenger was waving frantically, as she said, 'Scuba-diving? I've done a little of that, enough to get my PADI open-water certification.' She had tried to persuade Dean to do the course with her, thinking they could dive together in the warm waters of the Caribbean on their honeymoon, but he had only gone a couple of times before dropping out, claiming trouble with his inner ear. Privately she had thought he was scared. He had never coped well with a new challenge.

'So you're a water baby?' The moonlight caught the shining jet of his hair and turned the grey eyes to mercury as he turned to look down at her. 'That doesn't surprise me. I had you down as gutsy as well as beautiful.'

'Flattery will get you everywhere,' Marigold said as lightly as she could manage.

'I wish.' It was very dry. 'And it is not flattery. I told you before, I only tell the truth.'

'That would make you a man in a million,' she said with a trace of bitterness she couldn't quite disguise.

'Just so.' He smiled lazily. 'It's nice you've recognised the fact so quickly.'

And then he stiffened as he looked down the drive, his voice gritty as he said, 'Who the hell is that, driving like a maniac? He's just caused Charles to swerve and nearly go off the road. I don't recognise the car.'

Marigold followed the direction of his gaze and then swallowed hard. *She* recognised the car and it didn't belong to a him but a her.

Emma was driving the smart little sports coupé her doting father had bought her the year before, and she executed a flamboyant halt in front of the house which sent gravel scattering far and wide. 'Goldie, darling!' She was calling even as she unfurled herself from the leather interior. 'I've had a nightmare of a journey.'

'It's Emma,' Marigold murmured desperately. 'She wasn't supposed to arrive for another couple of days.'

'Lucky you.' It was caustic, antagonism bristling in every plane and line of his hard male face as narrowed eyes took in the tight leather trousers and three-inch stiletto heels, the dyed blonde hair and carefully made-up, lovely face.

'I was waiting outside the cottage and one of the cars

stopped and told me you were here,' Emma continued as she walked towards them, speaking to Marigold but with her big green eyes fixed on Flynn. 'Darling, I *had* to get away from London. Oliver and I have had the most *awful* row and I never want to see him again in all my life,' she finished dramatically, before adding, as though she had suddenly realised her lack of manners, 'Oh, I'm Emma Jones by the way,' as she held out one pale beringed hand to Flynn.

He made no effort to reach out and take it, merely nodding as he said, 'Maggie's granddaughter. It figures.'

Emma stopped abruptly. She was used to men going down before her shapely figure and batting eyelashes like ninepins, not having them growl at her with a face like thunder. However, Emma was made of sterner stuff than she looked, and her voice didn't falter as she said, 'What exactly does that mean?'

'I was a friend of your grandmother's and cared about her; I think that says it all.'

'Really.' Emma lifted her small chin and slanted feline eyes, but it was obvious she knew exactly what Flynn meant when she said, 'Daddy said there were some rather rude individuals in this neck of the woods.'

'Daddy was right. And this particular rude individual is now asking you, politely, to get off his property,' Flynn said evenly.

At some point during the discourse Marigold had disentangled her hand from Flynn's arm and now she said hurriedly, 'I'll get my bag if you want to wait in the car for me, Emma.'

'Sure.' As Emma turned and began to saunter away, Marigold fled into the house, grabbing her bag from where she'd left it in the drawing room and retracing

er footsteps into the hall, where she found Flynn wait-
ng for her.

'You don't have to go.'

'I do.' Marigold bit her lip. 'You know I do.'

'Can I see you tomorrow?' he said quietly.

'I don't think that's a good idea.'

'I disagree,' he said, still very softly. 'It's an excellent
dea.'

'Please, Flynn—'

'What are you so scared of anyway, Marigold? Is it
ne? As a man, I mean? Or is there something more?
Something in your past concerning this ex-fiancé of
ours? Did he ill-treat you in any way?'

'You mean apart from sleeping around in a way that
nsured everyone knew but me?' Marigold asked deri-
ively, and then she paused, taken aback at her own bit-
erness. Right up until this moment in time she hadn't
ealised how deep the wound had gone, and for a second
he hotly resented Flynn forcing her to see it. She didn't
vant to think of herself as damaged or a victim, she
hought furiously. She had to get the victory over this.

'I have to go.' She gestured towards a scowling
Emma, sitting looking at them from the gently purring
oupé. 'Emma's waiting.'

'Damn Emma.'

'I have to go.' She backed into the doorway and out
eyond, running to the car in a way that played havoc
vith her injured ankle.

Once Marigold was inside the car, Emma wasted no
ime in leaving, her speed indicating quite clearly she
vas mortally offended even if she had handled the sit-
iation with surprising coolness. *What an awful man!*
They hadn't got out of the drive and onto the lane be-
ond the gates before Emma let rip. 'How dare he talk

to me like that? And what were you doing in his house anyway?'

'I beg your pardon?' OK, so Emma might be upset but no way was she going to apologise for being in Flynn's home. 'I wasn't aware it was out of bounds,' Marigold challenged quietly.

Emma sent a swift glance Marigold's way and her tone was less confrontational when she said, 'Of course it isn't; I just wasn't aware you knew the owner, that's all.'

'I don't—I didn't,' Marigold corrected. 'It happened like this...' She explained the circumstances of her first meeting with Flynn, leaving out his comments relating to Emma and her family and finishing with, 'I think he thought quite a bit of your grandmother, Emma.'

Emma shrugged offhandedly. 'I barely knew her,' she admitted indifferently. 'I know she drove my parents mad with her refusal to go into an old people's home and that she had a load of flea-ridden animals, but my father usually visited her on his own.'

'How often was that?' Marigold asked quietly.

'Now and then.' It was cursory. 'She had plenty of friends hereabouts.'

'It's not like family though, is it?'

'Don't *you* start.' Emma skidded to a halt by the side of Myrtle and Marigold could almost see the small car flinch as the sports car missed her bumper by half an inch. 'My grandmother had the chance to go into a home where she would have been looked after and which my parents could have visited more easily, but she insisted she wanted to stay in the cottage. My father is a busy man; he's got an important job. He can't waste time running about all over the place, besides which he and Mother entertain a lot—important people, necessary for is position at work. Anyway, they didn't get on, my grandmother and father. Just because my father was unable to attend my grandfather's funeral, my grandmother said she'd never forgive him.'

'Why couldn't he go to the funeral?' Marigold stared at Emma's disgruntled face and wondered why she'd never realised that she really didn't like this girl at all.

'Pressure of work,' Emma said perfunctorily. 'You have to make sacrifices if you want to get to the top.'

'Yes, I suppose you do.' Marigold opened her door as she added, 'I'm leaving in the morning, Emma; there are things I need to do at home. Are you still intending to sell the cottage?'

'I might be.' Emma glanced at her as they walked to the cottage door whereupon Marigold handed the other girl the front-door key. 'Why?'

'I'd be interested in knowing how much you want for it, that's all.' Somehow she couldn't bear the thought of Emma owning the beloved home of the young, sweet-faced bride in the photograph, or selling it to someone who wouldn't appreciate the blood, sweat and tears old Maggie had put into the last years. 'Along with the furniture, the pictures, everything,' she added quietly.

'All that old rubbish?' Emma looked at her as if she was mad, and she probably was, Marigold admitted wryly to herself. 'Whatever would you be interested in that for?'

'It fits the cottage, that's all.'

'Doesn't it just!'

Marigold slept the night on the sofa in the sitting room despite Emma's insistence that she could share the bedroom, and by nine o'clock the next morning she was on her way back to the city. If she had stayed any longer there would have been a very real possibility of her and Emma having a major fall-out, and she didn't want that. Not so much because it would make things difficult at work as because she felt old Maggie was relying on her to buy the cottage and make it a real home again.

It might be fanciful, Marigold admitted as her car chugged cheerfully along, this link she felt she had with Emma's grandmother, but she felt it in her bones and she couldn't get away from it.

As she drew nearer to London, Marigold found she couldn't stop Flynn from invading her thoughts as he'd done all night; his image in her mind seemed to increase with the miles. He had accused her of being scared of him; was she? she asked herself, hating the answer when it came in the affirmative. She had run away this morning, she acknowledged miserably; for the first time in her life she had run away from something—or, more precisely, someone. Admittedly she would have left the cottage after her conversation with Emma; it had grated so much she couldn't have stayed and pretended everything was all right as far as the other girl was concerned, but she should have popped to see Flynn on the way and told him she was leaving. After all he had done for her it would have been courteous if nothing else.

But… She gritted her teeth at the but. She'd known deep in the heart of her but not admitted till now that she'd wanted to see him too much as well as not at all. How was that for a contradiction? she thought ruefully.

Was she thinking of buying Emma's cottage because it would mean Flynn would be her neighbour? Marigold tried to take a step backwards and answer her question honestly. No, she didn't think she was, which was a relief. But neither did Flynn's presence just across the valley make her think the notion was impossible, which if she wanted nothing at all to do with him, wasn't sensible, was it?

Oh, this is crazy, stupid! Why was she tearing herself apart like this over a man she hadn't known existed a week ago? He probably wouldn't give her another thought once he found out she'd gone—if he bothered to enquire, that was.

Marigold honked Myrtle's horn long and hard at a smart Mercedes that cut her up from an approach road and felt a little better for letting off some steam.

If her buying the cottage worked out—great. If it didn't, so be it. Either way she'd still put her plans for the future into operation and go self-employed. One stage of her life was finishing, another was just beginning, and it was up to her what she made of things.

She was not going to think of Flynn Moreau any more. He was a brief interlude, a little bit of Christmas magic maybe, but Christmas was over, as was her flirtation with Flynn. She nodded resolutely to the thought and then, as she caught the eye of the passenger in the car alongside, pretended to be nodding along to a song. Look at her, she told herself crossly once the car had changed lanes and disappeared, she was going barmy here! Enough was enough. Decision made. Autonomy for the immediate future and definitely, *definitely* no men in her life.

Marigold spent the next two days of the holiday cleaning her small flat in Kensington from top to bottom, and catching up with several domestic jobs she had been putting off for ages. She didn't allow herself to think, keeping the radio or TV on at all times and ruthlessly curtailing any stray thought which crept into her consciousness and might lead down a path to Flynn.

She returned to work on Wednesday morning with her notice already typed and in her bag. Patricia and Jeff were sorry to accept her notice but promised her work on a freelance basis, and after she'd agreed to stay until the end of March all parties were happy. Emma was on holiday until the new year and Marigold wasn't sorry, despite her desire to set the ball rolling with regard to her purchase of the cottage. The other girl's callous attitude about her grandmother had bothered Marigold more than she would have liked.

The first day back at work was quiet, what with quite a few firms having taken an extended break until after the new year, so for once Marigold left the office on time and was back home before six o'clock. The phone was ringing as she walked into the flat; it was her mother, insisting she join the rest of the family and friends for a New Year's Eve bash at her parents' home.

After promising her mother she would think about it—an answer Sandra Flower was not particularly happy with—Marigold managed to put down the phone some twenty minutes later; her mother having bent her ear about everything from her cleaner's bad leg to the state of the nation.

Marigold hadn't taken one step towards the kitchen for the reviving cup of coffee she'd been literally tasting for the last few minutes, when the front doorbell rang followed by an imperious knock a second later.

'Give me a chance...' Marigold grumbled to herself as she went to the door, pushing back her shining veil of hair with a weary hand. The hard physical work in the flat over the last two days, added to the twinges her ankle still gave which kept waking her up in the night, had caught up with her after a day at work and she was

looking forward to a long, hot soak in the bath with a
glass of wine, followed by an early night.

'Hello, Marigold Flower.'

It was Flynn. Bigger, more handsome and twice as
lethal as she remembered, his dark hair tousled by the
strong north wind which had been blowing all day and
his grey eyes narrowed and faintly wary. He looked
tired, she noticed with a detachment borne of shock.
Exhausted even.

Marigold said faintly, 'How did you know where I
lived? Emma didn't...?'

'No, Emma didn't,' he assured her drily. 'Let's just
say Emma took great pleasure in slamming the door in
my face and leave it at that.'

'You *were* awful to her,' Marigold said weakly, still
trying to take in the fact he was right here on her doorstep.

'She got off damn lightly and she knows it.' Flynn
was dismissive.

'So how *did* you find me?'

'Process of elimination. There aren't too many
M. Flowers in London, and your number was about the
fifth my secretary tried. Your answer machine provided
the name Marigold...' Dark eyebrows rose above brilliant eyes. 'Do I get invited in?' he asked softly.

'Oh, yes, of course.' She was so flustered she nearly
fell over her own feet as she quickly stepped to the side
and ushered him through.

'I've been in London for the last thirty-six hours,' he
continued quietly. 'Emergency call from the hospital.'
And then he stopped in the doorway of her small sitting
room, glancing round appreciatively as he said, 'This is
charming.'

'Thank you.' Marigold had spent every night for a

month painting and papering her tiny home in the immediate aftermath of the break with Dean, needing the hard work as therapy to keep her from caving in to the pain and rage and bitterness. She had gone for bright, bold colours to offset her internal bleakness, and the sitting room with its radiant yellow walls reminiscent of sunflowers and pinky terracotta sofa and curtains on a pale wood floor was daring and adventurous. 'I like it.'

He turned to her, his grey eyes smiling. 'It suits you.'

Oh, wow, he was something else. Impossible, dangerous and more attractive than any man had the right to be. Marigold sternly took hold of her wildly beating heart and said evenly, 'Why are you here, Flynn?'

'To see you.' He stated the obvious with a wry smile. 'You never said goodbye, remember?'

'You came here to say goodbye?'

'Not exactly.' he pulled her against him, bending quickly and kissing her with hard, hungry kisses that brought an immediate response deep inside her. He kissed her until she was limp and breathless against him and then raised his head, his voice slightly mocking as he said, 'No, not exactly, but then you knew that, didn' you? Just as you knew I'd follow you.'

'I didn't!' she said indignantly, her voice carrying the unmistakable ring of truth.

He frowned, tilting her face upwards with a firm hand. 'Then you should have,' he said softly, without smiling.

Probably, but then she wasn't versed in all the intricate games of love like his more experienced women friends. She was just herself; a not very tall, rather ordinary, hard-working girl with the unfortunate name of Marigold Flower. And she dared not let herself think this could mean anything.

'I came to ask if we could try getting to know each

other for a while,' he said smoothly, reading the confusion and withdrawal in her face with deadly accuracy. 'OK? No heavy stuff, just the odd date now and again when I'm in town. Dinner sometimes, a little sightseeing, visits to the theatre, that sort of thing. Just being together with no strings attached.'

She stared at him uncertainly. What exactly did all that mean? Did the dinner dates end up in bed? Was that part of the getting to know each other? 'As...as friends?' she asked shakily.

He looked down at her with a wry expression which made him appear twice as handsome. 'Is that what you want?'

She nodded quickly. 'I'm not ready for anything more.'

He was still holding her chin in his warm fingers and now his gaze intensified, pulling her into its mercurial depths until she felt he was drawing her soul out for inspection. And then, quite unexpectedly, he smiled his devastating smile, drawing her against the hard wall of his chest so that his chin was resting on the top of her head. 'Good friends,' he qualified lazily.

The warmth of him, the smell and feel was sending her heady, and over all the surprise and shock and uncertainty was an exhilaration and excitement that he had sought her out, that he was *here*. And she was glad. Too glad. 'I'll make some coffee.' She drew away slightly and after one moment of holding her close he let her go.

'I could use some.' He stretched powerful shoulders beneath the big overcoat he was wearing. 'It's been a hell of a day. A bad accident is never pretty but when the injured party is only eight years old it takes on a different picture.'

'The emergency call?' she asked quietly. His voice

and face had changed as he'd spoken, and suddenly his exhaustion was very evident again.

'Uh-huh.' He shook his head wearily. 'And it could have been prevented if the parents had checked the boy was strapped in. How can you expect an eight-year-old to remember seat belts when he's taking his new remote controlled car to show his grandparents?'

'But he's going to be all right?'

'Two major operations in the space of thirty-six hours and two pints of blood later, yes, he's going to be all right. But it was touch and go for a time and we came damn near to losing him more than once.'

'You haven't been working for thirty-six hours?' she asked as the reason for his exhaustion really hit home.

'More or less.' He shrugged offhandedly. 'It's an all or-nothing type job.'

He was an all-or-nothing type guy. 'Have you eaten yet tonight?' Marigold thought gratefully about the extensive spring clean of the last couple of days and the sparkling fridge newly stocked with food.

He shook his head. 'I think I ate some time yesterday but it's been coffee and biscuits in short bursts today. I was going to suggest I take you out for dinner if you're free?'

She stared at him. He was dead on his feet. 'Did you drive here?' she asked quietly.

'Taxi.'

'In that case I'll get you a glass of wine while you take off your coat and make yourself comfortable,' she said briskly. 'Lime and ginger pork with stir-fried vegetables OK?' It gave her great satisfaction to see the way his eyes opened in surprise. She might not be a Bertha but she could still rustle up a fairly edible meal when she wanted to.

'That would be great,' he said softly, the tone of his voice bringing a tingle to her skin. 'If you're sure?'

Sure? She hadn't been sure of a thing since the first time she had laid eyes on Flynn Moreau! 'Quite sure.' She smiled in what she hoped was an efficient, I'm-totally-in-control type of way, walking across to the little living-flame gas fire and turning it on full blast as she said, 'Sit down and get warm. Red or white wine?'

'Red, please.'

He was shrugging off his overcoat as she turned, and the perfectly ordinary, non-sexual action sent nerves racing all over her body. It was worse when she returned from the kitchen with the wine. He had clearly taken her at her word regarding comfort. His suit jacket was off and he'd loosened his tie so that it hung to one side of his pale grey shirt, the top buttons undone to reveal the dark shadow of body hair on his upper chest as he stood inspecting a photograph of her parents.

For a moment Marigold forgot how to walk, and then she managed to totter over to him without spilling anything. 'Your parents?' he asked, inclining his head at the photograph.

Marigold nodded, handing him his glass of wine as she said, 'It was taken last year.'

His eyes returned to the picture of the entwined couple; the man grey-haired and somewhat sombre as he stood with his arm tight round his laughing wife, who was petite and sparkling.

'I like it because it sums them up very well,' Marigold said softly with a great deal of love in her voice. 'Dad is a solicitor and very correct and proper, and Mum— well, Mum's not,' she admitted ruefully. 'But they think the world of each other.'

'It shows. Are you close to them?' he asked as he raised his eyes, watching her.

'Yes, I think so. Perhaps not quite so much in the last little while since I moved out and got a place of my own, but that change was necessary as much for Mum as me,' Marigold said quietly. 'She always wanted lots of babies but there were complications after me. Consequently I became the focus of all her attention and because we're very different that caused problems at times. But we're fine now. She accepts I'm an independent adult with my own way of doing things...mostly,' she added with a smile. 'How about you? Do you see much of your parents?'

'Not much.' He turned back to look at the photograph as he said flatly, 'They divorced when I was five, got back together when I was eight and divorced again when I was approaching my teens. They've had several marriages between them since then. My mother married Celine's father when I was eighteen, which is when Celine and I met for the first time. It was her father's third marriage.'

Marigold didn't know what to say.

'Our parents lasted three years but by the time they divorced Celine and I were close. We understood each other, I guess, having had the same sort of fragmented childhood.'

Marigold nodded. It hurt more than she would have thought possible to hear the other woman's name on his lips, which was a warning in itself.

'I was brought up in an atmosphere of too much money and too little purpose.' He was speaking more to himself now than her. 'I needed to break the cycle before it broke me, hence the medical profession. I could put something back there, you see, do something lasting.

The idealism of youth.' He glanced at her, a cool smile twisting his mouth. 'And it turned out that by some fluke I found my niche. I was a good student, and neurology had always fascinated me. The rest, as they say, is history.'

Marigold wanted to ask him more about Celine; when they'd realised they'd fallen in love; when they'd got engaged; what had caused the break-up. But she realised the brief glimpse into his past was over when he raised his glass, his voice changing as he said, 'To Maggie.'

'To Maggie?' She stared at him in surprise as she raised her own glass.

'Of course. Without the cottage being left to Emma we wouldn't have met, so we have Maggie to thank for it.'

'If Emma hadn't suggested I use it for Christmas we wouldn't have met,' she corrected factually.

'If you think I'm toasting Emma, think again.' He grinned with a sexy quirk of his sternly sensual mouth and she acknowledged defeat.

'To Maggie,' she agreed quickly, taking a great gulp of wine for much-needed support before she backed away from him, saying, 'Sit down and relax while I see to dinner. The remote for the TV is on the coffee-table,' before she turned tail and fled into the fragile safety of her small kitchen.

Once the oven was on and she had placed the pork loin steaks in the roasting tin, Marigold quickly made the glaze, mixing together lime rind and juice, soy sauce, honey, garlic, ginger and the other ingredients before she poured the mixture over the chops. She popped the tin into the oven and finished her glass of wine, pouring herself another before taking the bottle and walking into the sitting room to see if Flynn wanted a refill.

He was half lying in a somewhat awkward position on the sofa, as though the onslaught of sleep had caught him unawares—which it probably had, Marigold thought dazedly through the frantic beating of her heart. One hand was thrown back over his head and the other was still round his empty glass, and she was breathlessly aware she was seeing him vulnerable and defenceless for the first time.

He looked different in sleep; younger, more boyish, the deep lines round his eyes and mouth less pronounced, and his thick dark eyelashes adding to the illusion of youth. Not so his body; the broad, muscled torso and powerful thighs spoke of a man in his prime, and even sleep couldn't negate the flagrant maleness that was an essential part of his appeal.

Marigold moved forward, she couldn't help it, even though part of her was objecting that if their positions had been reversed and she had been asleep she would have hated Flynn being able to examine her at leisure.

His suit was beautiful and clearly wildly expensive, as was the silk shirt and tie, but he had looked just as good in the old jeans and sweater he'd worn to bring in the Christmas trees, she thought faintly.

She looked at his mouth, relaxed now but still so sexy it made her want to put her own lips against it, and at the hard, square male chin where black stubble was clearly visible.

What would it be like to be made love to by this man? Even the thought of it made her weak at the knees. The firm power of his naked flesh, the warmth of his body heat, the delicious and unique smell of him encompassing her in wave after wave of exquisite pleasure...

She knelt down by the sofa, telling herself she only wanted to remove the glass from his nerveless fingers and put it safely on the coffee-table, where she could fill it with wine ready for when he awoke.

This close, his aura of masculinity was disturbingly sensual, the combination of brooding toughness and little-boy susceptibility almost painful. She took the glass very slowly, easing it out of his fingers and placing it on the floor by the side of the sofa without turning to the coffee-table. She found she couldn't tear her eyes away from the sleeping face. His childhood, the break with Celine, the things he saw every day in his work must have all contributed to the cool, distant, cynical expression which veiled his countenance when he was awake, but like this she could almost imagine those things had never happened.

She touched the rough male chin very lightly with her lips, she couldn't help herself, and when there was no response, no stirring, she dared to move upwards to the firm mouth. She had never found over-full lips attractive on a man and Flynn's were just right; cleanly sculpted and warm. She shut her eyes for just a moment, knowing she had to move away and return to the kitchen, and when she opened them again silver orbs were staring straight into shocked violet.

She seemed to be incapable of doing anything but look back into his gaze, shock freezing her reactions, but then his arms came round her and she found herself drawn upwards and onto him so that she was lying half across the big, powerful frame. 'Nice…' It was a contented male murmur and he was holding her so closely, so securely, there was no point in struggling. She didn't want to anyhow.

His mouth teased at hers as he stroked over her compliant, soft body, exploring her curves and valleys with a leisurely enjoyment that sent tiny thrills cascading down her nerves and sinews. Languorously her head fell back to expose the curve of her throat as his mouth searched lower, and then it returned to her lips, the kiss more urgent as he made a low, deep sound of satisfaction in his throat.

It was as he moved her hips, drawing her against him in a manner that guaranteed she couldn't fail to become aware of his body's arousal, that she became aware of what she was allowing. She stiffened, but immediately he sensed her withdrawal, his voice soft and husky as he said, 'It's all right, sweetheart, it's all right. I'm not an immature boy who is going to insist on more than you want to give. Relax…'

'I…I have to see to the dinner.' She sat up, her voice breathless, and he made no effort to hold on to her by force.

'Damn the dinner.' But his voice was lazy rather than annoyed.

'I brought you some more wine.' She stood up quickly, her cheeks flushed as she endeavoured to straighten her clothes and brush back her tousled hair.

He sat up straighter himself. 'That's very kind.' It was mildly amused, and made Marigold feel about sixteen years old.

'The glass is by your feet.' She stepped back a pace as she spoke. 'Help yourself to the wine. I'll just go and see to the vegetables or the pork will spoil.'

'Heaven forbid.'

She gave a weak smile and scurried into the kitchen, furious with herself. How could she have kissed him like that? she asked herself angrily as she took out her aggression on a hapless onion, slicing it with savage intent. After all she had said about being friends she practically had to go and eat the man! Talk about sending mixed signals. And she just *hated* women who did that.

Did he call all his women sweetheart?

The thought came from nowhere and stopped her dead, and she stood for a full thirty seconds, staring at the carrots waiting nervously for her ministrations after they had seen her behaviour with the onion.

And then she shook herself irritably. It didn't matter if he did or not, she told herself firmly. By his own lips he was just going to ask her out on the occasional date when he was in town in order that they could get to know each other a little better. She thought of the hard, hot arousal she had felt against the soft flesh of her belly before she had sat up, and her cheeks burnt with brilliant colour.

Their getting to know each other had taken a giant step forward all of a sudden, but that had been her fault, not his, she reminded herself honestly. The poor man had been utterly exhausted and fast asleep and she'd leapt on him like a raving nymphomaniac!

She groaned faintly before taking a long, hard gulp of the wine, just as the poor man spoke from the kitchen doorway, his voice somnolent. 'Need any help?'

'No, I'm fine.' She slung the onion into the oil heating in her large frying-pan and went to work on the carrots without turning round. 'I'm sorry I woke you,' she added quickly. 'I didn't mean to. I was only going to pour you a glass of wine...' Her voice trailed off. Buy that, buy anything.

'I'm glad you did—wake me, that is.'

She could feel his eyes on the back of her neck and she just knew the wretched man was grinning, although she didn't dare turn round. 'As you're awake now, could you perhaps set the table in the sitting room?' she asked primly. Her little pine table was tucked away in a small alcove and she rarely used it except when she had a guest, but it was just the right size for two. 'You'll find mats and glasses and everything in that cupboard.' She turned and pointed to the wall cupboard by the kitchen door as she spoke, studiously avoiding his eyes.

'Sure thing.'

Which was probably exactly what he thought *she* was tonight after the little scenario in the sitting room, Marigold thought tightly.

However, once she had served up the pork and vegetables ten minutes later, garnishing the aromatic food with fresh slices of lime, she had calmed down sufficiently to face him with a bright smile as she walked into the sitting room, carrying the two plates.

'Wow!'

She had cooked plenty—he'd had the look of a hungry, as well as exhausted, man—and her reward was in seeing his face light up at the sight of his loaded plate. 'Hazelnut pie and ice cream for dessert—shop-bought, I'm afraid,' she said lightly. 'Or there's some cream rice pudding I made yesterday if you prefer?'

'Got any strawberry jam to go with the rice pudding?' he asked hopefully, totally unsettling her again as he pulled out her chair for her to be seated before sitting down himself.

None of her other boyfriends, Dean included, had treated her with such old-fashioned courtesy, and it was very nice—too nice. She didn't dare get used to it. Not that Flynn *was* a boyfriend, of course, she clarified silently. 'Strawberry jam? I think so.'

'Great.' He grinned at her and she wondered how many of his female patients fell in love with him at first sight, or whether there were any who took a little longer.

Whether it was because Flynn put himself out to relax her or the two glasses of red wine she had consumed on an empty stomach Marigold didn't know, but she found she thoroughly enjoyed the rest of the evening.

The meal was leisurely, finishing with coffee and brandy after dessert, and Flynn was nothing more threatening than an amusing, agreeable companion who regaled her with fascinating and often hilarious stories about his life and work. She had the sense to realise he was giving her the success stories and upbeat moments, and that there was a darker side to his work, but she just went with the flow, enjoying every second. Much of his humour was self-deprecating and it was a surprise to find he could poke fun at himself, mocking his position and status and the esteem in which he was held. It was also very endearing, and more than once Marigold had to take a hold of her susceptible heart.

When he made noises about leaving round eleven o'clock Marigold braced herself for a passionate goodnight kiss, or even maybe the veiled suggestion that he could be persuaded to stay given half a chance. Instead Flynn rang for a taxi and put on his jacket and coat, kissing her once—but very thoroughly—before walking to the front door.

'Will you let me buy you dinner tomorrow as a thank-you for tonight?' he asked softly as they stood on the threshold.

Marigold nodded; the kiss had left her breathless.

'Eight-ish?'

She nodded again.

'Goodnight, sweetheart.'

And he was gone.

CHAPTER EIGHT

THAT night was the first of many spent in Flynn's company. He wined and dined her, taking her to the theatre, to various nightclubs, to parties and for meals out with his friends.

If he was in London at the weekends they would browse in art galleries and book shops, go for long walks along the Thames or spend the day at the private gym and leisure centre of which Flynn was a member. Lunch at charming, out-of-the-way places; tea at the Ritz; dinner at the Savoy—they did it all, and not once in the weeks leading up to the beginning of March did Flynn act as anything other than attentive escort and charming friend.

It was driving Marigold mad.

It was useless to tell herself that he was acting this way because *she* had insisted upon it, that she'd laid down very definite rules and boundaries because of her conflicting emotions where Flynn was concerned, and that this was the best, the very best way to proceed.

Every time he took her hand or pulled her against him, every time he kissed her goodnight or sat with his arm round her or stroked her hair, she waited for him to make the next move. And he didn't. He just didn't!

Most nights, and especially following the evenings when she saw him, Marigold tossed and turned for hours before she could fall asleep, her mind racing and her body burning. She tried to convince herself her restlessness was due to all the changes occurring in her life, and there were plenty of those.

Emma had agreed to the sale of the cottage as soon as she had returned to the office in January. Apparently she had had a dreadful time there; being unable to light the fires without filling the cottage with smoke, struggling with the ancient stove and blocking the sink were just a few of the mishaps she'd suffered.

The final straw had occurred when a mouse had decided to investigate the bedroom one night, Emma had reported, and then added insult to injury by choosing one of Emma's sheepskin slippers for a nest.

In view of the isolation of the cottage and not least Emma's new-year decision to travel round Europe for a while with one of her friends, purportedly to recover from her broken heart at Oliver's exit from her life, the asking price for the small house was very reasonable. A sizable bequest by Marigold's maternal grandparents some years ago which she had resisted touching until now meant she could afford a fifty-per-cent deposit on the cottage, and after she had shopped around a little she found a bank who were prepared to put up the rest. The deposit meant her mortgage repayments were gratifyingly low, and, with Emma including all the furniture and household effects right down to her grandmother's dustpan and brush, her immediate outgoings would be negligible.

Marigold had given notice she would be vacating the flat at the end of March, which was when she intended to move to Shropshire, and had printed myriad copies of her CV with an accompanying letter explaining she intended to freelance in her new location, and sent them to every contact she'd ever made. To date she'd had several promising replies which could lead to work in the near future but, apart from the partners at her present firm promising they would continue to leave the new designs for the greeting cards in her capable hands, nothing concrete.

And then, at the beginning of March, several events happened within the space of twenty-four hours and with a speed which left Marigold breathless.

At ten o'clock on a blustery March morning the cottage finally became hers; at eleven o'clock she was contacted by a small firm on the borders of Shropshire who had been given her name by their parent company in London. Would she be interested in a new project they were considering regarding a range of English countryside calendars, cards, diaries, notelets, et cetera?

Indeed she would, Marigold answered enthusiastically.

They would market the proposed venture very much on the lines of a 'local country artist' thrust, which was why she had been approached. They understood she was moving to Shropshire shortly?

At the end of March, Marigold confirmed, her heart beating excitedly.

Her CV stated Miss Flower had already had the experience of setting up a new section within her present firm. If their scheme was successful—and they had every reason to think it would be, as their parent company was intending to back them to the hilt—would Miss Flower be prepared to think about spearheading the development of this work?

Miss Flower would be only too delighted!

At three in the afternoon of the same day the telephone on her desk rang for the umpteenth time. Marigold picked it up, a lilt borne of the happenings of the morning in her voice as she said brightly, 'Marigold Flower speaking.'

There was a brief pause before a male voice said quietly, 'Marigold? It's Dean. I...I wondered how you were?'

'Dean?' If the person at the other end of the line had been the queen of England she couldn't have been more taken aback.

'Don't put down the phone.'

His voice was urgent, and Marigold wrinkled her brow before she said, 'I wasn't going to.'

Dean must have taken her honest reply as some form of encouragement, because he said with intensity, 'I've missed you. Hell, I've missed you more than words can say. I was such a fool, Marigold. Can you ever forgive me?'

She held the telephone away from her ear for a moment, staring at the receiver blankly. And then she said, 'It happened and I found it hard at the time, but it's in the past now, Dean.'

'But do you forgive me?'

Did she? Marigold considered for a second and realised she'd barely spared a thought for Dean and Tamara in the last two months. 'I've moved on,' she said steadily, 'so that must mean I forgive you.'

'I'm not with Tamara any more. She drove me mad half the time. Always wanting attention and never satisfied with anything. She wasn't like you, Marigold.'

Two spoilt brats with egos to match. No, she could imagine things might not have gone too well.

'I know I hurt you but there's never been anyone like you, you have to believe that,' he said softly. 'You've always been my anchor, the one person I could count on.'

She had to stop this. She didn't want to be anyone's anchor, she wanted far more than that, and she realised with absolute clarity that Dean would never be able to give of himself. Dean was what mattered to Dean. 'Dean, if things had been right between us you wouldn't have gone with Tamara in the first place,' she said steadily. 'It was just as well we found that out before we got married.'

'No, no, that's not it at all.' He sounded desperate and she was surprised to realise she felt sorry for him. It was like listening to a child, a selfish child who had broken his toy in a tantrum and was now demanding that it be put back together. But the toy had been an engagement, a commitment to get married. Flynn had said she could die waiting for Dean to grow up and he had been absolutely right. She had done her stint of babysitting him.

'It was your decision to go off with Tamara,' Marigold said firmly, hating the conversation with its distasteful connotations. 'And frankly I think it was the best thing for both of us. You obviously weren't ready for marriage and it would have been a disaster. There'll be someone for you in the future, Dean, but it won't be me. Goodbye.'

She put down the phone on his voice, her heart thudding fit to burst. It rang again almost immediately but she didn't pick it up, letting the answer machine click on. 'Marigold? Pick up. Please, Marigold, pick up.' A few seconds' silence followed, and then his voice came again, a petulant note creeping in as he said, 'I know you're there. Look, if you want me to grovel I will, but you know we're meant to be together. You love me, you always have done. I need you.' A few more moments of silence and then the receiver was replaced at the other end.

Marigold became aware she was holding her breath and let it out in a big sigh. Six months, and he expected he could pick up where he'd left off all that time ago at the drop of a hat. It would be laughable if it wasn't so tragic.

She sat staring at her paper-strewn desk, her mind racing on. He hadn't once asked her if she was with anyone—that clearly hadn't crossed his mind! It was incredible, but he thought she had sat at home just waiting for his call since they had finished! He didn't know her at all, but then she hadn't known him either. Which was scary.

It wasn't the first time she'd thought along these lines and the faintly panicky, disturbed feeling which always accompanied such reflections brought her nibbling at her lower lip. There *were* people who got it right and stayed together all their lives—her parents were a prime example—but there were plenty who got it terribly wrong, as she would have done if she'd married Dean. How on earth did you know if something was going to last or not?

She took a sip of the coffee Emma had brought everyone a few minutes before the call from Dean had come through, and grimaced. Somehow Emma managed to make perfectly nice coffee taste like dishwater! The thought of the other girl led her mind on to the cottage and then Flynn, and she knew her previous deliberations had nothing at all to do with Dean and everything to do with Flynn. She was in too deep. She liked him too much. This getting to know each other as friends hadn't been such a good idea after all.

She stood up restlessly, walking across to the big plate-glass window and looking down into the busy London street beneath. Dean had hidden his real self from her and she hadn't had the experience or where-withal to recognise the signs of his deceit. But compared to Flynn, Dean was like a little boy, so how on earth could she ever know where Flynn was coming from? She had made one big, big mistake with Dean; she didn't need to make another. Even without the spectre of Celine forever hovering in the background, Flynn Moreau was way, way out of her league.

All the excitement regarding the cottage and the wonderful offer of work faded, and she had the ridiculous urge to burst into tears. Instead she turned away from the view, marching back to her desk and attacking her mountain of paperwork with resolute grimness. No more thinking; no more ifs and buts. She had work to do.

She left the office later than usual, and almost got blown away by the wind as she stepped onto the pavement outside the building. There was a storm brewing, a bad one, she thought as she raised her eyes to an angry sky.

She did some shopping on the way home to the flat, struggling into the street of three-storey terraced houses with her arms feeling as if they were being pulled out of their sockets. She had just put the bags on the doorstep, delving into her handbag for the front-door key as the wind howled and the darkness surged all around her, when a hand on her shoulder nearly caused her to jump out of her skin.

'Sorry, did I make you jump?'

'Dean!' She'd swung round and knocked one of the bags full of groceries flying, and as they scrabbled about retrieving the food she said tightly, 'What on earth are you doing here? I thought we'd said all that needed to be said this afternoon.'

'I had to come.' He straightened with the bag of shop-

ping clasped in his arms, and as she stared at him
Marigold wondered why it was she had never noticed
how weak his mouth looked. He was good-looking, in a
boyish, charming manner, but almost... What was the
word? she asked herself silently. Foppish. That was it.
He was almost too well-dressed, too well-groomed. *And
she'd planned to marry this man.*

'Dean, there's no point to this.' She held out her hand
for the bag but he ignored it. 'Please, just go.'

'You don't mean that.' He moved closer, causing her
to step backwards until she was pressed against the front
door. 'You can't. We're meant to be together.'

The hell they were! The words sounded so like something Flynn would have said that Marigold blinked, as
though she'd heard his voice. 'It's taken you long
enough to find that out. It was the end of August we
split, wasn't it?'

He stared at her, taken aback by her tone. He had
clearly expected her to fall into his arms in grateful sur-
render after he'd made the big gesture of coming to her,
Marigold thought grimly. She was relieved to find she
didn't feel a shred of emotion at seeing him again beyond mild irritation. Hearing his voice so unexpectedly
this afternoon had been a shock and it had upset her a
little, raking up all the trauma. Now, faced with Dean
himself, she knew he meant nothing to her any more.

'I'll make it up to you, Dee.' His pet name for her
was annoying but that was all. 'I promise.'

He was still amazingly sure of himself, although
Marigold thought she had detected just the slightest
edge of uncertainty behind the arrogance, which made it
all the more surprising when he suddenly lunged forwards, his free arm grabbing her as his mouth descended
on hers.

For a moment Marigold was too startled to react, but then out of the corner of her eye she was aware of a vehicle pulling up on the road below them. She knew who was inside. Even before her eyes met ones of silver ice, she knew it had to be Flynn. It was fate, kismet.

She pushed Dean away, her voice sharp as she said, 'Don't! Don't touch me.'

'But Dee…' And then, as he saw her eyes were focused on something beyond him, Dean swung round, the shopping bag still in his hand. And then he saw the stony, cold face looking at them.

Marigold saw the metallic gaze take in what appeared to all intents and purposes a cosy shopping trip, and with the kiss on the step she half expected Flynn to order the driver to pull away.

Instead the door swung open and Flynn unfolded himself from the rear of the taxi cab, his height and breadth swamping Dean's slim five feet nine. 'Hello, Marigold.'

If one hadn't been looking into his dark, angry face, Flynn's voice could have appeared perfectly normal, Marigold thought a touch hysterically.

'I just stopped by for a quick visit,' he continued with the softness of silk over steel, 'but I can see you're otherwise engaged.'

In spite of the fact that Marigold was aware how bad it looked, she found she bitterly resented Flynn's assumption that she had been a willing participant in the kiss. And it was the knowledge of her own contrariness which made her voice brittle as she replied, 'Dean was just leaving, as it happens.'

'Really?' Flynn acknowledged the other man for the first time, his eyes scathing as they flicked over Dean, and in spite of the awfulness of it all Marigold knew a moment's amusement at the scandalised expression on her ex-fiancé's face. Dean had just had a salutary lesson in the fact that he was replaceable, and she hoped it might prove a warning to him in his dealings with the opposite sex in the future. 'Don't let me keep you,' Flynn said with distant chilliness, before his gaze returned to Marigold.

There was no further attempt at persuasion. Dean thrust the bag at her, his face like thunder, before he disappeared off down the street without a backward glance.

'That was Dean,' Marigold said weakly. She suddenly had the nasty feeling she had a tiger by the tail.

'So you said.' It was acidic.

'I didn't know he was going to be here. He phoned me this afternoon and then just turned up on the doorstep. I didn't...I mean I didn't want...' She stopped abruptly.

'Are you trying to say you didn't ask him here or invite him to kiss you?' Flynn asked evenly.

'Yes.' Which was stupid really because in view of the way she felt it would have been the easy option to let Flynn assume there was something between her and Dean, and thereby finish this 'friendship'. Flynn was not a man who understood the concept of sharing!

'Good.' He walked up to her, oblivious to the taxi driver, who was watching developments with interest. 'I'm pleased.'

'You believe me?' she asked weakly, astonished.

'Of course I believe you.' He smiled, a wry twist of his stern mouth. 'Didn't you expect me to?'

'I...' Her voice trailed away. She didn't know what she'd expected. 'I—'

'OK, I can draw my own conclusions.' He kissed her swiftly, lifting her chin with warm, firm fingers before adding, his voice very dry, 'I can see there is still some progress to be made.'

'What?'

But he was walking towards the taxi driver, bending down as he asked the fare and paying the man with what was obviously a handsome tip from the way Marigold heard the other man thank Flynn.

She watched him, her feelings so turbulent she hardly knew herself. She cared about this man and he was going to break her heart if she didn't finish this affair now, tonight. He had invaded her life with deadly intent, and even now she asked herself, why? He could have any woman he wanted—apart from the one who held his heart, Celine—so why bother with her? Was it because she'd made it plain she wanted nothing to do with him in the beginning, or just the way they had struck sparks off each other, mentally as well as physically? Right from the first time she had seen him it had been a love–hate relationship.

Her thought process hiccuped and died, leaving her in a state of suspended animation as she stared at the big figure in front of her. And then, as reason returned in a hot flood, she told herself, You don't! You do *not* love Flynn Moreau.

But it was too late. The truth she had been subconsciously denying for weeks was out in the open. Marigold wasn't aware of the blank despair which had turned her eyes navy blue, she only knew she mustn't betray herself by word or gesture.

'He's upset you.' Flynn was in front of her again, his handsome face unsmiling as he took in her drawn countenance. 'What's he been saying?'

'Who? What?' Marigold made an enormous effort and

pulled herself together. 'No, it's fine, really. He…he just told me he and Tamara have broken up. He wanted…'

'I think I know what he wanted,' Flynn said drily. 'And you told him to go paddle his own canoe, right?'

'My phraseology was a little different, but basically, yes.'

'You won't regret it.'

No, she wouldn't. Not with Dean. 'Flynn…' It was too soft, too trembling and feminine. She had to appear more in control. Marigold took a deep breath and her voice was firmer when she said, 'Flynn, we have to talk. About us, I mean.'

'There's an us?' One eyebrow quirked and his mouth lifted at the corners in a sexy smile. 'And I didn't know!'

'Please, Flynn.'

Something in her voice stilled the smile. His head tilted, eyes surveying her searchingly before he said, 'Inside. It's too cold and windy out here to deal with life and death issues.'

Once in the flat Flynn deposited the shopping he'd insisted on carrying in on the kitchen worktop, before walking through to the sitting room, where Marigold had just lit the fire.

'So.' He had on his big charcoal overcoat, undone, over an expensive grey suit and cream shirt, and looked every inch the powerful, dynamic and brilliant surgeon. He folded his arms over his chest, leaning against the wall just inside the door as he surveyed her unblinkingly. 'Let's have it.'

Please let me get through this without bursting into tears or disgracing myself in any other way, Marigold prayed desperately. I can't be with him on his terms, and any other way is out of the question. 'I think we ought to have a break from seeing each other,' she said stiffly,

rising from where she'd been kneeling in front of the
fire and seating herself on the sofa.

'Why?'

'Why?' Well, of course he would ask that, she told
herself crossly as she heard her voice echo his. She just
didn't have a reasonable answer, that was the thing. 'Because I'm not ready for a relationship so soon after my
engagement finishing,' she attempted quickly.

'Don't buy it,' he said coolly. 'What's the real reason?'

She didn't answer immediately and his eyes narrowed.
'The truth, Marigold, and I shall know if you're lying,'
he said softly.

'I…I'm not like your other women.'

He gave her a hard look. 'Flattering though some men
might find it to be compared to a sultan in a harem, I'm
not one of them. I wasn't aware I had "women" plural.'

'You know what I mean.'

'No, Marigold, I do not know what you mean. If
you're insinuating I conduct my love life like a bull let
loose in a field of cows—'

'Flynn!' She was truly shocked.

'The truth, please.'

'You…you're thirty-eight years old and used to full
intimacy in your relationships.' She couldn't believe
how priggish she sounded. Neither, apparently, could
Flynn.

'Marigold, you haven't the faintest idea what I'm used
to within a relationship,' he said coldly. 'Now, if this is
your way of asking me if I've slept with women in the
past then yes, I have. Hell, as you've just pointed out so
baldly, I am a mature man, not some boy, wet behind
the ears. However, I have never indulged in a promis-

cuous lifestyle, neither have I taken a woman to my bed who was not willing.'

She could certainly believe that. She stared at him miserably. No doubt they had been queueing up since Celine was crazy enough to let him go. 'The thing is…'

'Oh, not the thing again, please.'

The mocking note in his voice was the last straw, but it had the welcome advantage of putting iron in her backbone and fire in her eyes. All right, he wanted the truth, did he? He was darn well going to get it! 'I don't want to be someone who drifts in and out of your life,' she said tightly, 'that's all. That kind of lifestyle might suit some women just fine, but it wouldn't do for me. It might be old-fashioned but I would want to know that there at least is a chance of something permanent in the future if things worked out right. You…you're a closed and shut book.'

'I think the expression is an open and shut case.'

She glared at him. He knew exactly what she was getting at. She would not be a passing obsession, someone he wanted for a short time until the next challenge caught his fancy. And that was all she was, a challenge. If she'd gone to bed with him when he'd first wanted her to she might well be out of his life by now. And she couldn't cope with it. She loved him, and if she let him into her body as well as her heart she would never survive him leaving her.

It was when she'd met Flynn that she'd understood Dean had been all wrong for her, even if she hadn't admitted it for ages. From that first day Dean had ceased to matter. It was as simple, and as frightening, as that. She suddenly had the overwhelming desire to wail her head off, but controlled it rigidly.

'Marigold, correct me if I'm wrong, but wasn't it you

who insisted we keep each other at arm's length? Friends and no more? Don't tell me I'm now getting flak because I concurred with your desires?'

The word shivered over her and, although she was sure she hadn't betrayed herself, she was aware of the silvery eyes honing in on her. 'Come here,' he said softly.

'No, I need to make you understand we can't carry on like this. We live different lives; *we're* different. There's no meeting point. It's better to finish now...'

He moved, reaching her in a couple of strides and pulling her up from the sofa and into his arms. It was no gentle kiss; there was a well of frustration and pent-up passion that he hadn't let her see before, and Marigold was instantly aroused in spite of herself.

She found herself clutching him closer, accepting his kiss with a hunger which matched Flynn's, her mouth greedy for his. In seconds they were utterly lost to anything but each other, Marigold's arms tight round his shoulders as Flynn arched her backwards, his lips burning her throat before they moved back to take her mouth.

Somehow Marigold found that her coat was on the floor and then Flynn was nuzzling at the soft swell of her breasts above her low-cut lacy bra, her blouse open, although she had no recollection of Flynn undoing the tiny square pearl buttons. She was aware of the harsher material of his overcoat against her as he continued to ravish her flesh, the scent of him, the overall power and bigness of him, but only on the perimeter of her mind. The feverish need which had taken hold of her within seconds of his mouth taking hers had blurred everything but the desire to get closer and closer.

The soft pads of his fingertips had found her taut nipples under their flimsy covering and he was rubbing them gently, causing her to moan in her throat at the pleasure the small action produced. His body was imprinted against hers, his hard thighs and strong legs feeding the heady rush of sensation which had taken her over. She could feel his heart slamming against his ribcage and the tiny tremors shivering beneath her hands on his muscled shoulders, and knew he wanted her every bit as much as she wanted him.

He crushed her closer to him, lifting her right off her feet as he sank down on the sofa with her in his arms, settling her on his lap, his mouth never leaving hers. 'So soft, so warm, so perfect...' His voice was a thick, low murmur against her lips and she revelled in her power over this alien individual who had exploded into her life. 'You're sending me crazy, do you know that?'

For her answer she pressed herself against the solid wall of his chest, seeking his mouth with an urgency that was mindless.

'I want you, Marigold, but not like this. I want us to be able to take our time, can you understand that? I want to possess you so completely there'll be no room for anything but me in your head and your body. I want to marry you...'

The words hung on the air, shivering like tiny, crystallised raindrops caught in the delicate strands of a spider's web.

'What?' She drew back a little, staring at him dazedly. 'What did you say?'

'I want you to be my wife.' His hard looks had softened into such tenderness her breath caught in her throat. 'I agree with you, we can't carry on like this, not without me losing my sanity,' he added ruefully. 'You say we lead different lives so let's remedy that and lead one life together. You can still have your work, you can have the cottage as your studio if you like, somewhere where you can work peacefully and without interruption when I'm in London. When I'm home we can spend as much time together as we can.'

He had got it all worked out, she thought wonderingly. He must have been thinking about this for some time. 'But...but you never said anything before,' she murmured weakly.

'You made it clear I had to try the softly, softly approach,' Flynn said drily, 'and I can understand that after what you've been through. But you were right in one thing, Marigold—I am thirty-eight years old and frankly my time of stealing the odd kiss behind the bike sheds is long since past. I would have taken you to bed within days of us meeting if you had been willing, I admit it but you weren't ready—in here.' He touched her forehead lightly with the tip of a finger.

'Flynn...' Her voice trailed away as she looked into his eyes, which were lit from within by a light which had turned them the hue of mother-of-pearl. 'Are...are you sure?'

'As you have so succinctly pointed out, I've been around long enough to know what I want and from whom,' Flynn said softly. 'But I never asked any of the others to marry me.'

Except Celine. The thought hammered in her mind for a second before she pushed it resolutely away. She couldn't begin to work this complex and highly intelligent individual out, but he was offering her more than she had ever dreamed he would. And she loved him. In fact she loved him so much she didn't know how she would have managed to live without him. And now she didn't have to.

'So what's your answer?' he said very quietly. 'Think

carefully before you speak but one thing is for sure; I'm not letting you go out of my life and my patience is exhausted. I need to make a statement to any other young whippersnappers like your ex that might be sniffing about, too—a statement that you are mine.'

A statement to other men? Was he mad? Did he really imagine she had them queueing up in droves? 'It doesn't look as if I've any other option than to say yes, then,' she said softly, her mouth tremulous. 'But I don't understand—'

He had cut her voice off with a long and passionate kiss, only lifting his mouth from hers when she was trembling against him, melting and soft. 'What don't you understand?'

'Why you want me,' she said with touching honesty.

He stroked the smooth silk of her cheek very gently. 'Then I'll have to make you understand,' he said huskily, his eyes telling her of his desire more eloquently than any words could have done. 'But now is not the time.'

He glanced at his watch. 'Hell, I've got to go. I only intended to call by briefly to explain something, but there's no time now. I've got to go. I'll ring you, OK? In the morning before you leave for work. It's important we talk.'

'Yes, all right.' She was bewildered, but he was already lifting her away from him and standing to his feet, clearly anxious to be off. 'Are you going to the hospital now?' she asked, already knowing the answer. She had noticed the expression which had come over his face before when he was heavily involved in a case—a kind of veiled urgency, as though part of him was already in the operating theatre.

'Uh-huh.' He kissed her again, long and hard. 'But I'll ring you in the morning,' he reiterated.

That meant he was probably going to be in Theatre until the early hours; the case must be a serious one that couldn't wait. No doubt even now the patient was going through the rigorous checks and procedures Flynn insisted on before he operated.

'You go,' Marigold said quickly, wanting to make it easy for him, and then, for the first time since they'd met, it was she who reached up on her tiptoes and kissed him.

Flynn swept her close again for one last scorching embrace before he left, buttoning his coat as he went.

For a full minute after Flynn had gone Marigold just leant against the front door, staring dazedly about her tiny hall. Of all the events of the day, Flynn's proposal of marriage was the most amazing and she just couldn't take it in. She ran their conversation through in her mind as though she was listening to a recording to convince herself it had actually happened.

Marigold Moreau… She blinked, putting her hand to her wildly beating heart. He had asked her to become his *wife*.

She tottered through to the kitchen and made herself a strong cup of coffee before taking it through to the sitting room. She couldn't eat anything, not yet, she was too excited and worked up. Oh, Flynn, Flynn… The enormity of it began to sink in. *Marriage*. It had all seemed so simple when he was here and holding her tight, but now she found herself wondering why he had asked her to marry him this particular night. Had she forced him into the proposal by the stance she had taken tonight and the way she'd been over the last months? Refusing to sleep with him? If so, she didn't want it to be like that. That would be like a form of sexual blackmail and never, not for a second, had she planned that.

In fact it had never crossed her mind that Flynn would ever ask her to become his wife; there was Celine Jenet, after all.

Marigold brushed her hair away from her hot face, shutting her eyes tightly for a moment or two as she struggled with her turbulent thoughts, and the more she struggled the more the old doubts and fears raised their heads.

Had Flynn said he loved her? She thought back to the emotion-charged minutes they had shared, her racing mind desperately seeking reassurance. No, he had not. Not in so many words. But the way he'd looked at her had been a declaration in itself, hadn't it?

Or—a little voice in the back of her mind asked probingly—was it that she wanted, *needed* to believe it had been a declaration?

Her head was whirling after a few minutes, and another cup of coffee—black this time and as strong as she could stand it—did nothing to clear her head.

She needed to switch off for a few minutes. Marigold reached for the TV remote, and as the little screen in front of her lit up she sank back against the soft cushions of the sofa, utterly spent.

She couldn't remember a thing about the programme which was on—she must have sat in a kind of stupor through most of it—but her attention was caught by the short clip introducing the next feature, an awards ceremony of some kind. 'Tonight promises to be a glittering occasion for those in the fashion world...' It went on in the same vein for a moment or two, but then Marigold sat up straight as the announcer said, 'And among those flying in this afternoon was Celine Jenet, who has only recently announced her retirement from the catwalk.' There was the briefest of pictures of a smiling Celine exiting the airport terminal, but it was the tall, dark man who had his arm round her waist who caught Marigold's eye.

Flynn. Marigold's hands went to cover her mouth, and she pressed hard against her flesh as she stared uncomprehendingly at the screen before the picture changed, showing more celebrities and flashing cameras and crowds cheering outside some building or other.

This afternoon. That was what the announcer had said. Celine was here, in London. With Flynn.

'No. Oh, no.' It was a whimper and Marigold heard herself with a feeling of self-disgust, but she could do nothing about the pain and shock swamping her.

Was that where Flynn was tonight? With Celine at this gala occasion? She clicked off the TV, her head swimming. And she had actually encouraged him to leave her, thinking he was going to the hospital.

A tide of nausea rose up in Marigold's throat and she found herself having to take deep breaths to control the sickness. How could he do this to her? Lie to her like this? How could he *propose* and then go straight to another woman, to Celine? He was as bad as Dean. A sob caught in her throat and she stood up, beginning to walk backwards and forwards as she tried to think what to do. History had repeated itself, it would seem. Was there something the matter with her? she asked herself wretchedly. There had to be. Something had to make these men think that she was stupid.

But...but what if by some hundred-to-one chance she had got it wrong? Maybe, just maybe he had met Celine at the airport for old times' sake? It was possible.

She knew she was clutching at straws but she couldn't help it. What if Flynn had been telling the truth and was at the hospital tonight? It didn't have to follow that because he had been with Celine that afternoon he was with her at this function tonight. But how could she find out for sure?

Bertha might know. Marigold's heart began to thump hard and she didn't wait to consider further, reaching for the telephone and dialling the Shropshire number which was written in the little book at the side of it. It was only as the receiver was picked up at the other end she realised she could have called the hospital; Bertha might have been told to deny he was with Celine.

Marigold thought quickly, and then said, 'Bertha? It's Marigold. I was calling to speak to Flynn but I've just remembered, he's with Celine, isn't he? I'd forgotten. It's been a hectic day with one thing and another and I'm not thinking straight.'

'That's all right, dear.'

She hadn't denied it. *She hadn't denied it.* 'I'll call him on his mobile later,' Marigold said hurriedly before Bertha could start chatting. 'I'm in a mad rush. Goodbye for now.'

She put down the phone without waiting for Bertha's reply and then sat staring at the receiver blankly. She hated him. She really, really hated him.

She looked up the number of his London flat and dialled slowly. It was the answer machine on the other end of the line but she had expected that. She spoke clearly and concisely when the bleeps stopped. 'Flynn? It's Marigold. I hope you had a nice evening, you and Celine. Oh, just one more thing. I wouldn't marry you if you were the last man on earth. OK? And for the record I never did trust you, so don't think you fooled me for a minute. I don't want to hear from you or see you again. Goodbye.'

She put down the phone, blew a strand of hair out of her eyes and burst into tears.

CHAPTER NINE

MARIGOLD didn't know at what point she eventually fell asleep, but she had cried herself dry by the time she fell into bed at gone midnight and was exhausted in mind, body and spirit. Nevertheless, she tossed and turned for what seemed like hours before drifting off into a troubled slumber.

When the telephone began to jar her back to consciousness it took some time for the insistent tone to register. She finally surfaced, pulling herself up in bed and reaching for the receiver as she tried to focus blurry eyes on her alarm clock. Five o'clock in the morning?

And then, as a furious male voice bit out her name, it all came flooding back and she remembered. Flynn and Celine!

'What the hell is that message supposed to mean?' Flynn sounded more angry than she had ever heard him.

Marigold desperately tried to gather thoughts that were still buried in layers of cotton wool. 'I would have thought it was pretty obvious,' she managed fairly smartly, considering her heart had just jumped up into her throat at the sound of his voice.

'You know about Celine?'

Marigold blinked, unable to believe her ears for a moment. He wasn't even going to *try* to deny it? Perversely that made her madder than ever. 'Again, I would have thought that was obvious,' she said icily.

'Then what was with the crack about a nice evening?' he snarled savagely. 'And me fooling you?'

She had never heard him like this, not even when he had thought she was Emma. He obviously didn't take kindly to being caught out. 'I said you *didn't* fool me,' she reminded him cuttingly.

'You also said you didn't want to see or hear from me again a few hours after promising to become my wife,' he grated, 'so what the hell is this about? And don't say you think it's obvious because it damn well isn't, not to me. I've been up for twenty-four hours and I'm not in the mood to play games, Marigold.'

Games! He thought this was a game, did he? And he had obviously only just got in. 'You told me you were at the hospital last night,' Marigold said, refusing to let her voice quiver.

'So?'

'So I saw a clip on TV of Celine arriving in London,' Marigold said tightly. 'You were with her. And Bertha said you were with her last night.' Well, she had in a way.

'Wait a minute, let's get this straight. You said you knew about Celine?'

'I do. There was a programme about the fashion awards, all very glitzy and glamorous,' Marigold said scathingly.

'And you think Celine was there last night?' There was the briefest of pauses. And then his voice had changed to a soft, icy tone when he said, 'And you phoned Bertha to see if I was with Celine at this do? Is that right?'

'Yes.' There was something wrong here. Her stomach curdled with horrible premonition.

'You could have called me on my mobile, or phoned the hospital if you wanted to talk to me direct, Marigold.'

'You...you weren't at the hospital.'

'Did you check? Before you talked to Bertha?' he asked, still in the quiet, deadly tone which was sending chills of foreboding all over her body.

'No.'

'I wasn't worth one phone call.'

'It wasn't like that,' she protested faintly.

'The hell it wasn't.'

'I thought—'

'I know what you thought, Marigold. You were sure I was fooling around with Celine last night so you called Bertha to check up on me. Damn it, I've been such a fool. I thought I could make you love me the way I love you, but you never gave me a chance, not really, did you? Apart from the physical attraction between us I don't think you even like me.'

'Flynn, that's not true.'

Her genuine distress didn't impress him at all. 'You believed I would ask you to marry me and then go out and spend the night with another woman.'

The contempt in his voice cut Marigold to the quick, the more so because it was the truth. What could she say, what could she do to make this right? Whatever had occurred during the day she believed Flynn had been at the hospital last night. He hadn't been with Celine.

And then he proved her wrong when he said bitterly, 'I *was* with Celine last night, Marigold. I left her at four this morning. She's in Intensive Care after having a tumour the size of a golf ball removed from her head. When she comes round—*if* she comes round—she'll probably have to learn to walk and talk again; she might be blind or worse. She should have been operated on weeks ago but some charlatan of a doctor she visited missed all the signs of a tumour and told her she was having migraines due to stress.'

Marigold was frozen with horror.

'She came to see me yesterday for a second opinion; she was never intending to go to any function. I knew I had to operate immediately from the tests I did in the afternoon but until we opened up the skull no one realised how bad it was.'

'Flynn, I'm so sorry.' Remorse and shame were strangling her voice. 'I don't know what to say.'

'There's nothing left to say.' It was terribly final. 'I was fooling myself all along there was anything real between us.'

'No, please! Listen to me. I didn't understand—'

'No, you didn't, but then I wasn't important enough to you for you to make the effort, was I?' he said bitterly. 'If you thought I was capable of behaving like that then there is no hope. I've tried to show you myself over the last months, Marigold. The inner man if you like.' It was said with cutting self-derision. 'I've never pretended to be perfect, but neither am I the slimeball you've got me down for.'

'I haven't. Flynn, I haven't.' She was crying now but it seemed to have no effect on him at all.

'You are going to have to trust someone some time, Marigold,' he said flatly, 'but it won't be me.'

He meant it, she thought sickly. She'd lost him.

'Goodbye, Marigold.' And the phone was put down very quietly.

The next few days were the worst of Marigold's life. She got through the working hours by functioning on automatic pilot, but once she was home, in the endless loneliness of her little flat, there was no opiate to the pain of bitter self-reproach and guilt.

She picked up the telephone to call Flynn a hundred times a night, but always put it down again without making the call. What could she say after all? She'd let him down in the worst manner possible and there was no way back. She hadn't even given him the opportunity to defend himself before she had sailed in, all guns firing. He must have got home from the hospital, exhausted and mentally and emotionally drained, and then had the welcome of her telephone message.

If she said she loved him now he would never believe her—she certainly hadn't acted like a woman in love, she flailed herself wretchedly. Love believed the best of the beloved; it was generous and understanding and tender.

She deserved his hatred and contempt. She deserved all the pain and regret.

This orgy of self-recrimination continued until the weekend, and then two things happened which jolted Marigold out of her hopelessness, the first event instigating the second.

At half-past nine in the morning on a cold but bright Saturday Marigold answered a knock at the door to find Dean on her doorstep, an enormous bunch of flowers in his hand. He spoke quickly before she could say a word. 'I've come to ask if we can still be friends, just friends,' he said quietly, not sounding like himself at all. 'It was the truth when I said I missed you, Dee, and I don't want it to end like this. I know you're involved with someone else and I don't blame you, but I'd like to think we can still ring each other now and again, meet for coffee, things like that. What do you think?'

She stared at him in astonishment, seeing the genuine

desire for reconciliation, and then surprised them both by bursting into tears.

Two cups of coffee and a couple of rounds of toast later Marigold found herself in the extraordinary position of—having cried on Dean's shoulder—being encouraged by her ex-fiancé to chase after another man. 'If I thought there was the inkling of a chance of us getting back together I wouldn't be saying this,' Dean admitted wryly, 'but there isn't, is there?'

Marigold shook her head, her mouth being full of toast and Marmite.

'And I feel a bit responsible you didn't trust Flynn as you would have done if I hadn't played fast and loose,' Dean said in such a way Marigold suspected he expected her to deny he was to blame.

'Good, you should,' she responded firmly after swallowing the toast.

'Yeah, right.' He drained his coffee-cup, aware the time of Marigold seeing him through rose-coloured spectacles was well and truly over. 'So, go and see him. Talk to him face to face. Tell it how it is. Grovel if you have to. If you don't you'll spend the rest of your life wondering if things might have been OK if you'd just tried.'

Marigold stared at him. Comfort came in the oddest ways and from sources you least expected.

Once Dean had left she ran herself a hot bath and lay soaking in strawberry bubbles as she considered all they had said. If someone like Dean, essentially pretty shallow and selfish, could make the grand gesture he had made this morning, it surely wasn't beyond her to do something similar for Flynn, was it? OK, so Flynn might cut her dead or reduce her to nothing with that cynical tongue of his, but what did that matter? If that happened she deserved it, and she had no pride left after the misery of the last few days. She would do anything, *anything* to show him how sorry she was.

He had said he loved her, in that last terrible phone call, and she believed he had. Perhaps he still did? Perhaps she hadn't destroyed everything? And even if Celine *was* his first love she didn't care any more. It was *her* he had proposed to a few nights ago, *their* future he had been thinking about.

Marigold had rung the hospital a few times, enquiring after Celine, but each time she had got a standard formal reply. 'Miss Jenet is as well as can be expected.' The last two days she hadn't rung at all, but once out of the bath she picked up the phone and dialled the number of Flynn's home in Shropshire.

'Bertha?' She took a deep breath after hearing Flynn's housekeeper's voice. 'It's Marigold. I'm ringing to ask how Celine is.'

'Oh, hello, dear.' From the tone of Bertha's voice she knew nothing about their break-up, and this seemed to be borne out when Bertha said, her voice a little puzzled, 'Why don't you ask Mr Moreau, dear?'

'He's so busy.'

'Oh, you don't have to tell me! He'll be ill if he carries on, but hopefully now Celine is on the mend he can relax a bit more. She's still progressing little by little, dear, but she was awake more yesterday and her speech is all but back. It's a blessing her eyesight hasn't been affected, isn't it? I think that's what was worrying Mr Moreau the most.'

By the time Marigold put down the phone a few minutes later she was trembling with reaction. Celine was all right; she was going to get better. According to Bertha, Flynn was confident he had removed all of the tumour and the prognosis for the future was good.

She was going to go round to his flat as soon as she was dressed. She had to see him now, today. She needed to make him understand she loved him, really loved him, and then the rest was up to him. If he couldn't forgive her... She dared not let herself think about that. If she did she would revert to the soggy mess of the last few days, and right now she had to be strong.

After blow-drying her hair into a shining, sleek shoulder-length style, she stood for some time surveying the contents of her wardrobe. She needed to look smart but not too smart; feminine and appealing but not too obvious.

Eventually she chose a pair of new smart brown trousers with her brown boots, teaming them with a white cashmere jumper which had been wickedly expensive but always made her feel good. She made up her face with just a smidgen of foundation to hide the paleness of nerves, and stroked a couple of coats of mascara on her eyelashes.

She couldn't compete with Celine in the beauty stakes, she thought soberly, and she wasn't going to try. This was her; five feet four, brown hair, blue eyes, and capable of the utmost stupidity as her behaviour a few days ago had proved. Would he talk to her? She shut her eyes tightly and prayed for strength. She'd make him!

As the taxi pulled into the beautifully kept grounds of the private hospital Marigold did a few deep-breathing exercises to try and combat her wildly beating heart.

She had gone to Flynn's London flat first but when there had been no answer had assumed he was at the hospital. Of course, he might not be, she reminded herself nervously, but he was bound to turn up here sooner or later. Considering the taxi had run up a bill equal to a small mortgage, she wasn't budging further anyway!

After paying the taxi driver, she squared her shoulders under her brown leather jacket and marched purposefully to the reception doors, which glided open at her approach. She waded through ankle-deep carpet to where an exquisitely coiffured receptionist was waiting with a charming smile. 'Can I help you?' she purred sweetly.

'I would like to speak to Mr Moreau. Mr Flynn Moreau,' Marigold said firmly.

'Do you have an appointment?'

'No, I don't have an appointment.'

'Then I'm really very sorry but—'

'I'm not a patient of Mr Moreau's,' Marigold said quickly. 'I'm a friend. I'm sure he will want to see me when he knows I'm here.' She was getting better at lying, Marigold thought a trifle hysterically. That one had come out as smooth as cream.

A couple of men walked down some stairs at the far end of the reception area, obviously from the Middle East as their flowing robes proclaimed. They looked as though they owned a couple of countries apiece at least.

'Mr Moreau's secretary is not in today but I'll see if I can contact him,' the receptionist said pleasantly. 'I'm really not sure if he is in the building.'

Oh, yes, right, Marigold thought disbelievingly. If Flynn thought she was a poor liar he ought to listen to this woman!

'Who shall I say wants him?'

'Miss Flower.' She was not going to give her first name to this vision of sophistication!

'If you would like to take a seat, Miss Flower , I'll see what I can do.' The receptionist waved a pale beringed hand with long, perfectly painted red talons in the direction of several pale cream sofas some distance away, and Marigold had no choice but to smile politely and comply.

She could see the woman talking on a telephone from where she was seated but was too far away to hear what she was saying, although once or twice the heavily made-up, almond-shaped eyes looked her way. As the receptionist replaced one telephone another rang at the side of her, and she was once again engrossed in conversation.

The Middle Eastern gentlemen had been standing talking in low voices, and as they now departed in a swish of long robes and exclusive perfume Marigold glanced about her, trying not to appear overawed. Money might not be able to buy good health but it certainly made being sick more enjoyable! She knew Flynn worked in the public sector at the local hospital as well as this private one, and the two places must be like two different worlds. Suddenly panic was making her throat dry. She should never have come. This was a big mistake. Celine was far more suited to his world than she was and now the other woman was ill Flynn might well be hoping they would get back together again.

'Hello, Marigold.'

For the first time in her life she knew what it was to have her heart stop dead as the quiet, deep voice sounded just behind her left shoulder. She swung round so quickly she nearly fell off the sofa, and then jumped to her feet in a totally uncool way. 'Flynn! I...I didn't hear you.'

He raked back an errant lock of hair from his forehead, a slow gesture which suggested his air of calmness was deliberate. 'Sophia said you were here asking for me.'

He looked terrible. As handsome as ever and so sexy he should be certified as dangerous, but there was a grey tinge to the tanned skin that spoke of extreme exhaustion and his mouth wasn't just stern but drawn and tight. A sudden thought crossed her mind and she said quickly, 'Celine? She *is* all right. Bertha said she was getting better.'

'Celine is fine.'

He was wearing a pale blue shirt and his hands were thrust in the pockets of his suit trousers, his tie hanging askew as it so often did. She felt such a flood of love rise up in her that she wanted to cry. Instead she said shakily, 'I'm sorry to bother you here but I had to talk to you. The…receptionist said she didn't know if you were here or not.'

He shrugged powerful shoulders. 'It's been a hectic few days. There was a bad pile-up on the motorway and I've been to-ing and fro-ing between hospitals.'

She nodded. So that was why he looked dead beat. For a moment, a crazy moment she had just wondered if it was because he had been thinking about her.

His eyes narrowed slightly as they focused on the silky veil of her hair for a moment before taking in her smart trousers and the figure-hugging cashmere sweater. 'You're obviously on your way out to lunch some where,' he said dismissively. 'How can I help you?'

For a second she almost turned tail and ran in the face of his cool indifference, but something in the way he was standing, the faintest indication that his hands were balled fists in his pockets, caused her to stand her ground. 'I'm not going out to lunch,' she said evenly, her voice not shaking any more. 'I came to see you.'

'Why?'

It was now or never. 'To tell you I love you,' she said very clearly.

'Go home, Marigold.'

But she had seen his eyes flicker and the grimace of pain—fleeting but definitely there—that had twisted his mouth as she had spoken.

'Not until I am sure you understand how I feel,' she said thickly. 'If you walk away now I shall follow you. I'm not afraid to cause a scene.'

She saw his eyes widen just for a moment and then he took her arm, his voice grim as he said, 'This is ridiculous but if you insist you had better come to my office. This is a hospital, in case you'd forgotten.'

His office was sumptuous with a view over bowling-green-smooth lawns and mature trees, but Marigold didn't notice the decor. Once Flynn had shut the door he walked over to his desk, perching on the edge of it as he waved her to one of the visitor's chairs in front of it. 'I'm due in a meeting shortly so I can only spare you five minutes.' It was the cool, calm voice of a stranger, unemotional, cold.

She ignored the seat and walked across to stand right in front of him, so close she could see the five o'clock shadow on his chin although it was only midday. She touched his face lightly and though he didn't move a muscle she knew he had tensed. 'You need a new blade in your razor,' she said softly.

Her words were followed by a silence which slowly began to vibrate, an electricity in the air that was almost tangible. He remained perfectly still as he said, 'I've been up since two in the morning; complications with one of the road-accident victims. I've got an electric razor in my desk; I'll use that later.'

She put her arms round his neck. 'Flynn,' she said

quietly, 'please forgive me. I love you with all my heart. Please marry me.'

She could feel him begin to tremble but his voice was perfectly under control when he said, 'You don't have to do this, Marigold. I'm a big boy, I can survive rejection.' He reached up to remove her arms from round his neck but she hung on tight, nearly throttling him.

'Listen to me,' she said fiercely, her heart suddenly blazing with hope because she knew, she *knew* he still loved her. 'I love you, I do. I loved you almost from the beginning but I didn't dare admit it to myself. It was too soon after Dean for one thing but that wasn't really it. I knew you had the potential to hurt me in a way Dean never could have done, that was the thing.'

'The thing again.' He was trying to be mocking but it didn't come off and they both knew it.

'And then I heard those women talking about this girl that you still loved, this beauty who was always there in the background. It was my worst fear come true. And she turned out to be not just some ordinary woman but Celine Jenet, one of the most beautiful women in the world. I could understand how no one could compare with her. I thought you were waiting until she wanted you again.'

'Wanted me again?' His hands weren't trying to untangle hers now but holding them against his neck. 'Marigold, it was me who broke off the engagement, not Celine. I realised I loved her like a sister, a best friend, and after a time she came to realise that that wouldn't have been enough. If we'd married we would have made each other very unhappy.'

Why hadn't she considered it might have been Flynn who finished it? *Because she loved him too much.*

'I was jealous,' she whispered, her eyes shining with

tears. 'And I didn't trust you. I don't deserve another chance...'

He slid off the desk, pulling her into him and kissing her until she was drowning in bliss. 'I love you, Marigold Flower,' he murmured huskily. 'I'll always love you. I loved you when I thought you didn't love or want me, and it was slowly crucifying me. I've never felt this way before. I have lived for thirty-eight years without knowing what real love was, until I met you. Do you believe that?'

'Yes, yes, I do.' Her eyes were shining and his mouth sought hers again, his hands moving over her body, touching her with sensual, intimate caresses.

'You're everything I've ever wanted, although I couldn't have said what I was looking for until I saw you. Then it all came together in a moment of time, and I knew. Does that make sense, sweetheart?'

'I don't know.' Marigold didn't know anything when she was close to him like this, except that she never wanted to be anywhere else in the whole of her life.

'And you fought me every inch of the way.' He took her mouth again in a long, hungry kiss. 'I was the enemy, and whatever I did, however I tried to show you that we belonged together, you wouldn't give in.'

He made her sound almost brave, Marigold thought ruefully, when really she had been muddled and confused and frightened to death half the time, frightened of her feelings and the desire she'd felt every time he touched her.

'Ask me again.'

'What?'

He had pulled away slightly to look into her radiant face, and now his voice was soft and husky when he said, 'Ask me to marry you again. And before you do I want you to know that it will be forever. Once I say yes, there's no going back, Marigold Flower. Whatever happens you're mine.'

'Flynn Moreau, will you marry me?' she asked gently, cradling his face in her hands as she let him see all the love in her heart. 'Will you be my husband and the father of my babies? Will you grow old with me and watch our grandchildren play through mellow summer days, and will you still be my love?'

'Yes,' he said, his voice gruff.

And she kissed him.

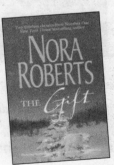

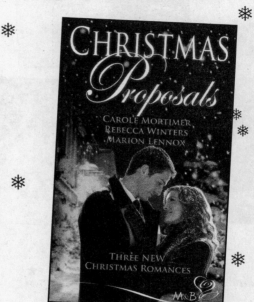

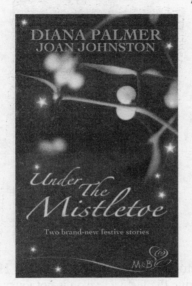

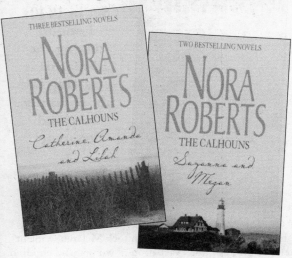

Set in 1940s London during the Blitz, this is a moving tale about family, love and courage

Queenie McLaren and her daughter Laura have long had to protect each other from Jock Mclaren's violent temper. In 1940, the evacuation of women and children from their homeland in Gibraltar is the perfect chance to escape, and Queenie and Laura eventually find themselves in London during the height of the Blitz.

During the darkest of war years, mother and daughter find courage in friendships formed in hardship, and the joy of new romances. But neither of them has yet heard that Jock is in England – and he won't rest until he's found them…

On sale 20th October 2006

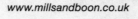

www.millsandboon.co.uk

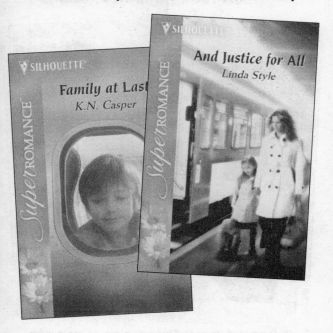

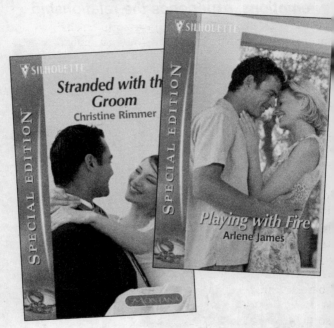